Philip Gilbert Hamerton

Modern Frenchmen

Five Biographies

Philip Gilbert Hamerton

Modern Frenchmen
Five Biographies

ISBN/EAN: 9783743306479

Manufactured in Europe, USA, Canada, Australia, Japa

Cover: Foto ©Raphael Reischuk / pixelio.de

Manufactured and distributed by brebook publishing software
(www.brebook.com)

Philip Gilbert Hamerton

Modern Frenchmen

·

Modern Frenchmen.

FIVE BIOGRAPHIES.

BY

PHILIP GILBERT HAMERTON,

AUTHOR OF "ROUND MY HOUSE," "THE SYLVAN YEAR," ETC., ETC.

Quam bene vivas refert, non quamdiu.
SENECA.

BOSTON:
ROBERTS BROTHERS.
1890.

UNIVERSITY PRESS:

JOHN WILSON & SON, CAMBRIDGE.

PREFACE TO THE AMERICAN EDITION.

THERE are some curious passages in the Life of Harriet Martineau, which may throw light on a subject very closely connected with the present volume. When Miss Martineau's reputation was established, and she had given up novel-writing, Charlotte Brontë persuaded her to try her hand once more upon a story which was to be published anonymously by Smith & Elder. The novel was begun, and the manuscript of the first volume sent to Mr. George Smith, who received it warmly, and predicted a great success; but, as the work advanced a little further, he declined the publication altogether, on the ground that it was favorable to Roman Catholics. The story must be true, as the biography which contains it was issued by the publishing firm in question. There is also a story about Charles Dickens of a very similar character. Miss Martineau had written a tale for "Household Words," but Dickens declined it on the ground that one of the characters was a priest *and yet a good man*, a combination which he considered inadmissible, because it might help the influence of Romanism.

I suppose neither Mr. George Smith nor Charles
Dickens would have published the present volume.
They acted upon a principle which is often tacitly
accepted as a rule of conduct, but very seldom avowed
openly, — the principle that it is an error in policy to
recognize in any way the merits of those who differ
from us.

If mankind were really and hopelessly in a state of
war, in which all justice, truth, and honor were permanently suspended, and life had but a single purpose,
to do the enemy as little good and as much injury as
possible, then, of course, in a conflict where the pen is
the best weapon, it would be the error of a dupe to use
it to the enemy's advantage. The proper course in such
a warfare would be to avoid with the greatest care any
recognition of an opponent's merits, to exhibit his errors
and failings in a light at once odious and absurd, to give
him credit for no motive that could do him honor, to
ascribe his actions to the basest self-interest, and to
deface whatever beauty might adorn his character.
This is constantly and habitually done in the ruthless
antagonism of low controversy, where justice is avoided
as carefully as generosity, and the object of the speaker
or the writer is to injure, by fair means or by foul, all
sects and parties but his own.

Such a temper and such conduct as those which I have
just been describing are not at all repugnant to the ordinary instincts of mankind : they are, indeed, only too perfectly human. The natural instinct of a man is to do
what harm he can to his opponent, even when the op-

position is simply religious, political, or intellectual, and is free from the antipathies of race. The notion of justice is quite foreign to this primitive human instinct : the idea of sympathy with those who differ from us is of still later growth ; and yet, without sympathy, justice itself must be cold and incomplete. Imagine an attempt to give an account, without sympathy, of such a character as that of Henri Perreyve ! He lived habitually in a condition of very pure and elevated sentiment ; and, if you refuse your sympathy to the sentiment, you cannot describe the man, you cannot even understand him. I may be asked how I can feel sympathy with sentiments not my own. The answer is easy. The sentiments, if not exactly my own, may be much nearer to mine than the intellectual condition which accompanied them. Perreyve and I would heartily agree in the love of truth, in the sense of satisfaction in the performance of duty, in the feeling of dissatisfaction when falling short of its full performance, in the admiration for an ideal elevation of character, and the humble desire to gain a little of such elevation for ourselves. We should heartily agree in an unfeigned contempt for all worldly advantages in comparison with the far higher pleasure of fulfilling our own vocation, we should be equally willing to do loyal service when the claim upon our time and effort was undeniable. If, after this, we went further, to the application of these general principles, we should immediately encounter those differences which are the result of circumstances and of intellectual situations. Though at one in the love of truth, we should not be

of the same opinion as to what was historically true ;
though, agreed in the desire to do our duty, we should
differ about the question, In what does duty consist ?
We should alike have a reverence for the ideal, but should
discover on comparison that our ideals were not identical.   To take a single example, our opinions about the
mother of Jesus.   For Perreyve, she was the queen of
the Sciences, a supernaturally lucid intelligence, to whom
science and art were open without an effort ; for me, she
possessed whatever science and art may have been accessible to the popular mind in her time and country.
No reliable information has reached me about any exceptional scientific knowledge in the wife of Joseph the
carpenter ; and, in my complete ignorance on the subject, I conclude that she probably knew very much what
was known to others of her sex and country and class.
Again, Perreyve speaks elsewhere of her extraordinary
beauty.   I know nothing about this except from Raphael,
and I know that Raphael drew from Roman models
whom he deliberately idealized.   Am I, then, to apply
to Perreyve that familiar alternative of "knave or fool"
which men apply so easily to those who think differently
from themselves ?   Certainly not.   Perreyve's idealization of Mary is nothing but an extreme instance of
what we see every day,— the common tendency of human
nature to attribute all imaginable merits to an object of
admiration ; and the less men really know about the
object, the more liberally will their imaginations adorn
it.   Such an idealization is compatible not only with
soundness of mind, but with brilliant intellectual power :

indeed, it is probable that there is hardly a single intellectual man now living in the world who has not in this way idealized some woman, more or less, by attributing to her a degree of intelligence and a range of information considerably beyond her real capacity and acquirements. This is what I desire to insist upon. We are all idealists more or less in some corner of our brains, and we ought to be able to bear with the idealisms of others. Compare the real Queen Victoria with the ideal! The real person, in this instance, is a lady of high culture and irreproachable character, anxious to do what is right; but there are many other ladies in England of whom this may be said, and whose characters excite no enthusiasm whatever. The *enthusiasm* inspired by Queen Victoria, and by all good and many bad sovereigns in monarchical countries, is due to the idealizing tendency of the human mind, and to nothing whatever else. Nay, it is not even necessary that there should be, or have been, a living human being to be clothed with the splendors of the ideal. A mere mental conception has often done equally well. The gods of Greece were simply mental conceptions, and yet the Greek enthusiasm about them was so very much in earnest that it went ill with those who spoke lightly of these imaginary beings and their attributes, and to incur the suspicion of scepticism about the reality of these popular conceptions exposed a Greek to the terrible accusation of impiety. Even in our own day, we see many Frenchmen renounce the monarchical ideal, which transfigures a crowned human being, for the idealization of a mere mental conception called *la*

République, a conception which the sculptors are set to realize in colossal statues, and which already exists as a mighty imaginary woman, from whom all good things are to be expected, in the fanciful brain of the people.

I can imagine some very earnest Protestant telling me that I am a dupe in praising a Roman Catholic priest, because the Church of Rome is the sworn foe of that which is dearest to a man of letters, — the liberty of thought and expression.

The answer is that, by cultivating the love of justice in the public mind, of justice towards all, including priests of every denomination, a writer is in fact rendering the best service to liberty of thought, because that condition of public opinion which has accepted the idea of justice as the director of its influence is the best of all possible safeguards against sacerdotal tyranny. Again, it is only in complete ignorance of history that we can look upon the Roman Catholic priesthood as the one great danger to mental freedom. Some of the most intolerant laws that ever disgraced a statute-book have been passed by Protestant parliaments. The English Conventicle Act, which punished by fine, imprisonment, and transportation, all meetings of more than five persons for any religious worship but that of the prayer-book, was passed by a Parliament whose Protestantism had been amply vindicated only twelve months before by the banishment of all Roman Catholic priests. This single instance may suffice; but the history of the last three hundred years abounds in evidence that the spirit of intolerance has not been confined to any particular sect. To be incessantly anxious about the encroachments of one, and careless about the influence of all others, would be the mistake of a general who thinks only of a single outpost when he is threatened in flank and rear.

Surely, the world is old enough by this time to have got over the first violent instinct of antagonism which a difference of opinion would arouse to unreasoning animosity. Surely, people may now endure to hear the simple truth, often the beautiful truth, about those who are divided from them by the barriers of usage, nationality, and tradition!

A biography is like a painted picture: it ought not to be a coarse, rough sketch, or a caricature. If the painter feels some admiration for his subject, the result will be the better for his admiration, provided that it is not strong enough to overcome his judgment. He should be able to recognize, and willing to represent, whatever is really characteristic of his hero with the simple clearness of a conscientious artist. He should state opinions fairly, but it is not his business to controvert them; he should not pass in silence the errors or failings of his subject, but it is not his business to excite public odium against them. I have compared the work of the biographer to that of the painter, but it may frequently bear a nearer resemblance to the humbler employment of the picture-cleaner. There may be cases when his duty is not so much to paint a new picture as to make one that has been already painted more clearly visible, by removing what obscures it, whilst reverently respecting and carefully preserving those delicacies of tone and detail, those thin glazes of transparent or semi-transparent color, on which both its beauty and its truth depend.   This is not to be done by scraping down to the bare canvas, and it is not to be done by daubing additions ; but it may be accomplished by method and patience, united to watchful care.

Of the men whose lives are narrated in this volume, three died young, — one passed middle age, and one reached old age in the plenitude of his faculties.   The old man, the sculptor Rude, is, in my opinion, by far the greatest man of the five, and perhaps the only one to whom greatness may be properly attributed, but all the five are men of power and energy and of high character, and they have all had influence on the present generation, which is more closely and immediately felt than that of the distant immortals, and which is far from being exhausted.   In giving to Rude alone the epithet *great*, in the highest sense, I ought to add that one or two others of my subjects would probably have deserved it, had they lived beyond middle age.   Victor Jacquemont, with his indomitable energy and industry, and the wonderful acuteness of his intellectual faculties, would almost inevitably have attained to indisputable greatness in science ; and Henri Regnault, with his strong memory, keen observation, and evident manual power, might have taken a great rank in art, equivalent, possibly, to the rank of Eugène Delacroix.   Perreyve was evidently not a man of great intellect, and I do not see that he had the greatness of religious power and leadership as Lacordaire

had it, for example, or even as John Henry Newman un-
doubtedly has it still; but the influence of his character,
with its remarkable purity and singleness of purpose,
may be wider than that of greatness itself. It is doing
good still in two very different ways: it is detaching
many Roman Catholics from the political reaction and
making them more tolerant, both towards Protestantism
and towards free thought; whilst, on the other hand, it
has won the respect of many outside the Church, and
made them less indisposed to recognize what is really
good in her. Such characters, when they happily become influential, are like oil upon the tempestuous
waters of religious and political animosity, and, if they
were more numerous, we might reasonably hope for a
future in which the different religious communities might
pursue their various ideals in peace, alike protected by
the secular power, whilst those who are unable to attach
themselves conscientiously to any one of them might
lead lives unembittered by contumely, and devote themselves, like Rude, to the austere duties of home and
family; or, like Jacquemont, to science and humanity;
or, like Henri Regnault, to their country in her need.

P. G. H.

Sept., 1878.

PREFACE TO THE ENGLISH EDITION.

IN selecting the subjects of these five short biographies, I have been guided chiefly by feelings of personal interest, from a belief that when the writer is interested there is always some probability that the reader will be so too. I do not intend to convey an indirect lesson against international injustice, being fully persuaded that the old British scorn of Frenchmen, and of all foreigners whatever, is now dying out of itself, and giving place to an intelligent desire to know something accurately about them. Such men as those whose lives are narrated here are certainly worth attention, especially for one characteristic which is common to all of them, and which gives a certain unity to my book, I mean vigor and intensity of life. They may be sometimes misdirected, but they never become dull, languid, or indifferent: they work with all their intelligence, they love with all their hearts, and they keep their bodily powers in full activity, not the activity of the athlete, but of the gentleman. My five modern Frenchmen are, I am well aware, superior to the average of their countrymen, and it is probable that no country or city which ever existed has ever brought its average citizens up to this level, or to any thing approaching it ; but at the same time I may add that my little list of five does not by any means exhaust the catalogue of modern Frenchmen whose lives I would willingly write.   It would be easy to compose another volume about other modern Frenchmen not inferior to these ; and amongst living men, too modest to look for any thing like notoriety, I have very frequently recognized qualities which belong to my present heroes, — the simplicity of Rude, the fire of Henri Regnault, the industry of Ampère, the sociability of Victor Jacquemont, the purity of Perreyve. These qualities may, I think, be increased to some extent in ourselves by the study of those lives in which they shone with a more than ordinary lustre, and it may be an acceptable service to make such lives more generally known.

I may add, with regard to materials, that my biographies are founded, wherever possible, on letters ; and, when these were wanting, on accounts furnished by near friends of the subject.   In the cases of Jacquemont and Ampère, the letters were delightfully abundant ; in that of Rude, they were unfortunately rare.   In all cases alike, I have been careful to sift and compare my materials, and believe that the strict accuracy of the narratives may be relied upon.

MAY, 1878.

CONTENTS.

MODERN FRENCHMEN.

VICTOR JACQUEMONT.

IT is almost an indiscretion to read the letters of
Victor Jacquemont; for he wrote in the confidence
of private friendship, and was so far from anticipating
publicity that he even disapproved of quotation from
his correspondence, and endeavored to forget that his
friends exchanged his letters amongst themselves.
Even such a limited degree of publicity as that resulting from the circulation of a single manuscript amongst
those who knew and loved him would have been
enough, if he had allowed his mind to dwell upon it,
to put a drag upon his pen, and prevent it from running
along the paper with the careless felicity and the remarkable swiftness which distinguished it. If Jacquemont could have foreseen that a day would come when
hundreds of his most frank and intimate letters would
be in the hands of ten thousand readers, he would have
written with more reserve, and we should have lost one
of the few really perfect opportunities of studying the
nature of the man. It is fortunate that Jacquemont's

obscurity during life — obscurity, I mean, so far as the European public was concerned — left him to the last without the slightest suspicion that whilst hastily scribbling, often amidst circumstances the most adverse to literary composition, he was writing what would be afterwards one of the most famous books of autobiography in the world. In the·cabin of a ship rolling and pitching on the Atlantic, under a thin tent in the freezing air of the snowy Himalaya, and beneath the pitiless blaze of summer in the plains of Central India, he wrote with the same vivacity, the same frankness and ease, the same unfailing charm. Victor Jacquemont's literary facility would be a fortune to a professional man of letters, and yet he never knew that he possessed any literary talent or skill ; he thought of himself simply as a wandering *savant* writing to his friends to beguile his loneliness, to cheat the sense of distance by turning his thoughts to those he had left in Europe, and to keep the friendships he valued alive until his return. The energy of his literary faculty found a happy exercise in letter-writing ; and, when he sat down with a supply of paper before him, he covered sheet after sheet with a rapidity which is surprising in itself, and is much more surprising when we consider the admirable quality of what he wrote, — the light and elegant yet perfectly constructed language, nimble and active as a gazelle ; the keen observations on men and things which follow each other in such abundance ; the profound yet genial philosophy which pervades both narrative and criticism ; and the delightful mixture of vigorous thinking with tender feeling, or alternation from one to the other. One day, being at sea, he felt an impulse to write to M. de Tracy, and gave his pen its liberty: the letter now occupies forty-two pages of print. On another occasion, being on the bank of the Hydaspes, he covered fifty-eight sheets in a day,—a wonderful feat of penmanship, if we consider nothing but the swiftness of the hand. There are hardly any corrections in his manuscripts, even in his scientific journals; and, when letters and journals went to the press, the only errors that had to be set right were those of the printer. Here, then, is a natural gift of writing, a natural communicativeness with the pen; but the gift was not cultivated consciously. The inborn talent was never developed into an art: it was simply an intellectual activity which satisfied certain needs of Jacquemont's richly endowed nature, after the physical activity of travelling. He would ride for several hours, and then sit down in his tent to relieve his mind by the facile exercise of the pen. When weary of the dull society on board ship, he had the same resource. Yet, although literature was to him a mere play of the mind after the fatigues of scientific labor and the hardships of travel, his production in a few years was by no means inconsiderable. Four volumes of his letters have been published; and, besides these, there are six quarto volumes of his scientific journals. This is much indeed, considering the kind of life the author was leading when he wrote.

The personal appearance of Victor Jacquemont was peculiar and remarkable, so that people who had once

seen him remembered him afterwards without difficulty.
His height was five feet ten inches, French measure,
which is equivalent to six feet four inches, English.
This fine stature was not, however, accompanied by any
corresponding development of the muscles, which in his
case were the reverse of athletic, yet wiry and capable
of surprising endurance. He loved the warm, tropical
air, and said that, although his long, thin body could
hardly be compared to a rosebud, he felt as if it made
him bloom. He amused himself, in his letters, by describing his meagre person in the flowing robes of the
East, surmounted by a pale face with spectacles and a
long moustache, shaded by a great, wide-brimmed straw
hat. The spectacles betray, what was really a misfortune for an ardent traveller and student, the defective
condition of his sight. He declared that seeing was
not to him a physical pleasure, but simply a satisfaction
of the mind ; and his own imperfect experience led him
to the erroneous conclusion that sight was the most ob-
tuse of all our senses. In other respects, he was better
gifted. His long limbs were not moulded like those of
a Greek statue, but they were good for use, — the proof
being that he could walk fifteen leagues a day without
fatigue. He could maintain health and strength on
short rations, — a most valuable accomplishment for a
traveller. To conciliate the good-will of strangers, Nature had endowed him with a singularly musical and
persuasive voice, to which few could listen without
yielding to the charm, and which was a means of conquest for him as beauty is for a woman. Besides these

gifts, he had all the courages : the courage of the nerves, which can retain perfect self-possession in danger; moral courage, which is not to be cowed by the ostentation of splendor and power ; and the courage of the intellect, which will not be deterred by toil, and looks truth straight in the face.

In 1830, Victor Jacquemont's father was seventy-four years old. He had all his life been a moderate liberal in politics, and so incurred the suspicions of the police during the despotism of Napoleon I. Fouché ordered his house to be searched, took away his books and papers, and put him into prison without trial, keeping him closely confined in a dark and narrow room for the space of eleven months. During these months, his son Victor, then a child eight years old, went twice a week to the prison, and there was taught to read and to write. There were no grounds for suspicion against the prisoner except that he had been a liberal member of the French parliament, and was the friend of some eminent men whom Napoleon did not like. He was a man of cultivated intelligence, gifted, like his son, with a remarkable facility as a writer. It is said that he never made an erasure in the manuscripts of his voluminous works. His scholarly accomplishments — for he had been Director of Public Instruction, and was a Corresponding Member of the Institute — enabled him to give an effectual direction to the education of his son. Victor afterwards studied medicine, but less with the intention of following it as a profession than as a part of his extensive general education. He pursued chemistry

in earnest, in the laboratory of the famous chemist
Thénard; and there an accident happened to him which
affected the course of his whole life. Whilst engaged
in an experiment with cyanogen, he was suddenly interrupted by the entrance of an idle visitor, and somehow
broke the vessel containing the deadly gas. The ema-
nations produced such an effect upon the larynx that for
some time laryngean phthisis was apprehended; and, to
avert this, the patient went to stay in the country at La
Grange, the well-known residence of General Lafayette,
who was a friend of his family. His recovery was slow,
but satisfactory; and, in order that it might not be inter-
fered with, he devoted himself chiefly to those scientific
studies which can be pursued in the open air, including
botany and agriculture. The early maturity of his
mind is proved by a letter addressed by him, at the age
of nineteen, to a friend of his, M. de Tracy, an agricul-
turist at Paray. He had been travelling in Picardy and
Artois, and had made it his business during this excursion to observe the farms and plantations. He gives a
résumé of these observations in the letter to M. de
Tracy, which occupies thirteen pages of print, and is as
thoroughly business-like a document as if it had been a
report prepared for a Minister by an agent of twice his
years. Besides this excursion, he made many others in
the most picturesque regions of France and Switzerland, but much more in the spirit of a man of science
than with the feelings of an artist. There was an artistic element in his nature, but it had nothing to do
with the sense of sight: the artist in Jacquemont was

altogether musical. He delighted in music, and understood it.

The poisonous cyanogen had driven Victor Jacquemont away from Paris; and now another evil, as dangerous to his moral well-being as the gas had been to his bodily health, was to drive him away from France. No details about this are known to the public; but it is known that in the year 1826, at which date he was twenty-five years old, a hopeless passion took possession of him, that he struggled against it with all the energy of his will, and finally sought safety by placing the Atlantic Ocean between himself and the lady who had enslaved him. The indifferent reader may smile at this, for strong passions are uncommon in these days, or at least not often avowed, and those who suffer from them are likely to incur more ridicule than sympathy; but when the passion of love first takes possession of such a man as Jacquemont, and the obstacles are not to be overcome, he must either conquer it by sheer strength of will, or waste his manhood in the vainest of all longings and regrets. Jacquemont, like all ardent and energetic natures, had at the same time strong passions and a strong will to govern them; but the inward battle was not won without suffering.

Who the lady was, we have never been told; but there is a passage in the correspondence which refers to country rides on horseback, to wild gallopings on the heather, in despair. He speaks, too, of a lady who galloped one foggy morning; but when they met their horses went more quietly, and he noticed that there had been

tears in her eyes.   If this incident refers to the serious
and dangerous passion which Jacquemont was fighting
against in 1826, he must have met the lady in the country during a visit to some château in a wild and lonely
part of France, — a region of heather and rough roads.

Victor Jacquemont had two brothers, named Porphyre
and Frederic.   Porphyre was ten years his senior, and
Frederic two.   The eldest was an officer in the army, a
captain of artillery ; the second was in business in the
West Indies.   The captain had a warm fraternal affection for his youngest brother, which was heartily returned, with a perfect trust and confidence, and lasted,
unchilled by absence, until death put an end even to
epistolary intercourse.   Towards Frederic the sentiment
of confidence and friendship was not so lively; nevertheless, when Victor determined to leave France, his
first thought was to visit his brother in the remote
West Indian island.   Porphyre accompanied him to
Havre, from whence he sailed to New York on an
American vessel, and thence to St. Domingo.   There
are some amusing letters about this first experience of
the sea, but I have not space for details of this kind.
Jacquemont, as a man of science, was rather taken
aback by the condition of the ship's medical stores.
There were twenty-four drugs, all in confusion, and no
scales to weigh doses.   The system of administering
these medicines was not regulated by the malady to be
combated, but by the quantity of the drugs in store.
Whatever the ailment, the rule was to administer the
drug of which the stock was greatest ; and the sailors

had the most perfect confidence in this system, which seems to have answered admirably. Without presuming too much upon his medical and surgical knowledge, Jacquemont never hesitated to use it when he knew more than any one else within call; so he acted as surgeon on the ship, and took care of a young sailor whose arm was accidentally broken. Besides this occupation, he had plenty to do in improving his knowledge of English.

No one with so lively an intelligence as that of Victor Jacquemont could land in a country entirely new to him, and different in almost all respects from his own, without receiving very strong impressions; but I think it better to defer the consideration of these until I have to consider his criticisms of other nations, which will supply materials for a comparison. He landed at New York on the eighth of December, 1826, stayed there until the twentieth of January next year, and then sailed for Port-au-Prince, where he arrived a month later, after a slow but pleasant passage, during which he could study quietly. He enjoyed the increasing warmth of the voyage southwards, and felt himself in a state of physical well-being highly favorable to the labors of the mind. This physical serenity had probably also a beneficial influence in enabling him to bear more easily the love-sorrow which had driven him to distant shores. The tone of his letters from the West Indies is calm, and their practical philosophy reminds one of Montaigne. It was always rather a habit with Jacquemont to talk about his bodily state in very intimate letters, not in the least from any morbid tendency, but merely because he was wise enough to know that little can be done in this life without health, and that for great performance something even more than ordinary health is needed. He always aspired to, and often enjoyed, that happy equilibrium of the organism in which the body obeys the mind without effort, and the mind goes to its purposes without hindrance. No sacrifice of mere pleasure appeared to him too high a price for such a condition as this. "I bear life lightly," he wrote from the West Indies. "The climate here is perfection, and I desire no change. Every constitution has its own needs, and mine are marvellously satisfied here."

Victor Jacquemont stayed three months at Hayti, with his brother Frederic ; and during this sojourn an event occurred to him which had nothing to do with the West Indian islands, but diverted his attention to the East. A letter reached him from the administration of the Jardin des Plantes at Paris, proposing that he should undertake an expedition in India for the purpose of studying its ethnology, geology, and botany, in the interest of science in general and of the Jardin des Plantes in particular. He had some doubts at first about the sufficiency of his intellectual preparation for a task requiring such a variety of knowledge ; but a feeling of confidence, if not in what he knew already, at least in his powers of acquisition and determination to learn more, at length carried the day. He wrote to accept the offer, and by so doing sealed his own fate and assured his fame, accepting, though he knew it not, an early death and that posthumous celebrity which men vainly call immortality.

After a second sojourn in New York and some excursions in the Northern States, Victor Jacquemont returned to France in the autumn of 1827, and at once set about preparing for his Indian expedition. The day of departure came at last ; and the separation from his father and his brother Porphyre has been minutely described by an eye-witness, M. Prosper Mérimée. There was a striking resemblance, on one or two points, between Jacquemont's character and what we are accustomed to consider the typical English character. Like the English, he was energetic and ready to go anywhere ; like the English, he was stoical, and had a great dislike to the betrayal of tender emotion. " The last day that he spent at Paris," says M. Prosper Mérimée, " I dined with him and with his father and his brother Porphyre. The repast was any thing but gay, and yet a stranger would not have suspected that this united family was on the eve of a long separation. When the hour of departure had come, Victor embraced his father, and said : ' I hope you will take care of your health. Avoid taking cold.' 'Don't be anxious. Send us news of yourself when you can,' the father answered, as he removed his spectacles, and took a volume of Walter Scott, which he read alternately with some metaphysical book. An old servant burst into tears. Victor went down the stair rather faster than was his wont. When he had taken his place in the mail for Brest, he took my hand and said, in as firm a voice as he could command, ' You will go to see him often.' He was so young, his health seemed so robust, there was in him such a happy mixture of resolution and prudence, that no evil presentiment occurred to me."

The traveller sailed from Brest at the end of August in the year 1828, he being then twenty-seven years old. The ship, *La Zélée*, was a man-of-war, bound for Bengal, with the new governor of Pondicherry on board, M. de Meslay; and our hero had his berth in the same ship, on account of his official capacity as a naturalist with a mission from the government. The *Zélée* had most respectable qualities, but she was slow, and the voyage before her was very long; for her first destination was Brazil, after which she was to recross the Atlantic from Brazil to the Cape of Good Hope, and then sail up the Indian Ocean to the Bay of Bengal, — rather a roundabout way of getting from France to Pondicherry, especially if we compare it with modern steam locomotion through the Isthmus of Suez and across the Indian Peninsula. Having so much sea-life before him, Jacquemont quietly took up his residence on board ship, and set to work at his studies with great energy. "Not much work (of a studious kind) is done on board, yet more than I should have believed. I am seldom alone in reading and writing of an evening, when a pretty lamp hanging from the ceiling sheds its light on our great, green-covered dining-table, and our room seems like the prettiest of studies. Here I make long sittings, and always feel some satisfaction after them, for I work easily and pleasantly. I mix my readings so as to rest myself by change, and they are all of them like a light embroidery on the grave business of learning Persian." In another letter, he compares the uniformity of life at sea to that of the cloister, — a uniformity which would harmonize well with a studious life, if sailors could be studious, — but "the day drags on, wasted in idle talk." Besides this inconvenience, Jacquemont complains that a ship-of-war is far noisier than a merchantman. Horribly shrill whistles are used instead of words of command ; even the drum is used, and on fine afternoons the cannons thunder during the artillery exercise, or one is disturbed by volleys of musketry. At first, all these noises put out our Oriental student considerably ; but he soon got accustomed to them, and such is the effect of habit that after a while he hardly noticed them at all. Worse than whistles, drums, cannon, and musketry, was the intolerable affliction of universal singing, from which the only escape was to jump into the sea. It gives one a strange notion of the discipline on board a French man-of-war, but Jacquemont affirms that on the *Zélée*, without respect for the presence of the governor of Pondicherry, about fifty voices of officers and men were perpetually singing the songs of Béranger, each vocalist in his own key, and without even keeping to his key. Most studious persons would have found this hard to bear ; but imagine the effect of it on Jacquemont, who was not only a student, but a musician with a fastidious and cultivated taste ! After a while, he began to long for better-informed society than that of the officers, whose ignorance, by his account of it, was something

wonderful. Taken out of the naval school at sixteen, and put on board ship without having had even
time to visit their families, they had been sailing about
ever since, with only a few months' leave. They were all
good enough sailors, and could work the routine business of their profession ; but they had not "even the
most superficial ideas of astronomy, mechanics, or
natural philosophy generally." No one on board knew
accurately the difference between the barometer and the
thermometer ; and, notwithstanding their voyages in the
Mediterranean and elsewhere, not one of them knew
a word of English or Italian. In short, Jacquemont
affirmed that these officers knew nothing but their
trade. They had, however, one very great recommendation : they lived together in the most perfect fellowship
and good humor, and admitted Jacquemont into their
society with a cordiality which he appreciated.

At Rio, his feelings of humanity, always very sensitive, were outraged by the arrival of several slave-ships,
with crowded and miserable cargoes covered with horrible maladies ; whilst in the city on the shore, by way of
contrast, glittered the wealth and luxury which call
themselves civilization. Moral evil afflicted and irritated Jacquemont, though he did not weakly shrink
from the contemplation of it; and, if the kidnapped
negroes excited his pity, he felt both contempt and disgust for their masters, "with their external European
varnish of elegance and politeness, their gold lace, their
diamond stars, their ribands, their titles, their ignorance,

their cowardice, and their dishonesty." He calls Brazil "the abomination of desolation, with its hundreds of viscounts and marquises, and no respectable middle class." He does not much respect the French colony either, which consists of modistes, tailors, and hair-dressers; and he speaks English in order not to be confounded with them. Let us hope· that Brazil has improved since 1828, and is now better worthy of its present manly and enlightened Emperor.

By way of varying his experience of sea-voyaging, Jacquemont witnesses three things on the *Zélée* in which few would much desire to participate; namely, a collision, a naval engagement, and a good rattling tropical tempest. The collision took place, in a very lumbering fashion, in the port of Rio itself, where there is abundance of sea-room. A merchant-ship was riding quietly at anchor, when the *Zélée* boldly ran into her, and smashed both spars and oaken ribs, but luckily no bones. This kept the travellers a week longer at Rio, during the repairs. The naval engagement took place to the east of the Cape of Good Hope, and only amused the crew of the *Zélée*, though it might have been rather serious for the other vessel, which was English. The *Zélée*, more zealous than the occasion warranted, delivered one broadside, and was ready to deliver another, when the enemy, who had fired no guns at all, made signals of submission. Jacquemont, being the only man who could speak English, was sent to board her with a party of sailors armed to the teeth, and with a collection of loaded pistols in the boat beneath their feet. There was no occasion for the pistols, however, as the enemy turned out to be nothing but a most peaceful Liverpool merchantman, with a cargo of goods and three passengers. The captain and crew were extremely civil, but rather alarmed. The only harm done by the broadside was a broken yard and a torn sail. Jacquemont pretended to scold the Liverpool skipper for having come near another vessel in the night, and the skipper made most humble apologies for the broadside that had been directed against him. The passengers were prodigal of friendliness, not desiring a second broadside, and made Jacquemont drink some champagne. The worst of this adventure was an accident that happened to one of the French sailors, who broke his arm, which had to be amputated, and Jacquemont tied the arteries. He was always cool and ready when any services were required of him.

The *Zélée* went on so slowly that they called her a wooden shoe. It had taken her sixty days to go from Brest to Rio de Janeiro, and seventy-four days from Rio to Bourbon Island. Here the *Zélée* would have rested for some days after her great labors, but she was caught in one of those fearful storms which demolish houses and cover the coasts with wreck. The *Zélée* went out to sea again, for more safety; lost some spars, all her boats, an anchor, and part of her bulwarks; and shipped so many seas that she had three feet of water between decks, which flowed into the hold. However, not a life was lost, though the only two officers on board remained sixty hours at a stretch on deck without sleeping. Meanwhile, Victor Jacquemont, lucky fellow, was comfortably established on shore as the guest of a wealthy colonist, the only impediment to his happiness being anxiety for his books and instruments on the ship, which fortunately took no harm. The deliberate *Zélée* occupied forty days from Bourbon to Pondicherry, making exactly one hundred and seventy-four days from Brest to India. The almost intolerable tedium of so long a voyage had been much alleviated by friendly intercourse with M. de Meslay, the new Governor of Pondicherry, and Jacquemont's fellow-passenger. With this " King of Yvetot," as our hero called him, he remained a guest for a time in the palace of that Indian Yvetot, and thence sailed for Calcutta, always on board the leisurely and inevitable *Zélée*, arriving there on the 5th of May, 1829. She had started from Brest on the 26th of August in the preceding year!

In the interval between Jacquemont's return from America and his departure for India, he had been to London to make use of some introductions in order to facilitate his future travels in our Eastern possessions. He had been received in London with the greatest kindness, and had brought away fresh letters of introduction, enough to open for him every palace and every bungalow between Cape Comorin and the Himalaya. During this stay in London, one of the East India Directors had given Jacquemont a dozen letters, and when the young traveller had returned to Paris he was surprised to receive a thirteenth from the same person. In the interval, this Director had been to see our hero's

friend, Mr. Sutton Sharpe, and had asked for his word
as a gentleman that Jacquemont was not a spy of the
French government. After this assurance, the additional letter had followed. "The others," said the
Director, "are such as one gives sometimes, but now
he will have such a letter as is *never* given."

The time had now arrived, the *Zélée* having come to
the end of her wanderings, when these recomménda-
tions were to be used to the best advantage. Our hero
accordingly, like a true Frenchman, clothed his long
person from head to foot in ceremonious black, and set
foot on the soil of British India, after which he immediately got into a palanquin, and had himself carried to the
residence of Mr. Pearson, the Advocate-General. Here
he was suddenly introduced into an immense drawing-
room, where sat three grandly dressed ladies and an
elderly gentleman in light clothing, all occupied in being fanned in a complicated manner. Unluckily, Jacquemont's mind had begun to occupy itself with the novelty
of what he saw, so that he could not retain his command
over his meagre colloquial English, and all the speech
he could make consisted of these few words : —

"I spoke a few words of English formerly, sir ; but I
perceive I have forgotten the all, so help me !"

Who could resist such a frank appeal ? Both the
elderly gentleman and the three ladies helped, and so
effectually that immediately afterwards the foreign visitor "was swimming in English like a little fish in the
river." Let us pursue the narrative in his own words : —

"I delivered my letters of introduction, not counting

upon them with much confidence; for they were second-hand or third-hand letters, yet they gained me an invitation at once. Then I was asked if these were the only introductions I had brought to Calcutta; a question I answered by exhibiting a monstrous parcel which made a bulge in my pocket, and which, charged beforehand like artfully prepared fireworks, opened with some desultory squibs,—a doctor, or captain, or merchant; then, becoming gradually more brilliant, came to a judge, then to the chief justice, then to a member of council, and finished by way of *bouquet* with the name of Lady William Bentinck and the Governor-General, five times repeated. Every chair came nearer to mine, and I was overwhelmed with questions and kindly offers."

A note from Miss Pearson to Lady William Bentinck was answered immediately by an invitation to call at the vice-regal palace, where Jacquemont was received with kindness, and kept to lunch and invited to dine the same evening. Lady William soon discovered that Jacquemont knew friends of hers ,in Paris, and from that moment the ice was broken. The Governor-General came in after her ladyship had been talking an hour and a half with Jacquemont, read the letters of introduction whilst they sat at lunch, and at once frankly admitted the young foreigner to an acquaintance which soon ripened into a warm friendship, notwithstanding the great difference of age and the still greater disparity in social rank and position. That first day at Calcutta is interesting as an illustration of Victor Jacquemont's character, of the ease and tact with which, in an embarrassing position, he won valuable allies by the use of his two great social arts, which were: first, the most absolute abandonment of every thing like false pretension; and, secondly, courage in exercising his own abilities whenever he felt it to be necessary. In a letter to his father, he describes the vice-regal pomp and state, the servants in long white robes with turbans of scarlet and gold, the uncertain light amidst distant columns, the brilliant splendor of the table with its magnificent fruits and flowers, the unseen, remote orchestra, executing "with rare perfection" the sweetest symphonies of Mozart, the lightest melodies of Rossini. Jacquemont has the place of honor; but, instead of being confounded by surroundings so new to him, he simply enjoys his dinner, and the splendor, and the music, and especially the conversation. He thinks the time has come for talking, and he talks easily and fluently in French, in English to the best of his ability. From that evening, Jacquemont was a frequent and favored guest at Government House. A fortnight later, the Governor-General went to the country, and Jacquemont was of the party. At Barrackpoor, they gave him a pretty cottage to work in; and Lady William would have him with her on her elephant. "She seemed so well pleased with our conversations on the summit of this walking mountain that she would have no other companion in these outings during our stay at Barrackpoor." In the evening, after dinner, the Viceroy had his turn with Jacquemont, the two sitting together, not on an elephant, but on a sofa, and talking about India and the United States.

There are some bits of English in the early letters from England which prove that Jacquemont had not yet mastered our language, but this did not prevent him from soon becoming the fashion at Calcutta. Besides being the fashion, he was very strongly liked, — *loved* perhaps would be the more accurate word, — for the charm of his manners and the fearless openness of his disposition. The legal and judicial families, the Pearsons, the Ryans, the Greys, received him more as a son than as a foreign visitor; the officers treated him like a brother; and everybody tried to facilitate his studies and insure the success of his enterprise. But as I felt compelled to pass hastily over Jacquemont's visits to New York, so I perceive it to be necessary to get quickly out of Calcutta. We will return to some of these hospitable Anglo-Indians at a later period, when we shall have to speak of Jacquemont's opinions and impressions about the English and other nations. I may mention one friendship formed at Calcutta, not with an Englishman, but with a Spanish refugee, Colonel Hezeta, an old companion in arms of Lord William Bentinck during the Peninsular war, and greatly esteemed by him. Notwithstanding Jacquemont's hearty appreciation of English kindness, it is evident that a closer *sympathy* existed between him and Hezeta than between the French traveller and his English friends. But this, again, is a part of my subject which may be reserved for the present.

The reader will remember that our hero's commission from the Jardin des Plantes was to study "the ethnology, geology, and botany of India." As to ethnology,

all parts of India were equally interesting to an observer
fresh from Europe ; but this was not the case with
regard to botany and geology. Jacquemont's studies in
these sciences, and his ardor for fresh discoveries, urged
him irresistibly to the mountains. His plans of work
included a complete exploration of the Himalayas,
"from the Indus to the Brahmapootra ;" but this gigantic
project was judiciously divided into two parts. He intended first to explore the north-western portion of the
chain, and then, after travelling in the peninsula, to
resume if possible his mountain work at a later period,
and complete it from west to east. He enjoyed the
idea of concentrating his labors "on a space so magnificently marked out by Nature herself," and this
seemed to him far better than mere desultory wanderings in Asia ; so he renounced a dream once entertained
of travels in Persia and Asia Minor, in order to give
his whole strength to his magnificent Indian enterprise.

He had health enough for the work, if only it would
last ; and he was determined if possible to keep his
health by prudence : he had knowledge enough for the
acquisition of more knowledge ; but had he money
enough ? Of private fortune, he had none whatever,
and his allowance from the Jardin des Plantes was
absurdly inadequate. The learned professors who were
trustees of that museum had sent Jacquemont forth
upon his mission with an income of £240 a year ! He,
with his economical habits and absolute ignorance of
Indian life, had at first imagined that his work might be
done on this ; but he had not been a fortnight at Cal-

cutta before the falsity of his position was made plain
to him. The expenses to be incurred arranged themselves under three heads : 1. Personal; 2. Travelling ;
3. Scientific. The allowance from Paris would cover
the first, with care ; but whence was the money to come
for the two others ? There was, however, no pressing
pecuniary anxiety for the immediate present, as the
traveller had been saving money on the slow *Zélée*, and
had spent very little whilst enjoying English hospitality
at Calcutta. He therefore made up his mind to start
as soon as possible, and travel as economically as he
could ; but, before setting out, he wrote a long letter to
the trustees who had appointed him, setting plainly
before them the difficulties of his position, — going into
minute detail like a man of business, which he was.
To show, for example, that scientific expenses might be
considerable, he mentions that a predecessor, M. Dus-
sumier, spent £360 on the preservation of nothing but
his Indian fishes. The idea that a traveller could explore all India for scientific purposes, and make collections for a national museum, on the beggarly pittance
of £240 a year, is an idea which could only occur to a
council of French officials.

Jacquemont's first purchase was an old white horse,
which he got for £40; but before his departure the
white horse fell, so he was sold, and replaced by a
vigorous little Persian stallion, of a red color, which
turned out to be most serviceable, and only cost £25.
The more Jacquemont knew this animal, the better he
liked him, and after long travel he said : " His walk is

remarkably rapid and easy to the rider, and he can travel far at a gallop when necessary. I can throw the rein on his neck and read a book, arriving without fail at my journey's end as if I were a letter in a post-bag." Both rider and horse were animals of great stamina and endurance. Now and then they had little tiffs, which generally ended in an empty saddle, but without any diminution of mutual regard. However, notwithstanding these accidents, Jacquemont pleasantly affirmed that he was too bad a horseman, too unclassical, to fall often.

The pen of Cervantes would be needed for any adequate description of our hero (who, in nobleness, poverty, and bodily presence, was not unlike a sounderminded Don Quixote), as he rode forth from Calcutta on those wanderings that were to make him famous. He was clothed in a long, nankeen dressing-gown, over which he wore a robe of coarse silk, as the old knights wore silk over their armor; and his great straw hat was covered with black silk also. He quitted Calcutta in the evening (Nov. 20, 1829), and a *Friday* evening, — day of evil omen! After riding five leagues on the Persian horse, he was already so far in advance of his cook that supper was not to be hoped for, so he supplied its place with two biscuits, — a foretaste of the meagre cheer that awaited him. These details of his beginning interested him so much that we find them all in his letters. The first night, having reached a bungalow, he slept in it, roughly arranging his camp furniture in the empty room with a new feeling of admiration for European inns. After that, he discovered that his little tent was much more snug and cosey than the four bare walls of a bungalow; that it could be much better lighted with his single candle, and felt more cheerful and homelike: so he remained faithful to the tent ever after. A traveller may become attached to a tent, as a yachtsman to the cabin of his yacht; and it becomes a familiar home to him, with a mute welcome of its own, after every weary day. Besides this, to lodge in a bungalow cost four shillings a night, with two for service; and our hero was not sorry to economize this outlay. Notwithstanding this cheerful beginning of camp life, Jacquemont arrived later, like most travellers, at a strong conviction that houses are an excellent invention, and declared that he should prefer a shake-down on the floor of an inn to his little mountain tent, shaken and threatened by the freezing winds of the Himalaya.

Our traveller's establishment was, as nearly as he could make it, in proportion to the smallness of his means, though magnificent if compared with that of Don Quixote; for Jacquemont had six servants, all counted, which, as he facetiously remarked (comparing small things with great), made exactly a thousandth part of the vast travelling establishment which moved with the Governor-General. A bamboo cart drawn by oxen carried the baggage, with the exception of the tent, which was borne on the back of a solitary ox. The six servants, however, did not include the ox-drivers: they were employed exclusively in the service of their master and his steed; one carrying his gun, another his cooking apparatus, another a ration for the horse, and so on. Of course, Jacquemont had never been served by such a numerous establishment of domestics in his life ; yet such is the effect of comparison, that he felt himself poorly provided because an English captain of infantry would not travel in India with less than twenty-five servants for his tent and palanquin and person. The English officer's tent was also very different from Jacquemont's, being heavy and comfortable and capacious, whilst our hero's canvas house was of such modest dimensions that he called it "the smallest tent in India." He laughs at its smallness more than once, and declares that it is too little for him to go inside, and that the best way to use it would be merely to fold it and sleep on the folded canvas. He had no hammock, but possessed a substitute in a light frame with canvas stretched upon it; and he often slept on nothing but a mat.

Jacquemont's daily habits when marching were as follows. He breakfasted at four in the morning on half a pound of rice, boiled in milk and sugared. From that time until dinner, he had nothing to eat, but drank a cup of milk whenever an opportunity offered, his cook having orders to seek for milk in every village on the way. The tent was pitched every afternoon, and then the cook prepared dinner, which invariably consisted of a fowl or other bird (an old peacock, on one occasion) in rice (*en pilau*) with plenty of rancid native butter, but no bread, his drink being water, or water with a few drops of brandy in it. Sometimes in the evening he consoled himself with a cup of tea, either when the temperature fell too low, or when he had writing to do and wanted to keep himself awake. In this way, Victor Jacquemont expended no less than forty shillings a month on the pleasures of the table, including the illicit profits of his cook. The perfect novelty of this kind of life, the complete severance from his own past, the strange customs and speech around him, made the traveller sometimes doubt his own identity, and suspect that, in the land of the transmigration of souls, some other soul had taken possession of his body.

Whilst travelling northwards in this way, the little caravan averaged more than eleven miles a day during a period of four months, which is a very high average for ox-travelling over so considerable a space of time. The usual ride on travelling days was twelve or fifteen miles, but this was sometimes much exceeded. At other times there were serious difficulties to overcome, as in the two days' march preceding the arrival at Rogonotpoor, in a sandy region, with fifty extra men to help the oxen by main force, and after the sands a river had to be crossed, and lo! beyond the river was no road, nothing but bush!

On arriving at Agra, Jacquemont discovered that there was a Roman Catholic bishop in the place, a native of Tuscany, to whom our traveller sent a polite note in Italian, requesting the honor of an audience. The answer was courteous in the extreme: so Jacquemont went at once to the episcopal palace, a little mosque in ruins, which the bishop dwelt in by permission of the Government, and here he found *monseigneur,*

a magnificent man as tall as himself "with five times
his bulk," and the finest beard Jacquemont had ever
seen in his life. A Scotchman accompanied him; and
as the bishop lived in poverty and simplicity, like a prelate of the early Church, the consequence was that no
Briton in Agra would believe him to be a bishop at all.
Our countrymen called him only *padri*, a spoiled Portu-
guese word, used in India for priests of different denomi-
nations. The bishop was therefore rather pleased to be
called *monsignore* (the conversation was in Italian) before a British witness. Notwithstanding his poverty
and his episcopal rank, he betrayed neither embarrassment nor pride, but hospitably invited his visitors to
pot-luck, and little luck there seems to have been in the
pot! They did not accept, so the bishop ate his dinner
in their presence, and the conversation turned on his
diocese. Jacquemont asked about the numbers of his
flock; and the prelate answered, " *La caldaja è molto
grande ; ma . . . la carne molto poca.*" * Now it so
happened that, as the genial prelate was pronouncing
these words, he was pursuing at the same time with his
iron fork the remains of a meagre *fricassée* in an enormous pewter dish ; and the accidental *apropos* of the
metaphor made Jacquemont laugh very heartily, the
bishop as heartily joining him. Meanwhile, the Scotchman, not understanding Italian, asked Jacquemont to
explain the joke; but when it was explained to him he
remained quite grave and solemn, and when they had
left the episcopal presence he expressed the opinion

---

* The pan is very big, but there is very little meat in it.

that it was very unbecoming, especially in a clergyman, to speak thus of Christian souls. The story is very like a bit out of Don Quixote, except that Cervantes could never have invented the Scotchman.

At Delhi, Jacquemont was received by no less a personage than the Great Mogul, who had never seen a Frenchman, and attentively studied the living specimen before him, from which he probably arrived at the erroneous conclusion that all Frenchmen were six feet four inches high. Jacquemont, being of a humorous disposition, had much ado to prevent himself from laughing at the absurdity of his own appearance; for, as a Frenchman, he had put on his black trousers, and, being in the East, he had been solemnly invested with a garment of honor like a flowery muslin dressing-gown, whilst his gray hat was turned into a turban by the vizier, and the Great Mogul himself completed the beauty of it by adding two ornaments in false jewelry. Jacquemont was conducted to the palace with great pomp, for in lieu of his own single horse and three oxen he was supplied by the English Resident with a regiment of infantry, a strong escort of cavalry, and an army of attendants, with a troop of elephants, richly caparisoned, in the rear. The Great Mogul asked if there were a king in France, a question which looks like wit, but was only ignorance. He also inquired if the French used the English language, thus betraying more ignorance. In consideration for the condition of the Oriental mind, the British Resident introduced Jacquemont as a conquering hero, a lord victorious in battle, *saheb bahadour,* which title he bore in the East. They do exactly the converse at Oxford, when they compliment a successful soldier by dubbing him D.C.L.

The English at Delhi obeyed the orders of the Governor-General with hearty good-will, for they treated Jacquemont with the utmost kindness and attention. On his departure, he was accompanied for two days by a hunting party of English gentlemen, and was mounted by their care on the finest Arab in those parts, so that he might ride pleasantly after the wild boars, which he did without accident, notwithstanding his " unclassical " horsemanship. Later in the same month, he joined a greater hunting party, and belonged to it for a fortnight, enjoying the kindness and cordiality of the English sportsmen, though his abstemious habits enabled him to do but scant justice to their good cheer. At Pattialah, they had a great hunt with the rajah's elephants, killing hundreds of hares and partridges, but no larger game. However, the novel scene amused Jacquemont, who threw himself heartily into the enjoyment of it. The merry company went with him as far as Saharunpoor, where he found a wretched botanical garden, under the direction of the resident physician, who made himself very useful by taking care of the traveller's collection and all superfluous things left behind at Saharunpoor, as he lightened his camp for the mountains. Faithful to the main purpose of his enterprise, Jacquemont had been doing scientific work ever since his departure from Calcutta, writing his observations and collecting specimens by the way. The first collection, formed between Calcutta and Delhi, had been left at Delhi under English care ; and now the second was left at Saharunpoor with the doctor, who also took charge of Jacquemont's Persian horse, which was sent back when its rider reached the Himalaya.

At the age of twenty-one, our hero had visited the Alps ; and now, in spite of the strength of a fresh impression, he at once perceived their superiority in grace, beauty, and interest. Although the vegetation of the Himalaya bore a close resemblance to Alpine vegetation, it was not so well placed for the adornment of the landscape; and this Indian scenery had not the broad valleys, the blue lakes, the rich meadows and pastures of the more picturesque Switzerland and Savoy. It is a consolation for holiday travellers, whose excursions are confined to Europe, that they may find within its limits the most beautiful scenery in the world.

In a letter to M. Victor de Tracy, dated the 26th of October, 1830, Jacquemont gives the following brief but clear description of the Indian Alps : " The Indian Himalaya may be compared with some regions in Europe. It is covered with forests whose trees bear a family likeness to those in the forests of the Alps ; namely, pine, fir, oak, cedar, and sycamore, growing in different proportions, according to the height of their situation. Above the limits of the forest, dwarf shrubs, willows, and juniper bushes are scattered on verdant pastures, and this zone reaches up to the line of eternal snow. Towards Thibet, however, the whole land is so elevated that the bottom of every valley is higher than

the forest limit on the southern slopes of the chain.
Vegetation, reduced to some dwarf shrubs, thorny,
stunted, and spreading low, and to a few sapless plants,
forms here and there a dark-colored patch by the side
of a torrent; the slopes of the mountains are covered
with nothing but their own *débris;* the immense horizon
includes no pleasanter prospect than a monotonous ster-
ility and desolation, surrounded by a wide circle of
snowy crests." *

In other letters, Jacquemont recurs to the impression
produced upon his mind and feelings by the scenery of
the Himalaya. "I have seen fine things," he says; but
he complains that what he had seen could never either
rouse his soul to admiration or soften it to tenderness
like the mere recollection of the Alps or the hills of
Central France. Nor was this due to the magic of the
native land, for even the hill scenery of St. Domingo
filled the traveller's mind with these tender recollections.
In such comparisons, although not an artist and little
gifted with any of the artistic sensibilities, Jacquemont
touched upon the most subtle and delicate influences of
landscape in nature and art. Why do we feel powerfully
stimulated or deeply moved by one order of scenery,
when another leaves us indifferent? The *ubi patria est*

---

* I shall have more to say of Jacquemont's literary abilities towards
the close of this study, but cannot help remarking here what a perfect
piece of writing the above quotation is. Not a word is wasted or out
of place; and the paragraph is so comprehensive that it conveys a clear
idea of a wide extent of country. Let us remember, too, that it was
written hurriedly, in a private letter to a friend, without any view to
publication.

of Tacitus does not answer the question. Jacquemont
was not born in St. Domingo, nor Turner by the Lake of
Lucerne.

Few travellers have had more of that sustained and
resolute heroism which steadily pursues ill-rewarded
labor in spite of adverse conditions. In the Himalayan
expedition, he was more poorly fed than ever, and the
necessities of mountain travel had caused such a reduction in his few comforts that his camp was little better
than a bivouac, and he suffered both from cold and
hunger, as well as the physical strain of hard pedestrianism ; yet his scientific labors went on day by day,
and all his hours were occupied. Four times he crossed
passes at the height of eighteen thousand feet, and
once he pitched his tent a thousand feet higher than
the summit of Mont Blanc. When exhausted by fatigue
and ill with the change of diet, — for the bag of rice
was empty, and could not be filled again at that altitude,
— he still endeavored to climb the snowy slopes to the
zone where all vegetation finally expires. The air was
so rarefied that he could not walk thirty paces without
difficulty of breathing and exhaustion. His men so
dreaded the toil in the snow that they mutinied, when
by deeds and words he re-established his authority, and
went on, like the hero of Longfellow's "Excelsior," but
with a more definite purpose. He had thirty-five porters with him (mountaineers), five domestics, and an
escort of five soldiers; yet few European travellers in
India have been so wretchedly fed and lodged. His
dinner had been boiled rice (so long as the rice lasted),

a piece of kid insipid and tough, and water from the nearest stream. He drank a little brandy at dawn only, to warm himself. The little tent was very thin, and the cold night wind from the snowy summits filtered through the tissue of it, came in gusts and squalls under its rim, and blew icily on Jacquemont as he lay on his hard bed without a mattress. This is what he suffered from most, the night cold ; for his constitution loved the sun like an orange-tree, and a low temperature was to him like Dante's frozen hell: so that his nights were miserable, though he was rolled like a mummy in fifteen yards of thick Thibetan flannel.

Notwithstanding the general dryness, the rainy season caught the little expedition, in the month of June, on the southern slopes of the Himalaya, and added to its other discomforts that of a thick, damp mist, which so obscured the daylight that Jacquemont could hardly see to write in it. Then came the rain " by bucketfuls," and the traveller marched away from it towards the rainless vales of Thibet. Here, at the worst, he found only wearisome winds and fogs.

A hardy spirit of adventure now urged our hero to penetrate even into the Chinese Empire, — an excursion of great difficulty, for he had to carry twelve days' provisions (sufficient for the journey and the return), and he had sixty men to keep. For five days they advanced without seeing a single village, and they had to cross two chains of mountains which exceeded the height of eighteen thousand feet. The utmost altitude reached during this expedition was above eighteen thousand four hundred feet, and here Jacquemont found quantities of new plants and organic remains, and made many observations, " which," as he said, " were an ample reward for the trouble and fatigue of the expedition." The special scientific purpose of this excursion was to see if there were not strata with shell-fish in them even there. These were found, and many new plants into the bargain.

Writing to his brother Porphyre, from the camp on the frontier of Chinese Tartary, Jacquemont describes the climate, and gives some details about his way of living: " There is a moderate amount of snow in winter, which is without thaw four months running : it hardly ever rains, but there comes a hurricane every day, at three in the afternoon, which lasts far into the night. I often awake long before dinner, frozen in my five rugs." His food consisted of coarse wheat cakes, the wheat half ground and with the bran in it, and a smoked mutton ham, of which he expected ultimately to devour the bone, as there was so little difference in hardness between it and the flesh. The expedition was not without danger ; for, although the troop included sixty men, only one-tenth of that number were combatants, and armed opposition was to be expected. Whatever little opposition they met with was overcome by Jacquemont's happy mixture of tact and audacity. He fired bullets into a tree, drank a spoonful of flaming brandy in the presence of the Chinese officer and his men, spoke to them with an air of offended dignity, and gave them some tobacco.

It is not hardship, it is not fatigue, that alarms or

discourages a man of spirit in such expeditions as this: the real enemy is sickness. During the whole of his Himalayan expedition, the worst hours for Jacquemont were passed in his tent in a forest, after a seven hours' march, when he was suddenly seized with horrible pains in the intestines, — pains so intense that they almost brought on delirium. Two days' march lay before him without a human habitation, and his band had only just provisions enough to carry them over this interval. These are the real trials of a traveller, — to be fit for nothing but a sick-bed and medical care, and yet forced to march forwards, forwards, on food entirely unsuited to his condition !

The Himalayan expedition lasted eight months, the summer being spent on the north side of the great range, chiefly on the banks of the Sutledje, or in exploring its tributary, the Spiti. During all this northern journey, such was the dryness of the atmosphere that Jacquemont never once detected a trace of dew. The land is not absolutely rainless ; for there is a little rain in spring, and a slight drizzle at rare intervals in autumn, but that is all. In winter there is a little snow. The scientific results of Jacquemont's northern excursion were a collection of plants unknown on the southern slopes of the mountains, a collection of minerals, and an abundance of observations. He passed to the south side in the beginning of October, descending first to Simla and travelling thence by the lower valleys to Saharunpoor, where he had left many things, and where his Persian horse awaited his return.

During seven months, Jacquemont had not heard or
spoken any European language, nor slept in a house,
and his table had been as solitary as it was ill-provided.
On his return to Simla, he found that his nomadic
habits clung to him still, so that a nervous restlessness
took possession of him as soon as he tried to be seden
tary and settle down to his writing, — a restlessness
which nothing but movement could relieve. This was
rather a serious inconvenience for a man who had to
settle arrears of correspondence with friends in Europe,
Asia, Africa, and America, and whose notion of letter-
writing was so magnificently liberal both as to quality
and quantity. Many a filial affectionate page did he
write to his old father, with abundant details about himself and his work, assuring him that the tall, lank body
was in good trim ; that he had not lost so much as a
tooth ; that he had a long moustache now, of an afflict-
ing color (the moustache was red), long hair, a very
brown face, the appearance of perfect health, and its
reality. It was hot at Simla, compared with the temperature of the high mountains ; so Jacquemont dressed
in white during the day, but in the evening, out of deference to his English host, he appeared in ceremonious
black silk stockings, dress-coat, every thing except
breeches, on which poor Jacquemont dared not venture on
account of the meagreness of his calves. " Had they
but been as well developed as my shoulders," he exclaimed regretfully, " 1 would have adopted the *culotte ;*
but under present circumstances I am not philosopher
enough for that ! "   Let it not be supposed that the love

of science had caused our hero to forget the graces and elegances of polite society! He kept a dress-coat somewhere in a box, — a coat which had none of the awkwardness of a new one, for it had been two years in use, including eight months at sea, and a fortnight of actual immersion in salt water during the storm at Bourbon. "It is one of the seediest coats in existence," said its proprietor; "yet the English pay me the most marked attentions in spite of it!" Nevertheless, he began to think seriously of providing a successor, and even of going so far as to order a new suit, in thick Chinese silk, "black and economical."

Jacquemont might reasonably look forward to much English hospitality, judging from the cordiality of the reception which had been hitherto given him everywhere. At Sabathoo, he had been the guest of Captain Kennedy, who treated him, I was going to say, "like a brother;" but men seldom treat their brothers half so well. Here, too, he made the acquaintance of Fraser of Delhi, who travelled with him southwards for two days; and a manly affection soon established itself between them, — an affection which afterwards became one of the strongest of all Jacquemont's attachments. During the journey between Sabathoo and Mahan, an accident happened to our hero, which exactly resembles one that occurred in an Indian defile to the present Governor-General, Lord Lytton. Jacquemont's horse was climbing a steep road on the edge of a precipice, when the ground gave way under his hind legs. He clung hard to the earth with his fore feet for half a minute, and then, being

able to cling no longer, fell backwards into the abyss.
As soon as the rider came to a consciousness of his situation, he found himself perched in a stunted, thorny tree,
with no worse injury than a blow on the head, received
from the horse as they fell over together. He expected
to see the horse dashed to pieces on the stones at the
bottom of the ravine ; but, lo ! the animal also was stick-
ing in a tree which grew conveniently lower down, and
waiting patiently, unhurt, till they fished him up with
ropes. Lord Lytton's accident was a precise repetition
of this. At Meerut arrived the news of the French
Revolution of 1830, just when Jacquemont happened to
be there ; and all the English officers, civil and military,
became suddenly possessed by such feelings of enthusiasm in favor of constitutional liberty in France, that
nothing would satisfy them but a banquet given to our
hero as a living representative of French liberal aspirations. His host, a colonel of cavalry, wounded at
Waterloo, was so enthusiastic that he embraced Jacquemont and burst into tears. Every Englishman in
Meerut wanted to shake Jacquemont's hand, which (he
declared) was oftener squeezed than that of M. de la
Fayette, in America. All this enthusiasm led to the
drinking of much champagne at the banquet. The champagne caused more enthusiasm still. Tri-color draperies
and flags hung over the festival ; the hero of the evening
wore tri-color ribbons on his breast, and so did all the
Englishmen in sympathy, rejoicing together over the
fall of that very white flag which English blood and
gold had helped to restore in France. Many a speech

was made. The honored guest launched out into a grand oration, in the English language, on liberty, the tri-color, the Imperial eagles, and the Gallic cock, ending with a brilliant and effective peroration on the alliance of France and England. The British officers at Meerut seem to have taken a peculiar pleasure in making Jacquemont deliver English speeches. It so happened that during his stay in the place there were several great military inspections. He was invited to each of these, and also to the inevitable banquet which followed ; the banquet never ending without a toast to the health and success of the traveller, with the kind wish that he might sometimes, though amongst strangers, forget the distance which separated him from his native land.

Towards the end of August, in the preceding year, when our hero was on the frontier of Chinese Tartary, at a distance of twenty-five days' march from the most advanced British station in the Himalayas, a Tartar courier had succeeded, by dint of much running and climbing, in overtaking his little band, and had delivered a packet of letters, amongst which there was one which turned out to be of the very greatest importance, as it affected the whole course of his future travels. This letter came from M. Allard, a French officer, who at that time was in the service of Runjeet Singh as generalissimo of his armies, and who now with great courtesy offered to facilitate Jacquemont's travels by every means in his power, and most especially by his influence with Runjeet. "I have learned," he said, "through Dr. Mur-

ıay, that a French traveller has arrived at Simla, who
is at the same time distinguished by his scientific attainments and by the mission intrusted to him.   This piece
of news makes me hope that an old officer might possibly be of use to one of his countrymen in regions so far
from their native land. . . . Make use of my services as
frankly as I offer them : it will be the countersign of our
nationality."   Here, at last, was the voice of the native
land in all its sweetness, made audible even to the
utmost confines of distant India.   Jacquemont's heart
was touched ; and he answered with a full expression of
his feelings, saying that the plains of the Punjab interested him little, but that if Runjeet could be induced
to let him travel in Cashmere, that would interest him
much.   On returning to Simla from the mountains, our
traveller found a second letter from M. Allard, recom-
mending him to get letters of introduction to Runjeet
from the Governor of Delhi.   In consequence of this
correspondence, Jacquemont resolved to get to Cashmere, if he possibly could ; and, when once the resolution
was taken, he used all his influence to further its accomplishment.   He wrote to Lord ·William Bentinck for an
introduction to Runjeet, begging to be described, not as
a victorious general, but simply as a doctor of medicine,
which was much nearer the truth, as he had received a
medical and scientific education.

At Delhi, the British Resident, by Lord William's
order, introduced Jacquemont personally to Runjeet's
representative there, in the warmest and most flattering
terms of recommendation that the Persian language

could supply. Here he left his collections, well preserved and in good order, not having money enough to
send them on to France, and so started on his expedition to the Punjab, with Cashmere for his ultimate purpose, towards the end of January, 1831. Resuming his
old camp habits of exercise and abstinence, which had
been interrupted of late by British hospitality, he resumed also the vigorous health which he had enjoyed
in the mountains. Even the irregularity of camp life
was a benefit to him. He pitched his tent on the battle-
field of Paniput, where he shot an old peacock, which
supplied an undesirable roast, washed down with brack-
ish water. From Kurnaul, he wrote to a friend : " Six
days of open-air life on foot and on horseback have
completely set me up again. Like a true Mussulman,
I have sworn myself to a total abstinence from spiritu-
ous liquors. I live like the natives, and find it to be
the *régime* which suits me best."

From Loodeeanah to Lahore the stages of the journey
were regulated by Runjeet Singh, who sent an officer
with thirty horsemen to greet and escort the traveller.
He crossed the Sutledje in some state and pomp, mounted
on an elephant and surrounded by his escort of cavalry.
On the opposite shore of the river, he was received by a
squadron, in order of battle, with military honors ; the
said squadron escorting him afterwards to his tent.
Here Runjeet's representative, Shah-el-Din, soon arrived, accompanied by several officers, and humbly offered
Jacquemont a bag of money, which, of course, the ill-paid
emissary of the Jardin des Plantes was only too happy

to accept; whilst the attendants came in a little procession, each man bearing an offering, such as a basket of fruit, a pitcher of cream, a pot of preserves, &c. The next day, Jacquemont, who was always careful of his dignity, did not invite Shah-el-Din to travel by his side, so he followed at a distance of two or three miles in the rear with his escort. When the camp was pitched, however, Jacquemont received a message from that officer, and afterwards a visit, during which the same ceremony of the money-bag and other presents was repeated. He began to wonder whether there was to be a quotidian money-bag so long as the journey lasted. The next evening, and the next, confirmed this pleasing expectation, for still did Shah-el-Din renew his obsequious visits, and offer his little sack of silver, whilst his attendants came with a daily offering of provisions, that threw far into the shade the stringy kids of the Himalaya, the hard mutton ham of Thibet, and the tough old peacock of Paniput. "Hitherto," said Jacquemont, "I have always been annoyed by the slowness of Indian travel, but Runjeet Singh has arguments that would reconcile me to the pace of a tortoise." — "You will be wanting to know," he writes gayly to his father, "how much there is in the sacks;" and then he tells him the sum, namely, a hundred and one rupees, — a daily allowance equal to more than a fortnight of poor Jacquemont's pay. He declared it made him begin to be avaricious!

At length, however, this pleasing journey drew towards its close; and, when Jacquemont's party got within two leagues of Lahore, they were met by a carriage and four, containing M. Allard and two other European officers in the service of Runjeet Singh. Allard and Jacquemont leaped to the ground, and embraced each other with the effusion which might be expected of two Frenchmen under such circumstances. Then Jacquemont got into the carriage; and after passing through a wild bit of country, rich in ruins, like the neighborhood of Delhi, they came to a delightful oasis — a royal garden of roses and lilies, with walks bordered by orange-trees and jessamine, and many fountains playing in their basins. In the midst of this charming spot stood a little palace, furnished with the greatest elegance and luxury; and this was to be the traveller's temporary home. Jacquemont was not much given to poetical description, yet the letter in which he tells all this reminds one of " Lallah Rookh." He had travelled on her road from Delhi, in Oriental pomp and state ; and now, at the gates of Lahore, a palace was assigned to him, worthy of the Princess, herself. Here a repast awaited him, splendidly served ; and when evening came his new friends left him alone, "in the enchantment," as he wrote, " of a dwelling which realizes the magic palaces of the ' Thousand and One Nights.'"

Then came Shah-el-Din, having announced the traveller's arrival to the king, who now sent exquisite grapes of Caboul, delicious pomegranates, other fruits in rare perfection, and also the ever-acceptable bag of silver, which this time contained five times as much as on the preceding evenings! A splendid dinner was served by a band of domestics in silken liveries, and so the wonderful day came to an end, and Jacquemont slept in the royal house, — more comfortably, let us hope, than under that thin tent by the snow fields of the wind-swept Himalaya!

The next day was a memorable one in our hero's existence, for he made the acquaintance of that remarkable soldier and sovereign Runjeet Singh, a man who, had it not been for the too close neighborhood of the colossal British power in the East, might have played amongst the Princes of India a part not less predominant than that of Napoleon amongst the dynasties of Europe. Jacquemont had no opportunity of studying Runjeet as a military chieftain, for he did not accompany him on any warlike expedition ; but he had the most ample opportunities for observing Runjeet's acute and original mind. It is probable that no European ever knew the wily sovereign of Lahore so thoroughly as Jacquemont came ultimately to know him. Of all Indians, he had the most lively and insatiable curiosity ; a curiosity so eager that it compensated, in the opinion of his visitor, for the apathy of all other Orientals. His talk was a series of interrogations. "He asked me," said Jacquemont, "a hundred thousand questions about India, the English, Europe, Bonaparte, about this world and the next, about heaven and hell, about the Supreme Being, about Satan, about the soul, and a thousand other subjects." Before Jacquemont's arrival, Runjeet suspected that he was an Englishman ; and after it he may still have imagined, for some time, that his strange visitor had more practical purposes than those scientific pursuits which must have been unintelligible to an Oriental. Might not this visitor be an agent of the English government? However, after the very first audience, as Jacquemont was leaving his presence, Runjeet said frankly (thereby revealing his former suspicions), "Decidedly you are not English. An Englishman would not have changed his position twenty times, would not have gesticulated whilst speaking, his voice would not have had your variety of tones, your high notes and low notes, and he would not have laughed as you do." Are not these remarks acute for a man living at such a distance from France and England? They precisely hit upon the most salient external differences between the natives of the two countries.

Runjeet soon discovered that he had found a treasure in Victor Jacquemont ; a living encyclopædia, always ready and very generally able to answer amply and clearly the questions put to him ; so different from the taciturn, monosyllabic English, who kept their information to themselves and answered with "yes" and "no." The French traveller, on his part, though sometimes wearied to death by Runjeet's incessant interrogations, was strongly attracted by that gifted and vigorous character. Jacquemont knew too much of men and their ways to be prevented from recognizing the qualities of such a potentate as Runjeet because his faults were equally visible : on the contrary, he observed him day by day with the eye of a naturalist who is interested in some dangerous creature, yet able to watch the operation of its most evil instincts without being disturbed in his studies by his sentiments of moral indignation. "This model Asiatic sovereign," said Jacquemont, "is far from

being a saint. He is without scruple when his interest
does not require him to be faithful and just, but he is
not cruel. He will condemn a great criminal to mutilation, to the loss of his ears, his nose, or his hand; but
he never condemns to death. He is brave in the extreme,
a quality not common amongst the Princes of the East;
but, though always successful in his military enterprises,
it is to his treaties and his perfidious diplomacy that he
owes his elevation from the condition of a plain country
gentleman to the throne of the Punjab and Cashmere.
In reality a sceptic, he professes the religion of the
Sikhs; and, besides that, goes annually to pay his de-
votions at Amritsir before the tombs of Mahometan
saints. He is shamelessly immoral, casting aside the
Oriental veil of mystery, and showing himself in public
in the worst of company."

It was on the 16th of March, 1831, that Victor Jacquemont took leave of Runjeet, who gave him a khelat of
the first class, — a khelat being nominally a robe of honor,
but in reality consisting of various presents. That given
on this occasion included a pair of magnificent Cashmere
shawls, in color like the lees of wine, another pair less
magnificent, and seven pieces of silk or muslin; "these
last," said the receiver, "being of extraordinary beauty."
To these things Runjeet added a jewel composed of
stones unskilfully cut, but precious, and not like the pastes
of the Great Mogul. The value of the whole present
was £500. But Runjeet's largesses did not stop here.
The excellent old habit of giving bags of silver was renewed to some purpose, for the bag this time contained

eleven hundred rupees ; and promises were given of further money-bags in the course of Jacquemont's travels to Cashmere. About the same time, he received a letter from the Jardin des Plantes, informing him that his pay was increased by £80 a year, so that his pecuniary prospects were brighter than they had ever been since the beginning of his travels. Jacquemont's feelings had been deeply wounded at not receiving any letter from the administrators of the Jardin des Plantes ; and now they were somewhat soothed by the date of this their first communication, May 19th, 1830, it having taken ten months to reach him. Those were not the days of fast mail steamers and the Suez Canal !

Our hero's camp equipage was considerably augmented by the combined forethought of M. Allard and the generous sovereign of Lahore. A guard of cavalry and infantry, camels to carry the tents and baggage to the foot of the mountains, porters to carry them afterwards, a secretary to write letters to Runjeet, — all gave evidence of his interest in his new friend. It is not always easy for travellers to get away from sovereigns who take a fancy to them ; and Jacquemont experienced some difficulty of this nature, for he was invited to a royal hunt, but firmly declined the honor. M. Allard looked into every detail of the traveller's wandering household, discovered every deficiency, and remedied it. Their parting was painful to Allard ; for Jacquemont had brought France, *la patrie*, with him to that place of exile, and took it away ·with him when he departed.

When he got into the hill country on the road from

the Punjab to Cashmere, our traveller found that, not-withstanding the increase in his band, such campaigning was still far from luxurious. They struggled on through a deluge of rain, which of all evils is the most discouraging to him who travels with tents, especially when it lasts day after day. "The tents become prodigiously heavy; the camels that carry them slide at every step on the sodden soil, and often put their hips out of joint, which they do only too easily; the ox-wagons with the heavy baggage bury themselves in the mud; all the servants, drivers, and soldiers are out of spirits; they become as if they were deaf and dumb and half paralyzed." Besides the rain, Jacquemont went through a terrible thunder-storm, he being in his tent at the time, which was rimmed with lightning as he lay on his low bed. Lightning never *seems* so dangerous as it does to a person in a tent at night, with the electric fire encircling him as it flashes round the tent-pegs like a flaming serpent in the grass.

Rough travel is romantic when we do not see its details, and pleasant enough in reality when the details are all in order; but it tries the patience of a leader most severely when things go wrong and cannot be remedied on the march. That excellent Persian horse, which was never ill, never tired, never dispirited, now fell lame because he had lost a shoe and the road was rough and stony. Two horses belonging to the cavalry escort fell down a precipice and were lamed. It was impossible to keep up a strict camp discipline in such terrible weather. The men dispersed, in the rainy nights, in search of better shelter, and could not be got together again in the morning. The mehmandar * managed to fall in such a manner as to break his arm, and Jacquemont walked for three hours on very rough, steep ground before he discovered him. The man was built like Hercules, but so wretchedly afraid of pain that it was impossible even to examine the bone. The physical labor of such travelling would be exhausting of itself, without any mental toil or care. The geological work kept Jacquemont constantly on foot, hammer in hand, every now and then leaving the road to climb some neighboring hill and get the direction of the strata with his mariner's compass. The road itself was nothing but a narrow, stony track, tunnelling its way through a dense wood of thorny shrubs. Sometimes, for want of sufficient foresight, the whole band ran short of provisions in places where none could be procured. To crown all these pleasures of travelling, Jacquemont was taken prisoner, in a very polite and respectful manner, by an outlaw who dwelt on the top of a hill with three or four hundred soldiers, all in rags and desperate with hunger. This man, Neal Singh, was an officer in Runjeet's army; but his pay had been stopped, and so had that of his men, for a space of three years, during which he said that his soldiers had lived on the grass of the fields and the leaves of the trees, without renewing their clothing. His crime was the refusal to give up

---

* A Persian word which Jacquemont translates by "gardien de l'hospitalité." This official in the present instance represented Runjeet Singh's hospitable care for his late guest during the journey to Cashmere

the hill-fort which he now occupied; and he looked upon Jacquemont as a convenient hostage who might be detained on this Hill of Hunger until the king sent all arrears of pay. In a word, Neal Singh thought that the capture of Jacquemont gave him the opportunity of treating with Runjeet *de puissance à puissance.* Whilst the outlaw explained these matters to his prisoner, his followers gathered round, clamorous, with lighted match-locks. Jacquemont tells the whole story in great detail, — how he played the *grand seigneur*, and tried to over-awe the man in whose power he found himself, succeeding at last so far that he escaped on payment of a ransom of £50, with a promise of his protection at the court of Lahore. The bandit received his money with affectations of the deepest humility, begging his victim to touch the money-bag and touch his own hand as he received it, to prove that the gift was made in pure good-will, as an expression of satisfaction for his ser-vices. To this Jacquemont had to consent, and then the robber prostrated himself, declaring that he was the most faithful, the most grateful, the most devoted of his servants; nay, more, — if he might be permitted so to entitle himself, — the most inviolable of his friends! The comic element was not wanting at the end; for Neal Singh, at the moment of Jacquemont's departure, begged in a low voice for a bottle of wine, and received (what would at least be equally intoxicating) a bottle of raki from Delhi, which served for scientific preparations instead of spirits of wine.

The hardships of rough travel and bad weather now

began to tell on Jacquemont's health. An ordinary traveller would have had himself carried in a palanquin, and so would have spared his body. Even a scientific emissary, less zealous and conscientious than Jacquemont, would have economized effort by contenting himself with the knowledge that came easily in his way; but our hero was hard upon himself, and economized no effort. The day when his mehmandar broke his arm, he walked fifteen hours at a stretch, and felt so tired in the evening that he was unable to eat. In some of his marches, he had waded through four mountain torrents in the course of the day, ice cold (the water being really iced), and deep enough to take him up to the waist. His constitution was not equal to such a life as this for very long together; so, on the 27th of April, he arrived at Prountche "in a pitiable condition, spitting blood." His manner of dealing with himself in illness was invariably marked by his usual energy and resolution. He did not give way to despondency, but at once applied the best remedies in his power, or what he believed to be the best, however severe. This time he thought leeches ought to be applied; but he had none, so he set his men to seek them in the neighboring streams, and put sixty-five of them on his breast and epigastrium. To remedy the weakness occasioned by this great loss of blood, he had sheep killed, and ate as much mutton as he could, which in course of time entirely re-established him.

There was still snow in the pass of Prountche when Jacquemont crossed it at the beginning of May, but

this was a small matter in comparison with previous experiences in Thibet ; and he arrived safely at the famous
lake of Cashmere, being conducted to his residence in
a boat sent by the Governor. This residence was a
pretty pavilion of small dimensions, in a garden of lilac
and rose trees, shaded by immense Oriental planes, and
close to the water's edge. The camp was pitched
under the trees, and huts were rapidly erected for the
cavalry and their horses. Our hero considered himself
too great a man to pay the first visit to the Governor
(who was not of high birth) at his own residence; so it
was arranged that they should meet at a small palace
on the opposite shore of the lake, formerly the Trianon
of the Mogul Emperors, but now very seldom used.
This palace of Shahlibagh was *en fête* to receive the
distinguished stranger, who was fetched from his own
residence by a fleet of boats with a guard of honor.
On arriving, he found a beautiful garden with magnificent trees, many fountains playing, a crowd of people,
and very fine troops parading in a handsome and picturesque costume. There was the usual exhibition of
Oriental dancing, accompanied by monotonous music,
" graceful only at Delhi," according to our traveller.
"I stayed," he says, "as long as I found pleasure in
looking at the strange architecture of the palace, the
variety and brilliance of the warlike figures that surrounded it, the colossal grandeur of the trees, the green
lawns, the cascades, and, in the distance, the blue mountains with their snowy summits."

His own pavilion, though pretty enough, was a poor

lodging. The walls of it were of open work, like lace, as if no wind ever rippled the famous lake of Cashmere, and as if the temperature never fell below that of a midsummer night. However, it served as a convenient frame-work, to be lined with canvas, which protected its inhabitant both from the wind and from public curiosity. As a further protection against this last annoyance, a cordon of sentries was posted all round the garden, who did not shoot or bayonet intruders, but belabored them with sticks. This plan is excellent, and ought to be adopted in every camp.

Though an excellent writer about men and women (but especially about men), our hero was not very skilful in the art of describing scenery, and was himself perfectly well aware of this deficiency. "If I knew how to express what I feel," he says in one of the most charming of his letters, — "if I could only transfer to paper what I see so clearly in my own mind, — what charming word-pictures would I not make of these places that I visit in my wanderings !" In other letters, he suspects himself of having become less sensitive to the beauty of scenery than he was in earlier life. "There is in each of us," said a French writer, regretfully, "a poet who died young." With the lake of Cashmere before him, Jacquemont's mind enjoyed the present far less than the awakened reminiscences of the past. His memory recurred to scenes that had impressed him far more deeply ; to the Lago Maggiore ; to the lakes of the Bernese Oberland, Thun, and Brienz ; to Lake George in America, whose character he describes in the English word *loveliness*, not finding a French word to express it. He remembers the peaceful and grave impression received from the cold landscape of North America, and the "tumultuous pleasure" of his first gallop under a tropical forest in the West Indies. "I am no longer," he writes in his pavilion by the lake of Cashmere, "under the charm of the illusions which gave life to these dreams: the brightness of these flowers has faded; their perfume has evaporated. The world of reality is a poor affair: *there is a sentiment which makes us see it as it is not.*"

All this is profoundly true; and the truth of it is proved by evidence inaccessible to Jacquemont, — the evidence of art. The strict truth, "le monde comme il est réellement," chills a painted landscape like the presence of death. The "illusions" are the living soul of the landscape-painter's art: the truth which destroys the illusion is that opposite of life, the terrible *rigor cadaveris.* Jacquemont's scientific training had killed his landscape sentiment; and so we find him in the most wonderful scenes of the East, only wondering that they did not affect him more. Something of his indifference may have been due simply to the condition of his eyesight, which was bad when he left France, and had become worse since his arrival in India. But, whatever may have been the cause, it is certain that the scenery of Cashmere gave Jacquemont very little pleasure; so little, that he does not condescend to describe it at all carefully in his letters, and hardly ever mentions it without criticism. The passages in which he attempts a little description are brief and scattered,—provokingly so for a reader who wants to know what sort of a place the lake of Cashmere is. They have, however, the great merit of wasting no superfluous words in those empty phrases with which ordinary travellers prolong their uninstructive pages. The writer has not the enchanted vision of poet or painter; but he has a manly sense of reality, and tells his correspondents briefly and honestly the plain facts that he is able to perceive.

Amongst the trees, the Italian poplar and the plane predominate in the cultivated landscape, the plane reaching a colossal development, as we have seen already in the gardens by the lake. The vine is gigantic when cultivated; the forests are composed of cedar, fir, and pine, and the birch grows on the higher levels. The fir and the birch remind the traveller of Europe, and so do the water plants, the butome and buck-bean (menyanthes), the yellow water-lily, and our familiar species of rushes and reeds. The lake is clear and shallow; so very shallow, indeed, that there was no place deep enough for swimming within five miles of the pavilion. "It is only a sort of marsh," wrote Jacquemont, "which the Alps would be ashamed of, if it stagnated at the bottom of a Swiss valley." Whilst he remained in his pavilion, occupied during the day by sedentary labor, he kept his health by an hour's swim every evening, going in a boat to the place where the water was deep enough; but it was very warm, so warm as to afford little refreshment. He sometimes went to a small island with a palatial building on it, consisting of one great hall, which had

been a plaything of the Mogul Emperors, now shaded
by two immense plane-trees, out of four that had been
planted there. From this island, there are fine views
in every direction, — picturesque buildings in the distance, with noble old woods, one of which is a forest of
gigantic trees, the whole bounded by the grand lines of
the mountains. Jacquemont admitted this grandeur
of line, but declared that within the outline there was
not that wealth of picturesque detail which gives interest
to the Alps of Europe.

The hospitable sovereign of Lahore had commanded
that the traveller's table, even in distant Cashmere,
should be kept at the royal cost; but it did not quite
realize the gastronomic ideal of a Frenchman, even when
that Frenchman was the most abstemious of his race.
"I should almost enjoy good cheer," he said, "if I had
but bread and wine." He possessed some bottles of fine
old port, bought at Simla at a sale; but it was too strong
for common use, and he kept it for the cold of the mountains. His health in Cashmere was not very regular;
and he attributed this partly to total abstinence from
alcohol, promising himself a glass of wine every evening
in his next campaign. He had the strongest confidence
in his own regulations about eating and drinking, firmly
believing that his life was safe so long as he adhered to
them. The heat was more difficult to deal with. It
happened that the summer of 1831 was exceptionally
dry in Cashmere, from the failure of the periodical rains.
The streams ceased to flow; the rivers became like that
famous Manzanares, to which a French traveller sent a

glass of water in charity.   Jacquemont, who generally
bore heat so well, was overcome by it now, and either
worked with difficulty, or sat still to be fanned in his
pavilion, or had himself rowed out upon the lake, if
haply he might catch some wandering breath of air.

The body was overcome, but the mind remained clear
and resolute, and able still to call the physical man to
fresh exertion.   Without entirely abandoning his residence on the borders of the lake, the traveller made excursions in the mountains, of the most fatiguing description,
lasting from nineteen to twenty-five days each, during
which he lived in the saddle or on foot in the old rough
mountaineering way.   He reached the point of separation
between the waters of the Hydaspes and those of the
Indus, between Cashmere and Thibet ; he discovered a
lake at that time unknown in Europe, and the only deep
one of those regions ; he made many geological observations, found some new plants, and even a new quad-
ruped, an unknown species of marmot.   He received a
visit from a highland chieftain, who had a wife and a
daughter in captivity in Cashmere.   Jacquemont promised to beg their liberty of Runjeet, and was happy not
to be seized as a hostage, the more so as this chieftain
had a " tail " of two hundred armed men.   " He accompanied me," wrote our hero, " to the brink of a large
torrent, which is the limit of his contested lordship.
I would not have permitted him to come farther, in the
interest of his own safety ; and I was on the point of
telling him so, when he got down from horseback to
take leave of me.   He said with a smile that no muskets

could be more accurate, or carry farther, than those of
the two mountaineers who always walked on each side
of him ; that no sabre could be sharper than his, no
horse more active than his horse. Here was a figure
I shall never forget, — so fine-looking, gentle, and picturesque. Sir Walter Scott would not have invented
a better."

Jacquemont had begun his residence at the lake of
Cashmere on the 9th of May, 1831 ; and he quitted Cashmere for the south on the 19th of September in the same
year. It would be difficult to imagine a more romantic
way of living than his had been during those summer
months. Alone in the isolation of a dignity which it
was necessary to maintain for his own convenience, and
even for his own safety ; never once hearing the sound
of any European language ; never seeing one European
face ; in a scene of great historical and poetical interest,
and which, however inferior it may have been to the
loveliest lakes of Switzerland or Italy, was still one of the
most beautiful in Asia, with all the elements of rich
foliage, clear water, and magnificent mountain distances ;
his mind continually occupied in noble studies, his body
alternating between strenuous exercise and undisturbed
repose, — this traveller had passed such a summer as it
is given to few travellers to enjoy.

There had been a great increase in his establishment
since the days when he could put his baggage into an
ox-cart, and when his dinner-service consisted of two
plates. He had now an escort of sixty soldiers ; and
his baggage, including a fresh scientific collection, was

carried by fifty porters. There were also some living animals in captivity, including antelopes from Thibet, which died from the heat as the party descended towards the lowlands. Jacquemont did not suffer from this cause, but only dressed more lightly; and yet it became a forced march, as the mountaineers of those regions had never been completely subjugated by Runjeet Singh, and were dangerous. The distance between Bimber and Jummoo had to be done in three marches, during which Jacquemont was on horseback fourteen or fifteen hours each day; besides which there was no sleeping, as the camp had to be on the alert all night long. He had expected to be received at Jummoo by Goulab Singh; but in the absence of the rajah his eldest son had remained purposely to entertain the traveller, and the vizier amply provided for the wants of his wearied men. "Abundance reigns in the camp," he wrote from this place: "soldiers, domestics, and porters all enjoy the rajah's hospitality. The poor fellows had great need to pass through this land of plenty, after the privations and fatigues that they have endured since they left Cashmere."

A little later, Jacquemont met with Goulab Singh himself, who seems to have been as fond of instructive conversation as Runjeet; for he sat with the traveller far into the night, talking "about the mountains, about Cashmere, the immortality of the soul, about steam-engines, then about the soul again, and the universe." Goulab was so much pleased with this physical and metaphysical conversation that he begged Jacquemont to stay a whole day with him; when they talked again, and hunted, and Jacquemont shot a wild boar, from which the rajah's cooks prepared an excellent *déjeuner*, to the horror of the Mahometans present, who consider wild boar not less abominable than the domestic porkers of the Giaour. Before Goulab bade adieu to Jacquemont, he sent him sumptuous presents, — a fine white horse beautifully caparisoned, and a khelat of Cashmere shawls. "I shall take a real pleasure," wrote our hero just at that time, "in continuing my Indian travels on Goulab's horse, for he did not give it me merely out of etiquette, but evidently as a friendly souvenir." How little we can foresee even the nearest future! A month later, Jacquemont himself slew this noble-looking horse, with a bullet from his own gun. The brute was dangerous in various ways, both to his rider and his groom. He had mutilated the groom, by biting off one of his fingers.

Just at this time, namely, in the month of October, 1831, Captain Wade and two other British officers were sent by Lord William Bentinck on a complimentary mission to Runjeet Singh. Their business was to meet Runjeet at Amritsir, and thence to accompany him to Ropoor, where it had been arranged that a personal interview was to take place between the two potentates. Runjeet had got as far as Amritsir, when Jacquemont arrived ; and both stayed there some days. They had a private interview of a very friendly nature, during which the sovereign of the Punjab offered the young traveller nothing less than the vice-royalty of Cashmere! Jacquemont chose to take this as an amiable royal jest, and laughed at it in his own lively way. But was it really a jest? Our hero seems to have thought that Runjeet, who repeatedly pressed him to accept, wished to prove his philosophy, by seeing whether or not it would be able to resist the temptation of worldly grandeur; but is it not also quite possible that the astute Asiatic prince may have been a sufficiently good judge of character to desire eagerly the services of a man so energetic, so able, and so perfectly trustworthy as Victor Jacquemont, — a man whose society interested and delighted him more than that of any other European, and whose superiority he was quite able to recognize? Had not Runjeet already given a post of immense importance to a Frenchman, since M. Allard was commander-in-chief of his armies, with extensive powers of military reform? and had not his success in this experiment been such as to encourage him to make a second? Whatever may have been Runjeet's intentions, it is clear that he would have made an excellent bargain in securing such a rare combination of qualities and accomplishments as the young traveller whom chance had thrown in his way. Jacquemont's refusal, on the other hand, is intelligible from his own point of view. He was too prudent, too sober-minded, to let himself be dazzled, even by the splendors of a vice-royalty, so far as to give in exchange for it all that made life dear to him, — his scientific career, his European friendships, his closest family affections. He saw, too, the absolute uncertainty of a position which would be held in daily dependence on the good-will of an Asiatic despot, whose suspicions might be easily aroused against a representative at a distance, and whose notion

of good government was the unfailing extortion of taxes.
The most effectual motive which might have induced
him to become a satrap of Runjeet Singh was the possibility of wealth; but Jacquemont was already aware that
Runjeet's policy towards Europeans in his service was
to prevent them from amassing, in order to retain them
more completely in his power. The temptation, however,
must have been very strong, if, as Jacquemont was informed, the last viceroy of Cashmere received a fixed
income of £50 a day, and scraped for himself additional
"profits" to the amount of £140,000 annually.

The closing days of that October were passed by
our traveller in the midst of most striking scenes. He
witnessed a review of the active and picturesque Sikh
army, consisting of two hundred thousand men, encamped round Amritsir. In the midst of this mighty
host was the royal pavilion of Runjeet Singh, in the
centre of a court enclosed with walls of silk. Jacquemont was present, with Captain Wade, when the vassal
princes came to do homage to Runjeet as their suzerain,
each of them laying tribute at his feet "in monstrous
bags of silver and gold." After this ceremony, each
vassal put himself at the head of his own force, and rode
past in the pride and panoply of Eastern war. Each
body of men had its own peculiar aspect and its special
costume; but, if the leaders were variously accoutred,
they were alike in the display of princely or baronial
magnificence. "The chiefs are covered with gold, silk,
and precious stones, which glitter on the sombre ground
of a heavy coat of mail. Their head-dress is a pict-

uresque combination of the helmet with the turban
wound about it.   Their horses are as magnificent as
themselves, and the knights ride with a grace and audacity utterly unknown to our old riding-masters in
Europe.   As they passed before us, Runjeet cour-
teously told us the history of the most famous.   It was
a frightful catalogue of heads cut off, of tigers killed at
close quarters, and similar deeds of prowess."   Though
Jacquemont was not much given to the indulgence of
poetical imaginings, and seldom sought for comparisons
in the remoter ages of history or legend, these various
bodies of men, each in the costume of their own land,
carried his mind to Homer and the Grecian armies
before Troy; whilst the knightly appearance of the
leaders, in their coats of mail, reminded him of Saint
Louis and his chivalry.

As Runjeet continued his royal progress in the direction of Ropoor, Jacquemont rode for five days by his
side; and then, on the 21st of October, they finally separated, Runjeet ending their intercourse, as he had begun
it, with very munificent presents.   Travellers get into
the habit of saying farewell to temporary friends, and
their hearts ought to be hardened to such separations;
yet Jacquemont often felt them keenly, and admitted
in a letter "that he had been weak enough to feel a
momentary sadness on leaving Runjeet Singh."   This
expression is an instance in which he was trying to
be stoical, and it really means that the separation had
affected him considerably.   It was a strange friendship
between the intellectual Parisian and the barbarous

Eastern sovereign; but, although Runjeet had united in his career the ambition of a strong-handed conqueror with the dissolute habits of a voluptuary, he had his good qualities, and had acted towards Jacquemont in particular with the most consistent kindness and the most loyal good faith. The keen pleasure that he took in their conversations was flattering to the traveller's self-love, and we may readily imagine that both would separate regretfully when the last of their many dialogues had come to its inevitable end.

On the first of November, our hero arrived at Mondi, the rajah of which place had given him a pressing invitation. However, when he got there, the sentries opposed his advance; and he had to push forward by force. Deputations came from the town, earnestly soliciting the traveller to go no further, and promising that the rajah would pay him a visit the next morning, wherever he might choose to encamp. All the town was in a state of commotion and excitement, as if the foreign traveller had been an enemy; and yet he was treated by the authorities in the most friendly and respectful manner. The enigma was explained by the rajah's uncle, who came and told Jacquemont, with a piteous air, how the astrologers had discovered the same morning that it was an unlucky day; and, that if he and the rajah did not postpone their interview, it would entail fearful calamities on the monarchy of Mondi.

Our hero's importance as the Plato of the world, the Socrates, the Aristotle of the age, the high and puissant seigneur victorious in battle, all which titles had been

given him in the Punjab and Cashmere, now suddenly
collapsed when he recrossed the Sutledje and became
plain Victor Jacquemont once again, a wandering naturalist and underpaid emissary of the Jardin des Plantes.
At Sabathoo, he met his old friend Kennedy, an artillery
captain, who for the time being was ruler between the
Jumna and the Sutledje, with a regiment of Goorkhas
under his command. This Kennedy was a humorous
Englishman who loved a joke ; and, partly as a satire
on the recent greatness of his guest, partly to exhibit
his own skill in handling a regiment of infantry, he held
a grand review of his Goorkhas in Jacquemont's honor,
compelling him to sit solemnly on horseback in European costume as the companies marched past. The
men presented arms ; Kennedy himself saluted with his
sword, and called out, "Now, Jacquemont, take off your
hat and make a speech !" Our hero's vengeance was
to upset Kennedy's gravity by exactly mimicking the
usual tone of English inspection speeches, in an address
of studied absurdity, which Kennedy had not self-com-
mand enough to hear to its conclusion. He got out of
the difficulty by drowning Jacquemont's peroration in
the roll of drums, and dispersing the men before it
was over. "After eight months of absolute solitude,"
said the traveller, "any gayety is good, *even that of
the English.*"

Our hero's plan was to return to Delhi first, and, after
staying there long enough to pack and send off his various scientific collections, to travel gradually towards
Bombay. He reached Delhi on the 16th of December,

1831, in the evening, and discovered with pleasure that
his friend Fraser was at home in his big house, where
of course the traveller received the usual hearty Anglo-
Indian hospitality. Lord William Bentinck happened
to be at that time quite close to Delhi, with the enormous vice-regal camp, so Fraser had to attend him to
the limits of his jurisdiction ; and Jacquemont was left
to do his work quietly, without any other noise than that
produced by his own workmen as they nailed up his
numerous packing-cases. Some idea of the extent of
the different collections when united at Delhi, which
Jacquemont had from the first selected as his central
dépôt, may be formed from the length of time occupied
in the packing. He had fondly imagined that a fortnight would be amply sufficient for this business, yet it
gave the traveller and his workmen incessant occupation for no less than two months. They were two very
pleasant months. During the day, there was plenty of
work to do ; and, when evening came, Jacquemont went
to the town, on horseback in fine weather, in a palanquin when it rained, to dine with the Resident, Mr.
Martin, who enjoyed an allowance of £500 a year for
the expenses of his table, and conscientiously spent it, so
that his dinners were superior to the solitary meals in
the little tent. After dinner came a long talk till mid-
night, and then a ride back behind two running foot-
men with torches. And so pleasantly passed the days.

On his arrival at Delhi, the traveller had learned that
his friend, the Governor-General, was encamped close to
the town, and would pitch his tents that night at Kou

toub, on the ruins of old Delhi, ten miles off: so he went to Koutoub, and spent two days there with Lord and Lady William Bentinck, who received him even more kindly than at Calcutta. During these two days, they had long conversations about the Punjab, Cashmere, Paris, and other countries and places.

But, of all his English friends, his host at Delhi, William Fraser, made the deepest impression on Jacquemont's heart. "You know," he wrote to a lady, "that I do not prodigally bestow the sacred name of *friend*. Well, I have given it to a man whom I may have mentioned in a former letter. His name is William Fraser. I have just been living for six weeks under his roof; and on his account Delhi will remain the tenderest of my Indian souvenirs."

Fraser was British Commissioner at Delhi (head of the civil service in the province). He was fifty years old when Jacquemont knew him; and they first met at Captain Kennedy's, at Sabathoo, in November, 1830. The reader may remember that a sudden friendship sprang up between them, and that they travelled together for two days. During those days, each was going out of his way merely to prolong their talk; and when they separated it was with the hope of meeting again. Fraser was one of those superior persons, who incur the imputation of misanthropy because they live on a higher intellectual level than those about them, and consequently suffer from a very real though involuntary isolation. For once, in Jacquemont, he had found a man who could understand him; and Fraser became, in what was real society for him, "the most sociable of men." "He is a thinker," wrote his young French friend, "who finds nothing but isolation in the interchange of words without ideas, which is called conversation in Anglo-Indian society; and the consequence is that he seldom frequents it. He has travelled much, and always alone, never having found a companion to his taste." After living thus in mental solitude to the age of fifty, William Fraser found companionship at last, for six weeks, all too short, whilst the young Frenchman stayed with him. When the time came for their separation, the apprehension of it was so painful to both that they tacitly agreed to avoid it, and Jacquemont was to get away "like a thief" without a word. However, when the dreaded moment came, and a servant told the parting guest that the camels were already gone and that his own horse was waiting, saddled, he forgot his resolutions, and went and pressed Fraser's hand. They parted in perfect silence, and Jacquemont went to Koutoub, where he encamped. In the night, a horseman came galloping to the camp with a letter from Fraser, in which he declared that the pain of separation was too much for him, and that he would follow his friend and travel a few days with him, even to the neglect of public duties. Jacquemont thought: "I wish he would come, but I don't expect him. It is only the sorrow of the moment that makes him write so: he has far too much business waiting for him, and he will not come." So he tried not to hope, and went and encamped at Gourgaon. Here he was walking in sadness and solitude in the midst of the great desert plain, when he saw a tall white figure advancing towards him from a distance. It was Fraser! The two friends dined together "like kings," though their dining-room was only the little travelling tent, "the smallest tent in India," and the feast was nothing but wheaten cakes and a jug of milk. They travelled together to Nhoun, which at that time was on the frontier of the British possessions, and there they separated for ever. Jacquemont was a very early riser, but one morning when he awoke and looked out of his tent, lo! Fraser's tent had vanished in the night. He had taken the sorrow of the final parting to himself, leaving his friend in the happy ignorance of sleep.

In February, 1832, Lord William Bentinck was still travelling in the north of India, after his interview with Runjeet Singh; and a meeting took place between him and Jacquemont, which I prefer to recount in the traveller's own words, — the more willingly, in this instance, as the passage was originally written in English, and may interest the reader as an example of the writer's skill in the use of our language. If we bear in mind that English was only one of four or five different languages that he knew at least well enough for practical purposes, we shall do better justice to his qualities as a linguist. Of his accomplishments in Oriental languages, few of us could form an opinion, if we had the materials; but he wrote Italian as fluently as English, and as well. The following quotation may present one or two instances of carelessness: a man writing a book would strike out such an expression as. " Never did I *receive* from them so kind a *reception*." * But Jacquemont was writing to a private friend, without the remotest idea of publication, and, no doubt, with his usual extreme rapidity. Another point may be noticed in his favor. His letter was addressed, not to an Englishman, but to a Frenchman who could read English ; and all who are accustomed to write a foreign language are well aware that they do so most correctly when addressing a correspondent for whom it is the native tongue. An Englishman will write more idiomatic French to a native of France than to one of his own countrymen, because in the first case he feels that his correspondent will have a sympathy with the intimate genius of the language that is wanting in the second.

"The Governor-General was then marching from Adjmeer to Agra:. his route was almost parallel to mine in opposite direction. I received from his camp an exceedingly flattering invitation to join it. Horses were sent to me, and stationed in the way, with horsemen to guide and to escort me ; and leaving my caravan on the 25th of February, long before daylight, I arrived before noon at the tents of the Governor-General, after many an hour of hard riding. Lord W. Bentinck was to stay two days in the place where I met him.

* Awkward as it is, this expression, *to receive a reception*, is not a Gallicism. It may be used in careless haste by an Englishman. I have just hit upon it in the *Daily News* (Jan. 2, 1878). The Athens correspondent of that journal telegraphs the following sentence : "The Queen arrived at the camp to-day, and *received* an enthusiastic *reception*."

However attentive he and Lady William had always been to me since the day of my arrival in Calcutta, never did I receive from them so kind a reception. I spent with them two days which I shall never forget. The camp was pitched in the weary desert of Rajpoota- nah. It appeared like a moving city. Though exceed- ingly averse to any thing like state, Lord W. Bentinck cannot dispense altogether with the pomp by which the former governors-general of India surrounded them- selves in their journeys. Many of the chief officers of the State must accompany him, to despatch the business of the various branches of the service. Every one of the heads of departments has a number of deputies and assistants. Then comes the personal state of the Gov- ernor-General ; then his escort, consisting of a regiment of infantry, one of cavalry, his life-guards, a light bat- tery ; and, after all, an immense number of camp- followers. The sight was quite new to me, and very interesting, as you may fancy. To welcome my arrival at head-quarters, my friend, the Alwur rajah, arrived there also on the same day. He had been informed that, after paying a visit to his Lordship, he might receive one in return, — an attention which had been paid by the Governor-General to all the other rajpoot princes except to him on a first occasion. The rajah expected also to receive a khelat, or honorary dress, — a distinction bestowed on many other chieftains of his rank. The reception afforded me an opportunity of see- ing a rajpoot court in all its gayety and glittering. After the Asiatic exhibitions of the day, I sat on the evening by the right of Lady William Bentinck, at a large table, to a superb dinner. The party was numerous. An excellent band was in attendance in a contiguous tent. Lady William told me she had lately received from the Palais Royale *La Parisienne*, and desired it to be performed for me."

" What a strange concourse of circumstances! I felt inwardly grateful for it. I enjoyed it thoroughly. The evening before, at that time, alone in my little tent pitched in a solitary spot at the foot of a hill, sitting to my usual meal; a plain pillow; a single candle burning on my small table, often blasted away by the wind; no noise but the loud shrieks of the jackals about my cattle, bullocks, and camels,— every thing about me told of the country where I was. And but for twenty hours, what a complete change around! All the luxuries and refinements of Europe! Lord William, the next day, was able to command some hours of leisure, which we spent together in his tent, talking of this country, of its probable destinies, glancing, too, at Europe, and concluding by exclaiming how strange was our meeting *there*, and talking *there* of such things, — he, a man from England, one of the crowd there, absolute ruler of Asia; I quietly engaged in my philosophical researches amidst barbarous tribes!"

"On 27th, long before daylight, the tents were struck down. I found a horse and a couple of horsemen in waiting at the door of mine. I mounted; and, trusting to the good eyes of my guides and to the sure footing of my charger, I pushed forwards at a sharp canter, on a rough path intersected by ravines, and, changing horses and guides on my way, in a few hours I joined again my poor little wretched camp, where I could not but fancy that the whole of the two days past was a dream."

Such was Jacquemont's English, and very respectable English it is for a Frenchman. There are a few faults, yet the faults are not, in most cases, Gallicisms: they are deficient or superfluous English, betraying less an intrusion of the writer's native idiom than an insufficient familiarity with ours. For example, he says, "The tents were struck *down*," — a word too much, the idiomatic expression being, "The tents were struck." And he says, "A rajpoot court in all its gayety and glittering," — a syllable too much: he should have said, "in all its gayety and glitter." But, notwithstanding these and other little errors, few men can write a foreign language so well ; and our hero's proficiency seems the more remarkable, when we reflect that he lived for weeks, and even months together, in India, without hearing any English at all. In the Himalaya, he used no English after leaving Simla ; in the Punjab and Cashmere, he spoke English to nobody. Even when surrounded by our countrymen at the British stations, he constantly complains that they made him speak French for their own improvement.

The long journey from the vice-regal camp at Kalakoh, by Adjmeer and Aurungabad to Bombay, may be passed over briefly, as it offers little to interest the reader. His way of travelling was to divide his little

caravan into two portions, one with the baggage in the
ox-carts, the other a light personal escort which attended
Jacquemont as he rode to the right or the left for purposes of study and exploration. Both were vigilant, on
account of tigers ; but the only death from this cause
was that of a peasant, who did not belong to the caravan,
but was closely following it. There are indications, in
the letters written during this part of his travels, that
Jacquemont's health, notwithstanding his persistent
courage and cheerfulness, was not so regular as it had
been. The great transitions of temperature tried him
severely. He marched two or three hours in the night ;
and in the sandy deserts of Rajpootanah the air is so
dry and clear that the earth loses much heat by radia-
tion, and goes down to the freezing-point in the absence
of the winter sun, which nevertheless had sufficient
power to raise the temperature of the tent in which the
traveller spent his afternoons to about 95° Fahrenheit.
The natural consequence was a very bad cold ; and the
patient stopped three days to be nursed by an English
surgeon, who luckily happened to be at a British station
on his line of march. The notion of sitting inside
a small tent during the hottest part of the day is a
notion which could have occurred only to Victor Jacquemont. In the month of May, at Yedlabad in the
Deccan, he would sit writing in that little tent for hours
together, with the thermometer varying from 100° to
110° Fahrenheit, so that a jug of water beside him got
up to the temperature of a warm bath. He sat happily
in this heat, clad in a light bathing costume, in the full

enjoyment of his wonderfully clear mental faculties, and
of what, so far as his own sensations could inform him,
seemed to be a perfect physical condition.   As he
advanced every day farther south, and as the season
advanced daily nearer and nearer to midsummer, the
temperature of night and day became gradually more
equal.   In the valley of the Nerbudda, the night heat
had risen almost to an equality with the burning sunshine.   "The heat from the ground," wrote Jacquemont
towards the end of May, "darts into the face and eyes
like that from blazing straw at a little distance."   He
got so acclimated to this, that when on the high ground
of the Deccan the temperature *fell* to 100°, he had a
sensation of coolness.

On the 5th of June, he arrived at Poonah, where the
Governor of Bombay, then the Earl of Clare, happened
to be staying at his country house.   He kindly offered
hospitality to Jacquemont, who declined because he
wanted the free disposal of his time, and also, very
probably, because, notwithstanding Lord Clare's kindness, it must have been evident to the traveller, at their
first interview, that much intercourse would be profitable
to neither.   One of the first disagreeable things he
learned in the neighborhood of Bombay was that the
place was about three times as expensive for man and
beast as either Delhi or Calcutta.   "My three horses
are ruining me," he wrote; but it was difficult to do his
work without them.

During the stay of Jacquemont's little party at Poonah, there were many cases of Asiatic cholera ; and

amongst the rest one of his servants named Soudine was attacked by the disease. Soudine was twenty-five years old, and had been in his master's service a year and a half. His health had been always perfect, and his conduct strictly regular; but the most severe temperance is not a protection against that terrible malady. The reader is already sufficiently acquainted with the manliness and mercy in Victor Jacquemont's character to know that under such circumstances no consideration for his own safety would weigh with him for an instant in comparison with the plain duty to do what he could for the sufferer. Soudine had been to Cashmere with his master, and had never served another. He had been the most active and the most useful of Jacquemont's men; and now, when he lay prostrate under mortal disease, his master tended him as one would tend a younger brother, had him near his own room, and endeavored, though in vain, to combat the progress of the disease during the forty hours that it lasted. Writing an account of Soudine's death, his master said: "I should have regretted it more, if I had not always used him well; but during these two years I have seldom spoken to him roughly, and, though he was engaged at five rupees a month, it is long since I doubled it."

Jacquemont himself had a severe illness at Poonah, — a sudden and violent attack of dysentery, which lasted five days, and only gave way after very severe treatment. On his recovery, he made the following reflection: "A traveller in my trade has various ways of making a *fiasco*, as the Italians say; but the most complete *fiasco* of all

is to die on the road." To us this looks like a presentiment, though it simply bore reference to the attack of
dysentery. Jacquemont was not as yet aware of the
existence of a still more dangerous disease, which was
gradually fastening its hold upon him. The grim, un-
welcome visitor whom we see in Holbein's "Dance of
Death" was already in waiting, and the traveller's long
journey in this world had nearly reached its end.

Here is another strange detail. A journalist at Bombay had somehow heard that Jacquemont had been bitten
by a dog at Hyderabad. The truth was that the traveller
had never been bitten, and had never been at Hyderabad;
but the newspaper writer added an expression which
looks prophetic, though his facts were unhistorical.
"What a misfortune it would be," he said, "if M. Jacquemont were to die!"

If the reader will take the trouble to refer to a map of
India, he will find the island of Salsett near Bombay;
and, if the map is a good one, he will find Tannah on
the eastern coast of the island, on the shore of the little
strait which separates it from the Indian mainland.
Jacquemont arrived at Tannah, from Poonah, on the 22d
of September, 1832. His intention was to explore Salsett
and the neighboring islands, getting through the work
as rapidly as possible, on account of the unhealthiness
of the season there, and then to get back, about the first
of November, to the elevated and cool plateau of the
Deccan.

Salsett, like many other islands, is cultivated and inhabited round the shore, but wild in the interior, where

the hills rise to a considerable height ; and there are rocky solitudes in dense forests. Subterranean temples of mysterious antiquity are to be found in these lonely places ; and Jacquemont reached one of these after a very long and fatiguing march. But the principal object of his curiosity in Salsett was to settle a question in geology. It so happened that, just before leaving Poonah, he had received a memoir by Arago on the geological researches of Élie de Beaumont. Jacquemont's scientific zeal was always like a lamp, just ready to be lighted ; and Arago's pages kindled it. Notwithstanding the season of the year, which everybody knew to be deadly in the island of Salsett, he explored it thoroughly from one end to the other, in search of tertiary and alluvial strata, under a burning sun, in pestilential air laden with the germs of death. He exhausted himself by long marches, by constantly stooping to examine the ground he traversed, and by hurrying through his self-imposed task in order to get back soon to the high country to preserve what remained to him of health.

Although half a physician, and always ready to rely upon his own treatment of himself, which on several critical occasions had proved successful, he had been mistaken as to his bodily condition since the month of March, when he passed through Ajmeer. His notion was that, by severe temperance, a European could protect himself against liver disease in India. This notion became a fixed belief, expressed repeatedly in his letters. Jacquemont was convinced that the Anglo-Indians had liver complaints, not because the climate was deadly, but because they ate too much meat, and drank too much wine and ale and brandy. Having an absolute control over his own appetites, Jacquemont had lived by rule since his arrival in India, and believed that his abstemiousness was safety. He had always been subject to a certain sluggishness of the bowels, and unfortunately attributed what were really attacks of liver inflammation to a heating of the intestines. Even so late as the 27th of October, when prostrated by a violent attack at Tannah, the result of his exploration of Salsett, he was still in error as to the nature of his disease, and had recourse to his old remedies, to leeches amongst the rest, with which he covered his body before and behind. The attack had begun with dull, aching pains, after an exposure of twelve hours to the sun ; and he met it with a two-ounce dose of the horrible oil of palma-cristi. As neither that nor any other of his usual remedies had any effect whatever, Jacquemont had himself transported to Bombay, to the officers' hospital, where he passed the whole month of November. He lay in bed, suffering much at first ; but, as the weakness increased, the pain diminished, and the nights, though sleepless, were calm. He was now clearly aware of the nature of his disease, —abscess of the liver,—and expected its fatal termination. He employed his time in settling all the details of his affairs, and in writing to his friends, when his failing strength permitted. To his brother Porphyre he wrote : —

"Nothing is so cruelly painful, when we think that those we love are dying in a distant country, as the idea that they have to pass the last hours of their existence in loneliness and neglect. You ought to find some consolation in the assurance that, since I reached this place, I have been the object of the most affectionate and touching care. Many good, kind fellows come to see me continually, indulging my sick man's fancies and anticipating my wishes. I mention Mr. Nicol first of all, and after him Mr. John Bax, one of the members of the Government, an old colonel of engineers called Goodfellow, a very amiable young officer, Major Mountain, and others whom I do not name. My good doctor, Mac Lennen, has risked his health for me. I have the most absolute confidence in his skill."

The first-mentioned of these Good Samaritans was Mr. James Nicol, an English merchant, who had been Jacquemont's host for some days immediately after his arrival from Tannah, before he was taken to the officers' quarters. Mr. Nicol had treated his suffering guest, whom he had never seen before, with all the affectionate solicitude of an old friend ; and he afterwards wrote an account of Jacquemont's illness, in French, for the satisfaction of his relations. In this account, he says that, during the whole time of his illness, the patient preserved "a tranquillity and a contentment of which he had never before witnessed an example." On the day of his death, Jacquemont sent for Mr. Nicol, who could not restrain his tears. On seeing this, the dying man took his friend's hand, and said to him : " Do not make yourself unhappy. The hour is at hand, and it is the accomplishment of my wishes. For the last fortnight I have

prayed for no other end. It is a happy event. If I were
to survive, it is probable that the rest of my life would be
made wretched by ill health. Write to my brother, and
tell him what happiness and tranquillity accompany me
to the grave."

Then he asked Mr. Nicol to see that his manuscripts
and collections were duly sent to France; and he entered
into minute directions about his funeral, expressing his
wish that the service should be conducted "as if for a
Protestant." He also dictated the words of the inscription upon his tombstone, probably to defeat any laud-
atory intentions of his friends. During the whole of his
last day, he retained the use of his mental faculties "as
perfectly," says Mr. Nicol, "as if he had been in good
health." At five o'clock in the evening, he said to his
friend, "I shall now take my last drink from your hand,
and then die." He lived an hour and a quarter longer,
after which he sank finally from exhaustion.

Whilst he lay there dead, his last farewell was slowly
crossing the Indian Sea, to be read long afterwards by
tear-dimmed eyes in Paris. Many a tear has been shed
since those days, over these simple words, by those who
have never seen the writer, and never heard his voice:—

"My end, if it is my end that approaches, is peaceful
and quiet. If you were here [he means his brother
Porphyre], sitting by my bedside with our father and
Frederic, I should feel heart-broken, and could not see
the approach of death with this resignation and this
serenity. Console yourself, console our father, console
yourselves mutually, my friends!

" But I am exhausted by the effort of writing. I must say Good-bye! Good-bye! Oh, how you are loved by your poor Victor! Good-bye, for the last time!"

"I am well off here," he said to Mr. Nicol, "but I shall be better in the grave."

He had received the cross of the Legion of Honor a short time previously, and was therefore interred with military honors. His funeral was attended by the members of the Bombay Government, by his recently won yet devoted friends in that place, and by many other persons. His wishes were minutely respected in every particular by Mr. Nicol, whom he had appointed to be one of his executors. A simple stone marks his resting-place, and on it may still be read his own modest inscription: "Victor Jacquemont, born in Paris, 8th of August, 1801; died at Bombay, after having travelled during three years and a half in India."* He did not mention his recent knighthood to the tombstone-reading public of Bombay, but he sent the cross quietly to his father.

To us, who know the end, many passages in the letters, in which the traveller indulges his anticipations of a happy meeting with Porphyre and their father, have a pathos far surpassing the calculated and intentional pathos of novelists and poets. Here is an extract from one of his letters to that beloved brother, Porphyre, written

* M. Cuvillier-Fleury gives the inscription in a slightly different form. According to him, the date of birth is given as the 28th, and not the 8th of August; and the date of death (Dec. 7, 1832) is given in the inscription. I have followed that given by the traveller's nephew, the present M. Victor Jacquemont.

in the month of May, in that fatal year 1832, in his little tent near Yedlabad, in the Deccan :—

"Oh, how delightful it will be to find ourselves to-gether after so many years of absence, which for me have been years of isolation! What a pleasure to dine, all three of us, or, better still, all four,* at our little round table, cheerfully lighted; to have soup and red French wine; and to leave the dining-room, only to go to your room or our father's; leaving others to seek their pleasure out of the house, whilst we shall remain at home by the fireside, telling each other all that happened when we were far apart. I have eaten alone and drunk water alone so long!"

Then come pleasant projects for a quiet old bachelor's existence with his brother Porphyre, when they are to walk out together, play trictrac together, and indulge themselves occasionally by hearing a little good music together. It seems almost a breach of confidence to quote this letter; for the writer ends by saying, "Of course this tender and ridiculous chatter is for you and our father only."

Now and then he recognizes the possibility of a less happy ending of his travels. Whilst as yet in perfect health at Samalkah, near Paniput, he writes : "I have left full directions about forwarding my scientific collec-tions, in case I happen to die during my travels. I could not forget this possibility. However great may

---

* The allusion here is to his brother Frederic, of St. Domingo, whom Victor loved and respected less than Porphyre, yet thought of frater-nally still.

be a man's confidence in his destiny, he cannot blind
himself to facts. The great majority of those who have
done work like mine in India have died here. Of course
I find all sorts of good reasons for not imitating them."
His two strongest reasons, as he believed, were severe
temperance and chastity. In the gayety of health, he
said it was rather a foolish thing to die at thirty; and
he had the vanity to suppose that he would live to a
much greater age, his notion being that death might be
resisted by self-control and strength of will. He criticised the English for having liver diseases. "All the
English," he wrote, "have diseases of the liver, which
are unknown to the French. I know what produces
them, — four immoderate meals a day. There is the
cause! I shall live on rice as much as possible. With
that *régime*, I have nothing to fear but intermittent
fevers; and I have a pot of quinine." And so, believing
himself safe from liver disease, he allowed it to establish
itself without opposition, whilst he took medicine for
another ailment. He compared himself with his predecessor, Duvaucel, who died in India, and flattered himself that he had played the game of travel more prudently. He also compared himself to an old vase, fragile
by nature, but hardened by knocks and accustomed to
fall without breaking: the similitude was a bad one; for
no vase that is really fragile is or can be hardened by the
blows of accident. On the isle of plane-trees in the
Cashmere Lake, he discovered that he was thirty years
old that day; and a scientific annual told him that it
was the probable half-way station in the journey of life.

He was astonished to think that half of life could be already over: he felt as if he had been born yesterday, and the thirty years were only like a dream. Alas! not only the half of life was over, but he was already living his penultimate year!

———

We have been so much occupied with the story of our hero's varied and adventurous life that time has been wanting for any adequate study of his character.

Victor Jacquemont was a stoic, but a genial stoic. Prosper Mérimée, who knew him intimately, said that this stoicism was neither a gift of nature nor an affectation in deference to the fashion of the day,* but that it resulted from reason, and was a conquest of self-discipline. The acquisition of this character was, in his case, the result of many combats, in each of which the victory was on his side, yet cost him dear. His theory was that a man ought to exercise himself continually in conquering his own desires, and that when he had to suffer he ought to find within himself an amount of endurance sufficient to meet the suffering. Closely connected with this stern and continual training of the will was an unfeigned contempt for luxury, or rather for that condition of the human mind in which it attaches importance to

———

* When Victor Jacquemont was a young man in Paris, the higher order of cultivated and aspiring youth to which he belonged were disgusted with the false sentimentalism of Rousseau and his imitators; and, by reaction from that, adopted a sort of English disdain for the expression of the feelings. This reaction against sentimentalism was a dominant fashion for a few years.

those minute and multitudinous details which in the aggregate make up the perfection of comfort. Here is a passage in a letter to his brother Porphyre, which sincerely expresses an unalterable conviction : —

" The English have habits of opulence and factitious wants without number, which would make them inevitably wretched in various situations where I shall find myself. I do not say this out of envy : no, it is from the bottom of my heart that I despise such an ignoble dependence upon things. I am sure, on the contrary, to find a charm sometimes in the somewhat antique and biblical simplicity of my caravan."

Here we have Jacquemont's view of luxury, — " an ignoble dependence upon things." He objects to it, because he perceives that it is an impediment to freedom and also to great actions. He did not object to those conveniences which are necessary to efficiency. He willingly accepted the services which save time, but had a contempt for mere self-indulgence in all its forms, and liked to get rid of cumbersome and useless *impedimenta*. He lived with a soldierly simplicity, but cheerfully. " I dine gayly," he writes, " with a piece of bread and cheese and a glass of wine, on the corner of my writing-table. . . . Setting aside all the cant of philosophy, I declare that I would rather not be rich. I believe that in my present condition I have more sympathy with men and things. In our *unfurnished* life, as the English would call it, there is more simplicity, more of the candor of truth, and therefore more poetry. . . . What an admirable receipt for happiness, to know how to do without things!" Mérimée said that Jacquemont was clearly aware that his scientific pursuits were not the road to wealth; but that he only esteemed money for the liberty which it gives, and that with his simple tastes and his contempt for the pleasures of vanity he asked nothing more from Fortune than the possibility of leading a philosopher's life.

Intimately connected with these ideas was a delight in sobriety, not at all from any harsh or uncharitable asceticism, but from a feeling that sobriety was morally more beautiful than its opposite, and also because he valued mental clearness and physical efficiency. His doctrine was 'that man, in a state of society, eats too much; and in this he was unquestionably right, as every physician knows. At Bourbon, he observed that the slaves who worked like horses, and had both the appearance and the reality of health, ate nothing but Indian corn and rice, except a weekly ration of codfish; whereas the whites, who expended no muscular force, ate from five to ten times that value of assimilable nutriment, digested it badly, and were either meagre or bloated in consequence. With regard to drinking, Jacquemont was not a teetotaller; but he drank water as a rule, and only allowed himself wine and brandy in the most moderate quantities, when convinced that they were necessary to his health. His cellar was easily supplied, and supplied for a long time. At Calcutta, he bought two dozen small bottles of brandy, of which he only consumed nine in twelve months. At Simla, he purchased a few bottles of port wine, and calculated that they would last him a year. He carried beyond reasonable limits the French habit of a long interval between meals. When on the march, he would travel often thirteen and sometimes fifteen hours without eating ; nor had he the common resource of tobacco, which puts off hunger, for he only smoked occasionally, and in the greatest moderation. Notwithstanding this extreme sobriety, he was not insensible to the pleasures of taste. There is an amusing passage in which he anticipates the delight of eating a *pâté* from France, and he gave some thought to the quality of the little wine and tobacco that he used.

His asceticism was always tempered by prudence : he did not lose sight of the essentials of human life. " I am without pity for my body," he writes in 1830 ; but then he adds immediately, " so far as the toils I impose upon it cannot radically injure health." He suffered terribly, as we have seen, from cold, in the Himalaya, yet had no thought of turning back till he had accomplished his purposes. He was manly in his habits without rashness, the only instance of downright rashness in his travels being that fatal exploration of Salsett; but that was a result of scientific ardor, and not of mere athletic temerity. He lived from reason, and not in conformity to the customs of those about him. At Calcutta, he did not follow English customs, but rose before the dawn and took his exercise whilst others slept. In spite of his unmuscular build, he had considerable personal strength, which his temperance and activity kept up to a pitch of regular serviceableness.

He could either walk or ride from morning till night. On the rough slopes of the Himalaya, he did his work on foot; at Agra, he tired three horses every day. "The variety of my studies and exercises," he wrote to M. de Tracy, "sometimes on horseback, more frequently on foot, sometimes on an elephant or in a palanquin, leaves no room for any kind of fatigue. I have never enjoyed more equal health."

He had a great esteem and admiration for industry and economy wherever he found them, and endeavored successfully to practise these virtues in his own affairs. "Work and thrift," he said, speaking of the life of nations, "these are the great matters; and liberty itself is precious only so far as it is used in labor and accumulation. Liberty is admirably employed in the United States; for the English race, which has peopled the North of the New World, is eminently industrious and orderly." He managed his own expenditure with such care that, at the time when he was poorest, he could write to his father, " I have had the admirable talent of remaining within my budget." At a later period, when his means were larger, he described his increased establishment, but added that it still bore the same strict proportion to his means. He had the moral courage, at the outset, to live on £20 a month, in the highest society in India. Jacquemont knew that with his limited means a close attention to money matters was essential to the success of his enterprise, so that he was parsimonious with a noble purpose.

His religion was more practical than dogmatic; for,

although nominally a Roman Catholic, he belonged to
a sceptical society and age, — "les hommes de 1830."
Some clerical newspapers have been hard upon him, and
even to this day strict Roman Catholics will tell you
that he had a cold nature. In a certain limited sense,
there is some truth in this. On the side of the ideal,
he had not the warmth of a saint or of a poet; he was
even less inclined than most men are to carry his
thoughts much beyond the boundaries of the visible
world. We must remember, too, that his letters, which
have been published without mutilation, were for the
most part addressed to correspondents of his own way
of thinking, and written with perfect freedom. It is
therefore easy to extract passages which may offend
readers who think differently. Sometimes offence may
be taken simply because the reader is not accustomed
to one kind of freedom, when he himself uses another
equally culpable, if culpability there be. I remember,
for example, a passage in which Jacquemont freely
criticises the way in which the femur of the camel is
articulated in the pelvis, which at first seemed pre-
sumptuous, because the Creator of the camel made the
animal what it is; but we are shocked by this simply
because we are not accustomed to hear any criticism of
bones. When Mr. Palgrave gives two pages to a most
severe criticism of the camel's mind, we are not shocked;
and yet the animal's brain is just as much God's work
as its pelvis.

Although Jacquemont himself said that he had not
religious faith in the usual sense of the expression,

he also said in the same paragraph, " Our tenderness ought to expend itself for the benefit of humanity : that must be our religion." He had in a high degree what the author of " Ecce Homo " has called the "enthusiasm of humanity," and carried it into practice. Mérimée said : " To be useful was with him an absolute principle, which had taken possession of his mind and reigned there without question. He was a slave to what he considered the first of duties, and looked upon every one as blamable who did not employ his faculties for the general good." Whenever an opportunity for usefulness clearly presented itself, Jacquemont accepted it cheerfully, and set to work at once, being often better qualified than most men by his scientific knowledge. On board ship, he acted as if he combined in his own person the qualities of a surgeon with those of a sister of charity. His love and sympathy were ready for all mankind. " How many good souls," he writes, " have I met with everywhere! A misanthropist, if he could have travelled with me, would have been cured of his malady." He had no desire to deprive others of their belief. " You are very happy," he wrote to a young lady, " to keep alive those persuasions which differ from mine ; " but then he cautions her against thinking uncharitably of heretics, who have a religion also, and one that is serviceable to the world. " I know some such," he adds, " who are stoics towards themselves, and angels of charity and indulgence towards others."

During his travels in different parts of the world, Jacquemont's feelings revolted against all cruelty and oppression. In Brazil, he actually witnessed the arrival of some cargoes of slaves from Africa, and was so painfully impressed by the sight that he remained ever afterwards an ardent enemy of slavery. Writing to a friend in office, he said: "If I were in your place, in the position which you occupy, I would make use of it for the suppression of those crimes. You are not afraid of going to extremes in doing right: say, then, that the colonial administration is accused of a criminal connivance in the slave-trade. If the administration acted loyally, it would prevent the importation of slaves." Then he goes into details, and shows how the thing might be done. Resuming the same letter at a later date, he says: "This lamentable question of slavery recurs to my mind incessantly. If you had seen, as I have, the slave-sales at Rio, you would be tormented without respite!" Jacquemont's humanity was large enough to feel sorrow for whole races of mankind. Glorious as was the discovery of Columbus, Jacquemont felt painfully its fatal consequences to the aboriginal races of America which the white man destroyed, and to those of Africa which he enslaved.

The Oriental system of government, by acts of cruelty and tyranny, was intensely repugnant to our hero's notions of justice. An Italian officer in the service of Runjeet Singh gave him some information about this, which made him deeply regret that he had not remained in ignorance. When Runjeet offered him the vice-royalty of Cashmere, one of his reasons for refusing was because he would have to inflict barbarous punishments, — "There were too many ears and hands to cut off." Nothing pleased him more, during his residence there, than his great reputation for justice. The people came to him voluntarily to settle their disputes, and he willingly made himself useful as an unofficial magistrate.

Though a man of science, and able to perform a surgical operation with perfect coolness, he had so much sympathy with pain that he disliked even the representation of it on the stage. He would have been totally incapable of vivisection. No man could be farther from every kind of effeminacy than he was, and yet his feelings of humanity towards animals deprived him of all pleasure in field sports. "I have not the heart," he said, "to kill inoffensive animals." Having shot a wild boar in a royal chase, he remarked that the feat gave him little or no pleasure, though it was his first wild boar.

One of the most marked peculiarities in this original and interesting character was the combination of genuine modesty with unfailing assurance. His modesty may easily be disputed by his enemies, who may quote many passages from his letters to disprove it ; for Jacquemont was fond of boasting humorously, to his intimate friends, about every little success that attended him either in society or in his adventures. It amused him immensely to call himself the modern Plato, the Socrates of the century, the Aristotle of the age, and by any other pompous titles with which Oriental hyperbole had recognized his abilities. He liked, too, to describe his lordly state in the Punjab and in Cashmere,

and the arts by which he kept up his dignity in the eyes
of the population. Many a passage may be quoted, in
which he frankly expresses the pleasure he felt in his
own skill, whether in carrying out some traveller's
project, in the mastery of a language, or in the management of men. Such passages a cautious Englishman
would have been careful to suppress, but there is nothing conceited in them. They are the exuberance of a
rich nature, rejoicing in the possession of extraordinary
powers. A man who could possess Jacquemont's mental and bodily activity without sometimes exulting in it,
would have no pleasure in life. He never expressed
such exultation except to those who loved him, and who
were glad to hear that he bore his labors lightly, and was
treated with kindness and confidence and honor. "I
am not timid," he said; "and perhaps, in the eyes of
some, I may be wanting in modesty, although in the
sincerity of my own heart I feel myself to be really
modest and exempt only from false modesty." It is
hardly to be expected that a strong man, thirty years
old, and more than six feet high, should have the graces
of timidity, especially after so much intercourse with
the world. He felt perfectly at ease in any society, and
was not to be put out of countenance by displays of
splendor which only amused him. In his intercourse
with great people, he resolutely made the conversation
interesting till they forgot the social distance and met
him with equal frankness, —a plan which succeeded
admirably when the great folks happened to be intelligent and weary of boredom (like Lord William Bentinck

and Runjeet Singh), but which would not have shaken
the majesty of stupid greatness. In a correspondence
between Jacquemont and a French lady, she laughingly
calls him "an impudent rascal ;" and he has the grace
to admit that there is some truth in the compliment,
but says, "After all, my impudence is only candor." *
We may add to this, that without unshakable self-
confidence, both in society and amidst the hazards and
anxieties of travel, Victor Jacquemont could never have
done his work. Sometimes he saved himself by cool
audacity when his force was insufficient. Here is an
incident, in the mountains, far from help : "My old Sikh
officer, Kadja Singh, pointed out to me, in an embarrassed manner, a score of rascals posted in front of my
camp, presenting their guns at us and refusing a passage. My horsemen proposed to ride at them with
lances, — an absurd notion that made me shrug my
shoulders. Instead of that, I wrapped myself in my
superb robe of white cashmere with flowers, sat down
comfortably in my arm-chair and began to smoke. In
this convenient attitude, I entered into diplomatic rela-

---

* The candor of his letters occasionally goes quite beyond what we
are accustomed to in English books ; but we must bear in mind that
they were private letters to the writer's most intimate friends. An
ultramontane newspaper treated Jacquemont's memory with great harsh-
ness and injustice, because he sometimes mentions a medical instrument
which was lost, and caused him some anxiety till it was recovered and
restored to him with Oriental ceremony. To this it may readily be
answered that the instrument in question was a most valuable safe-
guard for a traveller, and that, although Jacquemont's sense of the
ludicrous was tickled by the publicity accidentally given to it, the
inventor of that instrument was a benefactor of humanity, since it has
been the means of saving many a life.

tions with my enemies." The result was that, after praising them for their vigilance and patronizing them with airs of gracious condescension, he rode away majestically and unmolested. When riding with Runjeet Singh, he stopped the royal elephant and all the escort, to examine a plant by the wayside.

Although Jacquemont's character was one of the most truthful that ever existed, he did not hesitate to act a part before people who could never have understood him as he really was, however elaborately he had explained himself. In Cashmere, he had a reputation for sanctity, and willingly sustained it, which was not so hypocritical as it may at first sight appear ; for he could hardly have given a more accurate idea of his character to the simple inhabitants of the valley. He was temperate in the extreme, so is a saint ; he lived chastely, so does a saint ; he loved the virtues of charity, mercy, and justice as ardently as the holiest Buddhist or Mahometan, and probably understood the practice of them better than any Asiatic. It is impossible for a man like Jacquemont to make simple people really understand him ; and, so far as they can achieve the feat at all, they must do it in their own way, which is by taking some type that is familiar to them, and calling him by its name. One rule will be found to hold good with Jacquemont throughout : his frankness had no other limit than the capacity of his hearer to understand him. Suppose he had said to ignorant Asiatics, "I am a geologist and ethnologist," would it have conveyed any thing to their minds ? The impossibility of making himself known for what he really was, and the absolute necessity for making himself respected, led him occasionally into a sort of charlatanism quite repugnant to his real character. What he professed and practised habitually was an "exclusive esteem for absolute probity," and he carried this so far that he feared "to be amusing at the cost of truth." We know men by their admirations. Observe the points that Jacquemont admires in the character of Lord William Bentinck : —

"Though accustomed to scenes of carnage, he has preserved in its virgin purity that flower of humane feeling which too often withers amidst the habits of military life. Tried, too, by the most corrupting of professions, —diplomacy,—he has kept, like Franklin, his thoughts straightforward and his language simple and sincere. When I thought of the immense power of this excellent man, I rejoiced for the sake of humanity." There is an equally interesting paragraph, in another letter, about Washington : —

"He was not a very great general, nor an eminent orator, nor yet a statesman of extraordinary skill : he was better than all that, an honest man and a great citizen ! We ought not to give esteem or consideration, nor contempt or hatred, to the qualities of the intellect : talent is neither estimable nor inestimable in itself, it is morality which is estimable ; and immorality, with whatever rare talents it may happen to be united, deserves nothing but contempt."

Turning from the moral to the intellectual side of Jacquemont's character, I should say that its predominant qualities were a fine *curiosity* of the highest kind about every thing, and an openness on every side. He was not at all one of those specialists who shut themselves up in a narrow specialty, and become blind and deaf to the great interests of human life. Men of science are much exposed to this danger, especially when the science which they pursue, such as botany, for instance, can be entirely detached from history and politics. Jacquemont got a dislike to botanists for this narrowness, and avoided them, though botany was one of his own leading studies. He regretted that his labors in natural history left him such scanty leisure in India for the study of the various peoples whose origin he wished to investigate. Few men of his years have seen so much of mankind, and still fewer have made such careful observations and comparisons. Towards the close of his short life, he became a most acute critic, both of nations and individuals, seeing qualities and faults with equal clearness, and enumerating them with equal force. His criticisms of Humboldt and Cuvier, brief as they are, will be long remembered. I will not spoil them by translation, but give them in the original in a foot-note.* On the death of Cuvier, Jacquemont

---

* "J'ai reçu hier par M. Cordier le nouvel ouvrage de M. de Humboldt sur la géographie physique et la géognosie de l'Asie centrale, qu'il a visitée en 1829, et qu'on m'envoie de Paris, humide de la presse. Qu'il a de science et d'invention! Mais combien peu de *méthode!* Qu'il écrit mal, obscurément, péniblement, filandreusement! que ses phrases sont longues! que de parenthèses, notes et appendices pour expliquer l'obscurité du texte, comme si c'était du sanscrit! Que Cuvier est grand par la méthode! quelle intelligence parfaite! Tous deux manquent de simplicité. Cuvier laisse voir le sentiment de sa force; il est

associated him in his regrets with Sir Walter Scott, and took pleasure in recognizing the true *utility* of Scott's work. He then develops this idea of true utility, and affirms that Canova and Rossini were also useful men. Comparing Scott and Cuvier with a great manufacturer, whose usefulness no one denies, he observes justly that the manufacturer can be replaced, that if he had not been born some other would have done his work, whereas it does not follow that, in the absence of Scott and Cuvier, another author would have written " Waverley " or another zoölogist discovered comparative anatomy. Though a professional man of science, Jacquemont had a keen appreciation of literature, and read copiously and carefully in several languages. He had great intellectual energy, the sort of energy that a good lawyer displays when he grapples with all the difficulties of a heavy and complicated case. In all that he had to do, he took the wise precaution, which the vain and the indolent so generally neglect, of first ascertaining what had been already done, — a precaution which, simple as it may appear, often cost him weeks of the most weari-

coupable d'orgueil, mais avec une certaine dignité ; au lieu que M. de Humboldt, qui est le second homme du monde (du monde intellectuel, je veux dire), s'il n'est pas le premier, est, malgré cela, le plus fieffé charlatan que je connaisse."

The following passage about the personal character of Cuvier occurs in another letter : —

" Prodigieuse intelligence qui n'est plus ! Il a créé des sciences nouvelles, admirablement fécondes ; la géologie serait peu de chose sans son anatomie comparée. Il perfectionnait tout ce qu'il touchait. Mais il était égoïste et dur, dur jusqu'à la méchanceté, et les individus n'étaient rien pour lui. Il considérait le genre humain abstractivement, comme les géomètres sont enclins à le faire."

some drudgery. He was, however, so happily constituted that he could go through great labors cheerfully.
" My mind," he said, " although sometimes anxious, preserves an habitual freedom which makes work easy and
light for me. I feel myself in full progress, and one
is not unhappy with such a feeling as that." I have
spoken elsewhere of his extraordinary facility as a writer,
which enabled him to do as much in a day as other writers
can do in a week.

Like all great workers, Jacquemont had a keen sense
of the value of time. He detested the sort of existence
which people lead in cafés and steamboats, where any
useful occupation is so difficult as to be almost impossible. Although he happened (not from choice) to lead
an adventurous life, he disliked adventures as an interruption, and was never so happy as in the undisturbed
pursuit of his occupations. The time lost in the ceremonies of social intercourse was a constant vexation to
him. He rides round a city with a rajah, and notices
that it takes two hours : " Alone, I should have done it
in less than an hour."

He bore solitude easily, and said that when alone
his thoughts were full of sweetness and tenderness.
" A long studious retreat, entirely separated from the
men and things of Europe," would not, he thought, be
painful to him. When it came to the test, he found the
intellectual isolation easy to bear ; but he suffered from
the too long absence of those dear to him, and his imagination realized the distance from them too well. He
had the keenest possible enjoyment of enlightened and

intelligent society, in which he was everywhere a favorite ; but he had quite as strong a dislike, on the other hand, to the society of dull and stupid people, and had not the art of adapting himself to their ways. Prosper Mérimée, who knew him intimately, said that stupidity (and by stupidity Jacquemont meant nothing but the mental condition of all commonplace humanity) irritated him strangely, and that he seemed to think it almost culpable. He delighted in the society of intelligent Englishmen, such as Fraser, Lord William Bentinck, and Sir Charles Grey, with whom he would talk for hours and hours together; but the general tone of English society seemed to him unendurable. The ordinary English irritated him " by their prodigious indifference to every thing that lies outside of the narrow circle of their monotonous existence." He declared that he preferred the natives of the remote Cashmere valley. The " genteel 'stiffness " of manner which is considered the thing in England, and the habits of thought which correspond with it, were the exact opposite of Jacquemont's tastes, and he declared that "they crushed him." At Poonah, his irritation explodes in the violent exordium of a letter addressed to Colonel Hezeta, which is a fine bit of fury, worthy of Byron in a passion.* After all, Jacquemont

* " Ah les sottes gens que les gens de Poonah, mon cher ami ! Ils montent à cheval, vont en voiture, déjeunent, dinent, s'habillent, se rasent, et se déshabillent, s'assemblent en comité pour régler les affaires d'une bibliothèque commune où je n'ai jamais vu d'autre personne que moi-même ; dorment, dorment beaucoup et ronflent fort ; digèrent comme ils peuvent, pèchent sans doute autant qu'ils peuvent, lisent leurs gazettes de Bombay ; et c'est là toute leur vie ! Les sottes gens ! les sottes gens ! Le juge est une espèce d'idiot ; le magistrat, un en-

only says in his own way what Stuart Mill, Matthew Arnold, John Morley, and Mark Pattison have since said plainly enough in theirs ; besides, we must remember that he had not the precious advantage, which we possess, of concentrating it all in a single word. We can call dull people " the Philistines," and so relieve our souls, and have done with them.

Let it not be supposed, from the frankness of Jacquemont's criticisms of English society, in private letters never meant for publication, that he was ungrateful for the uniform kindness with which our countrymen everywhere received him. There are a hundred passages which express his gratitude most warmly, and prove that the sentiment was constantly present in his mind. He praises English hospitality as much superior to French, noticing especially its spirit of self-sacrifice to the guest : he appreciates English delicacy with regard to his pecuniary situation ; and his respect for the public character of the English breaks out in many a passage of sincerest eloquence. " Honor to English ministers," he says, "they keep their word !" — " The Englishman, beyond all men, has the capacity for command." He rejoices in the extension of the British power in Asia ; and, so far from exhibiting that jealousy of it which we find

ragé chasseur, etc., etc. L'homme de sens, c'est le général, qui a appris son métier, dans votre pays, contre nous, et, de plus, bonhomme. Les autres aussi peuvent être bonnes gens, mais quelles bêtes ! quelles nullités ! "

" J'ai essayé d'en faire causer quelques-uns de ce pays qu'ils habitent ; ils n'en savent pas plus que moi qui arrive, et ne parlent aucun de ses patois ; ils n'y ont pas voyagé, n'ont aucun désir de le faire ni de savoir. Oh ! les brutes ! les brutes ! "

in the lower portion of the French press, he constantly asserts that it is a benefit to the conquered races ;·contrasting the peace and security of British territory with the imperfect protection of life and property beyond what was at that time our frontier. He said that the English were awkward in their personal intercourse with Asiatics, did not know how to talk to them, and had no intellectual influence over them, but that no nation in Europe would have done so much for the natives of a conquered country. The great fabric of British power commanded Jacquemont's admiration. "The more I know of this fabric," he wrote, in our own language, "the more extraordinary it appears to me. No guess can be made at its durability: it may last centuries, and may be swept away in a few months. However, this I will foretell: *the British power in India will not perish by foreign aggression.*"

The severest of Jacquemont's criticisms of our countrymen relate to their carelessness in money matters, and the facility with which they went into debt. He compares this with the stricter condition of opinion in the French army, where debt is held to be so disgraceful that it is practically unknown. One of the numerous passages on this subject is an excellent specimen of Jacquemont's trenchant style of writing, when excited by moral indignation.* With his strong disapproval of

---

* "Voici comme ils raisonnent :

"'Je suis un *English gentleman,* c'est à dire un des animaux les plus brillants de la création.

"'J'ai quitté les joies de l'Europe, les charmes de la vie de famille ; j'ai dit adieu à mes amis pour venir habiter ce chien de pays.

debt, it was a matter of course that he should feel hostile to the cause of it,—the costly elaboration of comfort. So far from admiring this, he considered it a great and serious evil. "I do not conceal my opinion that the system of English life is nothing but a succession of errors, all fatal to happiness. They talk of *home* without ceasing; and this *home*, which they like so much, is the material side of their existence,—their sofas and easy-chairs. Our home, which we do not talk about, is in the heart. I tell them that the poor in our country have more pleasures, and pleasures sweeter and nobler, than the rich in theirs." In another passage, Jacquemont seems to imply that English luxury is always *more récherché* than French,—an error certainly in many respects, especially with regard to variety of dishes. The real distinction is, that in France you may live comfortably or barely, according to your means and your taste; whereas in England you have to conform to a certain standard of comfort, whether you like it or not. For example, if a Frenchman does not care about carpets, he need not buy any; but all Englishmen, in the educated classes, are compelled by custom to purchase carpets. Jacquemont had a well-grounded antipathy to all compulsory expenditure,—having small means and great purposes, and a firm resolution not to be thwarted by other people's exigencies.

"'*Ergo*, j'ai le dioit, par compensation, d'être admirablement nourri, abreuvé, vêtu, logé, voituré,' etc., etc.

"'Et, si mes appointements n'y suffisent pas, je m'endetterai pour faire face à cette nécessité.'"

The concentrated severity of this could not be surpassed in the same space.

He criticised other nations as frankly as ours, and his own countrymen did not escape remark. Dining with the French Governor of Chandernagor, he meets with "a collection of fellow-countrymen, probably very estimable and respectable people;" but he confesses that he would have been "much mortified," if an English officer had presented himself and been a witness to their vulgarity. He is ashamed of the French adventurers at Calcutta. It is evident that he had become so far Anglicized as to have acquired a taste for the society of gentlemen, and a certain intolerance of non-gentlemen. Further reflection might have convinced him later that it is not easy to keep up the refinement which he appreciated without a good deal of that expenditure which he thought superfluous.

The peculiar forms of vulgarity which flourished in the United States at the time when Jacquemont visited them were especially odious to him, because they appeared authoritative and overwhelming, like the vote of some great popular majority. He valued the blessings of high culture and intellectual freedom; and it was his conviction that these blessings were gravely imperilled by the tendencies of the middle and lower classes in America, which (so far as Jacquemont could judge from a short residence) were strongly imbued with what we should now call Philistinism. There is Philistinism in every country; there is plenty of it in France itself; and we cannot stamp it out, like the cattle-plague, by killing all the Philistines and burying them in quicklime on the spot. We must therefore reconcile ourselves to the

necessity of living side by side with large masses of
fellow-citizens who are contemptuously indifferent to
" the stars of mortal night" which shine in the higher
regions of literature and science and art. Jacquemont
could have made up his mind to this; he could have
selected his friends from amongst the .intelligent few,
and followed his own pursuits in privacy. What he
dreaded was such a complete predominance of Philis-
tine principles in America that a really cultivated class
could never thrive within the frontiers of the republic.
He was afraid that the habits of studious reading and
vigorous, independent thinking would be utterly stifled
and overcome by the other more visible habits of intense
money-getting and narrow-minded intolerance. No one
would have been more happy than Jacquemont himself
to learn that his anticipations of evil were not destined
to be realized, and that in another generation the more
thoughtful English writers would be more read in the
United States than they are in their native land. And,
whether we be English or American, we may easily for-
give Jacquemont his criticisms on our failings; for, in
his case, such criticisms were never suggested by the
narrow sentiment of international ill-will. They were due
invariably to his passionate interest in the well-being of
humanity everywhere, which made him anxiously apprehensive about the evils which menaced it, no matter in
what quarter of the globe. And I may affirm, without fear
of contradiction from any one familiar with that rare and
noble nature, that, although his death-bed on that far
Indian shore was blest with serenity and peace, it would

have been lighted by the radiance of a more perfect happiness if some credible voice could have told him that, long before this century drew to its conclusion, there would neither be a slave in the cotton-fields of America, nor a serf on the plains of Russia, nor a patriot in the prisons of Italy.

HENRI PERREYVE.

IT is probable that the name at the head of this paper
will be entirely unknown to the majority of readers
in England and America, and it is not a great name anywhere ; but it has gradually become familiar to a certain
class of minds in France, and is likely to be remembered
in connection with the religious and political life of the
Second Empire.   Perreyve was never an important personage ; but we should miss a great deal that is valuable
in human nature, if we confined our attention exclusively
to important personages.   Our loss would be equally
great, if we refused our consideration to all who differ
from us on politics and religion ; and a foreigner's views
of these subjects are always sure to be un-English, even
when he may nominally belong to the same denomina-
tions as ourselves. . You cannot reasonably expect Perreyve, or any other Frenchman, to have English views
about any thing whatever: the national habits of thought
will mould his opinions in one form or another, but never
in an English form ; and these habits of thought are due
to historical causes as well as to idiosyncrasy.   For
example, republicanism in England is associated much

less with. the love of liberty than with the desire for equality ; so that an Englishman who loves liberty is not by any means of necessity a republican. In England, political liberty is unbounded under the monarchy, which has indeed actually come to be one of its best safeguards; and, therefore, a lover of political liberty in England is always likely to be a loyal supporter of the throne. The only inducement to be a republican, in England, is the desire for certain social changes which may seem worth purchasing at the cost of social disorganization ; and very few Englishmen consider that such social changes, if desirable at all, are worth the risk and peril which disorganization would involve. The case is very different in the country where Perreyve was born and died. Nobody who knows France will hesitate for one moment to admit that every liberty-loving Frenchman, without a single exception, is a republican. He is so from sheer necessity, because the republic — the real, and not the nominal republic — is the only system of government which tolerates or promises the first elementary conditions of political liberty, — the rights of free speech and free printing, the right of public meeting, and the government of the country by its own fairly elected representatives. No monarchy in France can afford to permit the exercise of these rights, only a really representative government can permit them. So hostile is any thing like monarchy in France to every thing which an Englishman considers as his political birthright, that even a mere President, if he happens to be of a royalist temper, will try to restrain the sale of newspapers he does not like, will prohibit public meetings, interfere even in private "reunions," and set up a cabinet in defiance of an overwhelming majority in the representative chamber. It is beyond the scope of the present biographical essay to inquire into the reasons for this, but the fact is beyond dispute ; and an Englishman cannot judge a Frenchman fairly, unless he remembers it. Every one who holds English opinions about political liberty holds what all French monarchists condemn as radical opinions ; and there is no limit to the severity of the censure which they apply to Frenchmen who are guilty of no greater crime than this, that they desire for France the freedom which ought to belong to a civilized people in its maturity. A single instance may illustrate the difference between the two countries in this respect. A venerable English statesman received a working-man's club, in the spring of 1877, at his residence in Richmond Park ; and an address was read to his guests, in his name, which no Frenchman could have delivered in the same month without drawing down upon himself the attentions of the police, the abuse of the monarchical press, and the condemnation of "good society." Yet Earl Russell occupies his house by her Majesty's kind permission ; and it is probable that, of the six hundred working-men who were his grateful guests on that occasion, and who enjoyed the unrivalled beauty of the place which the aged statesman loves, and where he spends the evening of an illustrious life, there was not one individual who imagined that there could be any thing incongruous between the place and the address, —

the royal demesne and the rejoicing in the people's liberty.

I would ask the English reader, who in his own country associates the word "republican" with ideas of dangerous social disorganization, to try to put himself in the place of such a Frenchman as Henri Perreyve, who loved liberty next to religion, all but equally with religion, and who knew by the experience of his countrymen that there was no hope for it under the sceptre either of a Bourbon or a Bonaparte. What can such a Frenchman be but a republican? Perreyve, then, was a republican from boyhood to the day of his death. At the same time, he was a very earnest Roman Catholic. Here, again, we have to remember that we are not in England, that the subject of our study is not an Englishman. In England, he would probably have found all that he needed in the Established Church; in France, he happened to be born in the dominant religion, and adhered to it from a certain docility of mind in religious matters, which was quite compatible with much independence in secular affairs. A real Protestant is a person who has examined the evidences of religion for himself, and who accepts them because, after examination, he is satisfied of their genuineness and sufficiency; but there may be many in Protestant churches who not having time or learning enough for that, or the active spirit of inquiry, are content to take them on trust, in simple obedience to authority. Nobody who does this need feel surprised by the obedience and submission of a Frenchman, who was a born son of the Church of Rome. Such a simple submission of the mind is too common everywhere to excite surprise in itself; but it may seem remarkable in one who was perpetually expressing his enthusiasm for political liberty. An admirer of Perreyve, almost a disciple of his, told me that he was quite conscious of the contradiction in his own case, yet felt it impossible not to be ardently Catholic and ardently Republican, being unable to renounce his convictions in either direction. The inconsistency is more obvious to-day than it was before the utterances of the Vatican; but no inconsistency, however glaring, can prevent a man from having his own convictions and giving them hospitable lodging in his mind, where they have to get on together as they best can. The more perfect his honesty, the less will he be tempted to turn out any of his opinions, that he may appear consistent in the sight of others.

Henri Perreyve was born in Paris, in April, 1831. He lived in his own family, receiving his religious education at home, and at the church of St. Sulpice, where he was catechised. His general education went on at the same time at the Lyceum of Saint Louis, which he attended as a day-scholar. He studied philosophy two years at home, and began to study law. His philosophical studies were under the direction of M. Nourisson; his legal studies were directed personally by his father, who was a competent master, being Professor of the Civil Code at the Faculté de Droit of Paris. We are told that Perreyve's father was a distinguished Latinist as well as a learned jurisconsult, and that he watched over his son's studies with the most tender care.

The young man had an intensely strong ecclesiastical vocation from the beginning. He had the same passionate desire to be a priest that others have to be soldiers or sailors, famous authors or actors or artists. At a later period, when he discovered that he had the gift of eloquence, there are evidences of delight in this great power, and of a natural ambition to be famous and influential as an orator ; but there is no trace anywhere of any thing like worldliness in Perreyve's nature. To be a priest was what he desired, — a simple priest, but at the same time a thoroughly efficient one. This may seem to us a very moderate ambition, but it did not seem so to him. He had the deepest sense of the obligations of the sacerdotal character, and a great conception of its dignity. Though he belonged to a church where the ranks of the hierarchy are very sharply defined, where the mere priest is nothing but a common soldier under the orders of his officers, and a unit in an immense organization, he looked to this comparatively humble position as the most enviable lot on earth ; and the ranks and dignities of the church seem to have been as little in his thoughts, with any reference to his own future, as the woolsack is in those of an English attorney. From first to last, the sentiment of ecclesiastical arrogance was entirely absent from his mind. His daily prayer was that he might be "a good priest, humble and chaste, and serve his Master in obscurity or in publicity, in action or study, with tongue or pen." We are constantly meeting with this sentiment in his private memoranda, and in his most confidential letters. He had but one desire in his heart, and it was this.

The first full assurance of his ecclesiastical vocation came to him at the age of twelve, when he first took the sacrament. From that moment,-his future was decided in his own mind, and a lamp of enthusiasm was lighted within him which burned steadily and brightly to the last. There was little parental opposition to this vocation. The boy's mother hailed it with gladness as a mark of heavenly favor ; his father did not oppose otherwise than by requiring that Henri should complete his legal studies and take his legal degree. This is passed over somewhat rapidly in the biographies ; but it seems evident that the father was glad to employ this means of putting his son's ecclesiastical vocation to the test, and he may possibly have indulged the hope that the young man's ardor would cool with time, and that the legal studies might be of future use in a secular profession. Whatever may have been the father's private views (and it is scarcely conceivable that he should have imposed the study of law as a preparation for clerical life), his commands caused no rebellion, and there is no evidence of any dissension in the household. Henri submitted to the legal education, worked as well at it as if he had been looking forward to a future at the bar, and had the pleasure of writing to his father a very affectionate letter from Toulouse, on the 19th of January, 1852, in which he announced that he had successfully passed his legal examination. His father accepted this as a sufficient sacrifice of filial obedience, insisted no more on the subject, and left Henri to pursue his theological studies. His ordination as sub-deacon took place in May, 1856, and in the same month of the year 1858 he became a priest. He took the degree of Doctor of Theology in 1861, and died at the end of the month of June, 1865, aged thirty-four years and two months.

This brief outline of an ecclesiastical career, which was delayed in its beginning and prematurely cut short in its conclusion, will seem at first sight to offer few of the conditions of interest and none of the attractions of success. Young as Perreyve was when he died, there have been ecclesiastics of his age already advanced to high preferment, and with the splendor of episcopal rank within their reach. His life presents no worldly success of a degree sufficient to attract attention to his name. His profession gave him food and clothing, and nothing more, unless we count amongst its advantages that of admission to aristocratic society, which Perreyve accepted merely as a useful enlargement of his experience. And yet, notwithstanding this dearth of ornament and incident, this brief existence is more sure of being long remembered than that of many a prelate who has lived in magnificence, surrounded by the homage of his ecclesiastical court, the deference of lay officials, and the veneration of the faithful. Perreyve was one of those rare and fortunate persons who are gifted with the moral beauty which attracts and retains esteem, and with that inexplicable personal charm which draws to itself whatever loving-kindness there may be

in the social atmosphere, as certain crystals absorb
moisture from the air we breathe. He was gifted for
friendship and for persuasion. Few men have had
more devoted friends ; few men have exercised so evident an influence by oratory on audiences difficult to
move. The simplicity of his life's purpose was in itself
a constant source of strength. He desired only to be a
good priest, and hoped that his object might be attainable by his own efforts, with God's help. He lived,
therefore, in that very healthy state of mind which is as
nearly as possible independent of human aid and of
human opinion, — a state of constantly active aspiration, like that of an artist who cares only to do good
work, and is alike independent of the applause of the
press and the checks of the picture-dealer.

Whatever may be the advantages, to us who live in
the common world, of passing through that constant
succession of disillusions in which human life ordinarily
consists, few of us can be quite incapable of imagining
that sweeter and purer flavor which life might have had
for us, if we had been able to preserve, undiminished,
the fervor of our early enthusiasm. We may work, in
manhood, for what we believe to be right; but how difficult it is for us to throw ourselves heartily into the
conflict against evil, and to feel certain that we are not
likely, in some indirect way, to be doing more harm
than good ! It is this fear, unacknowledged, unex-
pressed, which takes the force from our speech and the
efficacy from our action. A man-child comes into the
world with a certain limited stock of vital energy and a

certain natural heat. If the heat is not chilled nor the energy paralyzed, the boy prepares vigorously for the work of his manhood ; and the whole life goes forward, year after year, with a perfect economy of its fire and force, even in what may seem the most prodigal expenditure. It was so with Henri Perreyve. His youthful enthusiasm animated him to the last. Instead of being checked by the cooler and more experienced people he met with as he grew older, it was respected by them as a divine gift, a sort of inspiration, — just as we should admire and encourage the growing genius of a poet. Nothing is more striking, in the brief records of his life, than the moral support he received on all hands, and the remarkable readiness with which people of all ranks, all ages, and the most various shades of religious opinion, at once recognized him as a person who ought to be treated with an exceptional degree of confidence and respect. Such is the influence of an earnest and beautiful nature ; but it is scarcely necessary to say that the sweetness of character which was Perreyve's greatest charm would have been difficult to preserve, if, whilst remaining equally honest and equally highminded, he had felt urged by conscience to any act of rebellion against his Church. The Church of Rome is a gentle mother, most tender and affectionate in all her ways to a son who remains docile and submissive ; but she has unfathomed wells of bitterness in reserve for the unhappy priest who ventures to dispute her authority in any thing, or to reserve for himself any liberty of action or of thought. Perreyve never felt the

weight of her authority. The submission of the intellect was natural ·to him in all that concerned his
religious faith, being bound up with his notions of duty
towards God.

It may be said with truth that Perreyve began the
practical work of his ministry in his youth ; for, in the
year 1848, when only seventeen years old, he and several of his young friends started evening schools for the
apprentices in the Quartier St. Victor at Paris, and he
himself was charged with the religious lectures. In
1850, his health broke down: he began to spit blood,
and was recommended to travel in Italy, with a physician, Dr. Charles Ozanam. The published collection of
his letters begins with this journey to Italy ; and it is
these letters which will supply the material for the
following brief account of his life, and of the impressions which he received from the men and things
he saw. The correspondence reflects his feelings and
impressions from year to year, and reflects them with
remarkable clearness, both because he naturally put
much feeling into his letters, from the earnest communicativeness of his character, and also because the letters
are for the most part addressed to very dear personal
friends, to whom he could be very communicative without impropriety, as they were interested in all he either
thought or did.

Throughout these letters, the most permanent characteristic is the intensity of the writer's affections, not
only for persons, but even for places and things. At
Lyons, he is sad, because his family once lived there, and

he had often visited the city in his early life. Now the
old friends are absent or dead, the property is in other
hands (a vineyard, with a tower, on the hillside), and
nothing is left but the mournful pleasures of memory.
Saddened by a visit to these scenes of childish happiness, — the wood, the garden, the little field where the
cow was kept, the strangely altered house, where he
finds some of the old furniture, nevertheless, — the
young traveller goes to Fourvières, and is pained by
modern projects of embellishment. The little old
chapel is to be enlarged, the altars enriched, the tower
rebuilt. All this only hurts Perreyve, whose affections
had attached themselves to the chapel when it was
small enough to be warmed by the burning tapers of
the pilgrims.

In Provence, he feels already like a wanderer in a
foreign land. Avignon, Arles, and the remarkably curious and interesting region round about, arouse in him
none of the happy energy of the real traveller, for the
simple reason that his affections are not bound up with
them in any way. So his heart turns back to Paris,
and he thinks of his own little room at his father's.

The same strength of affection makes him feel exiled
in Italy, although Italy is the chief seat of his own
Church. Even the Church herself seems strange to
him at Naples, and he writes about the southern aspects
of Catholicism, just as an English Protestant might write
about them. He says: "Our Gallican gravity has been
hurt by Pagan externals, and I could recognize nothing
of the Gospel in them. I feel tempted to call Naples a

Pagan city. Her mission seems to have been to preserve the genius of the ancient world. Unluckily, I stayed at Naples through the Holy Week. I compared the ceremonies practised there with the pious and severe ceremonies of the Church of France. I saw the frivolous and idle Neapolitan populace running from tomb to tomb, from church to church, a thousand times wilder, noisier, more jocular than the crowd of staring Parisians when there are public fireworks." Every thing in the world is relative, yet some English readers may feel surprised that any one could speak of the very advanced ritualism of ecclesiastical ceremonies in France as " severe." The passage is worth quoting, because it so decidedly exhibits Perreyve's tendency towards Gallicanism, and his love for seriousness and severity in public worship.

The young traveller was not entirely absorbed in ecclesiastical matters, for he became very enthusiastic at the tomb of Virgil, whom he calls "l'homme de bien qui ne chanta jamais que la vertu;" forgetting the antique immorality of the Eclogues. Possibly there may have been just a little innocent self-deception in this burst of enthusiasm about the Mantuan bard. A more genuine and perfect pleasure was a visit to the monastery of Monte Cassino, where he sympathized heartily with the industrious and intelligent monks who at that time were exposed to some persecution. The Neapolitan Government, hating intellectual labors, looked very sharply after these monks, stopped their correspondence, established a censorship over their books, and sent soldiers to seal up their libraries and break their printing-press. It is a curious evidence of the impressionableness of Perreyve's nature, that, although he, stayed at the monastery only a day, he formed a friendship there, as some have fallen in love at first sight, with a monk twenty-six years old, whom he describes as being full of knowledge and of high intellect. They had barely time to exchange a few thoughts hastily in the one day that they lived together, yet when they parted it was after long embraces, and Perreyve's eyes filled with tears. Monte Cassino may have impressed itself the more strongly on Perreyve's memory, that from his youth he had dreamed of a life combining religious faith with intellectual activity, and he found the two together there. His interest in the monks was increased by the tyranny of the authorities, whom he calls "the persecutors of free thought" — an expression remarkable as coming from one who was already in heart a priest of the Church of Rome, never herself very favorable to intellectual free-dom. His dominant idea, even at that early time of life, is expressed in a letter from Florence (March 18, 1850), in which he says: "I believe that what the world most needs in the present day is a class of young men at the same time moral, religious, *and liberal.* They may possibly be the salvation of France, and the transition, so often sought, between true social progress and the ancient doctrines of Catholicism." A little farther on, in the same letter, he speaks of his own willingness to give time and effort to strengthen the party, of whose members it may be said that they are at the same time pious and free and earnest for social progress, their religion not being a religion of slaves. This was the note of Perreyve's thought and aspiration from his youth. In him there was no real inconsistency between the passion for freedom and the devotion to the Church; for willing service is the most perfect liberty of all, and his ecclesiastical service was more than willing, being eager and joyous. The mistake of his life lay in the inability to see how few men can be *good* Catholics and feel perfectly free at the same time, and how dangerous to Catholic unity is the free action of individual intellects.

In the ardor of political liberty there was no such cause of embarrassment, and we may all sympathize with Perreyve in the bitterness of his disappointment when a respectable attempt at self-government in France was violently put an end to by the *coup d'état* of Louis Napoleon. "I shall remember all my life," he writes in February, 1852, — "I, a young man of twenty, cradled in radiant hopes, shall remember having seen a whole people, all France, sanctioning with its votes what every heart with the love of liberty in it must detest! I cannot bear to talk of these things, they have wounded me deeply. What are we to do or believe? I believe still what I believed before. If the happiness of humanity is to be in the application of the most comprehensive democratic forms, democracy itself is only possible when founded on Christian virtues. For the present, there is nothing to be done but to keep silence, turn away from shameful sights, concentrate inwardly those forces which

are powerless externally, and try to love good and hate
evil." In another letter, written towards the end of
April in the same year, he laments the intellectual inac-
tion and indifference which were such a remarkable
result of the establishment of the Empire: "What I
like at Paris is the intellectual activity, the life of discussion, the earnest interest in politics and literature.
There is nothing of all that now."

In August, 1852, we find him writing letters from the
Pyrenees, and exceedingly astonished at the first effects
upon strangers of that wonderful personal charm which
afterwards gave him so much influence over others.
He makes a little excursion into Spain, and meets with
many acts of kindness from people who have never seen
him before. "Is it credible," he says, "that, when I
could not get a seat in the public conveyance from
Bayonne to San Sebastian, two people entirely unknown
to me offered me a place for nothing in a carriage which
they had hired for a hundred and fifty francs? Is it
credible that I lodged three days at San Sebastian with
four kind souls, who first took me in from pity, then
kept me from a sentiment resembling attachment, and,
yesterday when I left them, gave me precious little gifts
for a remembrance, accompanied me as if they had been
my own sisters, and shed tears when I left them? Is it
credible that as I had chosen to go on foot from San
Sebastian to Renteria, to sketch by the way, and so
arrived tired and hungry, a gentleman whom I had never
seen, and shall never see again, made me go to his
house, introduced me to his family, treated me like a

son, and wanted to keep me to sleep in his delightful Spanish villa, rich with superb pictures of the very greatest schools? If I had had all my friends and relations in a line on this road to Spain, I could not have been more affectionately and generously treated."

Perreyve had plenty of variety in his life at this time, and went three times to the south of France in a single year. A visit to the Dominican monastery at Flavigny is interesting, from the traveller's evident want of sympathy with asceticism, — a feeling which may be detected in other passages of his correspondence. This time there was a little feast for the Dominican brethren, who were indulged with cakes and wine. "But how sternly severe their life is!" says Perreyve. "It is the only time that I ever saw a little general gayety and liberty amongst them. All the rest of their life is austere to a degree which frightened my weakness. Lacordaire made me dine in the monastery on the occasion of the festival, and I expected a merry meal; but they began by chanting the *De Profundis*, then the Father rang a bell, and all the monks who were to wait upon us prostrated themselves on the earth. Nobody breathed a word during the repast, and by way of dessert we chanted the *Miserere*." Then comes a remark worth noting: "There is something very seductive in the order of St. Dominic, and that is Father Lacordaire." This first impression deepened with time, and in after years Lacordaire loved Perreyve better and trusted him more thoroughly than any other man in the world.

Perreyve wrote to the Abbé de la Boissière, in August,

1853, that he had passed his examinations, and been received as an advocate. "At last," he said, "I am free!" This meant that he had fulfilled the paternal injunction of preparing himself for a secular calling, and was now at liberty to turn his attention wholly to the things of the Church. The very same letter in which he announces that he is an advocate curiously finishes with the other announcement, made at this time to several of his more intimate friends, that he had entered the little confraternity of the "Oratoire," a very active religious association, then in its infancy, in Paris, and unknown elsewhere, of which we shall hear more in the sequel.

In the summer of 1854, Perreyve being then at the Oratoire, the Archbishop of Paris, Sibour, who was afterwards murdered, visited the little community, and presided at dinner. At the end of this meal, a singular event occurred, which had an influence on the young Oratorian's life. The archbishop made a speech, and in the course of it fixed his eyes on Perreyve, expressing especial hopes for him. "I believe," said the archbishop, "that I read upon his forehead something which assures me that he will be the honor of my diocese." Then, speaking to young Perreyve directly, he continued, "I beg you to keep in your heart what I have said, until the will of God with reference to you shall be accomplished." There was nothing supernatural in the prelate's perspicacity; for Perreyve had a very open, intelligent countenance, which always attracted attention and won confidence.

He received the tonsure in 1854, and, in one of his frequent journeys, went to stay at the monastery of Notre Dame de Châlais, on the road from Lyons to Grenoble. We have said "on the road," but this may convey an impression that the monastery is more in the way of human traffic and intercourse than it really is. The actual situation of it is high amongst the rocks and pines. You quit the road at Voreppe, take mules, ascend for an hour and a half, and find yourself landed on a plateau of grassy lawns. After that, you ride still farther, under the shadow of perpetual rocks and pines ; and then you discover the monastery, hidden in this deep fastness of wild nature. Perreyve, like all exquisite modern natures, was keenly alive to the influences of sublime natural scenery; and it so happened that, on his arrival, these influences were enhanced by the charm of one of those beautiful hours which leave an impression on the memory for years. The sun was setting in a golden haze that filled the valleys of the Iser, lying far below the travellers. The bell of the monastery was tolling the angelus; and the mules stopped at the door of the chapel, the custom being "for new comers to salute first the real master of the house."

The days of Perreyve's sojourn in this place were full of a quiet delight for him. The very altitude seemed to lift him above the wretched interests and contentions of the common world. By a natural illusion, empires and emperors could be forgotten there, as if the arm of Napoleon were not long enough to reach so high ; and there was a sense of remoteness from terrestrial things

which suited an ideal nature willing to detach itself
from the earth.   The planet held him yet, however, not
by gravitation merely, but by the ties of a new affection.
The rocky ground which surrounded the monastery
soon became deeply attractive to Perreyve, when he had
made long pedestrian excursions with the brethren.
These walks, and his own hours of solitude, taught him
how happy a human soul might be in the midst of so
stern a land.   Sweetly serious, his mind enjoyed the
complete absence of the world's frivolity.   " Quel silence
de ce qu'il est vain d'entendre, et quelle harmonie parfaite des œuvres divines ! "

Amongst the excursions which could be made on foot
from the monastery was the ascent of a mountain, one
of the highest in Dauphiny ; and from its summit he
saw the chain of the Alps, with Mont Blanc surrounded
by his rocky spires, "like a monarch surrounded by his
guards."   He writes about this to a friend at the seaside, and wonders which of the two had been, at that
hour, in presence of the grander spectacle.   His mind
is too habitually theological to find any ultimate satisfaction in natural beauty : it rebounds to the divine at
once ; and he characteristically ends his letter with the
quotation, " Mirabiles elationes maris, mirabilis in altis
Dominus."   Then he makes private entries in his note-
book, following the same train of thought.   Ideas of
power lead him instantly to the feet of the Creator ;
ideas of purity and beauty conduct him as rapidly to the
Virgin Mary.   After strongly expressing his sense of
landscape beauty, especially of the Alpine purity, he

comes to the Virgin at once. "I know not how it happened," he says, "but, whilst a young Dominican monk and I were gazing together at these beautiful Chablais mountains, we were led to admire the beauty of the Virgin Mary." His mind is so occupied with religious conceptions that the external world seems only to exist for him as a suggestion of religious thought. Lakes and streams suggest this to him : the mountain stream is the broken and agitated life of man in the world, wretchedly narrow and forced on at speed, mingling and confusing the reflections of all that it hurriedly passes by ; the lake is restful and vast, with the fulness and peace of the larger life to come. There is nothing very new or very remarkable in these reflections, but they show the theological habit of mind. You may read through all the four volumes of De Saussure, who was constantly amongst Alpine scenery, without once finding mountain beauty likened to that of the Virgin Mary, or Lake Leman to the heavenly rest.

As Perreyve passed from youth to manhood, the twin ideas (for they were twins in his mind) of liberty and Christianity grew stronger within him, and found ampler expression in his letters. Liberty and Christianity were so bound together in his mind that he could hardly think of one without rekindling his enthusiasm for the other. In the agitation of the European mind which preceded the Crimean war, Perreyve perceived that the true solution must come from within the mind through changes of opinion, and not from without through military and political events. The solution which he himself always

proposed for public uneasiness was political freedom
along with faith in Jesus Christ. "At a time," he writes
in 1854, "when the attention of every one is directed to
outward signs, let us not forget that the ultimate solution of the problem is within us, and that sooner or
later, to-morrow perhaps, after great external commo-
tions, conquerors or conquered, we shall have to come
back to that. It may become a positive duty to speak
out, when there is danger in doing so. It will be more
a duty for us than for others, because we have received
from God two treasures very rarely united in the same
heart, the love of Jesus Christ and the love of liberty.
. . . I believe more than ever that when the terrible
day of the *last explanations* shall have come, in the
supreme hearing of the cause between the children of
this world and the children of God, if a voice may prevent complete separation and ruin, that voice will be
both free and Christian; in the midst of the general
confusion it will fearlessly assert justice and truth; it
will be full of love, even for those who have gone astray;
it will not pronounce anathemas, but a pardon; it will
call for liberty and social progress in the name of Jesus
Christ, in spite of menaces from those who care only
for the past and menaces from impious revolutionists."
Then he anticipates the possibility of meeting death at
the hands of those he most desired to serve, and hopes
to face it at least as courageously as the soldiers in the
war. The possibility really existed. If Perreyve had
lived to preach Christian liberty in Paris under the
Commune, he might have been shot with the archbishop

and others of his cloth. As for the courage which he
desired, he already fully possessed it, having served as
a volunteer whilst still a mere boy (at the age of seventeen), during the terrible "journées de Juin," five days
and five nights of danger.

Another danger menaced him already in 1854, that of
early death from pulmonary disease, or else, what had
greater terrors for him, a lingering existence on the
earth to be passed in impotent uselessness. The prospect of this possibility filled him with "a great and
bitter sadness." In October, 1854, he was seized with
congestion of the lungs, suddenly, in the public street.
He recovered from this attack, but felt his health broken.
When the malady was at its worst, he had accepted
death, not merely with resignation, but with gladness.
It was far harder to accept the return to life with the
dread of "a future without force, useless, and disarmed."
He wrote to Lacordaire about this, pouring out the
bitterness of his heart. Of all the misfortunes which
can happen to an ardent and generous nature, there is
not one so terrible as physical failure before the work of
the life is done. In Perreyve's case, it was not even
begun. There had been nothing but hope and preparation hitherto, and now the hope was clouded, the preparation possibly vain. "Can you imagine," he says to
Lacordaire, "what such an existence may be for souls
who have looked forward to action and contest? A life
of cowardly rest, kept up artificially without being good
for any thing or anybody, and for the mere pleasure of
living a little longer! The idea of that has hurt me

more than all the rest ; and, though I try to think of something else, it haunts and devours me !"

The next year, in the month of July, his letters are dated from Eaux-Bonnes, and are more cheerful; but the tone is rather that of an invalid who has made up his mind to bear his infirmity than that of a convalescent rejoicing in the prospect of a complete recovery. He thanks a friend (the present Bishop of Autun) for kindly greeting, and says that it has brought back a little courage. "I am pretty well," he adds, "but the improvement is not very perceptible." Then he complains of bronchial irritation ; and, passing from the physical to the spiritual state, seeks the divine reasons for his affliction, and believes he has found them in the lesson of sacrifice which he is painfully learning, — the sacrifice of his own tastes and wishes. "God has severed me from all that I loved best in the world, — severed me perhaps for long. He has separated me perhaps from myself, by compelling me to cast out of my spirit so many desires, so many illusions, so many ambitious hopes that I had nurtured through all my earlier youth, and has taught me to pronounce, a little less badly than I once could, the great expression of the Apostle, ' Servi inutiles sumus.' " Then he speaks of the salutary influence of the mountains upon his mind. He says that they make him calm, which is the more interesting that the usual effects of mountain scenery are exciting. The sylvan world attracts his attention also, suggesting its own analogies. Young pine-trees, torn from their places by tempest or torrent, fall before their time, wither, and die unresistingly. The leaf is carried away and perishes without rebellion. These things obey the law, and the law must be obeyed. The application to his own case is obvious.

In August, 1855, he writes from Biarritz to a lady cousin, in a pleasant, amiable tone, wondering at his own capacity for enduring solitude. The same astonishment recurs in other letters about this time. ·He had believed himself disqualified by nature for solitary living, and is quite surprised to find how easily his mind accepts it. Neither at this period, however, nor at any other, is Perreyve in the least ascetic: he willingly enjoys simple and unforbidden pleasures, especially the priceless one of looking at natural scenery, and describes with astonishment the life of the Bernardine Sisters, whom he has visited in their convent, — a life unequalled for the rigor of its discipline even in the Church of Rome. The Bernardines give their time to the direction of fallen women who have repented, and whose highest reward is to become Bernardines themselves at last. They live amongst the dreary deserts of sand that stretch along the southern coasts, like the first anchorites in the deserts of Africa. They eat black bread, drink water, and *never speak, — never.* A Chartreux may speak once in every week : a Bernardine is silent as the dead.

Perreyve's delicate health kept him much in the southern parts of Europe, the cold Parisian winters being especially dangerous for him. He went to Italy for the second time in November, 1855, and, whilst

passing through Marseilles, visited the military hospital,
then crowded with wounded soldiers from the Crimea;
and this visit gave him "one of the great and profound
impressions of his life." Most of the wounds were
terrible, and much aggravated by the length of the
voyage from Sebastopol. Perreyve, who had a good
deal of the military spirit in his nature, and who had
perfect confidence in the righteous character of the
Crimean war, felt the warmest sympathy with these
sufferers, whose prospects in life were so utterly blighted,
and whose courageous resignation made him ashamed
of his own rebellion against his ailment. I take leave
to pause here, to note a remark he made. Every English reader must be perfectly familiar with the assertion
(one of the commonplaces of insular self-complacency)
that Englishmen fight for duty; that duty is their leading idea, as exemplified in Nelson's watchword at Trafalgar, and in Wellington's conduct through life: whereas,
the French have no conception of duty, but only fight
for glory, — *la gloire*, as they call it in their tongue.
Now I have not the slightest objection to English pride
in duty, provided it is not accompanied by the notion
that the word and the thing are a British monopoly.
Devoir means the same thing, I believe, and is the older
word of the two, seeing that "duty" is derived from its
past participle. Perreyve wrote that, in the military
hospital at Marseilles, many a soldier said to him : "J'ai
fait mon devoir, Monsieur le Curé; que la volonté de
Dieu soit faite ;" and then he adds, " Le mot de *devoir*
est dans presque toutes les bouches." After that, on

the same page, he describes the departure of reinforce-
ments for the Crimea with a kindly indulgence for that
" French carelessness which covers more serious and
often profoundly Christian thoughts." A *voltigeur* said
to him, as he went on board, " What luck, to have a fine
sail for nothing!" But five minutes afterwards the
same man added in a tone of great earnestness, "Chacun
son *devoir*, Monsieur l'Abbé ; " on which Perreyve remarks, " Toujours ce mot austère et saint ! "*

Perreyve was already (1855) in friendly communication with two very famous ecclesiastics, who did much
afterwards for his own fame by associating their names
with his, in different ways. One of these two, the great
Dominican Lacordaire, is well known in England : the
other, Gratry, is less known out of his own country.
Perreyve wrote long letters to both of them from Pisa,
—letters full of the affectionate yet respectful familiarity
which proves that a young correspondent is quite at
ease, and knows that he can count upon the sympathy
of his elders. He is quite frank with both about his
bodily and mental state. He tells Gratry that he feels
within himself an extreme delicacy of health, a sort of

---

* Mr. Ruskin seems to be under the impression that *devoir* is an old
French word that had influence in the Middle Ages, but has since given
place to a modern substitute, *gloire*, with a very different meaning. Mr.
Samuel Smiles, in his book on " Character," contrasts the English idea
of duty with the French lack of the idea. This is one of those pieces of
international ill-nature which scarcely deserve refutation, but writers
of influence ought not to perpetuate them. The word *devoir* is quite as
much in use as *duty*. A French school-boy calls his work his *devoir*: an
English school-boy calls it his task, lesson, or exercise. As for *gloire*,
it is seldom used except in the official military style, which nobody
accepts without deductions.

inward ruin, which will make him *malingre* for the
rest of his days; but that he can find comfort yet, if
God will continue to him, "as at present," the faculty of
loving a few good and beautiful souls along with himself, and the power of working five or six hours every
day. This, for the time, is the limit of his ambition.
Then he goes on to say how rich human nature is in
consolations, even when all seems shattered around it.
He had recently been suffering much, and his eyes were
too much fatigued for reading and writing, so that all
occupation outside of himself had become impossible.
In this condition, he was delighted almost to the point
of enthusiasm to find that he could still derive happiness
from mere thinking. He had never before so completely realized the value of this gift of thought. It
seemed to him that, whilst this last sanctuary remained
inviolate, the rest might, in the last necessity, be sur-
rendered; and that, so long as the mind enjoyed simply
the liberty of its own motion, happiness need not be
renounced.

Perreyve found his health better at Rome than at Pisa,
and the interest he took in the city made the external
world attractive to him still. The Coliseum had a fascination for him, from the memory of the early Christian martyrs who perished in its arena. There is a curious anecdote
in connection with these visits to the Coliseum. Perreyve was sitting there reading Michelet's Introduction
to Universal History, — reading, not in an intolerant
spirit, but with a proper ecclesiastical pity for the "unhappy lost soul" of the great historian, — when he came

upon a remarkable passage in which Michelet says that
he had willingly (*de bon cœur*) kissed the wooden cross
which stands there, in memory of the early Christian
victims. Perreyve was reading the book at a distance
of a hundred yards from the same cross, and involun-
tarily left his seat to go and do like Michelet, not in
memory of the martyrs, but for the benefit of Michelet's
soul,—"that poor soul which compelled God to quit it."
The anecdote shows exactly the degree of intolerance
which was compatible with Perreyve's kindness of heart.
He calls Michelet "an unhappy lost soul," but reads his
book, and wishes him no evil.

The Coliseum became a huge *cabinet de travail* for
Perreyve, who used to take a book (St. Paul's Epistles
most frequently) and some paper there, to escape from
friendly calls and importunities, only going back to his
lodgings in the evening. He soon had a multitude of
friends at Rome, and had also a patron, Cardinal Ville
court, a lively old Frenchman, who, in spite of his
ecclesiastical dignity, had the national love of a joke,
and often made one, in an amiable way, at Perreyve's
expense. Another and more serious side of the cardinal's character was his preference for simplicity of life.
On being promoted to the purple, he was so afflicted as
to lose sleep for a week, yet could confide the reason for
his sadness to nobody, the papal intention being secret.
His old servant, seeing his dejection, made daily inquiries, but got no answer save this, "Ah, my poor
Jean, something quite unforeseen has happened to us!"
At length, being free to speak, he said, "My poor Jean.

I am a Cardinal;" and the man knew not whether to laugh or cry, but ended by finding the change favorable to himself, as it placed him at the head of a cardinal's pompous establishment.

By the intercession of the Cardinal Villecourt, Perreyve had an audience of Pius IX., and was so impressed thereby that he gave a most minute account of it to Father Gratry, in a letter. The Pope was most amiable and benignant, first gave his hand to kiss and then his shoe, made Perreyve go down on his knees and talked to him in the most paternal way, like a confessor. The Pope knew all about the Oratoire (the new little confraternity to which Perreyve had attached himself), and said : "The Oratoire at Paris directed by the Abbé Pététot, who used to be incumbent of St. Roch ? Ah, there's a priest for you!"—and then descanted on the abbé's virtues, which led to a sort of general discourse on the priestly character. When Perreyve went away, the Pope blessed his ecclesiastical life "according to the will of God,"—an expression which the young invalid at once understood in its reference to his broken health, and to the possible abbreviation of his ministry.

It is necessary in this place to set clearly before the reader Perreyve's ecclesiastical situation in 1856. He had been obliged, by the state of his health to quit the "congregation" of the Oratory, which would have required his presence in Paris, where he could not bear the winters, and more constant labor in public speaking and other labor than his diminished strength could give. He had received the "simple tonsure," but had not taken holy orders, not being as yet even a sub-deacon. His superiors had discouraged the idea of the sub-deacon-hood, which for some time had been Perreyve's ambition; and, though with great sadness, he had resigned himself to this early cutting short of his ecclesiastical career. A little later, however, on a second application from him, a more favorable answer had been returned, and the matter was decided as he wished. He tells the news to his father "as a piece of news saddening for him, which will require an effort of resignation,"— an expression which proves clearly that M. Perreyve the elder was not, even yet, entirely reconciled to his son's passion for the Church.

The letters from Rome, soon after this, are filled with enthusiastic anticipations of the sub-deaconhood. The strength of the young man's "vocation," as we say figuratively, was such that he really believed himself to be called by Jesus Christ. "It is not we who have chosen him," Perreyve writes to a friend, "but he who has chosen us;" then follow many amplifications of this idea. He writes to a very intimate young friend: —

"Blessed be our Lord Jesus Christ for having, by the help of his grace and the strength of our friendship, protected our hearts against those passions which have been the ruin of so many at our age, and for having preserved us for the radiant and chaste light of this day!

"Blessed be our Lord Jesus Christ, who has not permitted the light of our first communion to be extinguished in us; who, by his grace, has caused our faith to increase with our years, who has caused the piety of the child to grow into the piety of the man, so that we have not to regret having ever quitted or betrayed him ! "

The strength and purity of the religious sentiment in these sentences will be recognized by every one. It is difficult to find anywhere in literature, outside of the Gospels and the Imitation, such a concentrated expression of religious satisfaction of the most blameless and amiable kind. There is in it none of the pride of the Pharisee, but a genuine quiet thankfulness that youth has been passed in purity, and that the ideal of childhood has grown into the ideal of manhood without rupture or rebellion. It is the satisfaction of

> That awful independent on to-morrow,
>   Whose yesterdays look backwards with a smile.

It is the exact opposite of that misery which sometimes found expression in the verse of Byron, and gave to his " Stanzas for Music " their immortality of mournfulness : —

> There's not a joy the world can give, like that it takes away
> When the glow of early thought declines in feeling's dull decay.
> 'Tis not on youth's smooth cheek the blush alone that fades so fast,
> But the tender bloom of heart is gone ere youth itself be past.
>
> Then the few whose spirits float above the wreck of happiness
> Are driven o'er the shoals of guilt or ocean of excess.
> The magnet of their course is gone, or only points in vain
> The shore to which their shivered sail shall never stretch again.

Perreyve at last announces to his mother that the ceremony of ordination has taken place, " a finer and more imposing ceremony than he had expected." The younger Ampère was present, stayed all the time, and (though not a believer like Perreyve) was so much moved as to press his friend's hands with tears in his eyes on leaving the church. The day following is Trinity Sunday, and the new sub-deacon officiates at mass, when he chants the Epistle, "trembling a little with emotion." The next incident of some importance is another interview with Pius IX., who begins to treat the young Frenchman as an acquaintance. In July, we find him back in France, at Eaux-Bonnes; and in August, at Paris, where in a letter to Lacordaire he criticises the sort of life people lead at the watering-places: "Nothing paralyzes the mind like the accepted habit of doing nothing. Life at watering-places is wonderful in this respect: one has nothing to do, and yet never an instant to call his own. It is idleness organized." He announces that the doctors have now better hopes for him. He talks about Cousin, the philosopher, with whom he had become intimately acquainted, and regrets to have judged him harshly and unfairly before knowing him. Perreyve had complained to Cousin that in his writings there was an implicit denial of the need of the supernatural in man, to which Cousin replied that he had never denied the existence of the supernatural, but had implicitly recognized it by distinguishing between the natural and the supernatural." At this time, Cousin went regularly to mass, and behaved very properly in church.

The next year (1857) finds Perreyve again in Rome, from January till after Easter, kindly received by the Pope, and much interested, as usual, in all he sees at Rome, — the remarkable men, the splendid ceremonies, the scenery of town and country.

It was from the lips of the Pope himself that Perreyve
heard the astounding news of Archbishop Sibour's assas-
sination in the church of St. Étienne du Mont.   The
assassin, this time, was a priest, and the event might
have happened in the most prosperous days of the
Church ; but it gave rather a sombre shade to Perreyve's
thoughts about ecclesiastical prospects.   His strictly
theological way of estimating events lead him to wonder
that the tears and prayers of the Church had not exercised influence enough with God to procure from Him a
miraculous interference by which the murderer's weapon
might have been turned aside.   Possibly the event, little
as it had to do with the future of the Church, may have
led Perreyve to look forward with gloomy foreboding ;
but, however this may be, we find him predicting times of
severe trial.   " Perhaps," he says, " I see matters on the
dark side, but many indications are clear and certain.
The Papacy will pass through terrible crises."   This, as
we all know, has turned out to be true; the temporal
power being gone, and probably gone for ever, yet the
wonder is to us how little the spiritual power, or influence, has been affected by this loss, and what a robust
vitality the institution still displays.   Unforeseen circumstances have strengthened the Papacy almost, if not
quite, as much as the loss of the temporal power has
weakened it.   Stephenson and Wheatstone little thought
that by their labors in steam communication and tele-
graphy they were fortifying, in the future, an institution
so little in harmony with modern science as the Church
of Rome ; yet these modern instruments have greatly

increased the unity of the Church and the despotic authority of its chief, by bringing all the national branches
of Catholicism more immediately under the direction of
the Roman Curia. Bishops are summoned to Rome
from all parts of the world, and they come over land and
sea; pilgrimages are organized all over Europe, and even
in America; the pilgrims arrive in Rome by hundreds
and by thousands, bringing with them offerings more
valuable than were ever laid before the throne of the
most puissant temporal prince. Scarcely a day passes
without news from the Vatican amongst the telegrams
of the great journals; and that palace in its garden, where
the Pope lives in voluntary imprisonment, has a degree
of European importance far exceeding that of any of the
lesser sovereignties. It is the last place in Europe where
the right of sanctuary exists. A law-breaker who takes
refuge there, and is received, is safe from the police of
Europe. The master of the Vatican has still his ambassadors at foreign courts, and counts his faithful subjects
by thousands or by millions in the very heart of the
countries to which his nuncios are accredited,—subjects
who give him an allegiance far heartier and more zealous
than the simply acquiescent loyalty they reserve for the
secular power of President, or King, or Emperor. The
master of the Vatican is the only person in the world
who can use vituperation to any extent, and in perfect
safety. He can insult any sovereign on the earth, and
the insulted sovereign has no redress. A king cannot
move armies and fleets to attack an old man in a garden;
he cannot, in royal decorum, reply in language which is

thought allowable when it comes from a priest. The Pope has the power of a man and the immunities of a woman, the resources of royalty and the irresponsibility of a private annuitant. Gradually, yet rapidly, an amount of treasure is accumulating in his hands which will give to him, or to his successor, the subtle and secret power of gold to a degree exceeding the wildest imaginations of romance.

Perreyve came to the conclusion that the French troops were superfluous, and that the Pope's virtues would protect the Papacy better than a foreign occupation. It may be doubted whether the Pope's virtues have done much for this; but there can be little doubt that his exceptionally great age has won for him more sympathy than his successor can hope for; and his policy of constant and bitter complaint, though not always dignified nor consistent with truth, may have been on the whole the wisest policy for a Pope dis possessed of the temporal power.

Just before leaving Rome, Perreyve saw the Easter ceremonies of 1857, which were in complete splendor, with a larger influx of foreigners than usual. The "Saint-Père" was "beau à ravir le cœur, et sa voix tout accentuée de ces notes plaintives et sonores qui charment les hommes et doivent plaire à Dieu." Perreyve writes a description of the Pope blessing the city and the world, which conveys in a few words more of the spirit and emotion of that remarkable spectacle than the most elaborate description. It would be a pity to spoil it by translation : —

" Vous savez tout le reste : cette volée de cloches interrompue par le roulement des tambours, ce grand silence de tout un peuple, tous ces fronts découverts, cet ange vêtu de blanc paraissant entre le ciel et la terre, ce coup de canon pour saluer la joie de toute la famille catholique, cette voix, cette belle, forte, tendre, et bien aimée voix flottant dans ce grand silence d'amour, et ces mains enfin si haut élevées vers le ciel retombant surchargées de bénédictions sur nos pauvres cœurs ! "

Perreyve was back in Paris in May; and his health broke down again in June, when he was seized with congestion of the lungs, during a retreat at St. Sulpice, preparatory to his ordination as a deacon. He held out till the day of ordination, went through the ceremony by a great effort, and then went home to bed, where he lay ill for several days. When his physical state began to improve again, he was crushed by the old discouragement. " Here is fresh evidence," he says, " of my uselessness, — a new humiliation for so many longings after activity and apostolic duty which a return of health always awakens within me, but which cannot be pure enough to please God, since He does not accept them." Notwithstanding this liability to pulmonary attacks, Perreyve was strong enough to speak well in public, and discovered, at Sorèze, in November, 1857, that he had the natural gifts of an orator. This happened on St. Cecilia's Day, in the presence of Lacordaire and a large assemblage, when our hero narrated the feast of St. Cecilia in the Catacombs, and took her life and martyrdom for his text. The young orator trembled with emotion, yet was master of himself in spite of this, and spoke eloquently. He had written nothing, but only thought over his subject, and forgot nothing that he intended to say. At a banquet which followed, Lacordaire proposed a toast to his " young eloquence, on which God had great designs." This revelation of so enviable a power (fully confirmed in the sequel) delighted Perreyve, and filled him with a new sense of responsibility. With that complete expression of deep feeling which seems possible only to Southern natures, he no sooner found himself in the solitude of his own room than he threw himself with his forehead on the ground, "devant Celui qui seul est digne d'honneurs." In a letter to a friend, he gives an account of his sensations when speaking, and of his surprise at his own powers. He had believed himself to be too impressionable for oratory ; but, after a few tremulous words at first, he became surprisingly calm and lucid, and could speak slowly and clearly, so as to be heard at a distance. He felt also that he would soon have the courage to let his eloquence take bolder flights.

From that moment, Lacordaire felt so strongly the value of Perreyve that he wished to have him permanently at Sorèze ; but Paris attracted him too much, — certainly not for its pleasures, but as a great field for a laborer who could understand the Parisian love of liberty, and wished to add to that passion the love of religion, which was equally strong in his own nature.

The one perpetual dread was the possibility of a total break-down in health. "My health is not bad," he writes from Hyères, in February, 1858, " but still weak, and threatening ruin on one side or another. What can I do in the diocese, with so few elements of power? I cannot tell." Then comes an expression well worth remembering : "Knowing myself and my own weakness, *I accustom myself not to disdain small labors and small results*, since it is probably in these minor regions that my life will have to be passed. I do not make myself miserable on this account. I have often told you that nothing in the world gives me a purer pleasure than to teach children their catechism ; and I feel that the day will come when, if it be necessary to renounce bolder schemes, I shall readily console myself in obscurity for not having realized the ambition of my youth." The author of these sentences little anticipated that, notwithstanding bodily weakness, he would become one of the most influential minds in the French Church.

Perreyve's ordination in the priesthood was fixed for the 30th of May, 1858, in the chapel of the Oratoire at Paris. He had become less morbidly anxious about his physical fitness. Seeing every thing always from a strictly theological point of view, he finds especial divine interferences where a physician would recognize only natural sequences. His disease is " sent." "God sends us this cross of weakness and powerlessness to teach us that there is but one thing in the world worth seeking, and that is to execute the divine will. The important point is not to be strong, learned, active, nor even to be in holy orders : what really concerns a man is to be in his place in the eternal monument which

God is building; and if our place is one of suffering, impotence, premature death,—*amen.*" He was so ill some days before that fixed for the ordination that it seemed doubtful whether he would be able to go through the ceremony. However, he bore it better than had been expected, and felt a boundless joy at this realization of all the longings of his youth. To him, the priesthood was in itself an almost unimaginable dignity; and it seemed to him "incomprehensible" that God should have raised him to the rank of his ministers. His letters, just before and after ordination, seem like the utterances of a soul exalted to the final beatitude. "Here at last is happiness! You know how much the hope of this blessed day had been often, long, and seriously threatened : now that it is realized, I ought to consider myself too happy, and willingly sing my *nunc dimittis.*"

Lacordaire came all the way from Sorèze to be present at the ceremony, and, when it had taken place, he asked the new priest to hear him in confession ; so that the great Dominican was the first person Perreyve met in the confessional. Lacordaire went over his whole life, from the age of six to the hour then present. It would be difficult to imagine a more interesting penitent, especially to the young priest who listened. Any student of human nature would give much to hear such an autobiography. The contest between faith and intellect never agitated a more passionately earnest soul. Strength of conviction, first on one side, then on the other ; courage indomitable ; ardor of youth lasting to full maturity; enormous power of influencing others; an eloquence that had moved Paris and agitated the Vatican; fame that had filled the great Roman Catholic world, — such were a few of the attributes of that remarkable being who poured his life's confession into the inexperienced ear of Henri Perreyve.

Another incident in the beginning of Perreyve's priesthood is the last religious service which his ordination enabled him to render to an old servant in his father's house; and I mention this the more willingly, that it is a pretty illustration of the relation between master and servant, as it used to be understood amongst good French people of the middle class, and is yet in many families. Perreyve writes to a friend: "Our poor old Rose died last Monday, almost suddenly, of apoplexy. The poor woman loved you, and I believe there will be something in your heart not altogether indifferent to her loss. It is a grief to me, and I consider that my childhood is buried in her grave. She had all the recollections of other days, with the liberty of the good old times, and that right of loving unceremoniously which is acquired by thirty-six years of devotion and of faithful tenderness. I was anxious that her funeral should be honorable, as if she had been an old aunt and an old friend. All our own people were present, and I was really touched to see so much promptitude in our friends to honor a poor servant-woman. I believe that God will have found her worthy of His rest: simple souls have easy ways to salvation. It seems to me that there was a happy predestination in the life of this poor woman, who came from the extremity of Silesia into France, found a family to replace her own, gave all her heart to love a child who became a priest, received from him the holy communion several times, and at last the sacrament on her death-bed." The sentiment here is Christian in the best sense, and beautifully human.

The state of the Abbé Perreyve's health in 1860 was at times delusively promising. He had still some reserve of strength, the energy of youth not having been entirely used up by the enfeebling progress of his ailment. At Eaux-Bonnes, in that year, he was able to ride rapidly a distance of thirty-seven miles on horseback, with no worse consequence than a little stiffness. It was probably the encouragement resulting from this test of his powers that induced him to ask Cardinal Morlot, three days afterwards, to send him as a chaplain with the Syrian expedition ; a request which does not seem to have been granted. A year afterwards, Perreyve was at Sorèze again, by the bedside of his dear friend Lacordaire, who, finding his end approaching, desired to settle his affairs, and, having resigned the direction of his Order, made Perreyve his executor, — handing over to him all his private papers, in the presence of several of his monks. It is not easy to imagine a more impressive scene, or a finer subject for some earnest and serious-minded artist. A life which had swung like a pendulum from one point to its very opposite, yet ever true to its own inward convictions, was now settling to perfect rest : the white-robed Dominicans, who had been as children to their fiery and masterful leader, were now grouped about him

simply as witnesses, whilst he handed the written con-
fidences of past years to one who, though not of his
Order, was dearer to him than the dearest of those who
belonged to it.

Lacordaire died in November, 1861, and a month
afterwards Perreyve, in Paris, shrank with apprehension
from the task of preaching at the Sorbonne, which was
now his clerical duty. His physical powers were giving
way; and, notwithstanding his remarkable success as a
preacher, he had no illusions as to his intellectual power
and wealth. "I perfectly understand my intellectual
situation," he wrote to a friend. " I feel within myself
a mediocre talent which is now giving forth its liveliest
flames, but which will soon exhaust itself. I feel nothing
profound within me, nothing greatly original or powerful.
When people compare my poor little self — and, I know
not why, it has been done several times publicly in the
course of the present year — with such names as those of
Lacordaire and Ozanam, I feel such a painful sensation
that I know not how to describe it. If I considered
myself a fit successor to men of that calibre, I should be
preparing for the next twenty years, if God grants them to
me, the bitterest of disappointments ; for after a certain
time of favor the cloth would be visibly threadbare.
Happily, I have no such illusion ; and I ask only to do
some good, as I may, — that is to say, in an inferior
scientific and intellectual rank, — to some young minds
who will pass through me, and afterwards go higher
than I."

The modesty of this is very exquisite. It is neither

false in the sense of under-estimation of self, nor a false pretension to modesty. It is the' sincere expression of a judgment too clear-sighted to be deceived by the delusions of self-love. The sentences just quoted are simply and accurately true. It is clear from Perreyve's published works that he had little intellectual might ; that he never could have become a great philosophical thinker, his reason being too easily subjugated by his affections ; and it may be doubted whether, with such faculties as he possessed, he could have maintained for more than a short time the great supplies of material which are necessary to keep up the fame of a considerable writer, or even of a brilliant orator, if he speaks frequently in one place. Perreyve, therefore, did not underrate his intellectual faculties ; but he entirely forgot, or was simply unaware of, his remarkable moral influence and charm. All men loved him, trusted him, listened to him ; and not only men, but even boys, and French boys. The Director of the great college of St. Barbe, in Paris, asked the Abbé Perreyve, in 1862, to give a lecture during Lent, once a fortnight only, on Sunday morning ; and it so happened that by this arrangement the students were kept in college longer than the time fixed by the regulations. If any thing could make a French school mutinous, it was this. So the Abbé got up into his pulpit, before a thousand boys and young men, every one of them out of humor. He had not spoken ten minutes before all the thousand listened with the most eager attention. Two days after that, a petition, signed by the elder boys, was presented to the

Prefect of the school, respectfully requesting that, "if the Abbé Perreyve's health and other duties permitted, he would give his lecture weekly instead of once a fortnight." Whether he was able to do so or not, the petitioners desired to express their gratitude. This document is dated March 11, 1862, and is probably unique of its kind. The reader is not likely to remember another instance of a multitude of school-boys, intensely fond of amusement and usually much deprived of it, asking to be kept in, to hear a succession of sermons, on the pleasantest holiday in the week, as Sunday is in Paris.

Such success as this would have been happiness for Perreyve, with a little health to enjoy it ; but in 1864 the grip of disease was tightening fast upon him. He observes sadly how many elements and *beginnings of felicity there are in us:* "We feel so clearly, so profoundly, that happiness would be possible, easy, that it is close at hand, — yet a little, and we should have it in perfection! But no: there is the grain of sand, the little deviation, that mere nothing which destroys all, and plunges us again in the distresses of a heart deceived!" Who has not felt this? Who but the hopelessly unhappy has not now and then felt himself so near to perfect felicity that one trifling change would be its absolute realization, — a little more health, a little more money, or the presence of one who is away?

It is not possible, whatever idealists may affirm, to be really happy in this world without sound physical health ; and the lack of that would have been enough to make

Perreyve's felicity imperfect, though all other elements had been present. His father, too, was suffering from a cruel and incurable malady. As to the son's case, the doctor at Pau reported "progress," to which the patient answered that there was progress in the ravages of the disease. Bright as were his hopes of another world, his regrets for this were painful. "I regret every thing," he says ; and then follows a list of little details, showing how dear his working life had been to him. "A priest," he said, " is a man created and put into the world for others. Brought back within the limits of self, he has no longer any reason for existence." In the extreme weakness of the last days, the mental faculties lost their energy, and there was a painful consciousness of the loss. The dying man tried to write, but could not, and felt a gloomy dread. "I am condemned to mere animal repose." This condemnation was not for long. On the 26th of June, 1865, he felt, probably for the first time, the fleshly horror of dissolution, which sometimes sub- jugates for an instant the noblest and bravest spirits. "I am afraid! I am afraid!" he said, — "J'ai peur! j'ai peur!"

This horror was the precursor of the last change, which took place an hour afterwards; and all that often- repeated, self-torturing questioning, "Shall I live to be of any use?" found its final answer and solution.

Henri Perreyve never once seems to have anticipated that he would be of any good in this world after his death : his modesty precluded any such hopes, so that his whole anxiety was concerning what he might be able to accomplish whilst he could keep his poor, fleeting physical health, or such semblance and mockery of it as he possessed. It is a pity he never knew that the service he desired to render would by no means come to an end with his mortal body. The influence of his character has been steadily increasing since, — an influence of a quiet kind, yet persistent. The sincerity and sweetness of his nature; his perfect self-devotion to what he thought the most worthy purposes; his earnest desire to reconcile religious faith with political liberty, — have endeared him to thousands of people in France who are seeking after a better spiritual life in combination with more perfect freedom. It seems to me that English and American sympathies may be counted upon beforehand for such a desire as this, even though Perreyve and his admirers belonged to the Church of Rome. Many in England and America who kindly wish well to France desire for her a firmer religious faith, and an assured constitutional freedom, which may make her safe against conspirators in high places as well as against the tyranny of the mob. As for Perreyve's Romanism, the most Protestant of my readers need not withhold his sympathy on that account. Born in England, Perreyve would probably have found full contentment in Anglicanism; for such natures as his usually become warmly attached to the religious system they find ready to hand. He belonged, by the accident of birth, to what he himself called "the Church of France," which happened to be affiliated to Rome; and, as this Church satisfied his religious

cravings, he felt no temptation to rebel against her.
His nature was docile and trustful and conservative, as
well as aspiring after an elevated moral ideal. Even his
passion for liberty was conservative, since in his youth
constitutional freedom had really been attained for a time
in France, though Louis Napoleon set his heel upon it.
In all his aspirations, Perreyve was steadily sustained
by the warmest human sympathy. Life is really worth
having in the sunshine of such friendships as those
which surrounded him. His juniors looked up to him
with love and trust, his seniors treated him as a brother,
and one or two of the greatest selected him as the most
trustworthy, in their opinion, of living men. The most
exalted personages in the ecclesiastical hierarchy took a
kindly interest in his character and abilities from the
beginning, predicting a remarkable future. Perreyve
breathed, not "for a whole year," like Stuart Mill, but
during the whole of his existence, "the free and genial
atmosphere of Continental life." He was simply and
happily ignorant of what Mill calls "the absence of
high feelings, which manifests itself by sneering depre-
ciation of all demonstration of them, and by general
abstinence from professing any high principles of action
at all, except in those pre-ordained cases in which such
profession is put on as part of the costume and formali-
ties of the occasion." Perreyve lived habitually and
easily in a condition of high feeling, which he kept up
by constant intercourse, personally or by correspondence,
with friends who cultivated in themselves, and encouraged in others, the same nobility of nature. Though a

Roman Catholic, self-dedicated to the priesthood from his earliest youth, he cherished no intolerance towards Protestants and unbelievers. On the few occasions when he spoke of other churches, it was usually to point a moral by a reference to the virtues which they exhibited, and which Roman Catholics would do well to emulate. The hardest word against English Protestants which I can find in all Perreyve's sermons is, " Our brethren who are separated from us ; " and he heartily praises their zeal in the dissemination of pure literature. Again, in another sermon, he says, " Never be afraid of the virtues of our separated brethren," meaning the Protestants, "and do not yield to the vulgar temptation of ignoring or casting a shadow upon them. Never be afraid of what is good : the good is always the road to what is true." Of course, he does not think it a fortunate condition for the Church of England that she should be separated from "Catholic unity ; " but he has no lack of charity, or of admiration either, for the members of that Church. " Poor Church of England ! Truly a flock without a shepherd ; full, nevertheless, of beautiful and noble souls which are hungry and thirsty for the truth, who will restore to thee thy place in the sacred unity which thou hast left ? " In writing of or to an unbeliever like J. J. Ampère, Perreyve fully recognizes all that is in common between them, and has no harsh or unkind things to say. He only affirms (which is natural in a priest) that intelligence, reason, and poetry do not bring the soul to God; that real religion is another thing than intelligence, reason, and poetry;

that real religion establishes an eternal and intimate
friendship between God and man. This is Perreyve's
"short method with the infidel," — different, as we see,
from the scoldings and calumnies which used formerly
to be considered good enough for him, and fit weapons
for a cultivated clergy to employ. Perreyve quite admits that unbelievers may be friends of Christ, but
friends of the outer circle, admirers at a distance.
"They cannot know either the sweetness of his *parole
intérieure,* nor the peace of his *promesses intimes.* They
sometimes understand the happiness of others : they
never share it." One could scarcely expect a priest to
speak more charitably than this of unbelief. The admission that unbelievers may be "friends of Christ" is
much indeed. The assertion that intelligence, reason,
and poetry do not produce the religious state, will
scarcely be disputed, if religion is understood in the
usual plain sense of the word. We know what religion
is, and we perceive that the intellect does not produce
it any more than an oak-tree produces grapes or roses.
The intellect produces *philosophy.* Then, again, the
poetic sense does not produce religion : it has its own
flower, of another beauty and a different perfume, which
is *art.* I need say no more about Perreyve's tolerance
and charity ; but I may fairly claim that a like tolerance
and an equal charity should be exercised in his own
favor by ourselves. Surely, we are not to be outdone
in liberality of sentiment by a priest of the Church of
Rome!

I much regret that limits of space, already rather

exceeded, do not permit a thorough analysis of Perreyve's literary works. He was not, as we have already observed, a writer of great mental force; but I have seldom read sermons, or theological books of any kind, from which with the help of a little charity and patience the reader may more surely gain that benefit so easy to feel, so difficult to define, which enriches the heart, if it does not satisfy the intellect. The preacher is so much in earnest, and has so much the gift of a certain persuasive eloquence, — the secret of which is a strong desire to remove all possible misunderstanding, — that it is difficult not to listen, even though he often says things which the critical sense in us can never by any possibility accept. For example, one of his finest sermons is entitled "Marie, Reine des Sciences," a sermon full of the eloquence that springs from feeling, and in it he elevates the Virgin Mary to the rank of a Christian Minerva by ascribing to her the royalty of philosophy and art. It is easy to understand that a cultivated age may desire to associate its culture with its religion, and we have heard certain cultivated persons express their regret that there is neither a Minerva nor a Muse in popular theology; but really, when we remember who and what the mother of Jesus was, — the wife of a poor carpenter in Galilee, far removed both by social and geographical distance from the scientific and artistic centre of the ancient world, — it does seem a violent stretch of imagination to make her in a special sense the Goddess of philosophy and art. By the incessant contemplation of an idealized person, people can make themselves believe that they know the person in detail as the poet comes in time to know his characters without distinguishing what is historical in them and what the fiction of his brain. In this way, Perreyve persuaded himself that Mary's mind was remarkable for intellectual superiority. "I hail you," he says, addressing her, "as the Queen of philosophers. I admire in you that admirable *ordonnance* of all the human faculties, which makes your soul the masterpiece of intelligence and reason." This is exactly the sort of compliment which Frenchmen used to address to Madame de Staël. But the love of hyperbole, which is a characteristic of Roman Catholic theologians, leads them to say things still more disturbing to the equilibrium of a Protestant judgment. For example, Perreyve has a whole chapter about *the Priest* in his book for the sick, and in this chapter he quietly affirms, not the permanent, but the intermittent godhead of the priest. " The Priest is God in Jesus Christ when he teaches ; " "the Priest is God in Jesus Christ when he binds and loosens the consciences of men ;" "the Priest is God in Jesus Christ when he transmits the invisible grace in the external rite of the sacrament ; " " but the Priest is God most especially at the altar, through, with, and in Jesus Christ, when he offers the sacrifice for the salvation of the people." It is the nature of passionate love to wish to lose itself in its object ; and, when the object is so exalted as to be worshipped, this desire has often led to a mystic identification of the adorer with the adored. Perreyve is not the first who has had these feelings or used this language. Even philosophers make use of similar expressions to indicate certain conditions of intellect and feeling. Nobody will suspect Feuerbach of Catholic mysticism, at any rate ; yet, in his intellectual mysticism, he says : " Existence out of self is the world, existence in self is God   *To think is to be God.* The act of thought, as such, is the freedom of the immortal gods from all external limitations and necessities of life." The audacity of statement is here quite as great as in the case of Perreyve, and in both cases it is nothing but audacity of statement, better avoided ; for what the priest and the philosopher really meant might have been expressed in a less extravagant way.   Perreyve only meant that the priest shared or represented a divine function ; and Feuerbach only meant that the thinker elevated himself above the world of matter by his thought. However, Perreyve makes a clear distinction between the priest, who is divine some-times, and the physician, to whom divine honors are never to be paid. "The Priest is God and man ; " " Honor the physician as man, and not as a god."   This establishes such an infinite superiority for the priest that his dignity seems scarcely compatible with humility. Hence we find Perreyve quite oppressed by the ideal splendor of the priestly office, and constantly praying for humility, as the virtue most desirable and most needful for a priest.

His popular sympathies were broad, and included all classes really known to him. He was a democrat in the best sense, earnestly desiring the elevation of the people to a higher plane of intellectual and moral life, as well as their political emancipation. The popular vices in thought, language, and action, were as unpleasing to

Perreyve as if he had been a born aristocrat; but instead of saying, "Odi profanum vulgus, et arceo," and passing by on the other side, he did what lay in his power to civilize the barbarism about him. He had been tempted in youth, from pure ignorance, to judge the highest aristocracy severely, as people have prejudices against a nation in which they have no acquaintances; but, when circumstances brought him into close contact with one of the greatest ducal families in France, he willingly acknowledged his error, and admitted that the aristocracy had qualities of which he had not been aware. The great ladies seemed to him "modest, pious, and charitable, and not nearly so proud as he had imagined." The misfortune of the aristocracy seemed to Perreyve to be want of occupation, especially in young men; but he found and approved a tendency to combat this by giving them a professional training. His liberalism was of the kind that wishes well to all classes. He was not one of those Frenchmen who say, or once said, "War to the castle, peace to the cottage!" but one of those who say, like M. Taine, "Peace to the cottage, and peace to the castle also!"

It may help the English reader to an understanding of Perreyve's position in the Church of Rome to say that if it had been divided, as the Church of England now is, into the three well-known sections of ritualists, evangelicals, and broad churchmen, he would have belonged to the last section, — I mean relatively. It may seem strange to readers not intimately acquainted with Roman Catholicism to speak of it as any thing else than ritualistic ; but there may be the love of ceremony or the love of simplicity even in a royal court, and, in spite of compulsory outward conformity, a close observer may detect ritualism or its opposite, anywhere, in the natural dispositions of men. Perreyve had too much of the artistic sense to be ignorant of the power of august architecture, music, and ceremony ; and he never undervalued them, but his opinion about them was exactly that of M. Rénan. He considered them aids to the popular imagination of things divine, but neither divine in themselves nor indispensable. " A little bread and wine in a dungeon," he says, " sufficed for the liturgy of the martyrs." Here are the two sides of his feeling on the subject, in a page written when sickness kept him away from public worship (exquisitely beautiful, as it seems to me), and in the answer to the regrets which it expresses : —

" Lord, I have loved the beauty of thy House, and the place where thy glory dwells. I have loved this beauty from a child. I have loved thy holy ceremonies, the austere harmony of psalms, the pomp of festivals, the incense rising to the vaults, the flowers about the altar, thy priests transfigured far off in gold, in perfume, and in flame, whilst taking from thy hands the benediction which they shed upon the people. I loved the retired place where I hid myself with my prayer, I liked to lose myself in the oblivion of my own existence and the clear view of thee only. I liked to remain alone after all were gone, when the brilliance of tapers was extinguished with the last echoes of the great organ."

Then comes the answer. Like the author of the "Imitation," he imagines the voice of Christ replying: "Symbols will pass away, my son; temples of stone will pass away; my sacraments themselves will become needless, along with faith and hope: but that which will endure for ever is worship in spirit and in truth, perfect charity, and the rest of souls in me. Regret not immoderately that which in the external temple would please thy senses and imagination. Remember that in the whole world there is neither temple nor tabernacle so dear to me as the soul of the just man."

I need hardly observe how beautifully the two sides of the question are expressed in these two passages ; in what a serene atmosphere the thoughts of the writer move, — how far above vulgar contention about forms. The recognition of their utility is ample; but equally clear is the understanding that they are not indispensable, and that there is something above them and beyond them.

And now, in conclusion, I desire to say a few frank words about the long and generous dream of Perreyve's life, — the union of Catholicism with liberty. In one of his eloquent discourses, he narrated with pride how, in the thirteenth century, when the most glorious cathedrals were built, the workmen did not forget to place the statue of Liberty in its niche; and how, at Chartres, the mediæval carver had taken care there should be no mistake about it by plainly inscribing beneath the statue the name of the new patron, — LIBERTAS. "Ah! gentlemen," said Perreyve to his hearers at the

Sorbonne, " how I love to read that word in the doorway of ' the old basilica, near to that tabernacle which is to-day deserted, through the misunderstandings of the time, but which will one day doubtless see humanity coming back wearied with its struggles and tired of its fruitless quests." The answer to this is easy. Whatever the Church may have done in the thirteenth century little concerns us who live in the fourth quarter of the nineteenth. It is one of the commonplaces of history that she resisted secular tyranny in ages when no other organization was powerful enough to offer such effectual opposition. But *now* — in our own day — is she the friend of liberty or its enemy? The modern Roman Catholic principle has been much more accurately defined by Monseigneur Ségur than by the Abbé Perreyve. It is briefly this, that peoples are subject to sovereigns, who rule by divine right, and who, in their turn, are subject to the Church ; that is, to the Papacy. The principle of parliamentary government is so odious to Monseigneur Ségur that he condemns it in language of uncompromising severity. He has the spirit of the Syllabus and the Encyclicals, which Perreyve would have had to submit to in silent repugnance, like many another, if he had lived. At the time of his fortunate death, il usions were still possible, and a Roman Catholic might yet speak aloud of liberty.

The truth is, that circumstances having changed, the policy of the Church of Rome has changed with them. In the Middle Ages, she could well afford to be the champion of liberty and the protectress of learning, because in those ages the doctrines upon which her own authority rested were called in question by none, or by so few that she had no anxiety on her own account. In our day, her position is different, and so is her policy. Her policy now is against political liberty, in all countries where she is dominant ; and she favors it only for temporary purposes in those countries where she cannot impose herself by force. She was the friend of Catholic emancipation in England, but when has she been the friend of Protestant emancipation in Spain ? She has asked for liberty of public worship at Geneva, but she has never granted it in Rome. She has long been laboring, and is still laboring with all her power, to overthrow representative government in France and Italy, and what there is of religious liberty in Spain. The clerical party, in those countries, is well understood to be the reactionary and absolutist party. The Church has given her hearty support to every tyranny that has existed in Europe in the present generation, on the single condition that the tyrant should be a Roman Catholic ; and she has combated every movement towards political emancipation. What Perreyve was constantly deploring as a general "misunderstanding" is really a very clear understanding indeed. Frenchmen and Italians understand with the most perfect clearness by this time — they would be hopelessly dull if they did not — that whatever political freedom they may desire for themselves and their posterity must be won in spite of the Roman Curia and the prodigious organization which it directs. Tender and beautiful religious sentiments, such as we have lately been admiring, have little to do with this stern contest for the mastery of Europe. To the friends of political liberty, the Church of Rome, whatever may be the beauty of holiness to which many of her sons and daughters have attained, is at once the most redoubtable and the most insidious of their foes. Even so recently as the year 1877 she made an effort against representative government in France ; and, though not permanently successful, she was still powerful enough to suspend it for five months, and to replace it by an incredibly vexatious form of personal tyranny which brought the country to the brink of civil war, and persecuted free speech with relentless jealousy, from the Atlantic to the Mediterranean, and from Belgium to the Pyrenees.

RUDE.

IF this little biography begins like a novel, the reader is respectfully requested to believe that there is no attempt to amuse him at the expense of truth.

There is a place about nine old French leagues east of Dijon, say twenty-seven miles, called Saint-Seine-sur-Vingeanne. The Vingeanne is a pretty stream, and Saint Seine is a quiet country village with an old château that belongs, or used to belong, to an old family which took its name from the place. The village also possesses an inn; and the reader is requested, by an effort of the imagination, to transport himself to the court-yard of this hostelry in the strange and terrible year 1793. He is not going to be troubled with any word-painting of a picturesque old French court-yard: we have appealed to his imagination already, and will leave it to supply the quaint roofs, dormer windows, pigeon-cotes, the picturesque external staircases, and irregular wooden galleries, which are often to be found in such places. Our own task, just at present, is a little bit of figure-painting.

It is very early in the morning, and there is nobody

in the court-yard yet, when a figure comes down the stair, and goes straight to a very big grindstone in a corner. It is a boy nine years old, but he is dressed like a man and a soldier. He wears a blue coat with a large collar turned back on the breast after the fashion of those days, he has a three-cornered cocked hat worn knowingly on one side, he has white breeches and black gaiters. He is armed with a sword of a size proportioned to his stature, and it is his anxiety about the state of the weapon which has made him such a very early riser. The sword is too blunt, he thinks, and so he means to sharpen it. Unluckily, the grindstone is big and heavy, and there is nobody to turn it. Why not wait a little till people get up, and somebody comes to help? The reason is that the helper would be a witness, and our young soldier has his own private reasons for desiring to sharpen his deadly weapon in perfect secrecy. So he sets the stone in motion, and then grinds a little till it stops, which happens inconveniently soon ; then he gives it another impetus, and so on. Whilst our hero is thus busily occupied, we may tell the reader who he is, and why he is so determined to have his sword so very sharp on this particular morning.

His name is François Rude, and the reader is not to suppose for a moment that the military uniform has been given to him by wealthy parents for his amusement, as uniforms and swords are often given at the present day to children who go to fancy balls. François Rude belongs to a real regiment, and the uniform which he wears is as seriously authorized by the Government of his country as that of a midshipman is in England.

He belongs to the famous Royal Bonbon regiment of the National Guard, which, although composed of very young soldiers indeed, who would be called children were it not for the respect inspired by their military ardor, considers itself of no small importance in the city of Charles the Bold. Every Sunday, at noon precisely, the Royal Bonbon regiment marches with music to the strange but beautiful church of Saint Michael, which was built by a friend and pupil of Michael Angelo, and there a member of the Common Council, with his official insignia, gets up into the pulpit and talks to his young hearers about their duties and responsibilities. After this discourse, the boys kneel on one knee, they raise their hands to their three-cornered cocked hats, a roll of drums fills the echoing vaults of the old church, and the Councillor in the pulpit pronounces a layman's benediction. Besides this weekly ceremony in the church, there is another ceremony, every second day, in the theatre of Dijon. The battalion on duty parades on the stage between the two plays, performing its evolutions round the bust of Robespierre or Marat, and singing the Marseillaise!

Let it not be supposed that the regiment exists only to show itself in church and theatre. It exists for a very serious purpose; namely, the manly and patriotic education of the youth of Dijon, and it takes itself *au sérieux*. Long orders of the day are read to it with all solemnity when under arms in the public square, faults are severely condemned, and acts of merit encouraged by public eulogy. Every week it marches into the country, and is exercised in one of the rocky valleys in the neighborhood of Dijon, and every week it is paraded in the public park to watch the exercises of the National Guard.

François Rude has been a year in the regiment now, and has accompanied his father from Dijon to Saint-Seine-sur-Vingeanne on a little business excursion. Unluckily, there is a barber in the village, who on the evening of their arrival considers the young *Royal Bonbon* a fit object for the exercise of his wit. He laughs more particularly at the sword, inquiring sarcastically about the uses of that weapon, and finally so exasperating the wearer as to draw from him that last answer of the brave, a challenge to mortal combat. Then the barber goes home to bed, and thinks no more about the duel; not so the *Royal Bonbon*, who lies awake with anxiety, especially about the sharpness of his sword.

Whilst he is sharpening it so early in the morning, his father sees him from the window, and sends for the adversary and his seconds. The jests begin again, but the boy gets so angry that they endeavor to soothe his wounded feelings by a formal apology. This he rejects with indignation, and, finding himself unable to obtain satisfaction by arms, quits the village of Saint-Seine sur-Vingeanne in disgust, and walks by himself to Dijon without a penny in his pocket, or any thing to eat, along all those weary nine leagues of road.

I cannot think of this wonderfully characteristic anecdote of those times without asking myself what some great painter or novelist, some Leslie or Thackeray, would have made of it. The scene in the inn-yard, with the boy in that curious eighteenth-century uniform, the barber with forced seriousness offering his apology, the by-standers laughing, would have afforded Leslie an excellent subject for his refined pictorial comedy. Thackeray would have written a delicious chapter about that Royal Bonbon regiment in the rich old Burgundian city, and, after getting such a capital start for the hero of his novel, would have gone on developing his life and fortunes amidst all the surroundings of a strange and exciting time. Less fortunate than painter or writer of fiction, the biographer may give but little liberty to his imagination; and if by chance, as in the present instance, reality itself should offer tempting materials, he is soon compelled to leave them behind for the sterner realities of life.

The little François Rude who wanted to fight the barber was not, as the reader may imagine from his susceptibility on the point of honor, a young gentleman of noble lineage. His father was only a blacksmith who lived at Dijon in a sort of court, or street without an issue, the entrance to which may be found by the tourist in the Rue Poissonnerie between number 15 and number 23; and here the boy was born, on the 4th of January, 1784. An iron balcony of forged work by the hand of the elder Rude may still be seen above a little café hard by; for Dijon is a place with artistic traditions, like the Italian cities; and the rigid rule of cast-iron has not yet entirely succeeded in substituting itself for the living

work of the craftsman's hammer. Rude the blacksmith
had, however, discovered a more profitable department
of his business than the making of iron balconies. He
had travelled in Germany, and, being an intelligent man
with his eyes open to the merits of things that were
new to him, had observed there a sort of chimney or
stove, which he thought might be useful in his own
country. On his return, he immediately began to make
these stoves, which were soon appreciated at Dijon, and
are now to be seen all over France, where they are known
as *cheminées à la prussienne*, or, more briefly, as *prussiennes.** The introduction of this useful innovation was
rewarded by a business which, though it did not enrich
the elder Rude, enabled him to maintain himself and his
family in decency ; and he naturally looked forward to the
time when, upon his retirement, his son would continue
the trade. Their military life went no farther than this,
that both belonged to the National Guard. The elder
Rude was a mounted artilleryman, and after the exercises
in the park he used to take his son on the pommel of his
saddle and ride back with him into Dijon : sometimes he
would perch him on a caisson. " It was hard when we
got to the pavement," Rude used to say, in after-life ;
" but we held on for honor's sake ! "

* The *prussienne*, as Rude introduced it, is a sort of sheet-iron box,
lined with brick and open in front, with a stove-pipe inserted behind.
It combines the advantages of the stove and the open fire. In the more
elegant *prussiennes*, the sheet-iron is covered with marble, and some of
recent invention are made entirely of cast-iron, enamelled ; but the best for
burning wood with great economy of heat are the simple old sheet-iron
ones which Rude introduced.

As soon as the boy was strong enough to work at the forge, his father made him put on the leather apron, and begin. The military career in the Royal Bonbon came to a premature conclusion by the disarming of that regiment, after the fall of Robespierre, during the reaction of Thermidor. Our hero was so indignant at this measure that he positively refused to be disarmed, and hid his musket, for those small boys had firearms. His existence, for the next six years, was prosaic : he worked all the time steadily at his father's forge. At the age of sixteen, an accident happened which changed the tenor of his whole life, and spoiled a business career which might have led ultimately to fortune in the profitable trade of an ironmonger. A piece of red-hot iron fell upon one of his feet ; and, though the burn was not very serious, it confined the lad to the house for a few days. As soon as he was able to go out, he took a walk in the streets of Dijon for his amusement, and it so happened that it was the prize day at the public school of Fine Art in that city ; for Dijon was an art-centre even then, with centuries of artistic tradition to look back upon. Well, young François Rude turned into the Art School, which was open to every one on the occasion of this public solemnity, and he was so deeply impressed thereby that he resolved, if possible, to become a student. His father yielded to his entreaties, but only on condition that he was not to make an artist of himself, and that any skill which he might acquire as a designer should be devoted entirely to *prussiennes*. On this understanding, the young student went to the Dijon Academy for two hours daily; namely, from six to eight in winter evenings, and from six to eight in the morning when the summer gave early daylight. Meanwhile, he worked steadily at his father's forge.

Young men gifted with an instinct for the plastic arts are not, as a general rule, remarkable for their love of literature. Few men read so little as artists. You may talk about books to busy men in other professions, to busy clergymen, lawyers, and physicians, but not, as a general rule, to the professional painter, sculptor, or engraver. There are, however, a few exceptions to this rule ; and Rude, from his early youth, was one of them. As soon as he had begun to cultivate his artistic powers, he became aware of his defective education, and by the effort of a will that recoiled before no difficulty he resolved to cultivate his mind by reading, whilst he cultivated his eye and hand by drawing at the Academy. He had a little chamber in the garret, and here he shut himself up at nights to read and draw in undisturbed tranquillity. How he managed for fire and light is a mystery, for his father was already apprehensive that this ardor for study might not be favorable to the family trade in *prussiennes,* and rigorously refused both money and candles ; but François had his own devices, and followed his own pursuits. He had his Sunday too, which on the continent is the day of recreation, the day on which friends and relations meet for social intercourse as they do on Christmas Day in England. It was hard to leave all his companions and shut himself up with a book, especially in a sociable place like Dijon ; but, when

François Rude had resolved to attain some high object he was ready to pay the price.* In this way, he gradu- ally became well informed ; and, as the habit of carefu', reading remained with him through life, the extent and ac- curacy of his knowledge often surprised the learned. H'' was helped in various ways by M. Devosge, who foundeô the Art Academy at Dijon, and was its first director. This M. Devosge not only looked well to the young stu- dent's progress in the drawing class, but also gave him paper and crayons to work at home, and the use of his private library. We may also have our suspicions that the same M. Devosge was the source of light for the eyes as well as of light for the understanding ; or, in other words, that it was he who provided the candles. This good friend took such an interest in Rude that he was constantly talking about him ; and an old house- keeper, when she came to fetch M. Devosge from the Art School, once stopped where the young pupil was sit- ting at work, and said to him, " Mais qu'est-ce que tu fais donc, Rude, que *notre monsieur* parle toujours de toi ? "

The answer to this question is that the boy already exhibited the incipient powers of an artist. He very

---

* It is strange that a young blacksmith should remind one of Lady Jane Grey, yet here we have the story of her youth translated from a patrician to a plebeian form, and from feminine sweetness to masculine resolution. This blacksmith's son recalls that story so beautifully told by Roger Ascham, how he found his pupil "in her chamber, reading Phædo Platonis in Greek," when the joyous company of lords and ladies were hunting in the park. and how she answered him, " I wist, all their sport in the park is but a shadow to that pleasure which I find in Plato."

soon won a gold medal for ornamental drawing (the first prize) and a silver medal (the second prize) for an academic study from life. He now began to believe that his accidental visit to the Art Academy on a former occasion, when he saw prizes distributed to others, had revealed to him his true vocation; and it was a favorite theory of his in after-life that the chance which led a man to do what he was best qualified for was the most important element in all successes. "Every one of us," he used to say, "is probably so gifted as to be naturally able to do some especial thing better than anybody else, and when this natural aptitude finds its outlet the possessor of it infallibly becomes remarkable; but with our system of education such aptitudes remain unheeded, and people do not even trouble themselves to inquire about their existence."

At this period of Rude's life, we have the singular instance of a blacksmith who was at the same time an academic gold and silver medallist; for, notwithstanding his rapid progress in art, he still remained obedient to his father's will, and worked patiently at the forge for years. At length, however, his good friend M. Devosge began to think it wrong that such a sacrifice should be continued any longer, and talked to the elder Rude with such effect that he consented at last to let François be entirely an artist. To us, who know what he afterwards became, this may appear simply the preference of a higher to an inferior calling, but the elder Rude would not see matters in that light. By great industry and some intelligence, he had won for himself that specialty of *prussiennes*, his son had partly learned the trade, which if not brilliant was at least a certainty, and now it was proposed that he should abandon it for an occupation which offered no sure prospect whatever, and which, notwithstanding a good beginning, the young man had still to learn. Just after he had given his consent, the father was struck down by paralysis, and was not rich enough to keep François whilst he studied : here, then, was a fresh complication. The young man met the difficulty by going to work at a house-painter's, where he did nothing but grind colors and paint windows.

The question now is, how a poor young house-painter, who has not yet even learnt the trade he works at, who has no money, whose father is paralyzed and unable to help him, is to become the greatest sculptor in France?

It came about gradually, by the kindness of others and his own industry and genius. M. Devosge, in the first place, was not the man to abandon his young friend when under a cloud of misfortune, so he got some good folks at Dijon to sit to him for their busts, and such was Rude's natural talent for his art that these attempts gave satisfaction. One of these busts led to another very valuable friendship. M. Devosge had been the intimate friend of Monnier, an engraver. Monnier died in 1804 ; and his son-in-law, M. Fremiet, was living in Dijon as comptroller of taxes, but besides his official position he was a man of high intellectual culture, a good writer, and a great character. M. Devosge suggested to him that it would be a good thing to have a bust of Monnier by Rude. M. Fremiet accepted the suggestion, and gave the commission ; but his kindness did not end here. ' Under the pretext that the young artist would work more easily in his house, he prevailed upon him to establish himself in a room there, and in a very short time both he and Madame Fremiet treated Rude as if he had been their son.

This may look like a mere trick of rhetoric, for people are not much in the habit of treating the children of others as their own ; but a circumstance soon occurred which put M. Fremiet's kindness to the test. When François Rude attained his majority, the conscription claimed him ; and he would have had to go for a soldier, had not his new friend generously interposed by paying the cost of a substitute. M. Fremiet was not rich, but it seemed to him that a great gift for art ought not to be lost to the world, and besides this he had a personal affection for Rude, and a desire to insure his happiness. The sculptor used to say in after-life that his feelings towards MM. Devosge and Fremiet were much beyond what is called gratitude : his heart was too full of love for both of them to have room for any such sentiment, whilst they on their part had no notion of being patrons or benefactors. He felt it his duty not to burden them more than he could help, and so started for Paris in 1807 with £16 in his pocket, to make his own way in the world.

M. Devosge had provided his young friend with a letter of introduction to Denon, and Rude had taken the precaution to prepare a statuette as evidence of his capabilities. The subject of this statuette was *Theseus* *picking up a Quoit,* and when Denon saw it he took it for a copy of an antique. On ascertaining the truth, he at once offered to protect Rude, and got him work to do on the bas-reliefs of the Vendôme column. Whilst earning his living in this way, the young student worked as a pupil under Cartelet, a sculptor eminent at that time; and six months later he was admitted to the École des Beaux Arts, the national school of art, answering to our Royal Academy. In after-life, he used to say that the teaching he received there did him nothing but harm, that the force of example made him abandon his early manner for a worse, and that the seven years during which he followed the official routine were the seven lost years of his life. He went even farther than this in his regrets, for he used to add that the long and persevering effort of his maturity had been to cast off the influence of the École, and forget what he had learned in it.*

It is very possible that the interest which Denon took in the young sculptor may have been at first awakened by feelings of provincial patriotism ; for Rude was a native of Dijon, and Denon was born at the nearest town to the southwards, — namely, Chalon-sur-Saône. He was a

---

* The reason for this divergence between the genius of Rude and the academic system of teaching was not any want of classic feeling in him, but quite the contrary. His mind, from the beginning, was more truly and vitally classical than the spirit then prevalent at Paris. The boy who modelled the *Theseus* was in happy and natural sympathy with the genius of ancient Greece, and the kindly teaching he got at Dijon from his good friend Devosge was better for him than the rigid and deathful compression of the public school.

very great man, indeed, in those days; and his protection
was well worth having. He was famous as the *savant*
and artist who had accompanied Napoleon to Italy and
Egypt; he had a high social position as a Baron of the
Empire ; and, besides the celebrity gained by his works,
he held a most influential situation in the art world as the
official director of museums and general superintendent
of all works of art executed to celebrate the victories of
Napoleon. His kindness to Rude was unfailing. So long
as Rude remained at Paris, he gave him work to do, and
guided him by friendly advice. When his young friend
won the great prize in 1812, with a statue of Aristæus
lamenting the loss of his bees, Denon recommended him
not to go to Rome at once, but rather to stay in Paris
till he had saved money enough to see Italy thoroughly
and at leisure. This good advice was acted upon until
the year 1814; but the events of that remarkable year
made Paris distasteful to Rude, and led him to claim
his right to be sent to Italy. When he got to Dijon, he
stayed there to visit old friends, and during this visit to
his native city an event occurred which had an unex-
pected influence upon his future destiny.

It was now the month of March, 1815. Marshal Ney had
gone to Lons-le-Saulnier on his way to stop Napoleon on
his return from Elba. Napoleon was marching northwards
by way of Lyons and Chalon-sur-Saône. Ney's regiments,
passing through Auxonne, were soon to arrive at Dijon.
This threw all the Dijon people into a state of intense
political ferment. France, at that time, was divided into
two great political parties: the Royalists, who desired the

restoration of the Bourbons ; and the popular party, which
at that time had no effective representative but Napoleon.
It may be well to offer, in this place, a few remarks upon
the realities which underlie the names and outward appearances of French politics. The contest, for the last
hundred years, has been between aristocracy and democracy; but there have been changes in the names of the
parties on both sides, which are very misleading to readers
of French history who have never lived in the country.
The aristocratic principle was represented, in the first
quarter of this century, entirely and exclusively by legiti-
macy, and in 1814–15 the democratic principle had for
its representative a man quite as hostile to liberty as
any legitimate sovereign could be ; namely, Napoleon.
After oscillating between these two, the country supposed itself to have found a sort of compromise in a
bourgeois monarchy, or monarchy to suit the middle-
classes, called Orleanism ; but, when Orleanism came to
an end, the old contest between aristocracy and democracy began again, the reins of government being seized
by the democrats in 1848. Now we come to a period of
French history in which the action of the two parties is
not so visible on the surface of public events. Napoleon
III. did not lead the democracy as Napoleon I. had done ;
for the popular party now desired not merely the abase-
ment of its enemy, but also liberty for itself, and it had
realized the truth that liberty can never be possible
under a despotism. At the same time, those who remained faithful to the aristocratic principle were beginning to lose hope in a Bourbon restoration, and to

transfer their allegiance gradually to the new dynasty; so that the fall of Napoleon III. after Sedan was looked upon as a misfortune for aristocracy, a view of things which would have greatly astonished the French aristocrats of 1814. Napoleon III. being out of the way, the contest between the two principles began again under new names. The popular party was now called Republican; and the aristocratic party, composed of Legitimists, Orleanists,* and Bonapartists, now called itself Conservative. Having no longer any king or emperor at its head, this party placed itself under the nominal leadership of Marshal MacMahon, whose ducal rank made him acceptable; but its real leader was another duke, with an intellect incomparably more subtle and crafty, and a character far more unscrupulous, — De Broglie. With the last great struggle between the aristocratic party headed by this duke, and the democratic or popular party, headed by Thiers, Grévy, and Gambetta, every reader of these pages will be more or less familiar. How it ended, in the last months of 1877, by De Broglie's fall from power, and MacMahon's submission to the will of the majority of the French people, we all accurately know. If I mention in this place events so recent and so familiar, it is precisely because the very strength of the impression they have created is likely to falsify our conception of the state of parties in the early

* The principle of Orleanism had been the government of the middle classes; but, when Orleanism ceased to exist, those of its adherents who desired liberty became republicans, and those who preferred monarchy to liberty retained the name of Orleanists, but sided with the aristocratic party against the republic.

months of 1815. The events of the present, so far from enabling us to understand the past, are often a great hindrance to our comprehension of what happened even at a little distance from our own time. For example, our present hero, Rude, was in 1815 an ardent supporter of Napoleon ; but he was not in the least what we, in 1878, understand by the word " Bonapartist." Remember that Orleanism was not invented then ; that republicanism had apparently perished in disorders to which Napoleon put an end, and in tyrannies more odious than his own ; that a child of the common people, with plebeian instincts, like François Rude (who a few short years before was a blacksmith), had no choice between supporting a form of royalty which was bound up with traditions of privilege, or else welcoming an emperor who, tyrannical as he was, did at least throw open the avenues of advancement on every side to merit. All clever and aspiring youths in the lower and middle classes were for Napoleon in those days. Even if he had never gone to Paris, Rude would have been for Napoleon ; and having gone there, having lived under the personal influence of Denon, who owed his advancement to the Emperor's recognition of his merits, it was not in the nature of things that he could take sides against the Captain and Sovereign of democracy.*

---

* What is said in the above passage about the "plebeian instincts " of Rude will be fully explained before the close of this biography. The expression is simply true, and is not intended to convey either praise or blame, either sympathy or antipathy. This is not the place to expound my own sentiments about aristocracy and democracy ; but I may observe that the word "plebeian" is not necessarily a word of either hostility or contempt.

There is a certain old tower at Dijon at the old palace of the Dukes of Burgundy, one of the loftiest towers in the world and one of the most beautiful. It was commonly called, in Rude's time, *La Tour du Logis du Roi;* for the palace was still classed as a royal dwelling. High above the tower turned a big weathercock painted pure white, the color, or negation of color, which belonged to the legitimate monarchy. Rude tried hard to get the keys of this tower, with the audacious intention of painting the weathercock with the tricolor of Napoleon. He was gifted with uncommon strength, agility, and nerve, and he would probably have succeeded in his project if the porter had yielded to his entreaties; but the man suspected something, and declined.

At length, the news arrived that the first of Ney's regiments was at the gates of Dijon. M. Fremiet, Rude's old friend, whose political sentiments were the same as his own, thought it would be well for the most energetic of their party to go and join the Emperor on his passage across the hills; for Napoleon had slept on the 14th of March at Chalon-sur-Saône, and was now travelling to Auxerre, by way of Autun and Avallon, through the narrow valleys of the Morvan. Rude was to get these friends of the cause together at a café close to the ducal palace, and there he found in a back room five resolute fellows with tricolor cockades. Just then they heard the trumpet of Ney's advanced guard; and the six went boldly out with their colors, and posted themselves in line, with their backs to a hoarding in front of the theatre. The critical moment had now arrived: a regiment of hussars came riding along the street, with white cockades and drawn swords.

When Rude, in after-life, used to tell the story of that day, he said that he and his five companions shouted "Vive l'Empereur," as the royalist cavalry came on. "They had nothing to do," he said, "but lower the points of their sabres, and pin us to the boards." The first troop merely looked at them, looked at their tricolor flags and cockades, and then turned aside to go down the Rue Rameau. The second troop came on.

Rude and his companions shouted "Vive l'Empereur!" louder than ever. This time the soldiers hesitated when they looked, and, on receiving the word of command to turn down the Rue Rameau, they answered, "Vive l'Empereur!" Men and officers changed their white cockades for the tricolor as soon as they could, and a few days later Marshal Ney himself accepted an enthusiastic demonstration from the balcony of the Hôtel de la Cloche.*

---

* This is the account of the conversion of Ney's troops which is received as authentic by the people of Dijon, but the account given by Thiers is different. According to Thiers, the Sixth Hussars (the regiment mentioned above), commanded by the Prince de Carignan, went at a gallop to Dijon *to raise the city against the king*, and succeeded in doing so. This, however, is dependent merely on a report from an officer "who had been on the Burgundy road," and is not the testimony of an eye-witness. According to witnesses who were in Dijon at the time, the hussars rode quietly into the city wearing the white cockade, and not the tricolor, which they would have worn if already in insurrection against the king. At the same time, they say that many old soldiers amongst them had tricolor cockades in their pockets ready to exchange for their white ones, and that officers were seen to pull a little string, which was ingeniously so contrived that it revealed the blue and red which turned the royalist white into the national tricolor. The exact truth would

M. Fremiet was one of the most enthusiastic advocates of the Empire; and during the Hundred Days he maintained it so heartily that, after the battle of Waterloo, he became a marked man, not sure of keeping either liberty or life. Under these circumstances, there was nothing for it but flight, and for some reason he preferred Belgium to Switzerland as a residence. It was necessary to get him away privily, and by himself ; but he only consented to this on condition that Rude would bring his wife and his little daughters to Belgium afterwards. These events became, therefore, of the greatest importance in the life of Rude ; for the duty he now accepted turned him aside from his intended student-life in Italy, and changed for better or worse the whole texture of his future career. But, whatever might come in the future, Rude's devotion to one who had done so much for him made him indifferent to selfish considerations ; so he cut off his moustache, put loaded pistols in his pockets, and set off at nightfall with M. Fremiet, with the intention of getting, if possible, to the village of Pont-de-Parry, which has since become celebrated in the Franco-German war. They took the most roundabout,

therefore appear to be that the hussars entered Dijon as royalist soldiers, but that very many of them were secretly favorable to Napoleon, and only watched an opportunity to declare themselves for his cause. The action of Rude and his five companions decided the matter, just as a pointsman decides in which direction a train shall go. The conduct of the hussars at Dijon, when Ney heard of it at Lons-le-Saulnier, influenced *his* decision, and we all know how important that was. So here we have young Rude mixed up with a great historical event, and acting his part with remarkable courage ; for he could not know that the hussars were disposed to take his side.

unfrequented ways, and, after wandering for some time in the woods, got to Pont-de-Parry at last, and passed the night there. Before going to bed, they bespoke a place in the Paris diligence (which was to pass through the village the next morning), of course under an assumed name. M. Fremiet duly took his place in the diligence ; and just then another drove up, that from Paris to Geneva, with David the painter in it, also a fugitive. Rude immediately recognized him, but was discreet enough not to let anybody perceive it.

The next thing the young man did was to return to Dijon, and devote himself to the ladies and children of M. Fremiet's family. There was his mother, eighty-five years old ; there was his unmarried sister ; there were his wife and two daughters. Rude employed his time at Dijon in making preparations for departure, and then accompanied the ladies all the way to Belgium, where he determined to share the exile of his friends, and renounced the pleasant Italian life of a *Grand Prix de Rome*, with all the brilliant prospects which at that time it offered to a young artist. At Brussels, he got some work to do, and hired an old abandoned chapel divided by a floor. In the upper part of this he established some pupils, and in the lower his own studio. This little art school soon became an influential academy, for Rude introduced principles of teaching which until that time had been unknown at Brussels. We shall have to say more about these principles afterwards ; at present, we have to follow the story of the artist's life.

The years had been passing rapidly since our young

hero left Dijon, with the letter of introduction from Devosge to Baron Denon. That was in 1807, when he was twenty-three years old. The next remarkable event in his life was the winning of the *Grand Prix de Rome* in 1812, a wonderful achievement for a young man who but a few years before had been a working blacksmith in a provincial city. Then he stayed in Paris to save money for Italian travel, but quitted Paris in 1814 for Dijon, and, instead of going to Italy, left Dijon for Belgium in 1815. He stayed there, working steadily, and living in friendly intercourse with the Fremiet family, for several years. This intercourse led to his marriage in 1821 with Mlle. Sophie Fremiet, his old friend's elder daughter. This was in several ways an exception to the usual French marriage customs ; for the union was founded on a long acquaintance and on mutual esteem, whilst pecuniary interest had nothing to do with the matter, either on one side or the other. As Rude was born in 1784, he was now of mature age (thirty-seven), and he knew his own mind and heart. M. Fremiet knew him thoroughly, and could appreciate both his talent as an artist and his character as a man. Both had strengthened greatly since the days when M. Fremiet exempted his young *protégé* from the con-scription.

. I have said little about Rude's personal qualities hitherto, both because we have been occupied chiefly with events, and also because his nature did not come to its full and magnificent maturity until somewhat late in life. It has been given to few human beings to reach a more perfect manhood. In him, both body, intellect, and character were alike robust. There is a certain appositeness in his very name, if we take it as it is understood, not by the learned, but by the peasantry of his native land. They would have said of him, " C'est un rude gaillard!" not meaning that he was rough or unpolished, but that he was strong. As to his polish, what shall I say? All who knew him are agreed that he was gentle, and yet he was not what we call a gentleman. His habits were too simple and laborious for the graces and elegancies of society, and there was a certain plebeian pride in him which made him unwilling to veneer his heart of oak with rosewood. To the day of his death, he remained resolutely plebeian, gracing himself with all the virtues and accomplishments that might be attainable by a man of the common people, but without the slightest desire to raise himself into any other social class. It is the same spirit, in another grade of life, which has sometimes led an English squire to refuse a baronetcy or a peerage. It is a spirit which, wherever it may be found, deserves our deepest respect, — a spirit which, if it could be more generally prevalent, would have the most beneficial consequences ; for it would lead the best men of each class to improve their class instead of toiling and struggling to get out of it. In most cases, a man of great ability, born in the ranks of the common people, does no good to his fellows, does nothing to elevate his class, for the simple reason that as soon as he earns money he pretends to be a gentleman. It never entered into Rude's mind to advance any such preten-

sion. All his life he considered himself simply a working man ; and his ambition was to do the best work he
could, and to be himself, in all things, the model of those
qualities which may be attainable in humble life. His
work was always the best he could do, and he spared
upon it neither time nor pains. He had a horror of the
hasty, unconscientious productions which French workmen call *pacotille* and *camelotte*, exactly the same feeling
that a first-rate cabinet-maker has with regard to goods
got up hastily for sale. Another plebeian virtue that he
cultivated was to be satisfied with a workman's wages.
A gentleman, or a would-be gentleman, thinks himself
ill used by Fate and Fortune if he cannot live in a certain style, and we know what that style of living costs.
Rude was absolutely independent of all the troubles
occasioned by anxieties of this kind ; for he asked no
more from Fortune than the ability to live like a workman who honestly pays his way. No expensive pleasure
tempted him, his pride was not in any form of luxury,
his dignity was simply human, and depended upon no
adjuncts. All the pomps and all the minor vanities of
the world were alike to him matters of unfeigned indifference. With the hardihood and simplicity of another
sculptor, Socrates, and an equally independent philosophy, he had a more substantial happiness ; for his
marriage turned out to be one of those rarely fortunate
unions in which a man of genius finds a refuge from the
world's injustice, and a protection against his own discouragement. Rude was so happy in love and work
that he could wait very patiently for fame, and enjoy

life thoroughly *en attendant.*   The routine of his existence
at Brussels was closely observed and recorded by one of
his own pupils, M. Feignaux.   It is the existence, not of
ı man who was waiting to live when fame and wealth
should come to him, but of a man who lived already in
the full enjoyment of his powers.

"He was dark-complexioned, strong, and robust,
graceful in his movements, and skilled in all bodily exercises.. He danced well, skated well, and swam well.
He fenced with such grace, address, rapidity, vivacity,
that he used to drive me to despair.   His temper was
very equal in its kindness and goodness.   He was sober,
courageous, and laborious, constant in his affections, in
his habits, and in his dealings with others, well disposed
and generous towards those whom he employed.   He
was gifted with a remarkable gayety, but the sallies of
his humor were always in good taste.   His modesty was
excessive.   I remember that one day he received a visit
from an archæologist, who was a professor at Haarlem.
This learned man, after standing some time in silence
before one of Rude's bas-reliefs, broke out into enthusiastic praises, giving the reasons for his admiration with a
fire and an enthusiasm rare in a Dutchman.   I never saw
Rude so ill at ease : he seemed as if he were trying to
excuse himself for the possession of his talents."

The gayety and cheerfulness mentioned by M. Feignaux increased, as may be expected, after the happy
marriage with Mlle. Sophie Fremiet ; and, though Rude
had been energetic and industrious before this alliance, he became doubly energetic after it.   Even the

disappointments which occur to every one, and of which Rude had his full share, were powerless against his unshakable spirit of cheerfulness. Many promises had been held out to him which were never realized, but which had entailed great labor on his part in many sketches and inventions ; and, when on each of these occasions he discovered that he had been deceived, he used to say to his indignant pupils, "What does it signify ? The really important matter for an artist is *to do.*" Then he would go to work again without the indulgence of a moment's discouragement, gayly singing an old French refrain, which grandly declares that it is only the weak who bend to the strokes of evil fortune. All his life he maintained the doctrine that art is its own reward, that the artist should harass himself as little as possible about any other ; that, if he has just means enough to enable him to work, he ought to find his happiness in *that*, which is itself an inestimable privilege. He was therefore in the highest and best sense an *amateur*, as all the greatest and noblest artists are. He did not work for money : he accepted money when it came, because he was not born rich, and could not follow so costly a pursuit as sculpture on his own means ; but the money was not his object, except just so far as it enabled him to work. He troubled himself just as little about public opinion, being neither elated by its attention nor soured by its neglect. Such a temper as that is worth more than fortune and fame to its possessor.*

* Amongst the disappointments alluded to in the text may be mentioned the following : The architect Vanderstraeten, in order to get

Rude's daily habits when at Brussels are described as follows by his pupil M. Feignaux: —

" In summer, he came to the studio at sunrise. At eight, his breakfast was brought to him. Sometimes, when very busy, he contented himself with one or two rolls of bread and a little brandy, at noon he ate another roll, and at three o'clock he went to his dinner. At four or five o'clock, he was in the studio again, and worked there until night. I used to go with him to the door, and he would say, when we separated, ' M. Feignaux, the first to awake calls the other;' but it always happened that, in spite of all I could do, he was before me. So we walked through the silent streets at three o'clock in the morning. During all the summer season, we began work at sunrise. On Sundays he went into the country with his family, but on Monday he was at the studio with his accustomed regularity. He liked to be read to whilst he worked, and one or other of his pupils read to him every day. In the evening, when the day's work was over, he drew and composed by lamplight, in the midst of his family, listening to music. What happy evenings they were, what affection and peace surrounded him !"

The reader may observe here an artful economy of

Rude's advice and assistance, encouraged him to believe that he would have various works to do which were never commissioned, and in consequence of these inducements the sculptor made models or drawings for many important projects, including great figures of Agriculture and Navigation, four great bas-reliefs, the external decoration of a theatre, and various models of heads and ornaments. As these projects were never carried out, the artist received no remuneration for them.

time. The sculptor delights in literature and music, but he manages so that these passions shall not steal an instant from his long hours of work. His pupils read to him whilst he models and carves, his wife plays to him whilst he sketches in the evening. The same economy of time may be observed in his readiness to begin work late in the day, when the earlier hours had been sacrificed to other duties. He had often to go to Tervueren, whilst the architectural works were in progress there. He would leave Brussels at four or five o'clock in the morning, in the worst of winter weather, go to Tervueren on foot, and return in the same way. "Anybody else," says M. Feignaux, "after having walked six leagues, after having been an hour or two in the building with the architect, standing or walking all the time in mud or snow, would have rested himself when he got home. Rude went to his studio, and said to me, 'M. Feignaux, we will smoke a pipe, and before dusk I shall find time to do this thing or that.'"

I have not space to go into a very minute account of the sculptor's artistic productiveness, and this is less a biography of the artist than a written portrait of the man. He found employment in Belgium, but was looked upon there as a political refugee, and received neither the honors nor the emoluments to which his extraordinary abilities might, in his own country, have entitled him. He attempted, on one occasion, to procure commissions from the royal family by making a bust of the king from memory, after observing him at church during the sermon. This bust he sent to the queen, and after the expiration of some months the receipt of the bust was acknowledged with a compliment ; but there began and ended all the encouragement he received directly from the royal family. He was employed by the architect of the royal palaces, where he executed many works, chiefly bas-reliefs and ornaments ; and he produced some works for the Belgian Parliament House. These labors just enabled him to meet the double expenses of his studio and his house ; but, notwithstanding the frugality of his way of living, he found it impossible to save money.*

* Here is a brief list of Rude's principal labors during his residence in Belgium, which may be of use to readers who travel : —

Palace of Tervueren.

1. Outside, on the principal front. A great bas-relief of Meleager's hunt with two hunting trophies, all in stone.
2. In the vestibule. A frieze of children with garlands of flowers and fruits.
3. In the rotunda. Eight bas-reliefs of the history of Achilles. Heads and figures placed in the ornaments of the ceiling.
4. In the great drawing-room. Two heads, Romulus and Remus, and warlike attributes in the frieze. Rude also designed, though he did not execute, the painted subjects in the ceiling.
5. In the dining-room. Figures holding shields over the doors.
6. A marble chimney-piece in one of the rooms, I think the rotunda, but the account before me is not clear on this point.

In the Royal Palace at Brussels.

1. In the private staircases. The ornaments of the ceilings.
2. In the vestibule. The arms of the Low Countries on the ceiling.
3. In the banquet-hall. A great frieze of allegorical figures with garlands, such as Commerce, Navigation, Abundance, Truth, &c.
4. In the ball-room. Figures of winged children playing on various instruments.
5. In the Queen's bedchamber. An elaborate marble chimney-piece, with a frieze of Loves playing with marine monsters. The supports have

His position was even worse than this simple statement can explain. Notwithstanding the commissions he had received, there was no substantial reason to expect even so much as a continuation of the modest prosperity which he had hitherto enjoyed. There had been a certain limited quantity of work for him to do in Belgium : he had done it, and might now very possibly find himself face to face with a degree of poverty approaching destitution. He had therefore no feeling of security, and was ready to accept any change which might lead to an improvement in his prospects.

In 1827, a French sculptor named Roman came to see Rude at Brussels, and the two friends talked over Rude's affairs with perfect frankness ; the result being an understanding that in four months Roman was to

heads dressed with fruits in their hair and bas-reliefs beneath them. This chimney-piece is one of the artist's most important works.

In the Parliament House.

1. In the First Chamber. Two Genii holding a clock-face in marble, for the chimney.
2. In the Second Chamber. Two winged Genii bearing the shield of the Low Countries. A figure a yard high, in metal, for a timepiece. The King's bust, in marble.
   The works in the Second Chamber were destroyed by fire soon after their execution, and Rude did them all over again.

The Mint at Brussels.

1. The pediment. Rude carved this in stone.
2. The great busts of Vulcan and Mercury.

For the Church of St. Étienne at Lille.

A carved pulpit, in wood, with five gigantic allegorical figures of Faith, Hope, &c., a bas-relief of the Stoning of Stephen, and, to crown all, an archangel eight feet high, and two angels.

come and fetch him, and they were to travel together to Paris. The appointment was kept with punctuality on both sides, and so it was that Rude returned to his native land after an exile of twelve years.

His position was not by any means brilliant. He had some reputation in Brussels, but none whatever in Paris ; he had no fortune, nothing in short to help him but his own intelligence and skill. He was beginning life anew at the age of forty-three, and he had a wife and son to maintain. Youth was gone, with its wonderful elasticity; but the enthusiasm of art remained in all its freshness, and the habit of industry was there in confirmed strength, after the labors of twelve strenuous years. Clearly, the first thing to be done was to win some reputation in Paris. The Salon of 1828 was to open in a few months : was there time to do any thing? Rude's old master, M. Cartelier, got him a commission for a statue of the Virgin for the church of St. Gervais ; so he set to work vigorously and executed this, finishing it entirely, and yet leaving himself six weeks for some work more in accordance with the classical tendencies of his own genius. In those six weeks, he executed in plaster the statue of Mercury putting on his talaria, which is now in bronze in the Louvre. I do not know any statue of Mercury, ancient or modern, which will bear comparison with this for the grace and energy of its inspiration. Many of the antique Mercuries are heavy and sleepy deities, with no life in them, unless it be latent ; and amongst modern sculptors there seems to be a very general persuasion that any young Academy model may

be turned into Mercury at a moment's notice by adorning
his head with the petasus and his feet with the talaria.
Rude's Mercury is so light, and strong at the same time,
that you feel how swift he must be, and how indefatigable ; he is ready to start, he needs no urging, his agile
form is leaving the ground already ; in another instant,
when the wings are fastened to the springing feet, he
will flash through space like a sunbeam!

Rapidly as this statue was executed, it presents no
appearance of haste or insufficient finish. Rude was
careful and slow in his work generally, but he had the
power of working with surprising rapidity when hurried.
In the list of his works in Belgium, the reader may have
found the two great busts of Vulcan and Mercury for
the Mint. M. Feignaux, his pupil, saw him make these
busts, witnessed the whole process from beginning to
end, and his account of it is this. He says that Rude
came into the studio one morning early, according to
his custom, and asked him to prepare clay. Whilst
Feignaux was doing this, the master occupied himself
with the construction of the armature (the internal skeleton of wood or metal which supports the clay) ; and
then he asked Feignaux to pose, not as a model, but in
order that the sculptor might refer to nature as he
worked. These arrangements made, Rude labored vigorously, and before the sun of that day had set the two
great busts were finished.*

* This equals the feats of rapidity which were performed by Rubens,
Landseer, and Turner. In all these cases, it is not the rapidity which is
wonderful, but the combination of quality with speed. The busts were

To return to Rude's labors for the Salon of 1828. He was ready in time, and exhibited. His work was appreciated, but it does not seem to have won any thing approaching to popularity. However, so far as the artist's own career was concerned, the success was sufficient, as it procured him employment. The next year he received from the Government the commission to execute a third of the frieze which goes round the Arc de l'Étoile, and the whole of the ornamentation was intrusted to him. He also got a commission for a marble bust of Lapeyrouse for the marine museum, and a bust of David for the Louvre.

That bust of Lapeyrouse, or rather the block of marble for it, had a powerful influence on the artist's future career. The Government had given the marble, which was larger than necessary, so Rude cut a piece off which had the shape of a prism. The possession of this piece of marble was a constant stimulus to the poor sculptor. "Make something of me!" it said to him continually ; and the answer was always, "What can I make of such an oddly shaped block as thee?" At length, after much pondering, it occurred to Rude that there was just room in it for a little Neapolitan fisher-

---

good enough to sustain the reputation of a master sculptor in an important public building, and were probably more effective at the intended distance than more polished work would have been. In the study on Victor Jacquemont, the reader has met with an example of the same rapidity in a writer. I have just read some reminiscences of Courbet the painter, in which one of his friends declares that he has seen him paint a landscape from nature a yard long in a single sitting with the palette knife. This might be fairly true in color and tone, but it could not have much form or texture.

boy playing with a tortoise; and, as soon as this idea had suggested itself, he determined to carry it into execution.

I have not said much hitherto about the sculptor's wife. Some characters describe themselves better in an authentic sentence than the art of the biographer can describe them in pages of the most careful writing, so Rude's wife shall speak for herself. The marble was there for the new statue; but what about the current expenses whilst the artist was executing it? A block of marble is not like a lump of clay: it cannot be fashioned between the rising and the setting of the sun. There were house expenses and studio expenses, the wages of the carver, and all to be paid — out of what? " If necessary, we will sell the linen off our backs ! " said Madame Rude. After that answer, we know the woman.

The statue was exhibited in 1833. It was an immense success. It may not be quite literally true that the sculptor, like the English poet, "awoke one morning, and found himself famous ; " but it is, I believe, the exact truth that at the beginning of a certain fortnight in the spring of 1833 our hero was a perfectly obscure artist, whereas at the end of the same fortnight he was the most popular sculptor in France. It was the time of the great warfare between the Classics and Romantics, and both parties claimed him. The Classics said, " This is the calm, unexaggerated art, the perfection of form that we desire : " the Romantics said, " This is not a servile imitation of Greek or Roman work, it is modern, and has the breath of life." The general public, outside of this warfare of the schools, was satisfied with the simple enjoyment of an exquisite conception realized with the most consummate skill and refinement. The Government set its seal to the general opinion by purchasing the work for the Luxembourg, and conferring the cross of the Legion of Honor on the now successful and celebrated artist.

There is a tragic element in human life which intrudes, like an awful shadow, at those times when happiness seems spread before us like a feast. You labor for twenty years, you grasp the prize at last, you realize the dreams of youth in statue, picture, or book, or you have become a ruler of men and have a great following in the State. It may be a superstition to believe that, at such a moment of attained fruition, some dreadful misfortune is more especially probable ; but it frequently so happens that, whether probable or not, such a misfortune occurs. Who does not remember a score of instances in which the cup has been turned to bitterness just when it reached the lips ? In Rude's case, the fame and honor won in that year 1833 found him stricken by a blow so terrible that it benumbed his faculties of pride and pleasure. His son had died before his statue was finished. The sculptor had courage enough to complete his work ; but his gayety was gone, and the merry playfulness with which, in any preceding year, he would have received the red riband, and the money, and the celebrity, had given place to a silent acceptance of an endless sorrow. Never, in after-life, could he bear to speak about his boy. Years afterwards, a young man from Burgundy, who had known Rude's son during his short visits there, came to the studio and mentioned this intimacy, thinking it might recommend him to Rude's good-will. The bereaved father, in whose presence all who knew him had carefully avoided this subject, looked at his visitor with an expression of such pain and reproach that it made him burst into tears.

We may remember this date then, the early months of 1833, as the time when Success and Sorrow both came to change the flavor of the artist's life. He was never to be merry again, but never again neglected : the wolf of poverty would be kept away from the door, but Holbein's grim skeleton visitor had entered it and taken away his boy. It is possible that this coincidence may have left in Rude's mind a certain contempt for fame and wealth, as vanities incapable of giving any effectual consolation. It is certain that few artists have worked in such a temper as that which now became the habit of his mind. He loved his art still, and labored in it manfully, but with the most complete unworldliness of motive. His saddened seriousness left no place for the minor satisfactions of the artistic career. Henceforth, the unfailing character of his mind was a sustained elevation and dignity, in which he took refuge to husband its powers of resistance. Firmly resolved to let no petty anxieties disturb his peace, he lived habitually aloof from the petty jealousies which torment the lives of artists, and willingly retreated into a laborious solitude, if that can be called solitude which was cheered by the faithful affection of a few most sincere friends and the devotion of a wife who had the birth and breeding of a gentlewoman and the culture of an accomplished artist.

Thiers was Louis Philippe's minister in those days ; and he had a delicate taste in sculpture, which he could appreciate and understand. He liked Rude's work, and gave him a commission of immense importance, nothing less than all the "grande sculpture" for the Arc de Triomphe. Rude made sixty sketches to ascertain what the Government wanted, and then some finished drawings. When it became known that the whole had been intrusted to one artist, the jealousy of his rivals was at once awakened; and Thiers was so plagued by them that he divided the commission for the trophies into two parts, one being given to Rude (the side looking to Paris), the other to Éten. After that came other intrigues which deprived Rude of the half of his own side, so that finally he only executed one of the four groups, the *Chant du Départ.* He bore these disappointments with his usual serenity, and considered that, as he liked to finish his work well, and the time was limited, it was perhaps as fortunate that he should only have one group to execute instead of four.

Most readers who have visited Paris will remember the Arc de l'Étoile ; and few will have seen it without feeling that, in spite of the good taste of its architecture and the finish of its figure sculpture, it still looks incomplete. So huge a mass needs some crowning ornament to come more lightly against the sky. On the occasion of an imperial *fête* during the Second Empire, a temporary eagle was erected upon it with outspread wings, and when the night came this eagle was splendidly illuminated. It is evident that the most appropriate ornament would be the same thing in a permanent form, — a gigantic eagle in gilded bronze, with wings displayed and talons grasping a globe; and it is curious that under the Second Empire, when such immense expenses were incurred for the decoration of Paris, this was not carried into execution. Louis Philippe wanted to put the Gallic cock on the top of the arch, which would have been an error for various reasons; and Rude boldly opposed the king on this point. Rude insisted upon the eagle; his advice was not taken, but at any rate he saved the work from the absurdity of being crowned by the noisy little sultan of the dunghill. The inappropriateness of the decoration would have been obvious to every one, as the arch is exclusively a monument to the fame of the imperial armies. Rude did not hesitate to say this plainly to the king.

The habits of the artist's life in Paris were exactly the same as they had been in Belgium. He worked all day incessantly, and refreshed his mind by intercourse with a few friends and by the still sweet, though now saddened, evenings in his own home. He remained faithful to his observance of the Sunday's rest, not so strictly, of course, as a Scotchman would observe it, but still in entire abstinence from labor and in harmless recreation with those who knew and loved him. To mark the difference more completely between Sunday and the other days of the week, he rented a little country house in a very quiet out-of-the-way village in the valley of the Bièvre,* where no Parisians went to disturb the rustic peace. Rude set off manfully every Saturday evening, and did the whole distance on foot: his wife and his youngest niece, Martine Vanderhaërt, whom about this time he adopted as a daughter, followed in one of the milk-carts returning from Paris to Cachan, the village where the sculptor's humble "maison de campagne" was situated. This weekly change of air and surroundings was probably beneficial to his health, which had begun to suffer from the malady of those who think and toil too much, and who feel the sorrows of life too acutely. Notwithstanding his naturally robust constitution, still apparently as strong as ever, the nervous system had begun to show signs of yielding; and from 1833 to 1842 it often tormented him with those severe sufferings, more difficult to bear than pain, for which people have no pity because they leave no trace. He worked on courageously in spite of them, though at times they became alarming; and it is possible that this perseverance may have laid the foundation of a later trouble.

The reader will remember that Rude's devotion to the family of his benefactor, in the year 1815, had prevented him from going to Rome, which his position as *Grand Prix* entitled him to do at the expense of the

---

* The Bièvre is a stream which flows into the Seine. It has since gained some celebrity from the studies of a landscape painter who loved it, the late Antoine Chintreuil

state. During the years of his residence at Paris, his annual excursion had been to see M. Fremiet at Mons. In 1842, he was persuaded to go to Italy, as his wife and friends thought the journey would be useful and pleasant to him. We may suspect that there must have been a little innocent feminine *ruse* on his wife's part to get him in motion towards the south, for she accompanied him as far as Burgundy, as if with the intention of sharing the whole excursion ; but, when she got into her native province, she suddenly discovered that the journey to Italy would be expensive, that she was not very well, and had better stay where she was, and that her husband must go on without her in the society of his friend M. Camille Bouchet. All this arrangement, probably planned long beforehand, betrays the craft and subtlety of a woman, and her affectionate self-denial.

The two friends travelled from Lyons to Arles by boat on the Rhone, one of the finest voyages in Europe, now generally abandoned for a corner in the night train. At Arles, they took boat again for Marseilles, and for the first time in his life Rude beheld the Mediterranean, which to his classic mind was like no other water in the world. The travellers seem to have gone to Naples first by steamer, coasting the shores of Italy from Genoa and Leghorn southwards. They walked incessantly, seeing the collections with the greatest interest; but Rude studied and admired works of art almost invariably in silence,* so that few of his remarks have been pre-

---

* On one occasion, being much tormented by a garrulous Parisian collector, whom he met in the Sistine Chapel, he endured the wordy

served.   They returned by Rome, Venice, and the Simplon.   Unluckily, for the reason just given, the materials for an account of Rude's impressions are so scanty that it is not worth while to dwell upon them.

A remarkable result of the Italian journey was that, after seeing so much of the real antique, the sculptor could no longer endure his composition of *Aristæus lamenting his Bees*, which had won him the prize in 1812. He consequently destroyed this figure, that he might be vexed by the sight of it no more.   The reader will please observe that it was precisely the clearer perception of the true classical spirit of antiquity which made Rude unable to tolerate any longer the pedantic pseudo-classicism of modern academic teaching.

Just at this time, a number of young men, who understood the work of his maturity, and who had been the pupils of another eminent sculptor, David of Angers, entreated Rude to open an *atelier* as a school for them, since that of David was now closed.   Rude had too much perspicacity not to see the defects of the system ; and, before accepting the proposition, he answered, with his usual clearness, to the following effect: "The word *atelier*, as the habits of the eighteenth and nineteenth centuries have caused it to be understood, signifies a sort of contract between the master on the one hand and the pupils on the other, by which the pupils tacitly undertake to learn, before all things, respect and adora-

enthusiasm for a time ; but a final outburst about Michael Angelo's glorious independence of the model was too much for him, and he said simply to his companion, "Allons-nous-en !" whilst he turned his back on the speaker.

tion for their teacher, to celebrate his merits, and copy his performances. The master, on his part, undertakes to use his official influence in their favor, to get work for them, and make the road to official honors easier for them, a contract which reproduces in our day the old Roman arrangement between the patrician and his clients." After this preface, Rude proceeded to explain that he would enter into no such tacit understanding, which appeared to him simply pernicious; and that his teaching, so far from imposing a set system, would aim simply at enabling the pupil to think and work for himself as soon as possible in perfect independence. To this the pupils answered, in a letter which was a model of good taste, reiterating their request, and that decided him.* The students were so numerous that, when Rude

---

* According to the French *atelier* system, the place where the pupils work is not the studio of the master. He works in his private studio, uninterrupted by his pupils, who study together on the mutual enlightenment principle, in a bare room, which he visits occasionally, and which may be miles away from his own residence.

The letter to Rude, mentioned in the text, is worth reprinting: —

"MONSIEUR, — Les élèves de l'atelier David, tous bien convaincus qu'il n'y a que M. Rude qui puisse continuer ce que leur maître a fait jusqu'à ce jour, viennent le prier de nouveau de vouloir bien les accepter pour élèves. Ils déclarent en outre à M. Rude que les paternelles et bienveillantes observations qu'il a voulu leur faire dans un esprit de sollicitude extrême, les ont vivement touchés; mais qu'après les avoir suffisament muries dans leur pensée, ils persistent toujours à ne vouloir d'autre maître que lui.

"En conséquence, ils s'empressent d'assurer M. Rude qu'ils ne cesseront jamais de faire chaque jour de nouveaux efforts pour mériter de plus en plus les précieux conseils qu'il voudra bien leur donner, et le prient d'agréer l'expression de leur profond respect et de leur inaltérable reconnaissance."

(Here follow the signatures.)

admitted them to work under him, they filled two large rooms. He directed this school of art for ten years, and through it exercised a great and beneficial influence on the French sculpture of the present day. The combination of classic grace with a lively sense of reality and a sufficiently marked individualism, which distinguishes the best French sculpture now, may be traced, in great measure, to Rude's precepts and example.

If this volume had been a work on art, I should have given a chapter to Rude's system of teaching, which I firmly believe to be the soundest of all systems ; and which, though the art he professed was that of the sculptor, is in its method and spirit just as applicable to painting. The old principle or habit was to begin with the study of detail, by making eyes, noses, ears, &c., to be afterwards agglomerated in the mind till it possessed the concrete notion of a human figure. David the painter taught in this way ; and no Frenchman, in David's time, taught in any other. Rude reversed this by beginning with the study of the whole in its proportions, taking the masses first and the details afterwards.*

---

* The same principle is applicable to the studies pursued in Universities, — to history, for example, — and it was very much insisted upon at one time by Jacotot, whose name is connected with it. Hence it has been inferred that Rude's method was adopted from Jacotot ; but this was not the case. Rude's method was simply the result of his own artistic convictions ; but after 1830 he came to know Jacotot personally, (when they lived as next-door neighbors in the same street, Rue d'Enfer, at Paris), and then there was a close agreement between them on the subject of education, and Rude applied Jacotot's method to the general education of his niece, Mlle. Martine Vanderhaërt, the result being so satisfactory that he was a zealous advocate of the method ever after.

The reader will now perceive how the principle may be applied to painting, even to landscape. If Rude had been a landscape-painter, he would not have begun with leaves and twigs, but with the great masses of foliage in their broad relations of light and shade. He taught his pupils to draw their figures life-size on great black canvases, with a piece of chalk at the end of a stick. This reminds one of Meissonier, who, though his pictures are small, makes his studies life-size.

An ardent admirer of Napoleon I., who lived at the village of Fixin, near Dijon, and had been a grenadier at Elba during the Emperor's exile there, determined to erect a bronze monument to his old master at his private expense. M. Noisot, the enthusiastic Burgundian who conceived this remarkable idea, was by no means a rich man; and the mere expense of casting the bronze, not to speak of the artist's remuneration, was of itself quite enough to make a serious breach in his fortune. Luckily for M. Noisot, Rude's own enthusiasm for the captive of St. Helena was equal to the occasion. Rude gave his time and talent for nothing, M. Noisot found the money for the casting, and the statue now actually exists in the place they selected for it. The site had suggested the work. During a visit which the sculptor had paid to the rural proprietor in 1844 at his country home at the village of Fixin, six miles from Dijon, they had taken a walk together on the elevated rocky ground of the Côte d'Or, and M. Noisot had expressed his regret that France had erected no monument to Napoleon since his death. "I should like to buy a statue of him, and place it just here," he said, "facing the Alps and Italy!" The fire of this enthusiasm was contagious; and the sculptor answered with a positive promise, "I will make your Emperor myself!"

Very few artists would have kept such a promise, when it came to the long labor of realizing the sudden idea; but Rude kept it faithfully, and the recumbent Napoleon in bronze was actually inaugurated on the rocky hill in September, 1847.

The Dijon people had the good taste to seize the opportunity and give a public banquet to the artist. Two busts were placed on the table: one of them was that bust of Monnier the engraver, which has already been mentioned in the earlier pages of this biography as the first commission kindly given to the young artist by M. Fremiet; the other was that of his earliest friend and helper M. Devosge, in his grave when the banquet was held, but succeeded by his son who sat at the head of the table as the rightful president of the feast.*

The reader may like to know what was the appearance of the hero of the day; he may like to have some description of him as he stood to return thanks for the honors rendered by his native city. Since Leonardo da Vinci, the arts have never been followed by a more remarkable-looking man. His body, which in earlier life had been that of an athlete, had now become too

---

* Rude's father had of course died many years before, but I cannot tell the reader at what date. It will be remembered that he was struck with paralysis when the sculptor was still very young, probably in the year 1803.

heavy for such feats as that which he proposed to himself when he wanted to paint, without scaffolding, the weathercock of the royal tower. Still, he was strong and active for an old man, a vigorous walker, and able to bear the long day of physical labor without fatigue. He stood erect, straight as a pillar, and looked as courageous as he really was. The head was magnificent. It had become extremely bald, retaining only a fringe of hair, like that of a monk; and it exhibited a superb cranial development, grandly modelled, with a great breadth about the temples. He wore a black velvet cap towards the back of the crown, leaving the forehead disengaged. The eyes were lively, frank, penetrating, and looked every one straight in the face, "but without aggression," says one who knew him. The eyebrows were thick and quite black, in contrast with an immense beard of the purest white, which fell in broad masses, like a cascade, over his powerful chest and down to the middle of his person. The nose was thick and strong, rather than refined, and the neck was "like that of a bull."

The vast white beard was so grand in its masses that no painter could see it without wishing that Rude had been a model instead of an artist, and hereby hangs a tale. Ingres, the famous painter, knew Rude well enough; but Madame Ingres did not know him: so one day, when he came to call, she made him sit down in the entrance, and went to tell her husband. "Who is persecuting me?" growled the painter, who hated interruption. "It is a river-god who is waiting," answered the lady, who had taken Rude for a model. The river-god overheard this, and so far justified his title that he laughed till the tears flowed down his cheeks. But, however advantageous a noble beard might have been to a model, such an appendage was, in those days, detrimental to an artist. It was not considered very respectable, it had a revolutionary aspect, the "respectable" world used the razor. The shaven Academicians excluded the sculptor, saying, "We cannot admit the man with the beard."

I have mentioned the two busts on the table. At that time, these busts were the only works by the artist in his native city. Notwithstanding the enthusiasm at the banquet, the people of Dijon had been sufficiently cool about their townsman's success in life, and (with the noble exceptions of MM. Devosge and Fremiet) had purchased none of his works. There is very little enthusiasm about the art of sculpture anywhere, so we cannot blame the Dijon people much. They probably had little confidence in their own judgment, and waited till the fame of the sculptor was beyond dispute : besides, we all know how small a place sculpture holds in modern life, how few private persons buy statues anywhere. A bust is the usual limit of such private purchasing as there is.

The common council of Dijon did what the circumstances seemed to require. It took upon itself to represent the public, and gave Rude a commission for a marble group, leaving the subject to his own choice. The sum allowed for this purpose was £1,200, not more than a fair price for the group which now adorns the Dijon

museum, yet a considerable sum for a provincial muni-
cipality to give. Rude took for his subject "Hebe
playing with Jupiter's Eagle," and produced one of the
most exquisitely refined, one of the most perfectly delicate and elegant works that give lustre to his native
land. It seems almost a contradiction that Rude, whose
own personal characteristics were pre-eminently those
of power, should have taken especial pleasure in the
grace of unmuscular forms, like the slight limbs of Hebe,
who is only just sufficiently developed to escape meagreness. The same taste, however, is exhibited in other
works of his, especially in the glorious figure of *L'Amour
Dominateur du Monde*, in which, with admirable tact,
he has chosen to represent Love as frail in himself, but
governing the world by his haughty and imperial air.*

Although Rude had been an ardent Bonapartist in the
time of the first Emperor, and had represented him in
the Fixin monument as on the rock of St. Helena, his
eagle fallen from the clouds and expiring convulsively
close by, the sculptor's Bonapartism ended with the
death of his hero, in whom he did not see the Emperor,
but the brilliant first soldier of the Revolution.† In
1848, this romantic admiration for the hero of Austerlitz
had become simply an historic enthusiasm, such as any
one may feel for a great soldier who will fight no more,

---

* This beautiful statue is now in the museum of Dijon, to which it
was bequeathed by M. Anatole Devosge, who presided at the banquet
of 1847.

† The Fixin statue is entirely military, not in the least imperial.
Napoleon is draped in the Marengo cloak over the uniform of the
Chasseurs de la Garde; the military hat and sword lie near him.

without influencing his opinion about the politics of the present hour. Rude's democratic instincts threw him naturally on the side of the republicans, in 1848. He declared himself " *démocrate radical,*" took the warmest interest in that premature attempt to found a liberal government in France, and in obedience to a desire of the new authorities rapidly made a colossal statue of the Republic to be placed under the cupola of the Pantheon. In the "*journées de Juin,*" this statue (which was nothing but an effective sketch on a colossal scale) was shattered, ominously enough, by the first cannon-ball, and the artist was never remunerated for his labor.

Little need be said about him as a politician. The whole of his political creed was an enthusiasm for popular rights, which in such a country as France made him inevitably hostile to the old monarchy. In 1848, French republicanism had the heat of metal just fused, which has not yet had time to solidify into its definite forms, and to cool as it solidifies. Without the enthusiasm of that epoch, the country would never have possessed the constituted liberties of the present ; but the republicans of those days, however useful as pioneers, were without political experience. Whether old or young in years, they were all politically immature. The republicanism of 1848 was a creed believed in passionately,—a creed that men were ready to suffer for and die for,—but it was not yet a practical philosophy. Silvestre spoke of Rude's political ideas as "generous illusions." We know very little about them, in detail : we only know that he was passionately earnest in politics on the democratic side.

and that sometimes, when talking on the subject, he would explode in .such fiery eloquence that his niece feared it might do him harm. In this as in some other matters, he remained unaffectedly plebeian.

But, whatever may have been the sculptor's political aspirations, they never turned him aside from his daily labor. He was not one of those artists, often met with in French towns in times of political excitement, who quit their work to go and talk about politics in cafés, from morning till night. Rude was still, before all things, the patient and laborious workman ; and, instead of taking rest as old age advanced upon him, he worked, if possible, harder than ever, having more commissions to execute, and still resolutely refusing to spoil his work by hurry. His way of life from 1848 to the year of his death was that of extreme retirement in the midst of Paris. He lived as he had lived at Brussels, working always from sunrise to sunset, even in the longest days, with only a short interruption for a simple repast. His amusements, as before, were reading and music, to both which he was simply a listener, though an attentive listener. Amongst the readings which he preferred were translations from the Greek and Latin classics, and the history of Napoleon's wars. A sculptor, constantly at work on clay or marble, has not time to give himself much intellectual culture ; and, notwithstanding Rude's creditable taste for literature, it would be an error to suppose that he ever acquired that easy familiarity with events and ideas which constitutes real intellectual experience. The letter in which he makes his political profession of faith is distinctly *not* that of a trained thinker. He rejects with contempt the idea of shades of opinion in politics, affirming that he has "never understood them." A trained thinker would not have written that: he would have been too well aware that, in matters of opinion, shades and tints are as various and as important as they are in Berlin wools; and that the classification by two or three primary colors, though convenient for simple minds, is both arbitrary and unjust.

These latter years of Rude's life were quietly happy. His health was regular, the nervous sufferings having worn themselves out, and left apparently no evil effect behind. He had given up his little country house in the valley of the Bièvre, because his niece had to be in Paris for her religious duties on Sundays, and it was not in the old man's tastes to separate himself much from his little household: however, as he retained his vigorous powers of pedestrianism, he often explored his favorite valley still.

So the time passed with him in the quiet routine of habit, until the Universal Exhibition of 1855.

Ever since 1848, the Jury for the Salon had been elective; and such was the general confidence in Rude's knowledge of art, and in his high-minded probity and impartiality, that his name always received more votes than any other, and he came out regularly at the head of the list. This was a profound satisfaction to him, as it proved in the most indubitable way how generally his judgment and his character were appreciated by artists of all kinds. Accepting the task imposed upon him as a sacred trust, he devoted himself, without the slightest consideration for his own health, to the very fatiguing labors which it imposed upon him. It was the same for the Universal Exhibition of 1855. He was on the Jury, and discharged the duties of the position with such a conscientious attention to the merits of the works of art before him that a dangerous degree of fatigue was the result. Instead of resigning his post on the first symptoms, he went on without regard to them, trusting to ultimate recovery when he had an opportunity for repose.

The exhibition in the Champs Élysées was at a considerable distance from Rude's home in the Rue d'Enfer, but he had always been accustomed to go on foot in Paris. Now, however, he found himself seized with sudden weakness on the road between the Exhibition and his residence, and this repeatedly, so that he was obliged to take a cab. Another symptom was that, whilst at work in his studio, he was observed to stop and turn pale suddenly.

The hand of Death was on him ; yet it kindly, as it were, refrained from exercising the last fatal pressure on the organs of life until the old man had received the reward of his long labors. By forty-seven votes out of fifty, the members of the international jury awarded to him the first of the four great medals of honor. It was a splendid recompense to receive in the sight of Europe, and it pleased the veteran immensely.*

* He had exhibited his Neapolitan *Fisher-boy playing with a Tortoise,* in marble ; his *Mercury putting on the Talaria,* in bronze ; and a bust of

On Tuesday the 30th of October, he was present at the official dinner given by the Minister of the Interior to the members of the jury. He felt unwell, and went home as soon as he could in a carriage. On his arrival, he had to sit down on the stairs, from an attack of faintness. The doctor recommended rest in bed, and noticed some symptoms of bronchitis. On the Saturday morning, Rude felt well again, asked for a basin of soup, dressed himself, and talked of going to the studio. After having taken the soup, he began to smoke, then he coughed and complained of feeling uncomfortable. The expression of his face alarmed Madame Rude, who sent for her niece's husband and the doctor. " I suffer here," said the patient, pointing to the heart ; then he stretched out his limbs, and all was over. This happened at ten o'clock in the morning, on the 3d of November, 1855, in the presence of Madame Rude and her nephew, M. Cabet.

And now came a trial for that heroic woman, such as few persons in the world of either sex would have the resolution to accept or the fortitude to endure. Her niece, who had been to Rude as a daughter, and loved him as a daughter may love a tender and indulgent father, was lying in the same house in a precarious condition, having just given birth to her first child. The doctors affirmed that, if at that critical time she had

---

his niece, Madame Cabet, in marble. Madame Cabet had been adopted by Rude, in her girlhood, when she was Mlle. Martine Vanderhaërt. M. Paul Cabet, her husband, was an able sculptor of the Dijon school. They were married in November, 1853.

to bear any strong emotion, the consequences would probably be fatal. And now let the reader imagine Madame Rude's position. If she communicated the dreadful news, she inflicted certain injury and probable death : if she simply stayed away from her niece's bed-side, the immediate consequence would be to produce a dangerous anxiety, which could not but go on increasing. There was only one safe course, but it required a degree of resolution almost beyond the powers of humanity. Madame Rude was told that she must hide her husband's death from her niece, and she determined to obey ; so she went to the bedside day after day, for fourteen long days, talking cheerfully, hiding her sorrow, never be-traying it by a tear or a tone of sadness, answering Madame Cabet's ceaseless questions about her uncle with fibs that she had to invent as excuses for his con-tinued absence ; wearing, not her widow's mourning, but the dress of happier days, talking with pleasant anticipation of the little feast they had all been looking forward to at the baptism, when Rude was to have been godfather, — an event which had pleased him as much as his great medal. All this might have been compara-tively easy, if Madame Rude had not loved her hus-band ; but she had loved him from her girlhood with an unceasing devotion, and his death was the most cruel blow that remorseless fate could have dealt upon her. Try, then, to imagine the heroic strength of will which could go through all that acting for fourteen days, to save a precious life ! In the authentic stories of womanly fortitude I never read of any thing more sublime.*

Madame Rude was a well-trained and able painter. Partly in consequence of their extremely retired kind of life, partly because she was overshadowed by the greater fame of her husband, she never received that degree of public recognition to which her qualities as an artist fairly entitled her. She painted portraits well; and she left at Brussels, in the royal palace of Tervueren, and in the library of the Duke of Arenberg, works of a more elevated character. Besides these, she painted other composed pictures after her return to Paris.

Rude is interesting as a strong and original character, even for those who take no interest in art. He seems almost out of place in modern times, with his antique simplicity and independence. In an age when men struggle frantically for the means of luxury, and use

---

* I remember a case somewhat similar, which came accidentally, twenty years ago, within the range of my own experience. I had to see a man in Paris on business, and was told by the servant that he was not at home, but that his wife would replace him. She did so, very efficiently, and in answer to my inquiries about him replied simply that he was absent. For several weeks every applicant was treated as I had been, — the gentleman was always "absent;" but his wife did what was wanted as well as he could have done it, had he been there. At last, it was discovered that the absent husband had really been dead all the time, and that his widow, who had a family of young children to provide for, had heroically taken this means of winning confidence in her own abilities. Had she openly announced her intention of succeeding to her husband, people would have placed no confidence in her, and gone elsewhere; but by the time his death became generally known she had won confidence enough to secure her children's bread. The reader may imagine the torture this widow subjected herself to, in answering everybody's questions.

their utmost ingenuity to advance in the world's estima-
tion by plotting for the praise of coteries and newspapers, Rude concerned himself neither about wealth
nor about notoriety, but was content to do the best work
he could, to preserve his own dignity, and leave the rest
to Fortune. You may often find artists and men of
letters who are content to suffer poverty that they may
pursue a beloved occupation, but the indifference to
notoriety is rarer. Rude was not indifferent to fame,
fairly and honorably won: the great medal of 1855 was
joy and gladness to him in the last days of his life ; but
he had an absolute disdain for the sort of notoriety which
is procured by scheming and intriguing, by giving dinners to journalists, by elbowing one's way in the saloons
of ministers, by flattering the occupant of a throne. He
belonged so little to his own age that he simply put his
best energies into his work, and was willing to let that
answer for him, never once doing any thing to push himself or advertise himself in any way whatever, either in
general society, in the cliques of artists, or in the press.
There has never been an instance, amongst celebrated
men, of a dignity more firmly and consistently maintained throughout the course of a long life. He did not
refuse to receive public writers into his house, he admitted them even to his friendship ; but it was always on
the expressed condition that they should not say any
thing about him or his works in print. This was his
way of protecting himself against the flattery of friends,
or the biassed appreciation of those who were grateful
to him for his kindness. M. Fremiet, his father-in-law,

was an able writer for the press, and wrote on art for ten years at Brussels, but never once mentioned Rude or his works, well knowing that praise from so friendly a source would be displeasing to the sculptor's delicate sense of what was becoming. He became accidentally acquainted with an eminent writer in Paris; and they liked each other so much that a close friendship would have been formed, if Rude had not resolutely denied himself this pleasure. " M. —— is a journalist," he said ; "and, if we knew each other better, the public would believe that his decisions were those of a friend, and I myself should think so too." He disliked *camaraderie*, which is bad enough in England, but a monstrous evil in France.* He had no fear of the venomous *éreinteurs* of the French press, and simply shut his door upon them when they presented themselves, telling them he would have nothing to do with swindlers. In this way, he paralyzed the action of his friends in his favor, and increased the acerbity of his enemies, whom he never attempted to conciliate. His conviction was that journalists, even when honorable and sincere, formed their opinions simply from a literary point of view, quite outside of all modes of thinking properly applicable to sculpture; and

---

* *Camaraderie* is the help given to each other by comrades, to the detriment of merit outside their little clique. For example, if in an Academy of Arts the Academicians were to elect comrades for friendship's sake, to the exclusion of more meritorious artists, that would be *camaraderie* ; and if in a literary journal the books or articles of a friend or contributor were mentioned as being important, when literary works of really greater importance, by outsiders, were passed over in silence, that would be *camaraderie* also, and of a bad kind, though nothing can *look* more innocent.

he cared so little for what any writer might have to say about him that, when a critic presented him with a reprint of his articles, in two volumes, the volume which dealt with his own works was found, after his death, with all the leaves still uncut. "I do my very best," he said; "and praises could neither make me do more nor better, whereas censure would trouble me. If my works are good, they will endure: if not, all the laudation in the world would not save them from oblivion." This may be true, but an artist has temporary and present as well as posthumous interests; and Rude injured both himself and his wife by his sturdy independence. He never would do any thing to be elected an Academician, though it is customary to "poser sa candidature," and pay visits to get votes. His independence and his pro-digious beard kept him out of the Institute.

Rude's philosophy about wealth was remote, indeed, from that which generally prevails in the nineteenth century. "I have not yet," he said, "met with rich people who consider themselves rich enough; and it has always been so, if we may believe the writings of the ancients. And why do men desire riches, if not to arrive at a state of contentment, at a feeling of satisfy-ing possession? But if every man, whatever may be his wealth, has never enough according to his own opin-ion, it is proved that this feeling of contentment does not depend upon riches in themselves. Can I hesitate between the two lines of conduct before me? One of the two would be to acquire a great fortune, a very dif-ficult thing to do, and I am not certain of success: if I succeeded, I should be no better off; for the example of all the ages proves that the more a man has, the more he desires to have. The other line of conduct would be to try to consider myself rich enough as I am, which costs infinitely less anxiety, and disturbs nothing in my way of life." Having argued the matter in this way with himself, he made his choice of contented mediocrity, and adhered to it. Just before Thiers fell from power under Louis Philippe, he said to Rude: "You have had a disappointment about the Arc de Triomphe: cannot I give you some compensation in a commission, whilst I am still a minister? You have never been to Italy: would you like a mission to Rome?"* Rude answered simply that he needed nothing. The day before, he had examined the state of his fortune, and found that his savings now gave him no less than forty-eight pounds of annual interest. Of course, with so handsome an income as that, a man needs no favor from any Government.

The moral and philosophical side of Rude's character directed his admirations quite as much as his artistic feeling. When at Rome, it pleased him to retrace the steps of Nicolas Poussin; and he talked of him continually, not merely because he liked his art, but because Poussin's character was remarkable for its integrity and independence.

Rude's disinterestedness showed itself in many actions of his life, but seldom more prettily than in the matter

---

* M. Silvestre says that Thiers offered £1,200 to Rude for his expenses in Rome.

of a statue of Louis XIII. at the age of seventeen, executed for a very generous and high-minded nobleman,
the Duc de Luynes. This statue, which was in pure
silver and the size of life, cost Rude £480 independently
of the cost of the silver, yet he only charged the Duke
£240. The Duke seems to have suspected that his
artist friend was really making him a present, for he
sent him £400. Here is another anecdote of the same
kind. M. Thiers had asked Rude to let him have a
reproduction of the Mercury for his private collection.
The sculptor accepted the order, and immediately set to
work upon a new and original Mercury, which he sent
to M. Thiers, charging for it as a reproduction. The
reader will remember that he executed the Fixin statue
of Napoleon for nothing, as a tribute to the hero's memory. In estimating the value of these generosities, it
may be well to remember that Rude's time was fully
occupied with remunerative work, and that he did not
give away the valueless hours of an idler.

His temper was full of courage, and singularly independent, of surrounding circumstances. When artists
complained to him that they could not find suitable
models, that it was difficult to get a studio sufficiently
well lighted, and so on, he refused to recognize these
difficulties, and declared that he would have carved
statues at the bottom of a well. He accepted all circumstances philosophically, maintaining that they always
presented a favorable side, if we only knew how to seize
it. The result, in many instances, proved that he was
right. The awkward triangular fragment of marble,

which anybody else would have rejected, led him to invent the Neapolitan *Fisher-boy with the Tortoise*, merely
because such a composition would go into the block;
and it made him famous, a success which may have
confirmed him in his philosophy. However this may
have been, he remained always a disciple of Epictetus,
and maintained that things had two handles, the art
being to seize them by the right one.

Some anecdotes of Rude have an antique flavor, and
seem as if quoted from Plutarch: others remind us of
the turbulent Italian artists of the sixteenth century.
He was seldom angry, but it happened to him occasionally to lose patience. Once, when fencing, his adversary
would never confess that he was hit; so Rude said,
"Let us remove the buttons from the foils, and the
blood will show," which it presently did. In 1848, a
big policeman was disrespectful to him in the street; so
Rude seized the man, and dragged him by sheer strength
to the nearest police-station to lodge his complaint.
He was occasionally subject to the same outbursts of
passionate energy in intellectual discussions. One day,
when speaking of a public man whose conduct he disapproved of, he became angry, and received this telling
rebuke: "He whom you blame so severely is wiser than
you, for he never loses his temper." "You are right,"
Rude answered: "in that he is wiser than I am; but, if
passion did not carry me away now and then, I should
not have the temperament of an artist."

If he had the passionate strength of the artistic temperament, he had, in an equal degree, its tenderness and

delicacy. On the death of his friend Roman, the sculptor, who had been an Academician, Rude's friends suggested that he ought to offer himself as a candidate for the vacant chair. " I could not bear," he answered, "to sit in poor Roman's place." We have already seen what an incurable wound had been left by the loss of his boy.

He never complained about the past, never uttered a vain regret. He considered those words idle and profitless which men employ in pleading against irremediable evils.

Rude's social characteristics were peculiar. In dress and manners, he was plain and simple ; and he belonged all his life to the plebeian order, which it was part of his philosophy not to desire to leave. Opinions may differ about his conduct in this respect : some may think that an artist, as he rises in his profession, ought to imitate the manners of the aristocracy. I think there is more dignity in Rude's adherence to his class. It would be a complete mistake to suppose that he was vulgar, that he aspired after no ideal of conduct or manners. He was plebeian, but not vulgar: the two things are entirely distinct. Rude had neither the aristocratic nor the democratic vulgarity. His difference from other men may be easily expressed. Most men, as they rise in a profession, try to push themselves into a higher class, and become imitations of what is positively or relatively some sort of aristocracy. Rude preferred to remain a plebeian, and to improve himself as a plebeian, .in the ways which might be accessible to a plebeian, without quitting his own order. He did not electro-plate himself with silver, but wrought the good steel of his own nature to a finer temper. He was a workman able to read his own language, and skilful in such amusements and accomplishments as were accessible without expense. He worked in iron when young, and afterwards in wood and marble. Whilst still a smith at the forge, he won a gold medal for ornamental drawing, the accomplishment of a skilled artisan. We do not hear much of his labor in wood ; but as a less gifted workman might have carved the flourishes on a sideboard, so he decorated a pulpit with allegorical figures, and surmounted it with gigantic angels. He had no objection to make a marble chimney-piece, but where the ordinary workman would chisel out a few mouldings, and perhaps a couple of brackets, or a coat of arms, fit for the house of a private gentleman, Rude carved his chimney-piece for a Queen's chamber with its frieze of Loves playing with marine monsters. In all this, he was simply the working-man developed to a higher perfection. Again, in his reading, he is a man of the people, who chooses his readings well : he knows no foreign tongue, he has no scholarship ; but, instead of wasting his time on the trash of the low journals, he listens to translations from Tacitus and Plutarch. I have mentioned his amusements, — all costless and accessible to the people. He is a first-rate skater, a powerful swimmer, a redoubtable fencer, an indefatigable pedestrian ; but we do not hear that he was ever a good horseman or a good shot. His one luxury was the workman's luxury, a pipe of tobacco ;

and he often began the day with a thimbleful of brandy, a common practice with the French *ouvrier*. His dress was generally a tight jacket; or else he might be seen in his shirt sleeves, and sometimes with bare arms, enjoying a good wash at the public fountain in the evening, "like a smith who has done his day's work." He would sit, of an evening, playing backgammon on the causeway in the Rue d'Enfer at Paris, just as if he had been in a country village. The reader may imagine how difficult it was to persuade a man of this kind to pay visits of ceremony, in correct costume, with gloves and a neatly brushed hat.

He retained to the last a sense of fellowship with the people, and a reliance on them which are rare in the middle class. When first he used to go to his country house at Cachan, his friends said, "We cannot go to the public billiard-table, there are too many quarrymen in the place, and they will be there, and be uncivil to us;" but Rude answered for the quarrymen's good manners, and it turned out that he was not mistaken, as they behaved well, and soon became quite courteous and polite, their courtesy being uninterrupted by any unpleasant incident during the ten years of Rude's weekly visits to the place. When he travelled on the steamer from Arles to Marseilles, he was hungry, and the steamer had no provisions for passengers, so the common sailors invited him to *déjeuner* with them. He accepted, and they behaved admirably, treating him with easy courtesy and deference.

The grandeur which impresses us in Rude is the

grandeur of a great character and a great talent; but we are not to expect, from a mind so constituted and so occupied, the qualities of a trained and precise thinker. His belief that mere will and industry can enable any man to accomplish any thing is a belief common enough amongst imperfectly educated men who have courage and industry; but no one of really cultivated intellect denies the variety of natural endowments.*   Sometimes he expressed the more moderate opinion, which is indisputable, that unless a man works he cannot find out what he is able to do; and from this he drew the moral that the artist must look to his own industry, and not to the criticisms of others, for the true revelation of his own powers.   All that he said in this sense is admirable, and worth preserving; but he got beyond his intellectual depth when he denied the inborn gifts.

His method of teaching, and his own technical practice, exhibit a mind both synthetic in its first conceptions, and singularly cautious in its processes of realization.   Though capable of wonderful speed when pressed for time, he was usually as careful about the measurements of proportions as a young beginner, and all the methods of his choice were slow and prudent in the extreme, making sure of each step with an almost painful solicitude.   His mind, as we have seen, was not Academic, but in a certain sense it was classical.   When travelling towards Italy with his friend M. Bouchet, he saw an old woman who sat spinning at her door.   Struck

---

* He used to repeat Jacotot's formula: "Qui veut peut. — Toutes les intelligences sont égales."

by the dignity and nobleness of her aspect, he said to his friend, "She is the mother of Ulysses!" When he sat at last on the shore of the Mediterranean and watched the white waves, he said, "Are not those the coursers of Neptune, and cannot you see out there in the distance the chariot of Amphitrite?"

Rude was a great man and a great artist. The French Government has lately (1878) paid a tribute to his memory by calling one of the rooms in the Louvre by his name. The next time, reader, that you go to Paris, ask for the *Salle Rude,* and see the *Fisher-boy playing with the Tortoise* and the *Mercury fastening his Talaria.*

We may remember Rude's doctrine that the simple privilege of doing art-work is in itself the artist's sufficient reward, his only real misfortune being whatever interrupts his studies.

"La grande chose pour un artiste, — c'est de faire."

JEAN JACQUES AMPÈRE.

THE maps of France do not always give the villages ; but, if the reader has access to any fairly good separate map of the Department of the Rhone, he will find a place called Poleymieux, or Polémieux, eleven kilomètres north by west of Lyons. It is in the region of the Mont d'Or, and a little more than three kilomètres, as the crow flies, from the right bank of the river Saône. There is a little country house there which has become famous for its connection with the two Ampères. André Marie Ampère, the illustrious scientific discoverer, was born in it ; and his son, Jean Jacques, the writer and traveller, passed his infancy there. The region about Polémieux is that of the Mont d'Or, which is one of the most beautiful parts of France. This famous hill (*Mons Auriacensis*) rises to the height of two thousand feet, and has three *mamelons;* the three being sometimes classed as separate hills under the names of Mont d'Or, Mont Verdun, and Mont Ceindre. Round about them are charming little valleys with villages nestling in them, and from their summits you may see the valley of the Saône (which in those parts is one of the noblest pieces of river scenery in Europe), the mountains of Dauphiné, and the distant ranges of the Alps. Few regions in the world are richer in natural charm ; and now, since the publication of the Ampère correspondence, the neighborhood of the Mont d'Or has pathetic associations for all who love either literature or science.

Although the subject of this biography is Jean Jacques Ampère, the well-known writer on Roman History, and our own contemporary, I will first give a brief account of his grandfather and his father, not only because they are interesting characters in themselves, but also because the peculiarities of Ampère, the writer, may be clearly traced to the influence of the two generations which preceded him.

His grandfather was a Jean Jacques like himself. This first Jean Jacques had been in trade on a small scale, and by strict economy had saved a little money ; he was also the owner of the house at Polémieux, and temporarily discharged the functions of a Justice of the Peace.

In those days, the days of the great Revolution, it required not a little courage to accept public functions of this kind. In the spring of 1793, Lyons rose in insurrection against the Jacobin club which tyrannized over it, and for sixty days the city resisted the army of the convention. Jean Jacques Ampère remained at his post as Justice of the Peace ; and, when Lyons was taken at last by the Republican army, he was one of the first to go to prison.

Going to prison under such circumstances was simply

entering the ante-chamber of the grave. Ampère was aware of this, and quietly occupied one of the few days which remained to him in settling his affairs by means of written instructions for his wife. His letter to her is still in existence, and it deserves to be kept as long as the fibres of the paper will hold together, or the last trace of the faded ink remain visible; for, in all the records of human care and sorrow, there are few finer examples of tranquil courage and thoughtfulness in the presence of death.

He goes into all the little details of their money matters, so that his wife, so soon to be his widow, may have as little trouble as possible when he is gone. In his desire that no injustice should be done by neglecting the payment of what he owes, he mentions every little thing which has not yet been paid for, even to a quarter of a pound of bread; the outstanding accounts together amounting to about £4, besides which he owes something for his keep and that of his sister-in-law during the siege, when they were fed by a good woman who trusted them. This statement of his affairs is treated as a separate document, and signed formally "Jean Jacques Ampère, juge de paix jusqu'à ce moment." After it comes a page of explanation about the state of his small fortune, and towards the close of this is an expression of feeling, but of feeling under the most perfect control; and the dignity of the just man, about to suffer an unmerited death, is never for an instant abandoned. This latter part is signed "Jean Jacques Ampère, époux, père, ami, et citoyen toujours fidèle." These

are not our usages, — we do not call ourselves faithful
husbands, fathers, friends, or citizens, — but let it be
remembered that these words were written in a time of
high public excitement, when the noblest and basest
feelings were alike in full activity, and that in Ampère's
case they were the simple truth. He was what he called
himself.

"I do not leave you rich," he said to his wife, "or
even in common comfort; but this cannot be imputed
to bad conduct or dissipation on my part. My greatest
expense has been the purchase of books and mathematical instruments which were indispensable to our son's
education; but this expense was in itself a wise economy,
considering that he has never had any other master than
himself."

The son here mentioned is the illustrious Ampère;
and the outlay for books and instruments was to lead
to ultimate results so magnificent that no human imagination could at that time possibly have foreseen them.
It is probable that, since the world began, no money
given for educational purposes was ever better applied.
It is like buying colors for Titian in his youth.

The condemned man had made heavy pecuniary sac-
rifices in the service of his country, but these he does
not regret: he regrets only that his country should have
"misunderstood" him, — a mild expression under the circumstances, when misunderstanding meant decapitation.

There is nothing about glory in the letter, but we find
that other word which Perreyve called "ce mot austère
et saint."

" Je n'eus jamais que le goût et la passion de mes *devoirs ;* je n'ai ni repentir, ni remords, et je suis toujours digne de toi."

Please observe that the word is used in the plural, a recognition that there are various kinds of duty. The simple provincial *bourgeois* who for years past has been quietly sacrificing his interests to the public weal, and is now going to have his head cut off because he has been faithful to the end, cheers himself with the approval of his own conscience, and can say to his wife, " Je suis toujours digne de toi." After his trust in God and his hope of the heavenly rest, his best consolation is that she will cherish his memory even as she herself has been cherished by him in life ; then he adds, with a sense of his own rights, " Ce retour m'est dû." He promises that, if the dead are permitted to concern themselves about those they have left behind, he will care for his wife and children still, when he is in heaven. He prays that the children may have a happier fate than his, and may ever have the fear of God before their eyes, — " that salutary fear which can keep us innocent and just in spite of the frailty of our nature." He says good-bye to his sister-in-law tenderly by her pet name, calling her " la Tatan," and wishing her the courage which he feels. His little daughter, Josephine, is to be kept in ignorance of the tragic nature of his end. Then comes a word for his son, intended evidently as a stimulus to the young man's energy in the battle of life which lies before him : " As to my son, I expect every thing from him."

It would be difficult, in a few words, to leave a better legacy to a son. The praise for his past life is conveyed so delicately, the trust in his future conduct and industry is expressed so handsomely, along with an implied confidence in his good abilities, that the boy could have little nobleness in his nature who was not stimulated by such an appeal to all that was good in him. Again, the words are few, and likely to remain in the memory. It is not a long parental lecture, but a watchword like Nelson's at Trafalgar, the two being identical in spirit.

The blood of this just man having been shed, his family was left to lament him. The first effect of the tragedy on his son André, at that time eighteen years old, was to paralyze his intellect for a year, during which he seemed like one in a waking dream, unable to work or think, unable to interest himself in any visible thing. At length came the awakening, in a strange, new pleasure at the sight of flowers; and after that he began to delight in the verses of the great poets. It was a new birth into a fairer world after a darkness like the darkness of the grave; and the freshness of revived sensation, acting upon the vigorous energies of youth, produced in André that high condition of the feelings which elevates men to the best enthusiasms, and makes them poets, lovers, or friends. And now comes the prettiest and saddest love-story of which we have authentic record.

It is an idyl of that lovely region about the Mont d'Or, — a true idyl, not invented like that which haunted

Byron at Clarens. Here, at St. Germain au Mont d'Or, the immortal verse would be true indeed : —

"Thine air is the young breath of passionate thought."

The place is a little village, not two miles from Polé-mieux, and here lived in the summer months, in a simple little country house, a family called Carron. They were not rich people : the head of the family was in business of some kind, probably at Lyons ; but, whatever may have been their social position, we can see quite plainly from the family correspondence that they were people of refinement and culture ; that the women of the family were gentlewomen, and that the mental atmosphere of the little country house was an atmosphere of bright intelligence, cheerfulness, and purity.

There were three sisters in the family, and one brother. The eldest sister was married already to a bookseller at Lyons ; the youngest, Élise, was unmarried ; and the middle one, Julie, was the object of young André Am-père's affection.

Julie was a fair girl with blue eyes and golden hair. She had been asked in marriage by a young physician, who rose to eminence afterwards, and died in 1813 ; but, although his love for her was perfectly disinterested, — for she had no dowry, — she could not return it, and he was disappointed. Ampère was more fortunate : the blue eyes answered his, certainly not with any thing approaching to his own ardor, but still sufficiently to keep that ardor alive. The awakening of the young man's spirit to life and thought after the dreadful incubus of tragedy which had oppressed it was like the flowering of a plant in the gracious sunshine of spring. Intellect and affections blossomed together in wonderful luxuriance. His power of learning, far surpassing the power of ordinary humanity, had made him, at the age of twenty, a prodigy of attainment. He knows as much about geometry and mathematics as the best teachers of the sciences in Lyons; he reads Latin and Greek, not as a schoolboy, but for his delight in noble literature; he writes tragedies and poems; he studies botany, chemistry, mechanics. One of the mightiest brains that ever existed was already in full activity, playing in the upper regions of intellectual endeavor as easily as a young eagle flies between mountain and mountain. This ardent spirit, so splendidly gifted, sought another of its ideals in love, and, being too pure and too elevated to satisfy itself with any of those temporary connections which degrade the mind and character instead of sustaining them, threw itself into that which is at once the supreme imprudence and the supreme felicity of human life, an engagement of pure affection, a love-match in which money matters were simply and innocently ignored. The young man has no trade but the ill-paid profession of teaching, he is utterly without experience of the world, he is timid, tender, and modest; but he loves his Julie, and will have her in spite of poverty.

He kept a diary in the year 1796, which gives us the earliest incidents of this attachment. The first of these entries is : —

"Dimanche, 10 Avril. — Je l'ai vue pour la première fois."

Then he borrows and lends books, Italian and French, as an excuse for going to the house where she is. Four months later, he begins to explain himself, — "to open his heart," as he calls it, — in consequence of which he is forbidden to return to the house in Madame Carron's absence, and has "but feeble hopes." The mother comes back ; and the borrowing and lending of books go on, as if the houses were *cabinets de lecture.* Here are extracts in September and October : —

"Lundi, 26 Septembre. — Je *la* trouvai dans le jardin, sans oser lui parler."

"Vendredi, 30 Septembre. — Je portai Racine. La mère était dans la salle à mesurer de la toile."

"3 Octobre. — J'y allai. Je glissai encore quelques mots à la mère. Je rapportai le premier volume de Sévigné."

All through the diary, the books come in delightfully. "Sévigné" is a capital book for the purpose, being in nine volumes, every volume giving an opportunity for a visit : besides which, they make *bouts-rimés*, which André is to fill up and carry back, — all which offer chances innumerable, but the timidity of the young *savant* always prevents him from making use of them. One day, he talks to Madame Carron, and has a little hope : another day, Julie returns to him the "Lettres Provinciales" "avec grâce ;" and the mother says, "It is a long time since we saw you," but the sister Élise speaks coldly. Julie leaves for Lyons. Ampère ventures to call, knowing she is there; and he calls on her mother again at St. Germain. She is very cool about him; and he is as awkward as a schoolboy, always blundering, staying when he should not stay, and committing those little social errors which excite the pity of all Frenchwomen, when they do not incur their contempt.

Science and love are strangely mingled in one of his entries. On the 24th of June, the Ampères go from Polémieux to see the eclipse at St. Germain. They walk about in a friend's garden, where Ampère sits near Julie, whilst Madame Carron and his mother have a mutual explanation at some distance. The interest of the natural philosopher carries the day against the ardor of the lover, and there is more about the eclipse in the diary than about Julie. The weather is cloudy, but the sky becomes clearer "at ten minutes past six, after the middle of the eclipse; nevertheless," Ampère continues, " I observed the end of it exactly at thirty-five minutes after six, as I had calculated with my watch and that of M. Périsse with a telescope belonging to M. Rapt."

The great and memorable day, however, was not that of the eclipse: it was the day of the cherry-tree, Monday, the 3d of July, which Ampère entered in capital letters in his diary.

The Carron family came to the Ampères' house at Polémieux at a quarter to four o'clock. They remain in the garden, and Ampère climbs the big cherry-tree and throws cherries down to Julie. Then he gets down from the tree and sits on the grass near Julie, with their sis-

ters ; and he eats cherries which have been on her knees.*
She accepts a lily from his hand ; they go together to
the little stream ; he gives her his hand to jump over
the wall, and stays with her near the stream, far from
Élise and her sister.   They walk a little, and see a
golden sunset ; and he gives her another lily, which she
accepts.   On the 10th of July, he goes to her home with
a basket of raspberries and currants, and some orchises
for Élise to put in her garden.   Julie and Ampère, with
his sister, go together into the garden ; and his sister
helps Julie to fold some chemises, whilst he reads to
them (of all things in the world) the discourse of M.
Derieu at the reception of the Ottoman Ambassador :
then he reads from two volumes, which are named.   On
the 18th, he takes another basket of currants.

Can any thing be more exquisite and charming than
these details ?   But to see them really as they were
would need the imagination of a landscape-painter and
a figure-painter in one.   Imagine the rich scenery of the
Mont d'Or in summer, the sweet valley far enough from
the city for the most perfect rustic peace, and these
young people in the quaint dresses of the eighteenth
century, enjoying a simple existence in which refinement was gracefully reconciled with industry ; imagine
Julie beautiful with her blue eyes and her golden tresses,
André full of the liveliest intelligence, the morning light
of genius in his look, the glow of a first pure love upon

* This reminds us of an early love affair of Napoleon I. in Corsica,
when he and his first love "ate cherries together," which was all he
remembered of it in after life.   Ampère's finer and better nature clung
more fondly to those sweet reminiscences of the golden time.

his cheek, and the gentle sisters and kindly old people
near them to complete the group, to whom after poign-
ant sorrow now came a happier time! Never did
painter or novelist adorn his work by the invention of
prettier details than these real ones, — the cherries, the
lilies, the books, the walk by the stream and the garden,
the golden sunset of that golden day!

On the 6th of August, 1799, André Marie Ampère,
still a minor, espouses "demoiselle Catherine Julie Carron, fille majeure," etc., which proves that she was the
older of the two.

They were married at Polémieux, that fifteenth day of
Thermidor, *an* VII.; and Ampére's friend Ballanche
delivered an epithalamium on the occasion, which only
shows what a prodigious distance separates our manners
and customs from the manners and customs of those
days. Ballanche begins by quoting, —

> *Felices ter et amplius*
> *Quos irrupta tenet copula, nec malis*
> *Divulsus querimoniis*
> *Suprema citius solvet amor die!*

and then delivers the epithalamium of his own composition, which is nothing less than a long prose poem about
love in marriage. A modern Englishman would rather
be shot at on his wedding-day than sit to be talked to
in such a strain, yet the whole thing is true enough,
undeniably true, and very well expressed besides, though
the style is old-fashioned now, and it is impossible to
read it without a smile. The epithalamium begins with
a joyous celebration of the happiness of getting married
when one is in love; and it ends with an appeal to duty,

in the anticipation of a life made happy "par la pratique des devoirs." There was another lucubration of the same kind for the evening, and yet a third for the next day! There were no wedding journeys in those days, and young couples had to go through these ceremonies for several days together. Another friend wrote a similar composition as a commentary on the epithalamium, and it has been preserved. All these writings look exactly like translations from antique poetry into prose. There are two passages which seem prophetic:—

"Et ces sources limpides, et ce ruisseau solitaire murmurant sous des berceaux de feuillage, . . . et la mystérieuse obscurité de ces lieux silencieux . . . *que de souvenirs seront un jour attachés à tous ces lieux !*"

This prediction is by Ballanche. That which I quote next is by the anonymous friend and commentator:—

"Ampère, *si même une longue et glorieuse carrière lui est destinée*, ne connaîtra jamais rien de comparable à ces heures, à ces courtes et heureuses années passées auprès de sa Julie, sur ce pauvre domaine paternel où il est né."

But one expression occurred in the first epithalamium which, unhappily, was a most mistaken prediction:—

"Jeunes époux, vous serez toujours unis."

Alas! never was wedded pair more cruelly separated! They were separated almost from the very first by poverty, and soon afterwards they were separated by death.

Their first trouble of this kind was in the spring of 1800. André had to live at Lyons to teach mathematics; and Julie had to go to St. Germain with her mother, because her husband could not afford to keep her at Lyons, she being then in a situation which required more attendance than his slender purse could pay for. He went to see her every week, but that was all.

In July, 1800, she gives birth to a boy, in Madame Carron's house at St. Germain. This boy is Jean Jacques, the subject of our present study. Whilst the young mother and her child are living in the country, the father is still at Lyons, earning precarious bread by giving lessons. "Our income is very uncertain," he writes, "pupils come and go, and we never know what may be calculated upon." These pecuniary uncertainties harass the young husband already, and incline him to think that, were it not for his wife and child, he would not much care to live.

The next event is the weaning of the child. Julie has nursed him herself, which has exhausted her. She is to come to Lyons, and André is full of anxious care about her journey. The river Saône is in flood, and not to be thought of; he objects to the diligence, and finally determines that Julie is to ride on a donkey, with a hot stone under her feet. He charges her sister most earnestly to remember the hot stone, which indeed she does, but after Julie's departure, when it is too late. It is a wonderful proof of the importance of a day's work to poor André that he does not go to fetch his wife himself. Perhaps François Delorme, an attached young servant of the Ampère family at Polémieux, may have led the donkey, or otherwise stimulated its movements. André and Julie lived together at Lyons after this, their child remaining in the country ; but poor Julie never really recovered her health. She suffered from weakness and internal pains, so that the doctor had to advise complete repose.

In the month of December, 1801, André Ampère was appointed teacher of chemistry and physics at the École Centrale of the department of the Ain. This school was situated at Bourg. His wife was too unwell to bear the removal, he too poor to refuse the appointment, which was worth a hundred guineas a year, so they had to accept the chronic misery of an involuntary separation.

They were divided then, she remaining in pain and languor at Lyons, he living in a boarding-house at Bourg, in a horrible isolation of the heart, eating at a public table with vulgar people whom he could not endure.* He tried to find a compensation in writing a diary for Julie, which goes into the minutest details of his life, day by day, almost hour by hour ; and, as with all his learning he was the simplest and most candid soul that ever lived, we know him from this correspondence a thousand times better than the people we see every day. The torment of his life is the ruin of Julie's health. She, on her part, is constantly fidgeting herself about innumerable little details, which she thinks her scientific husband is incapable of attending to. She asks a question which could only be addressed to a very

---

* This was at the beginning. Soon afterwards, he boarded at the house of M. Beauregard, the teacher of history, who cannot have got much profit out of him, considering the wondrous moderation of his charges, which amounted to *forty francs a month*.

poor man, — "Have you any chairs in your room?" thinking that it may be unfurnished, and knowing her husband's entire inability to buy furniture. She inquires, too, about his fire, — does he make a good fire? — is his bed comfortable or not? Again, as to his clothing, she does all she can to keep him decent; but it is not easy, at a distance. However, there is the carrier, called Pochon, whose wagon goes between Lyons and Bourg, doing the twelve leagues in ten hours when he does not stick in the mire (Macadam is as yet unheard of in France); and by Pochon's help things can be sent both ways. Julie makes a waistcoat for her husband with her own hands; she sends him an old coat to wear when he makes his experiments, and strictly charges him not to go out in it. " Mind about your chemistry," she says: "your blue stockings are burnt with that horrible acid which burns every thing." Try to look like a decent sort of a man, to please your poor wife." He on his part boldly affirms that he does not burn his clothes with acid, and that he carries on his chemical experiments with nothing but his breeches, his gray coat, and his waistcoat of greenish velvet; but at a later date he has to confess that his best breeches smell of turpentine, that his trousers have a hole in them, which gets bigger in spite of mending, and displays a piece of different cloth below.

Julie thinks as much about André's keep as about his dress. She urges him to buy a bottle of wine, to keep it by him, and drink a little when he needs it; and, when the bottle is finished, he is to buy another. He is not to sit up late at night, because the next day he has a head-ache.

The correspondence on his side is less practical, and dwells more willingly in the region of the sentiments and affections. He goes minutely into money matters, however, and recognizes the necessity for keeping a sum of money by him for unforeseen requirements, this reserve amounting to no less than ten or twelve francs. He sends most of his money to Julie, who has doctor's expenses to meet ; but the good doctor knows how poor they are, and, when she offers him a hundred francs, he will only accept fifty, though he has paid sixty-five visits. Notwithstanding all these petty details, which become beautiful when illumined by affection and self-sacrifice, André's letters are really love-letters yet, and all the simplicity and tenderness of his nature are revealed in them. He kisses what he calls "the talisman," which is her first letter to him ; * he kisses "the little picture," which is a small frame containing a campanula given by her three days before the great day of the cherry-tree ; he kisses a dried rose which he had received from her hand. He keeps these treasures with a feminine fond-ness in a little portfolio of rose-colored satin, with their initials in an embroidered monogram on the back. The rose-colored portfolio is still in existence, the dried rose is in it still, and the letters, and the campanula; but where are those true lovers ? Poor Julie! she was always dreading lest her absent-minded husband should

* He had been ill at Lyons when a bachelor, and had begged for a letter from Julie as a "talisman" This had been graciously accorded.

leave her letters about for other eyes to see them ; and
now they are in print, in all the booksellers' shops, and
on the stalls at the railway stations !

She never had strength to go to her husband at Bourg
even for one day, though the distance was but a dozen
leagues. He regrets this bitterly, because, if she had
only been there, she would have left recollections of herself by associating her presence with the locality in his
mind, and he might have gone to seek these associations
afterwards.

Poor Julie gets weaker and weaker. Her love for
André is in a continued *crescendo*, and her strength goes
down in an equally regular *diminuendo*, an inverse
ratio which she notices with melancholy humor in a
letter. She can hardly even write now, but is in the
hands of a good, friendly doctor who has known her
from childhood. Her only hope of a permanent reunion
with her husband is his appointment as teacher at the
Lyceum of Lyons ; but they have to wait long for this,
and life is ebbing away from her very fast. They have,
however, the vacation to look forward to. It comes at
last, in the late summer of 1802, which they pass together
at Polémieux, or St. Germain, with their little boy, —
two months, two happy and miserable months, in which
the felicity of the present is clouded by the shadow of
coming evil. In November, he has to leave her again
for his duties at Bourg, where he is wretched to think
that she is ill at a distance, but tries to console himself
by the still remote prospect of the Easter holidays. He
cannot even get away for a day to see her, as the exami-

ners are expected. Then the weight of anxiety settles down on his mind, and he is " hardly able to work." She has far the wiser and cooler head of the two, giving him the most judicious advice about his professional prospects, often treating him in quite a maternal way, and even playfully calling him her son. Much as she may desire to have him near her, she sees clearly that it will not do for him to present himself at Lyons before he is definitively appointed. Then comes a terrible silence. The last of Julie's letters has been received : she is living yet, but she can write no more! The next event of importance is the dissolution of the École Centrale at Bourg by the government, in consequence of which all the masters are dismissed. On the 17th of April, 1803, André Ampère, free from Bourg, and now sure of his appointment to Lyons, joins his wife again, and lives with her till she is finally taken away from him by Death.

This reunited wedded life of theirs lasted nearly three months. He watched her day and night with the tenderness of a lover and the care of a Sister of Charity. On the 24th of April, they went from Polémieux to Collonges on the Saône, the loveliest place on all that river ; and here he kept a little diary with brief entries, like those in that happier diary of the courtship. Now, alas ! instead of fruits and flowers, we have entries about useless medicines. On the 5th of July, Ampère gives his first lesson at the Lyceum of Lyons, holding at last the appointment so long looked forward to by both of them ; but all is joyless henceforward in his darkened

life. On the 13th of that same month of July, he writes
a long earnest prayer in French and a passage from the
Latin Bible. It is the day of their final separation.
" O God of pity," he cries in his anguish, " join me again
in heaven to her whom Thou hast permitted me to love
on earth ! " *

Here ends this tale of love and sorrow, and now let
us turn to Julie's child, Jean Jacques, who is the special
subject of our study.

The child passes his earliest years in the little country
house at Polémieux, tenderly cared for by his grandmother and his aunt, with his maternal relations living
two miles off, at St. Germain. The place was exactly
suited to the needs of childhood, — incomparably better
than an apartment on a fourth or fifth floor at Lyons.
It is difficult to convey to English readers an exact idea
of such a house, because in England nobody has any
thing exactly of that kind ; but let the reader imagine a
small, very old-fashioned dwelling inhabited by people of
cultivated tastes, who lived nevertheless in much simplicity. There would not be very much furniture in it,
— hardly any thing beyond what was absolutely necessary, — yet it was not at all a peasant's house ; for there
would be signs of the higher life in books, and even a bit
of tapestry or a picture. There was a charming old
garden for the little boy to run about in, well shut in
from the great world beyond, with plenty of shade for
the hot days of summer, apple-trees on each side the

* One who knew André Ampère well, J. J. Bredin, said of him:
" Never did a man love as he loved."

walks, and a bower of vines where André used to sit with his books and papers in a state of absolute intellectual abstraction. There were flowers also in the cheerful old garden, for the walks were bordered with pinks; and was it not here that André gathered the lily for Julie? There was the great cherry-tree, too, — a powerful attraction for a child; and not far from the garden flowed the little stream. With these pleasant and healthy surroundings, the little boy had plenty of feminine tenderness to watch over him, and compensate as far as possible for the loss of his poor young mother.*

André Ampère did not long retain the situation at Lyons which he and Julie had looked forward to with so much longing when it was to bring them together. Now that she was gone, he could not bear the place and wanted a change of scene. He became so thin and pale as to alarm his mother, who wrote to him very serious letters full of strong good sense to arouse his energies. In his present state of indecision and dislike to his former occupations, André is tempted to go into trade as a dealer in vitriol. His mother knows his absolute natural incompetence for commercial pursuits, and strongly dissuades him. Luckily for all parties, he gets an appointment in Paris as *répétiteur d'analyse* at the École Polytechnique, where he settles in November, 1804.

After this, there is an interesting correspondence between André Ampère and his mother, in which we catch glimpses of Jean Jacques in his childhood at Polémieux.

---

* All the details which I have been able to include in this imperfect description are authentic.

André sends him books ; but the *savant* is unlucky in this, as in most matters belonging to ordinary life, for Madame Ampère complains that the books are too expensive and too far beyond the child's years. There is a correspondence, too, between André and his sister-in-law Élise. She was certainly superior to Julie in intelligence ; she certainly understood Ampère better than Julie ever did, and it may be suspected that she would have loved him, had she been chosen ; but we see her always acting her sisterly part with perfect tact and delicacy.

For the next two or three years, André's mind is in a most unsettled condition. He is earnestly religious, yet his religion only agitates and disturbs him. Then he becomes perplexed by the painful side of his theology, and is landed in a region of doubt which harasses his mind exceedingly. His mental condition may be understood by a single example. He has never doubted the immortality of the soul, but he looks forward with a new horror to the moment when his soul is to be separated from his body. Whatever beliefs remain to him, he can no longer persuade himself that he is a real Roman Catholic. At the same time, an accelerated intellectual development is going forward in his mind, accompanied by intense intellectual labors, and by an ambition quite new to him, the desire for fame, evidently a morbid symptom in his case. He is full of all kinds of regrets : he regrets having quitted his post at Lyons ; he regrets the Catholic doctrines which he is no longer able to believe ; he regrets having left his boy, — all which feelings are really nothing but disguises of the one supreme regret for Julie. André's friends perceived his profound unhappiness, and thought there was no remedy for it but a second marriage, so they persuaded him to see a young lady at Lyons, who, in their opinion, was sure to restore him to happiness, as she had a great admiration for talent, and a tender soul. Ampère was in such a state of mind as to have scarcely a will of his own, and, being ready to catch at any thing that promised relief from his misery, just let himself be married. It soon became apparent that his new wife was a young lady who liked society, and thought that a man of talent would procure her a foremost place in it. She had not the slightest sympathy with her husband's intellectual life, which lay outside the limits of her understanding ; and, when she discovered that he was a recluse devoted to his studies, she made his existence as uncomfortable as a disappointed woman could. He took refuge in his work-room, and they met only at table, where she sat in a state of perpetual sulk, and would not answer a word when he spoke to her. His father-in-law informed him that, if he wanted to avoid a separation, he must sacrifice all his opinions to those of his wife. In short, after experiencing the pleasant side of the feminine nature in Julie, he now as fully experienced the disagreeable side, — a cold, sulky disdain hardening steadily into frozen feminine hatred. The contrast between the present and the past threw him into agonies of what he called " remorse," though he had done no wrong. The worst was that he became utterly incapable of work. " In spite of all my efforts," he said, "work has become absolutely impossible for me. I have not faculties enough to put two ideas together."

Whilst things were in this state, his family was increased by the birth of a daughter, after which event André Ampère reached the lowest depth of mental wretchedness, and went to his mother at Polémieux for consolation. There his friend Bredin met him, and listened to the detailed history of that deplorable second marriage. Madame Ampère, his old mother, saw that the right thing to do was to accompany him to Paris, and take the little boy along with them; and this is how it happened that Jean Jacques, instead of being educated in a village, under the shadow of the Mont d'Or, became a sharp-witted little Parisian, — a change in his destiny highly favorable to his culture, and to his future celebrity, but very probably not so favorable to his happiness.

A formal separation between André Ampère and his wife was declared by the Cour d'Appel in July, 1809. The husband had done all he could to prevent this necessity; but in vain. In the autumn of the same year, another blow fell on André in the death of his mother.

From this time, his life took its permanent shape and color. The agitations of early misfortunes passed away and left him in a calm sadness, with his magnificent intellectual powers quite unimpaired, whilst the practical power of labor, which had been for a while suspended, was at length completely restored. He was therefore able, notwithstanding the desolation of his domestic circumstances, to pursue the career of science in which he became illustrious. He had ambition, which was gratified both by his own discoveries and by the honor rendered to him by others. Even so early as 1812, he announced the principle of the electric telegraph ; and in 1814 he was elected *Membre de l'Institut.* Besides these and other satisfactions of his splendid scientific career, he had the very exceptional consolation of recovering his early faith in all the dogmas of his church. In the year 1817, and during the remainder of his life, André Ampère was one of the most fervent Roman Catholics in France, — a remarkable instance of submission in so powerful an intellect. The explanation is that, although his intellect was one of the strongest in the world, his sentiments were at least equally energetic ; and they found no satisfaction in scepticism, whilst Protestantism had no associations for him connected with the human affections of his youth.

As for Jean Jacques, he had such a taste for the catechism in his childhood that his grandmother's sister declared he would become ultimately *un père de la foi ;* but the prediction was not verified. A lady who knew him at Paris in his youth gives the following lively description of his character and talents : —

" Gifted with the happiest faculties of the mind, young Ampère inherited none of his father's aptitudes for the physical and mathematical sciences. He had a delicate and nervous constitution, a mobile imagination with a disposition for dreaming, an unsettled temper with sensitive feelings, a great need of affection, and a lively sense of natural beauty. Though his memory was very comprehensive, and his intelligence naturally quick, he was always a very bad learner in the opinion of all the masters who took part in his education."

The boy's natural incapacity for science astonished his father, who used to repeat that at eighteen he knew as much about mathematics as could be taught in those days. The elder Ampère, who had suffered so much inconvenience, and sadder troubles besides, from the straitened circumstances of the family, desired like most parents that his son should follow some lucrative occupation ; but there were difficulties in the boy's natural character, which was strongly inclined to literary pursuits. The simple truth was that Jean Jacques was a born man of letters, just as his father was a born man of science ; and neither the one nor the other had any of those talents which favor the accumulation of wealth.

The studies pursued by young Ampère in his adolescence were not confined to the strict university curriculum. He worked at botany, he read a great deal of German, and began to learn English. Besides these studies, he looked forward to enlarging his mind by travel, so that the whole field of his culture was already mapped out at an early age ; for he became afterwards accomplished in modern as well as ancient languages, and a traveller.

His father's desire that Jean Jacques should follow a lucrative pursuit led him when a young man to think a moment about entering into trade, so he put himself into communication with a M. Clément, a manufacturing chemist, who disenchanted him by what we should now call his Philistinism. M. Clément began by telling him that he must forget all he had learned in literature, to occupy himself with useful knowledge. " Useful, if he pleases," thought Jean Jacques, " but I shall never forget Virgil and Racine." The next thing M. Clément did was to attack the higher mathematical studies, by declaring that all which was taught at the École Polytechnique was useless in after-life. The only effect of these bits of worldly wisdom was that young Ampère's dislike to trade became confirmed into a positive antipathy. If all the higher attainments were to be cast aside as an encumbrance, and the mind exclusively concentrated on gain, he declined the bargain. "What ! " he exclaimed indignantly, "boys are taught all sorts of generous and elevated sentiments, disinterestedness is preached to them, their themes and translations are composed of nothing but maxims of wisdom and moderation, and, when this education is ended, they are told that all these principles are *un tas de bêtises !* " The elder Ampère writes to his son, and talks of mathematics, chemistry, and drawing for the following year, but omits all mention of literature. " You forget literary studies," was the reply : " do you imagine that I shall lose sight of them for a single instant? I hope the omission was unintentional." In August, 1816, Jean Jacques writes to his father, " The further I go, the more strongly I feel how wrong I should have been to follow commercial pursuits."

Young Ampère's susceptibility to impressions from

literature was extreme. Byron's "Manfred" produced such an effect on his imagination that it made him physically and mentally unwell for a whole week. "My dear Jules," he writes to his friend Bastide, "last week a sense of malediction was upon me, around me, and in me. I owe that to Lord Byron. I read 'Manfred' twice. Never in my whole life did reading crush me like that. It has made me ill. On Sunday, I went to see the sunset, and it seemed menacing like the infernal flames. I went into a church where the faithful were peacefully singing the Halleluiah of the Resurrection. Leaning against a column, I watched them with disdain and envy. In the evening, I dined with E——, and had to talk with Madame M—— about room-decoration. At nine o'clock, I could stand it no longer. I was in a state of bitter and violent despair, with eyes closed and head leaned back, devouring my own thoughts."

This is a curious instance of the tremendous influence which Byron exercised on the most eager and excitable young minds of that generation. There cannot be a doubt that, either from the nearness of the great Revolution and what followed it, or from the intense ferment of ideas which disturbed Western Europe in the beginning of the century, young men in those days were far more inflammable, far more ready to catch fire from the compositions of men of genius, than they are at the present day. The cool young gentlemen whom we see around us would read "Manfred," if ever they read it at all, with the most perfect self-possession; and, instead of losing their mental balance for a week after, would probably experience no further emotion than a feeble impulse toward criticism. I quote J. J. Ampère's account of his own state, because it shows how alive he was to poetical influences. There is the same vivacity (it will be called exaggeration by colder temperaments) in his sentiments towards those who influenced him personally. He writes from Berne to his friend Bastide, who had been ill and was now alone: " What are Venice and Illyria to me, when I am far from him who suffers in solitude ? Never let us be separated : life is so short, how can we waste it so ? What a frightful madness it is to separate ourselves one from another! And to think that I am two hundred leagues from you, and am going still farther into regions where you are not ! "

In an earlier letter to the same friend, he expresses a passionate repugnance to philosophy, and bestows upon it his hearty malediction : " How I do execrate philosophy : it is that which has brought me to a weariness of every thing. I really look upon it with horror and contempt. I will bear no more of it ! "

I have given these extracts simply to show the intensity of young Ampère's sentiments when on the threshold of manly life. His letters of those times reveal already that electric state, with its violent attractions and repulsions, which afterwards made his existence so strangely and perpetually unsettled.

He started on his first tour in 1820, and was mistaken enough to imagine that he would never wish to travel again, he who was destined to be a roamer to the end of his life! In August, we find him by the Lake of Geneva ;

and in September he visits the Lake of Brienne, where
his mind is full of souvenirs of Rousseau, especially on
the island. " A storm threatened : I noticed it only
from the light movement of the little waves which rocked
our boat. When we got near to the island, I heard all at
once an agitated movement in the crests of the highest
trees. We landed ; we walked upon the grass of the shore ;
we sat down by the water. A sad and sombre border of
fir-trees rose up like a great wall whose base was washed
by the water : round about us all was fresh and gay. I
fancied Rousseau, in his age, broken in health, walking
there at the same hour, a little before sunset, gathering
a few flowers, with pain upon his forehead. When we
embarked again, a livelier wind filled our sail and raised
the most beautiful waves : we passed in the midst of the
reeds without an effort, and as if by enchantment. I was
delighted. Night came, and the moon shone upon the
agitated waters. There was in her peaceful rays, in the
clouds which passed rapidly before her, in the serenity
of a great part of the sky, something sweet and yet
menacing, uncertain as life itself. We returned through
a thick forest, and passed by wooden houses and across
meadows. And now the rain is falling."

This was not written to be printed : it is simply part
of a letter to Ampère's young friend Bastide. I do not
quote it for any remarkable literary merit, but only
because there is a certain elevation in its tone, considering that it occurs in a familiar correspondence between
two young men. There is feeling here, and observation
besides : the traveller both looks and remembers. Most

young men of the present day, after such an excursion, would write much more briefly, and suppress their thoughts and feelings, if they had any. They would say : " At the Lake of Brienne, we took a boat, and landed on Rousseau's Island. The weather looked threatening, and when we got back it began to rain."

This tour in the autumn of 1820 included a botanical excursion in Savoy ; and the two companions, J. J. Ampère and his friend Adrien de Jussieu, pushed on as far as the Italian lakes, crossing the St. Gothard and going to Lugano by Bellinzona. Our hero wrote a lively account of the first impression of Italy to his friend Bastide. After the treeless desert of the high Alps, they began to descend, first through the zone of the pine-tree and then through the zone of the oak, coming finally to the vine, after which they were surrounded by the full beauty of a rich, inhabited country, with châteaux and country houses on the shores of a beautiful lake. This experience, the change from the arctic desert of the Alpine heights to the luxuriant southern land of Italy has been described before and since, but seldom with so much of the genuine traveller's emotion. Young Ampère does not say now as he said in August, " If our plan is realized, the desire for travel will never possess me again." He says now : " I am sure that I shall start another time. There is a delicious charm in the succession of places and aspects, in the long marches, in the fatigues and chance opportunities for rest." These are the words of the real traveller, and from that year to the year of his death J. J. Ampère was as much addicted to wandering as if he had been a born Englishman.

With these elements, we may begin already to understand J. J. Ampère's nature and character as a young man. He was a passionate student of several different literatures ; and a new passion, that of travel, had developed itself in him during his first tour beyond the boundaries of France. These two passions already distinguish him from the purely national Frenchman, who reads no language but his own, and limits his travelling to his own country. In these early years of his life, J. J. Ampère, like many young men of an ardent disposition and high culture, indulged the hope that he might be endowed with poetic genius, and wrote much in verse, even as a schoolboy. At twenty, he composed a tragedy, " Rosemonde," the fable of which was founded on the history of the Lombards in Italy. This tragedy had the extraordinary honor, considering the age of the author, of being taken *au sérieux* by the committee of the Théâtre Français,* who listened to it with good-natured attention. Notwithstanding this degree of encouragement, young Ampère's most intelligent friends did not think that he was intended by nature to be a dramatic poet ; and when his father asked Ballanche the direct question, " Do you think that my son is a genius ? " Ballanche was too honest to say yes. Notwithstanding

---

* For readers who are not intimately acquainted with Paris, I may mention that the Théâtre Français is quite an exceptional theatrical institution, maintained by the government in order to keep up a high standard of dramatic literature and acting, which it does very strictly, as an academy of dramatic culture and taste.

this absence of real poetic inspiration, which of all mental gifts is the most rare, we should not estimate young
Ampère correctly, if we left his poetic labors out of
account.   If not a genius, he was still a young man of
most brilliant abilities ; and his versifying was a not
unimportant part of his culture, both as an exercise of
imagination and a discipline in the use of language.
We may also take note of a certain success in his college studies, in spite of his want of discipline as a school-
boy ; for we find him carrying away the *prix d'honneur*
in philosophy.

We have now to quit J. J. Ampère entirely for a short
time, and direct our attention to a most remarkable and
very celebrated woman, who had an influence ón his
life which has seldom been equalled, for strength and
duration, in the long history of woman's influence over
man.

In the year when poor Julie Carron was born at
Lyons, 1777, and almost in the same month, another
child was born in the same city, and soon afterwards
baptized by the name of Juliette.   Julie Carron and
Juliette Bernard are both not merely celebrated, but
sure to be remembered centuries hence for their influence on transcendently great men.   Nobody can know
much about the elder Ampère without remembering
Julie Carron ; and the history of Juliette Bernard is so
closely interwoven with the literary and social history of
the First Empire that few remarkable women are so sure
of immortality.

Julie Carron was educated in the simplest and most

unworldly fashion, spending much of her time quietly in the country, in that sweet homely life of which we have had glimpses at Polémieux and St. Germain du Mont d'Or, — a life beautifully occupied, in its retirement, by household duties, good literature, and the observances of unaffected piety. The life of Juliette Bernard was a complete contrast to this. She was shut up almost in infancy in a convent at Lyons (l'Abbaye de la Déserte), from which she was suddenly removed at the age of twelve, and sent to Paris to be dressed as elegantly as possible and exhibited in her mother's *salon*, a place filled with a numerous and artificial society, her father occupying an important public position as *receveur général des finances*.

Here Juliette Bernard ripened rapidly into beauty, and beauty of that especially powerful kind which is heightened by all the graces of extreme civilization. Then came the terror of 1793 ; and M. Bernard sought protection for his daughter by marrying her to one of his intimate friends, M. Récamier, a banker, chiefly occu pied with his own pleasures.

Monsieur Récamier was between forty and fifty years old at that time, and his wife between fifteen and six· teen. He remained just the same after his marriage as before it, and the consequence was that husband and wife saw very little of each other. He was not a com· panion for her, she never had any children, and she sought compensation for the want of society in her mar· riage by forming many friendships, of a kind which, in justice to her memory, may require a few words of explanation. A career like hers is so entirely outside of common experience that the mere unusualness of it and the peculiar customs of her own intimate circle might easily awaken suspicions. Nearly all Madame Récamier's friendships were with men; but there is no evidence against her morality, and there is, on the contrary, some evidence in her favor. A lady who lived with her for years wrote of her afterwards as "the finished type of grace and purity;" another lady speaks of her untarnished reputation; and after a careful examination of the materials which have come down to us, and which are sufficiently abundant, my own conviction is that her nature was passionless, and that the leading motive of her life was simply the desire to exercise a supreme influence in a certain limited circle. She liked to be the queen of a little court, to live surrounded by sympathy, affection, and admiration. Her self-love was gratified by the intellectual eminence of those who gathered around her; and in order to retain them, which she did with astonishing success for years and years, she had recourse to certain feminine arts, which a very little study of that society makes plain to us. The most effectual of her arts was to take, or appear to take, the heartiest possible interest in a man's career; so that, whenever he wanted a little sympathy or encouragement, he came to her and talked about his fortunate or his unrewarded efforts, about his projects of study or travel, with the certainty of finding an attentive hearer and a kindly adviser. It is quite evident from her letters that Madame Récamier was not a person of any intellectual eminence herself; and yet she had so much tact, so much sympathy with intellectual men, that they remained under an illusion on this subject, which surprises us who never experienced her charm. The reader will remember a passage in which Henri Perreyve, by a stretch of imagination, attributed especial intellectual eminence to the Madonna; and I think it may be admitted that most men want to look up, if they possibly can, either to some ideal woman, as Perreyve did, or else to some real woman whom they innocently and unconsciously idealize, as J. J. Ampère idealized Madame Récamier. Let us confess that we want a degree of encouragement in our labors, which the frigid selfishness of our own sex and its limited sympathy are utterly unable to supply! Madame Récamier supplied this want with a rare degree of completeness, not only because she had inexhaustible sympathy, or the talent for imitating it in any required quantity, but because her stately beauty, her royal grace of demeanor, her exquisite tact and taste, made her interest in a man's occupations seem to him such a distinguished honor. The intercourse between this lady and her admirers became a sort of barter, in which the courtiers offered their homage, and the queen paid for it in gracious audiences and enviable distinctions. What has been said in defence of Madame Récamier's moral character must not be taken to imply that she made no use of her extraordinary physical attractions: on the contrary, I am fully persuaded that she knew their value, and availed herself of them as a means of keeping her singular little court together. Though passionless herself, she was not sorry to awaken just such a degree of passion in her admirers as might keep them in a proper condition of slavery to her will; but she made them control it, or she controlled it for them, and there were no declared jealousies nor out-breaks. The manners of the Récamier group were affectionate, and at the same time regulated by well-bred courtesy; for the queen could not tolerate errors of temper in her court, and constantly exercised her intelligence to prevent the development of rivalry into dissension. Those members of the little circle, who also belonged to Madame de Staël's little circle at Coppet, continued their Coppet practice of calling each other by their Christian names, which produces the oddest effect upon a reader of the present day, especially as their intercourse was in other respects guarded by a somewhat formal politeness. The reader who meets with extracts from their correspondence might greatly misinterpret the degree of their intimacy when he finds Camille Jordan calling Madame Récamier " chère Juliette," and she replies to him with "cher Camille." Sometimes she is called " belle Juliette," sometimes "aimable Juliette," and sometimes "belle et aimable Juliette" both at once. Nothing can be more contrary to French habits of the present day, which are formal and ceremonious in correspondence between persons of different sexes; but this is only the free-masonry of a little clique, which had a fancy for making itself into a sort of family by this practice.

The question naturally suggests itself, to what degree

these customs, and the remarkable position in society which was assumed and maintained by Madame Récamier, can have been agreeable to her husband? He really does not seem to have cared about the matter. He took it all with a serenity due partly to his knowledge of his wife's character and partly to the happy frivolity of his disposition. He thought it was her way to be a queen and have a court, and it does not appear that he disturbed his mind about it any farther. As for the brilliant intellectual talk which Madame Récamier liked to have going on about her, it probably bored him, and he felt happier out of its way. She, on her part, behaved to him with what people call "the strictest regard for propriety." She conducted herself like a lady who has duties to perform and means to go through them with irreproachable correctness. A crisis occurred in 1806, which put her good behavior to a severe test. M. Récamier was ruined, and his young and brilliant wife was henceforth to be like a picture without its gilded frame. If any thing could have vexed and irritated a woman who liked to shine in society, it was this. Financial ruin held out a gloomy prospect for one to whom social celebrity was the breath of life, and it is possible that she anticipated a much worse future than that which really lay before her; yet such was her self-control, and her determination to act the part of a well-conducted lady, that, although there was no affection between her and her husband, she skilfully avoided all useless recriminations, resigned her splendors apparently without an effort, and even consoled him under his misfortune. She got a letter on this occasion from her friend Camille Jordan, which was most affectionate and sympathetic; and it is a curious evidence of M. Récamier's freedom from jealousy that she read the letter to him, for his consolation.

To this brief and incomplete sketch of a most remarkable woman may be added a few words about her peculiar kind of worldliness. She was a worldly person, no doubt, in her own way; but it was a very refined and elevated way. To be sought by the distinguished, to be regarded by them with feelings of admiration for her beauty and of affection for her character, was the satisfaction which made life agreeable to her, and she was indifferent to the vanities of the vulgar. She bore misfortune with a dignity which never gave way for a single instant, and she had many trials. The most interesting society in Europe had become, from long habit, almost a necessity of her existence; yet, in 1811, she was exiled by command of Napoleon to a distance of forty leagues from Paris, and went to live with one servant and a child six years old, a niece of her husband, at the dull country town of Châlons-sur-Marne. The dread of Napoleon's power was so oppressive in those days that people avoided a political exile as men avoid a leper, but she bore her solitude and the dulness of the provincial town without a murmur. After ten months of this, she went to Lyons, where she met with one or two friends, and from Lyons she passed into Italy, where she lived chiefly at Rome

and Naples. The fall of the Empire in 1814 permitted
her to return to Paris after an exile of three years.*

Notwithstanding her poverty, Madame Récamier could
still contrive, by very strict economy, to live upon her
little income, and rent rooms to receive her friends.
Her most serious occupation was the education of her
niece, which went forward under her own eye, in all its
details, even in little household matters which are sometimes neglected by ladies of her rank in society.
Madame Récamier herself, though strict and orderly
about her expenses, had never possessed those practical
household accomplishments which are so common in the
middle classes in France; and she was very anxious that
her niece should be a thorough *ménagère*. She was
entirely above the two opposite vulgar errors which
would confine women to ornamental accomplishments on
the one hand, or else to household drudgery on the other.
She believed that the household knowledge was compatible with good mental culture, and she was determined that her niece should be wanting in neither. The
kind of life which Madame Récamier believed to be the
happiest and best for a woman was that which we have
already caught some glimpses of at Polémieux and St.
Germain du Mont d'Or, where the ladies read good literature, were thoroughly and unquestionably ladies in all
their thoughts and ways, and yet at the same time well

---

* The cause of her exile was simply that Napoleon objected to feminine influence, when it was not exercised in his own favor. For the same
reason, he had exiled Madame de Staël, whom Madame Récamier visited
at Coppet, a visit which irritated Napoleon. The beautiful Duchess of
Cheuvreux was exiled for having resisted an imperial order.

skilled in the useful labors of the house. These excellent home qualities seemed to her worth special endeavors for their attainment ; but what she most desired for her niece was a marriage of affection, which she considered far more conducive to happiness than the vanity of her own splendid but unsatisfying position. The reader may be glad to know that she completely succeeded in these good projects. I mention them because they throw some light upon what was best in her nature, and also because they give us a glimpse of that latent unhappiness which attended her singular mode of life.

I have said that Madame Récamier could still live sufficiently well to rent good rooms ; and this implies that her existence, though regulated by a severe economy, was still not without some of those elegancies which a lady does not easily relinquish. Unhappily, this modest degree of well-being was not destined to last for very long. A second financial reverse threw her into such a degree of pecuniary difficulty that it was impossible to keep up even this quiet manner of life ; and a second change, a new descent, had to be accepted. She bore this additional trial with her usual dignity and patience, and resolved at once to adapt herself to her altered circumstances. There was a religious house in the immediate neighborhood of Paris, called the Abbaye au Bois ; and, though she could not become a nun, she begged or hired a garret in the out-buildings of this establishment. Her own religious sentiments were gratified by the associations of the place ; and her choice of it marked at least a willingness to be considered as

retiring from the world. She was not sorry, perhaps, to
shield her reputation at the same time by her selection
of a religious building as her refuge. And now came
the most remarkable and (in reality, though not in outward appearance) the most triumphant period of this
extraordinary career. Wealth was gone, youth was gone.
Madame Récamier was now nothing but a middle-aged
woman living separately from her husband, in an out-of-
the-way garret, in a condition of avowed poverty; and
still, with the single exception of Madame de Staël, she
got more homage than any other woman in Europe.
With the materials in our possession, which are considerable, we who have never been brought within the
radius of her influence may have a difficulty in account-
ing for it. She had the reputation of the most tran-
scendent beauty, and her portrait by Gérard is still in
existence, — a portrait which was accepted as a likeness
by those who knew her, and yet it does not produce
upon the present generation the impression of a remarkably beautiful woman; and it is an open question
whether the lady on the canvas has any right to be
called beautiful at all. She is a fine-looking person,
une belle femme; but that is different. She looks healthy
and well grown, a well-developed, well-preserved specimen of humanity, which *poses* in a studiously graceful
attitude, according to what was thought classical under
the First Empire; but it astonishes us to think that her
face could make a fool of any man, yet she turned the
heads of the most experienced, and made slaves of them,
not for a month or a year, but for the term of their

natural lives. Again, as to her mental qualities, there can be no doubt that with reference to her aim in life she generally acted with great judgment ; * but this was more by feminine tact than by what could properly be called intellectual force. We have her letters, and what are they? She could write affectionately; she could be encouraging and sympathetic (it was her habit, her art, and each correspondent liked his own little dram of consolation) ; she valued her friends, and made it her business to preserve their friendship: but there is never a ray of real intellectual light in all her simple correspondence. She writes news, she acknowledges the receipt of news, she expresses her good wishes, she notices some very visible peculiarities on her travels, such as the numerous domestics of Italian grandees, and some oddities in their mode of life; but this is all. Now, if Madame Récamier had really been a superior woman, she had every imaginable stimulus to exhibit her superiority in her letters. They were addressed to some of the most cultivated men then living; and there was always a possibility that they might, at some future time, be made public.

The date of young Ampère's first meeting with Madame Récamier has been preserved by her niece, who was present. It was the 1st of January, 1820. The ladies were in their retreat at the Abbaye au Bois ; and there were only five gentlemen present (which was below the usual average), when young Ampère and his

---

* There is, however, one most remarkable instance to the contrary, which will be mentioned in its right place.

father arrived. André Ampère was by this time a great man ; but, besides this recommendation, he had the advantage of being the oldest and most intimate friend of Ballanche, who was a great friend of Madame Récamier, and she therefore gave him a particularly gracious reception. As for Jean Jacques, the mature hostess, being considerably more than twice his age, might have taken him simply for a boy ; but, young as he was, he had already some reputation for extraordinary attainments, and his conversational talent, which afterwards became one of his greatest powers, was already acceptable even in so exacting a circle as that of the Abbaye au Bois. He was dazzled by Madame Récamier, notwithstanding the extreme simplicity of her dress and the absence of all splendor in the little room ; and there is an anecdote of this first interview which reveals at once his boyish awkwardness and her delicate womanly tact. As she did him the honor to talk with him, he took a jasper paper-knife to play with, and managed so badly that he broke it. She, observing that the sight of the fragments embarrassed him, managed to get them, one after another, under her arm, as they lay on a little table, and to hide them away without his knowledge.

That evening fixed his fate. The hostess had only intended to be kind to the son of an illustrious man who was dear to her friend Ballanche ; but she was such a skilful artist in the use of feminine charm and influence, and her skill from long practice had become so much a part of herself, that she innocently subjugated poor Jean Jacques, who had never before talked to so sympathetic a listener. From that hour till the date of Madame Récamier's death, a space of nearly thirty years, Jean Jacques could never be happy for a week, and scarcely even for a day, unless he talked with her. Those who knew the lady already were not in the least surprised by this fresh evidence of her fascination: they were accustomed to see men subjugated, and an instance more or less excited scarcely a remark. Madame Récamier's niece, who was present, only makes the general observation that " few escaped from that all-powerful charm, of which the truest and most attentive kindness was the principal influence, and which, coming from an elevated and delicate soul, took hold upon what was best and highest in your own heart."

It has occurred to me sometimes, in thinking about this remarkable friendship, to wonder how much of it may have been due to the melancholy event which took place by the river Saône so far back as the year 1803. If Julie had lived, her child would have found in his own home that kindly sympathy and interest which only the tenderness of a woman can ever bestow in its perfection. His father loved him as a father may love his boy; but André Ampère was absorbed in his own studies, and was the most absent of men. The grandmother was dead; and, even if she had been living, still there was a certain austerity in her character which was not what Jean Jacques required. Of the maiden aunt, Josephine Ampère, we know little. The other aunt, the intelligent and high-minded Élise Carron, had followed her sister Julie to the grave quite prematurely. It is clear that young Ampère, living amongst men and boys, enjoyed at the age of nineteen very little sympathy indeed; and it is equally evident that his susceptible and delicate feelings, for he had the feelings of a poet without a poet's creative genius, were waiting to be touched by the feminine influence, as the strings of a silent harp are waiting for the fingers of its mistress. The first influence of Madame Récamier was evidently maternal. Jean Jacques had never known what it is to be listened to with full interest and full understanding by a woman; and, after all reserves about Madame Récamier's intellect, it is certain that she had acquired the habit of always seeming to understand her worshippers. Having once tasted this new pleasure, and felt its strengthening influence, the boy wanted to taste it again, as one returns to a wine which is at the same time tonic and delicious. She, on her part, being a mature woman, and surrounded by middle-aged men, found a pleasant freshness in the enthusiasm of a gifted youth, who, with his beardless face and simple ignorance of the world, looked even more boyish than he really was. There is no reason to believe that her culpability went farther than this, and at first she may have done more good than harm to Jean Jacques, by stimulating what was best in him, and by admitting him into the highly cultivated circle which surrounded her at the Abbaye au Bois; but such a friendship as theirs was dangerous for him, though not for her. " It is a great happiness," wrote one of the wisest clergymen who ever adorned the Church of England, "to form a sincere friendship with a woman; but a friendship amongst persons of different sexes rarely or never takes place in this country. The austerity of our manners hardly admits of such a connection, — compatible with the most perfect innocence, and a source of the highest possible delight to those who are fortunate enough to obtain it."* J. J. Ampère was formed by nature for such friendships, and in the course of his life he enjoyed the affectionate esteem and regard of several excellent women, eminent both for their intelligence and their position in society ; but his friendship for Madame Récamier was too predominant, absorbed too much of his time and thought, and reduced him to the position of a mere satellite among other satellites, going round and round the luminary which had become the centre of his earthly existence, without any hope of rest in an ultimate union. Again, whilst she with her passionless nature was always calm, her influence sometimes agitated him; and there were times in his life when he painfully felt his bonds, though he had no more power to break them than the earth has to liberate itself from the invisible tether of gravitation. Madame Récamier's worst fault in this intimacy appears to have been that insatiable appetite for homage which was part of her natural character; and young Ampère's most lamentable weakness was a total want of mental independence. He could master himself so far as to regulate his behavior, he could even, by a strong effort, command sufficient strength of will to banish himself for months from her presence; but his thoughts turned to her inces-

* Sydney Smith, in his Memoir.

santly wherever he went, and he never had an hour of freedom.

Towards the close of the year 1823, Madame Récamier went to Rome, with the intention of staying there some months, and took lodgings in the Via Babuino, opposite the Greek Church. It is scarcely necessary to inform the reader that her evening receptions went on just as if she had been at the Abbaye au Bois. "Every evening," says Madame Cheuvreux, "she was surrounded by intimate friends, such as M. Dugas Montbel, the Duke of Laval-Montmorency, M. de Givré, the Abbé Canova, Guérim, Léopold Robert, Schnetz, Delécluze, &c. Ballanche and Mlle. Amélie remain with Madame Récamier. Jean Jacques passes part of his days with them. And so the Abbaye au Bois was reconstituted in Italy."

Madame Récamier has been compared to a queen with her court, and the comparison is not inaccurate. By her beauty and tact, she exercised a sort of royalty; but this was only a part of her means of influence. She was also, in reality, though not in name, the president of a literary club, constituted, as the smaller French clubs usually are, for the purpose of conversation. The members of this little circle found it convenient to have her for a centre around which they might group themselves. She presided admirably well, and the deference with which she was always treated kept the members of the circle in order. Wherever she happened to be, any one member felt sure of meeting other members; and this is evidently the true explanation of the rapidity with which her circle reconstituted itself in Italy. If she had been an immoral woman, a circle of this kind could never have held together, for obvious reasons.

Jean Jacques immediately set to work to make the most of his time in Rome. Young as he was, he already led his own life, pursuing his studies with great ardor, and refreshing himself with pleasures as improving as his studies ; indeed, in such happy days as those he spent in Rome, the distinction between the two becomes difficult to define. " Rome is a very good place to work in," he writes to his father ; "and, if people spoke French there, it would be the right place for an École Polytechnique." Speaking of his own way of passing his time, he says it is impossible for life to be more fully occupied. He has an Italian master with whom he reads Dante and practises himself in speaking. He enjoys excellent weather, the finest winter known in Rome for years ; and he avails himself of it to study the ruins, thus beginning at his early age those long labors in Roman archæology, which were ultimately to be the materials for his most important work. He had the courage to begin a new tragedy, entitled " Rachel," which he calls " La Juive " familiarly in letters to his father. " When the fire of my admiration for Rome has subsided a little, I shall take the chisel and give the first strokes to the marble. I have been working on the plan." His father took the warmest possible interest in his literary projects ; and, when a few pages of verse were composed, they were sent at once to Paris for the too indulgent paternal criticism. The correspondence at this time is interesting, as a picture of the relation between father

and son. It is melancholy on the father's side; for Jean
Jacques is every thing to him, and his absence leaves a
dreary void. "Your absence," he writes, "produces in
me the same effect as the longing for the native land
on the Swiss and Lapps. Ballanche has spoken of the
celestial nostalgia, I am tormented by the paternal."
The young man, on his part, writes with the cheerfulness of youth amidst the excitement of new and interesting scenes. He promises to return, so as to pass the
following winter with his father, and talks in a tone of
affectionate pleasantry about the tragedy which he is
just beginning, and which he will read when they come
together. Then there will be the impressions of Italy
to recount; and meanwhile he tries to satisfy the paternal heart as well as he can by letters, those welcome
palliatives of absence.

To avoid the dangerous summer air of Rome, the
travellers go to Naples, traversing the dangerous parts
of the route with an escort of eighty Austrian soldiers,
and marching by moonlight to avoid the effects of the
heat and the malaria from the Pontine marshes. At
Naples, Jean Jacques is in excellent health. "I have
never," he writes, "enjoyed so much health and so much
physical well-being." His existence is that of a poet:
he passes part of his time on the water after sunset,
when the ripple plays gently about the boat, and every
stroke of the oar flashes phosphorescent light. "I do
not believe there can be any thing more delightful in
any place in the world," he writes: "the nights of Greece
and the East cannot be more beautiful. We shall go to

see Pompeii by one of these lovely nights. The illusion
will be more perfect in the ancient city at the hour when
all the inhabitants may be supposed to have quitted the
temples and theatres and to be asleep. I hope to write
here, for there is less to be seen than at Rome; and, in
the long, dreamy days on the seashore, the waves will
bring me many a verse."

Jean Jacques found so much happiness in this dreamy,
poetic life at Naples that it was difficult to tear himself
away from it. The days passed in pleasant study;
the evenings were spent happily on the water, or with
Madame Récamier's little circle; it was still permissible
to dream of a poet's fame, and in the mean while he
could afford to wait a little for the laurel, in the full
enjoyment of his youth. The influence of the natural
beauty around him, and also the still more powerful
influence of the lady whom he conversed with every
day, disposed him to a return towards religious sentiments. "I feel here," he writes to his father, "a return
to religious emotions and ideas, which in reality are what
is best in us; and, although my mind has a repugnance
for what is exclusive and terrible in certain beliefs, my
heart is more than ever disposed to humble itself, and be
tender under the hand of a just and good God." Then,
speaking of Madame Récamier, he says, "I owe her
whatever good sentiments I may possess." The truth
is that this lady, in a gentle, unobtrusive way, tried
at that time and constantly afterwards to bring Jean
Jacques within the influence of religious ideas. In
reality, the difference between them may not have been

quite so wide as she imagined; for, although he was not able to give intellectual assent to the dogmas of the Church, he earnestly desired to believe as much as he could, having a strong inducement in the pleasure which his more perfect orthodoxy would have given to his father and to Madame Récamier.

He left her at Naples early in November (1824), to return to his father; but the separation was very hard to bear, and he wrote the most despairing letters. He travelled by way of Rome, Ferrara, Padua, to Venice, his melancholy becoming darker and darker. Imagine some faithful dog that has been too kindly treated for its own good, and is now sent away to a distance; imagine what the dog would say if it could only write, and you have these letters. It is a curious evidence of the remarkable absence of enmity in the Récamier circle that one of the first persons Jean Jacques goes to see, on his arrival in Paris, is M. Récamier himself, to whom he presents a gift from his wife, a pin, with which M. Récamier is " charmed."

Having seen for the present enough of young Ampère's weakness, it may be right, in justice to him, to look now on his stronger side, which was a resolute intellectual industry. Few men whose lives are laid open to us in detail will bear so searching an examination as to the use made of the passing days. If happy, he works merrily, and enriches his mind even by his recreations; if unhappy, he works with determined energy to relieve himself from the pressure of painful thoughts. In either case, the result is always an advance; and this is how it came to pass that in his mature life J. J. Ampère was one of the most cultivated men in Europe. Even so early as the year 1825, the excellent intellectual habits, the well-chosen intellectual principles, which led to this result, were already formed or accepted; and it is scarcely too much to say that by their help he gained a clear advance of ten years over the majority of intellectual workers, who seldom attain to this steadiness in harness much before middle age. The three great needs of his life, as he himself defined them, were " friendship, imagination, and labor." Of these, the most disturbing was imagination, including the belief that he was a poet, which led to a waste of effort in versification. " All my time is my own," he writes from Paris in January, 1825 : " my work is prepared, but I have not the fire necessary for its execution. I sit down to my table and make a few verses, perceiving soon after that verses so manufactured are never good; and then I stop short for fear of disgusting myself with my work in spoiling it." Soon afterwards he writes, " For some time past, I have not been able to make a verse; " and again, " It would be too pleasant if one could always compose : one would produce many a masterpiece, and life would slip away happily; but alas! for one hour of poetic fervor, how many hours are pale and cold ! " This intermittence of productive power would not of itself be a proof that Jean Jacques had no poetic inspiration, for that is usually intermittent; but these lost sittings, these futile efforts, have a discouraging effect upon the mind. Ampère braced himself, after them, by the study of Hebrew and

Chinese. A fairly happy day was a day spent in peaceful work : a perfectly happy day was one in which, after energetic labor, came the longed-for conversation of the well-known circle. On the 14th of February, he writes : "What a good day it has been ! Splendid weather, which I admired from the garden ! I have made verses, read Chinese and Hebrew. If there had been only a little of the Abbaye au Bois this evening, all would have been completely to my taste." As to amusement, like most men who have tasted the superior satisfactions of congenial work, he found that mere pleasures were insufficient. "That which is only amusement," he writes, "is a very poor affair ; and, after all my attempts in that direction, I come back to my books, to my studies." One of his favorite pursuits at this time was to read the history of France by the light of the principal memoirs or contemporary chronicles, whilst he followed the literary history of his country, at the same time, by studying the principal literary remains of each epoch ; and in this way, at an age when most men are absorbed entirely by the present, he acquired the faculty, so useful to him afterwards as an historical writer, of throwing himself back into the past, and living in it by the intellect and imagination.

Madame Récamier's maternal interest in young Ampère's intellectual pursuits has been the means of giving us many details about his ways of work. Here is an especially valuable paragraph from one of his letters to her : —

"You like me to speak about my labors, to tell you

all my studies, as a schoolboy tells his mamma.* Well, here is what just at present seems to me the finest thing in the world, and an infallible means of arriving almost at universal knowledge. It is very simple, and consists only in remarking in each book that I read what are the most important points, to concentrate all my attention upon them, to engrave them in my memory, and endeavor to forget all the rest entirely. To this I add another condition, which is to read, on each subject and in each language, nothing but the best books. It seems to me that by this method it may be possible, without uselessly overburdening the mind, to acquire very accurate and very various knowledge. I have begun to apply this system to various works, and am delighted with it."

There is nothing very original in this, though Jean Jacques may have discovered it for himself; but the wonder is that he should have paid attention to such a matter so early in life. Young men rarely have any conception whatever of the necessity for economizing intellectual effort; and they seldom realize the truth that the carrying power of the memory is limited, and that a wise man will not burden it uselessly.

With all his love of learning, Jean Jacques hated pedantry, both in early life and afterwards. His tone was that of a genial, cultivated man of the world, who read much and observed much without losing the elas-

---

* The reader will observe how this confirms what has been said about Madame Récamier's art in attaching people to her by taking an interest in their occupations, and also about the maternal character of her friendship for Jean Jacques, which he recognizes himself.

ticity of his mind. His love of ladies' society may have
saved him from the hopeless dulness which is often the
penalty of learning, and the intelligent conversations at
the Abbaye au Bois may have given him a distaste for
intercourse in which there was less of sweetness and
light. At the end of January (1825), he dines with some
of the cleverest young men in Paris, "l'élite de la jeunesse française," and they seem to him "terribly pedantic."
He is irritated by the disdainful tone which they adopt
with reference to their own epoch, he is vexed by their
scornful inquiries, "Where is poetry to come from?
Who has genius?" He feels tempted to answer, "Have
genius yourselves, and let us see what you can do!"
When we remember that those learned youths were
despising the natural gifts of their countrymen exactly
five years before the brilliant epoch of 1830, it is enough
to deliver us from the gloomy forebodings of pedantic
criticism at all times.

Madame Récamier returned from Italy in May, 1825,
and went to spend the autumn in a rural retreat at the
Vallée aux Loups, which had been arranged by Chateaubriand when he composed "The Martyrs." From what
the reader already knows of J. J. Ampère, he will at once
infer that the young gentleman would exhibit strong
rustic tastes at the same time, and so it turned out; for
he went to stay at the village of Aulnay with one of his
friends, M. de Latouche, a dramatic author. Aulnay
was quite near to the Vallée aux Loups; so Jean Jacques
could easily walk over and take his place in the friendly
circle, which, wherever Madame Récamier happened to

be, immediately gathered around her, as bees do round their queen.

That Vallée aux Loups seems to have been a dangerous place, not on account of wolves, but from the facility with which a sentiment will grow and gain strength in the retirement of the country. Sainte-Beuve said that, in the summer or autumn following the first presentation of Jean Jacques at the Abbaye au Bois, Madame Récamier spent some time in the valley, and Jean Jacques went to stay there too with his friend De Jussieu, who had a small residence there. He returned to Paris a fortnight before she did; and, when he met her again at the Abbaye, she delicately hinted that country walks were somewhat dangerous, — that, if their stay in the valley had lasted longer, "there might have been a reason for apprehending the beginning of a romance for a poetic heart." Madame Récamier, at that time, had no notion that her young guest would make himself miserable about a middle-aged woman like her; but with a remarkable want of feminine perspicacity she imagined that J. J. had fallen in love, or had begun to fall in love, with her young niece, Mlle. Amélie Récamier, who was always by her side.* Thrown off his guard by the suddenness with which such an entirely new idea was presented to him, Jean Jacques lost for a moment his

* Sainte-Beuve, who knew Madame Récamier, believed that she really imagined her niece to be the attraction; but there is still a possibility that a clever woman like her might have feigned such a belief simply in order to clear up the situation. It is possible, too, that she might have looked with favor upon a marriage between J. J. Ampère and her niece, and that she may have taken this means of suggesting the idea to his mind.

habitual self-control, burst into sobs, and exclaimed, "Ah! it was not for her!" That crisis over, he had recovered, as we have seen, his modest position as one of the members (the youngest member) of the Récamier circle, and had had courage enough to deny himself even that satisfaction by returning from Naples to Paris, from a sense of duty to his father. The visit to the Vallée aux Loups in 1825 renewed the old danger. Jean Jacques could control his feelings in Paris, where he was simply one of a conversation party; but in the country he saw more of the lady, and this did him harm by making him feel too keenly the painful nature of his position, and that fatal throwing-away of his youth in a hopeless attachment, which in moments of bitterest frankness he acknowledged to himself, without having the power to withdraw finally from its influence. "What can I become," he asked, "with the faculties that I feel within myself, this need of activity, this energy for work, and that other something, I know not what, at the bottom of my soul, which extinguishes all, and is inflicting dull death upon me gradually? Oh! I know well what it is: it is a life badly begun, a wasted youth. Oh! if I could but have seen in her a friend only, if my heart had not worn itself in painful dreams, it would not have been languid and broken as it is now. I suffer through my own fault, but I suffer horribly. Full of the wish to work, I can do nothing. I try all the old remedies, languages, sciences, conversation, reading; and all has less hold upon me than in the past." Elsewhere he says, "In my purgatory, I do like Dante, who stimulated

himself when traversing the circles of pain by pronouncing the name of Beatrice."

Such a condition as this could not have lasted for
very long without weakening the foundation of the
mind and character, and it may have been a good thing
ultimately for the patient that his stay near the Vallée
aux Loups in 1825 brought his malady to an acute
crisis.   The lady, on her part, remained as cool and
self-possessed as ever.   She had her own policy to follow, which was to maintain her power over as many
subjects as possible ; and she was not going to sacrifice
this policy to the folly of the youngest of them.   Her
married life with M. Récamier was merely nominal.   He
had given her, at her father's request, the protection of
his name in the terror of 1793, a time when she was a
mere child ; but he had lived his own life since then, in
complete independence of hers, and with scarcely even
a pretension to the position of her husband.   For a moment, Jean Jacques conceived the hope that this marriage might be dissolved by a divorce, and that he might
profit by the dissolution of the tie, — an idea which only
betrays his boyish ignorance of the lady's nature.   In
1811, she had refused a royal suitor, Prince Augustus of
Prussia, who had indulged his imagination by the same
project.   Later in life, when a widow, she refused even
Chateaubriand, who had certainly more influence over
her than any one else.   As for J. J. Ampère, she looked
upon him simply as a clever and interesting boy, whom
she patronized by encouraging his studies, and by developing in her circle his considerable talent for conversa-

tion. He was a part of her state, as a young groom is part of a rich man's state, in a house where there are twenty servants (with the difference that he would not have been so easy to replace) ; and she did not wish to diminish herself by the reduction of her establishment, which would have resulted from his dismissal. She, therefore, whilst giving him little or no encouragement, used all her tact to calm him, and yet retain him in her service ; and, as she knew him better than he knew her, she so far succeeded that, from that day to the day of her death, he contented himself with her friendship, and, though he might be neither husband nor lover, remained devoted to her in age and infirmity with an unshakable fidelity. Poets have used the simile of brooks or flowers and the moon: such a simile could never have been more aptly applied than to the lives of this man and that woman. The uneasy current of his existence, twisting hither and thither, vexed by many obstacles, owed the lights which sparkled upon it and the shadows which were cast upon it to a luminary, cold, remote, unattainable, which shone with equal lustre on his rivals.

> The moon looks
> On many brooks :
> The brook can see no moon but this.

The elder Ampère infinitely regretted to see his son's strength of affection wasting itself year after year on a friendship in which he gave all and received a mere fraction in return ; and remembering the days of his own wedded life with Julie, the happiest of his existence, he

said to himself that if only Jean Jacques could be persuaded to love some good girl who would accept him,
all might yet be well, the young man's life would have
its centre in his own home, and his sentiments towards
Madame Récamier would subside into a reasonable
friendship.   André Ampère had found precisely the
young lady whom his best judgment approved in Mlle.
Clémentine Cuvier, daughter of the famous naturalist.
All accounts agree in describing her as a person to
whom a prudent man of cultivated intelligence might
gladly   intrust   his   happiness.   She   had   inherited
some of her father's rarest intellectual powers, as he
himself acknowledged ; and, though not beautiful, her
countenance had the " sweetness and light" which
always win regard.   André Ampère had an absolute
confidence in her, and it became the strongest wish of
his life that Jean Jacques should be her husband.   The
young lady herself, in the opinion of an observant
witness (Mlle. Amélie Récamier), would not have
been averse to this project.   Her manners, like those of
every well-bred young lady in her nation and class, were
extremely modest and retiring ; but she still betrayed a
certain preference for Jean Jacques in talking with him
about literature or science more willingly than with
any one else.   The same witness is of opinion that Jean
Jacques had a sentiment of " very tender respect" for
the young lady, which might easily have gained power
over his heart, had he not disliked Baron Cuvier's domi-
neering spirit, which made him aware that to become
his son-in-law would be equivalent to the sacrifice of his

independence. A passage occurs in a letter to his father, written about a year after his first meeting with Mlle. Cuvier, in which he says, " I had for a moment an idea which passed away like so many others, as others may possibly take its place. This is my nature; and it ought to be a reason for you to look with apprehension on the irrevocable state which you are anxious that I should enter upon. My head must have time to ripen and my character to form itself before I can engage myself for ever without madness." Behind these objections, the reader perceives the real one, which was the difficulty of finding in any young lady's society the charm of Madame Récamier's conversation. This was a terrible disappointment to André Ampère, whose letters about this time to his friend Bredin are quite painful to read. He speaks of being " torn " by these circumstances, of being " smothered with sorrows," and says that his scientific labors, successful as they are, cannot console him for the loss of all the happiness which he had dreamed of for his son. This grief lasted permanently ; and when in July, 1827, André Ampère learned that Mlle. Cuvier was engaged to be married to M. Duparquet, the news cut him to the quick. " I cannot express how much sorrow this has caused me," he writes to his son. A month later, before this project of marriage was realized, the young lady was suddenly taken ill, and began to spit blood. André Ampère saw her a few days after this, and was struck with her extreme paleness, and with an expression of melancholy upon her face. " Her sister had put a rose in her hair, which seemed half faded. All this gave me a gloomy presentiment." During another visit, he saw the young lady lying on a sofa, paler than ever, and with a great difficulty of breathing. Notwithstanding her engagement, she gave a painful pleasure to Ampère by showing, through her questions, a great interest in his son, then travelling in the north of Europe. " I felt," he wrote, "that I was listening to her for the last time; and her interest in you touched me the more, that the arrival of her betrothed did not prevent her from continuing her questions." She was never married, but died at the end of September, 1827, as much to the grief of André Ampère as to that of her own parents. During her illness, Jean Jacques said, " I would give all in the world to know that she was out of danger and happy with M. Duparquet." This last expression shows how completely he had abandoned the project of marriage for himself.

On the intellectual side, notwithstanding temporary suspensions of mental power which resulted from the troubles of his affections, Jean Jacques had the satisfaction of equipping himself very sufficiently. In 1825, he wrote the following account of his studies : " Now, for the first time in my life, I find leisure to do nearly all that I desire. I have applied myself to the study of mathematics, not to become a mathematician, but to open my mind to this sort of conception, and gain an entrance into a world of new combinations."

" As to languages, I am nearly sure now of knowing all which are worth studying. I read history to gain a conception of each epoch, and in order to interest myself in every thing which belongs to it."

These are few words ; but they trace out a very extensive field of study, already in the writer's possession, though not yet so fully cultivated as he intended it to be in course of time. His projects of study and labor were always on a great scale ; and although he retained a youthful absence of pretension, and was never at any time a pedant, or any thing like one, still he had vast intellectual ambition. Even so early as 1826, he had conceived the idea of a general history of literature, involving almost infinite study in different languages, and in different countries ; for long journeys were never an impediment to him, and he knew the importance of working on the spot. His Italian labors had already been well begun in Rome ; but Rome was too closely connected in his mind with certain experiences of sentiment for him to return to it willingly in 1826, so he prudently took the virile resolution of bracing his mind by a student's life in Germany, far from the Vallée aux Loups and the beloved Abbaye au Bois, in a land, too, where the circle of the Abbaye would not be likely to constitute itself, as it did in Italy. He quitted Paris on the 6th of August, 1826, without revealing this grave determination ; simply informing his friends that he was going to the Mont d'Or, near Lyons, with the De Jussieus.

When Jean Jacques travelled with his young friends Alexis and Adrien de Jussieu, they went a great deal on foot and out of the beaten tracks. Ampère was an excellent walker; but Alexis de Jussieu was much more than that, he was a wonderful runner, and could keep up with a diligence for hours. He did almost all the road between Mende and St. Jean du Gard (twenty leagues) on foot, running before the carriage except up hill, when he rested; but it was especially down hill that the postilions admired him. One of them, wanting to leave him behind, whipped his five mules to a gallop, but Alexis kept ahead of them. Who would not rather possess that young man's physical powers than the handsomest equipage in Paris?

At Avignon, they were rather horrified by learning that the room they occupied was the very chamber in which Marshal Brune was assassinated.* The innkeeper had sustained a siege of five hours to defend the Marshal, and was himself wounded by the stroke of a hatchet. His wife, his mother, and his daughter all died in consequence of the fear and excitement of that day.

The travellers went to Grenoble, through the mountains, sometimes travelling where there was not even a foot-path. In one outlandish place, they became objects of suspicion, and nobody would give them a lodging. When they begged to be allowed to lie on straw, the suspicions increased, and they were surrounded by fifty peasants and a policeman. At length, the *maire* appeared, luckily an intelligent man; and, when he had

---

* Marshal Brune was shot in August, 1815, by the ringleaders of a royalist mob, in the White Terror. The murderers were powerful enough to intimidate the local authorities, who signed a declaration that the Marshal had committed suicide.

talked a few minutes with the young gentlemen, he solved the difficulty by inviting them to his own house, gave them a supper and three excellent beds, and detained them afterwards for another twenty-four hours. This *maire* was a character, famous in those parts as the " King of the Mountains," where he exercised a beneficent despotism singularly independent of the Government, which he sometimes resisted in the interest of his people. Ampère speaks of him as a character whom Walter Scott might have invented, "simple, frank, loyal, and full of natural good sense." Jean Jacques next visited the Chartreuse, which strongly impressed him. Here is his description of the night service there : —

" We came back to a frugal supper (from a walk amongst the rocks), and then they put us in our cells till eleven o'clock. The sound of bells awakened us in our first sleep; and, whilst still dizzy with the sudden awakening, we passed through the long corridors, guided towards the chapel by religious chants. One little lamp burned by itself in the midst of the immense nave. All those pale faces under white cowls, lighted by a few lanterns; the gravity of the voices ; the lugubrious monotony of the litanies; the thought of these lives of solitude, prayer, and sacrifice, — oppressed the heart."

Each of the brethren has a bedroom, a little study with bookshelves, a workshop, turner's tools, and a little garden. Had it not been for their meagre fare, Ampère said he would almost have consented to become one of them.

After a six weeks' tour in France and Switzerland, he arrived at Strasburg on the 8th of October, 1826, and afterwards wrote an interesting letter to Madame Récamier from Coblentz, where his sense of landscape beauty was enchanted with new experiences in his boat voyage on the Rhine from Mayence. " There was not a minute to lose," he said, "for every stroke of the oar brought us to a new picture." This boat voyage lasted from dawn till moonlight; and during the whole of it, whilst *seeing* the castled crags and vineyards of the Rhine, Jean Jacques was travelling again in memory and imagination through those Italian scenes which were dangerously dear to him from their association with Madame Récamier. "Almost at every instant," he wrote, "the contrast of the climates, of my situation then and now, awakened in me melancholy recollections."

Ampère began by establishing himself at Bonn, where he was introduced to Schlegel, who received him well, but seemed at first to avoid literary conversation as a sort of pedantry, and to pose as knight and gentleman with servants in livery and the yellow ribbon of Sweden ; but soon afterwards he invited Jean Jacques to meet an Englishman, and these representatives of three nations talked together for six hours at a time " like magpies, or like people who have known what conversation is at Paris, and are transplanted together to Bonn." Ampère was lucky in arriving at Bonn just when Schlegel was about to begin a course of lectures on the German language and literature; and he was still more fortunate in being there whilst Niebuhr lectured on Roman History, a subject of special interest and importance for our hero. He had not been long at Bonn before he got into regular habits of life ; and, as his self-imposed exile in Germany was intended to be a course of discipline, he had the courage to take it as such from the first, and to seek his satisfaction in the strict fulfilment of his duty to himself as a student. The regularity of his labors soon produced a beneficial effect upon his mind ; and he not only made good intellectual progress, but he also found himself calmer and stronger morally than he had been during the two or three preceding years. He gave himself the innocent pleasure of writing an account of his studies to Madame Récamier, but there is no painful agitation in his letters.

"I have not an instant of *ennui.* I follow four courses of lectures every day, each of which gives me the same pleasure that you find in a new play. I frequently meet men of the highest merit, who are most kind and attentive to me. I read numbers of new books which interest me. I have the pleasant sense of progress. My imagination, which for several years has painfully tormented me, seems to be cured. My mind, given up to itself, is disposed for all tranquil sentiments, for all wise and generous resolutions. Well, in this equilibrium of the faculties, so long desired as a dream, in this life of my own choice, my thoughts still turn to Paris, to the time when I shall be there again. I hope that it may be possible to bring back with me the calm which I enjoy, and to embellish it by friendship."

"I have learned three things here," he says, towards

the conclusion of the same letter, "the extent of my ignorance, what I had to learn, and how to set about learning it."

"One is confounded," he says elsewhere, "with the indispensable equipment of knowledge that we *dispense* with in France." In February, 1827, he says, "For the first time in my life, I understand what it is to learn." His life at this time had the regularity of clockwork.

"At Bonn, all my days resemble each other perfectly. At half-past six, they come to light my stove and my lamp. I put on a dressing-gown, and read in bed till eight ; then I get up and work. At noon there is Niebuhr's lecture, at one o'clock I dine, at two there is Schlegel's lecture ; then I take a walk, and attend two other professors. At seven I study at home, and go out in the evening when I am invited to tea at some professor's house. Once a week, I go to the theatre. *Voilà toute ma vie.*"

Ampère's visits to the theatre were not likely to disquiet Madame Récamier; but he was apprehensive that she might be rather alarmed by his attendance at the lectures of German theologians, who then as now were pursuing their exegetic labors. On Shrove Tuesday, he went to hear a lecture on exegesis given specially for himself, and wrote to Madame Récamier that, even if it scandalized her, such theology was edifying enough for the *mardi gras.* This is only one of many little evidences that the lady tried to exercise a theological influence over her admirer, and keep him within the limits of Roman Catholic orthodoxy, but not, it must be

ıdmitted, with much success; for Jean Jacques had a too
omprehensive intellectual curiosity to confine himself
:asily within the teaching of a single sect: and as he
ʌisited other countries and learned other languages, so, in
:he same spirit of inquiry and comparison, he interested
himself in other theologies than that in which he had
been born.

He accompanied Schlegel's English friend Bonnard
to Cologne in the Paris diligence, the very same diligence which was actually to arrive in Paris on the following Friday; and he felt it hard not to go on, but
manfully returned to Bonn, in spite of momentary weakness. He quitted Bonn in April, after having formed
several friendships with Germans whom he greatly liked,
as soon as the difficulty of language began to be surmounted. He had met with so much cordiality and
kindness that it was impossible to quit the place without
regret. However, he was leaving interesting Germans
to meet the most interesting man in all Germany. "In
a fortnight," he said, "I shall be with Goethe."

It had happened some time before that Jean Jacques
had written two articles in the Paris *Globe* newspaper
about Goethe, which the poet had himself translated for
his Weimar journal. "I found the great man very kind,"
says Jean Jacques, "very simple, in very good health,
and very amiable." During his stay at Weimar, Ampère
saw Goethe very frequently, dining three times with him
in the course of a single week at those select little
dinners given to few friends, to which strangers were
seldom invited. What astonished Jean Jacques most in

Goethe was his general interest in every thing, and his knowledge of all that was going on both in France and Germany. Jean Jacques heard him talk for several hours together with a fire and *verve* "fifty years younger than his age." He talked about the last French vaude-villes as if he had just seen them acted, knew by heart the songs of Béranger, and missed nothing that was going on in Germany. Goethe, on his part, was greatly pleased with the distinguished young Frenchman. "Ampère," he said, "has placed his mind on such a high level that he has left far beneath him all the national prejudices, all the apprehensions, all the con-fined ideas of many of his fellow-countrymen : by his ways of thinking, he is much more a citizen of the world than a citizen of Paris. I foresee the day when there will be thousands of men who will think like him."

This prediction is already to some extent fulfilled, the highest culture becoming daily more cosmopolitan, be-cause it must necessarily take account of what other nations contribute to the common stock of knowledge or production ; and we have now the inestimable facility of railways. Unfortunately, war comes to counteract the reconciling effects of the nobler studies, and to revive national hostility, even towards neutrals. The war of 1870 not only made Frenchmen hate Germans, but it made them sore against the English, because they had remained neutral ; whilst the Germans despised the French because their army had been beaten, and they despised the English because their army was too small to be set against the forces of Germany.

"Goethe is prodigious," said Ampère : " he interests himself in every thing, has ideas about every thing, and is ready to admire whatever may be worth admiring. With his pure white dressing-gown which makes him look like a great white sheep, between his son, his daughter-in-law, and his two grandchildren, who play with him whilst he talks of Schiller, of their labors in common, of all that he wished to do, of all that he would have done, of his own works, his intentions, and his recollections, he is the most interesting and the most amiable of men. He is naïvely conscious of his fame in a manner which can displease no one, because he concerns himself about the talents of others, and is really alive to all good things which are produced in all departments of literature."

Ampère's last interview with Goethe left a strong impression on his mind. " The last hour that we passed together was really solemn and touching. We were seated on the same bench in the garden of a little rustic house, from which there is a view of the park, and where he wrote 'Iphigenia,' forty years ago. All the trees were planted by him : we were seated under them looking at the park, as it was lighted by the last rays of evening, the hour that you love best. He was serene and even gay, talking to me with that delicate irony which suits him so well. I thought to myself that this kind and amiable old man was the greatest of living poets, that he was very old, that it was perhaps a farewell ; for who knows if I shall ever come back to Weimar, and, if I come back, who knows if I shall find him there?"

" In the evening, I went to walk with several other people in the park; and we went near his little house. The window of his room was lighted : he was reading and working still. I was pleased to quit Weimar with this impression."

It was with reference to these letters about Goethe that Madame Récamier committed a lamentable and almost inconceivable indiscretion, which vexed Jean Jacques more than he could have thought it possible for any action of hers to vex him. Her niece gives some account of this, but omits all mention of his irritation. Madame Récamier had shown one of Ampère's letters from Weimar to Henri de Latouche, who asked her permission to print an extract from it in the *Globe* newspaper. To this she foolishly consented, and the extract appeared immediately, with some modifications which were any thing but improvements. Nothing could have been more disagreeable for Ampère. He had written to his correspondent in the *abandon* of intimate friendship, wishing to amuse her, and therefore talking about Goethe in a manner which would have been most unbecoming, if addressed to all the *élite* of Europe, — especially unbecoming on account of the great man's recent hospitable attention to him. Ampère had lightly criticised, or rather attempted to describe, a very fanciful work of Goethe's old age, which the poet had permitted him to read in manuscript. His description was by no means unfavorable, on the whole ; but he happened to mention "*bizarrerie*" and "*obscurité*" as amongst its characteristics, and he did not exactly like to see these words printed in a newspaper which was read by Goethe himself. The most distressing bit, however, in the reprint, was the following : —

" But you will believe, if I go on, that I have caught the *manie admirative* of the Germans for Goethe : nevertheless, I have not yet got to the point of the good lady with whom I am living here, who fell into raptures because the abundance of the great man's thoughts was such that he required a secretary ! To have a secretary, —that was unexampled !"

The words "*manie admirative*" were enough to wound the feelings of all literary Germany ; and the anecdote of the " good lady," though amusing, was not a thing to be printed, because she could be so easily identified at Weimar. " Do you think," asks Ampère, " it is agreeable to me to expose to the ridicule of a small town a respectable person in whose house, or rather in whose family, I have lived a month, who has bestowed attentions and cares upon me which are almost maternal, and who has given me several letters of recommendation for Berlin, for which she has been strangely rewarded ? In Weimar, it is as if her name had been printed ; for everybody knows where I lodged."

The letter goes on in quite a severe tone, and contains even this terrible sentence: "The moral is, that we must stick to principles ; and that if stealing is never permissible, which I have some little difficulty in admitting, it is far more certain that it can never be allowable to print fifteen hundred copies of what is written in the *abandon* of confidence and friendship." This from

J. J. Ampère to Madame Récamier! This from the worshipper to the goddess! Can there be any more *cultus* after this? Is not the idol overthrown, and seen to be only a woman, unreliable and indiscreet?

The irritation was extreme, and the foolish little feminine treason very hard to bear; but it did Jean Jacques immense good by loosening a little the chain which bound him to the Abbaye au Bois. He wrote immedi‐ately to the Chancellor Müller to beg his intervention to set matters right with Goethe. It is easy to see from his letter what a torture the whole business was to him.

He arrived at Berlin before the end of May, and remained there till the 7th of July, greatly enjoying the hospitality of the Prussian capital, where his father's European fame procured him an immediate welcome to the most interesting society, opening all doors. His own personal qualities, and the interest which intel‐lectual people always take in young men of high attain‐ments who evidently have a brilliant career before them, enabled him to use these opportunities to the utmost. "Your name is a talisman everywhere," he wrote to André Ampère. "People ask me if I am a relation of the famous Ampère, and I answer, as modestly as I possibly can, 'I am his son,' and then they make me a profound bow, of which I am very proud." As Jean Jacques lived with the most intellectual people in Berlin, and as at that time some of these happened to be in very high social positions, he saw Prussian high life also, dining several times with Prince Augustus (another worshipper of Madame Récamier), and meeting Humboldt at the royal table. He knew both the Humboldts, and most of the literary celebrities who were their contemporaries in Berlin. These social pleasures were, however, but a part of his occupations during his residence there. Wherever he happened to be, he had the happy faculty of setting to work immediately, and making the most of his opportunities for study. He was ardently pursuing all through this year his vast scheme of a general history of literature, and gathered in Germany an immense number of notes about antique European and Asiatic poetry ; whilst he endeavored at the same time to get light on Scandinavian literature, but found it more difficult, from a certain lack of materials. It may have been for this reason that he determined to visit Sweden, where he landed at Ystad on the 10th of July. He wrote as follows from Malmo, two days later, giving his first impression of the Swedish landscape, and of that *northern sensation* which one feels immediately on approaching the higher latitudes : —

" It is really a decisive step to cross the Baltic. The north begins here. These strong winds, this pale sun, that moon which I saw last night coming out of a dark cloud like the moon in Ossian, — all this has the northern character already ; and, when I remember that last week I found the climate of Florence at Berlin, it seems as if that were a recollection of another year."

The long northern twilight impresses him strongly when he lands at Gottenburg.

" We arrived here this evening at half-past ten, it being still light enough for us to distinguish every thing

perfectly. This twilight has a great charm, and produces a singular effect upon the mind.* The coast is
covered with rocks : we seem at the end of the world,
and are then delighted to find a noble river, on which
we enter a town which is quite new, with great, regular,
well-built, white houses."

The traveller's instinct of pushing on was strong in
J. J. Ampère, and we soon find him at Christiania, "a
little farther to the north than the Orkneys," as he writes
to Madame Récamier. Christiania is, in fact, in the same
latitude as the mainland of Shetland; but Ampère, being
in a travelling state of mind, was not satisfied without
seeing the interior. With four companions, he pushed
on as far as Drontheim, beyond the latitude even of the
Faroe Islands, but did not receive a very favorable impression of intellectual culture in those parts, as the
librarian showed him a Koran in Arabic, and affirmed
that it was in the Chinese tongue! A comparison between Sweden and Norway, being brief and interesting,
is worth quoting : —

"When you travel in Sweden, do not fail to go to
Norway; for Sweden is very inferior to it, so far as I
have seen. Here and there you may find some fine
views, but in general hardly any thing picturesque and
much uniformity. Nevertheless, I may say that the

---

* It would be difficult to speak of it more truly in a few words. The
northern summer twilight seems to turn the landscape into an ideal
world. Nothing in the course of my experience has left a more poetic
impression on the memory than whole nights passed slowly sailing with
faint breezes on a Highland lake in that weird and wonderful light
which is like the ghost of day.

uniformity itself had its charm, for that which is not pictorial may be poetical. I found great pleasure in being carried rapidly along in an open carriage amongst rocky heaths and pine woods without number. From time to time, a waterfall, a lonely lake, the sea advancing amongst the rocks, came to break the monotony of our impressions. But Norway announces itself quite otherwise. Christiania is placed in an admirable situation; and when, after having passed three days posting over bare lands, we saw its environs on the seaside all fresh and green, with country houses scattered about like those of Geneva, we felt something like the enchantment of travellers just arrived at Palmyra after having crossed the desert. If there were sunshine here, these fine coasts, these islands and promontories gently sloping to the sea, might, without profanation, remind us of *Mole di Gaeta*, or the Bay of Baiæ." *

This northern excursion ended by a return through Stockholm, which the traveller reached in September. In October, his letters were dated again from Berlin; and he returned to Paris through Saxony and Bavaria, after an absence of sixteen months.

The reader will remember that a more serious reason than a taste for travel had determined Jean Jacques to leave Paris and its neighborhood for a long absence. His real purpose was to bring his sentiments towards

---

* The reader who takes an interest in human sentiment about landscape will observe with some interest how *southern* and essentially classical the sentiment is here: he will notice the dislike to bare wild nature, the love of pleasant places with agreeable human habitations, the regret for the southern sun, the turning of the thoughts to Italy.

Madame Récamier within discipline, so that they might no longer be a source of torment and agitation in his life. In this he at last succeeded. It may have been partly the effect of absence and change of scene, partly the consequence of that indiscretion about the letter from Weimar; but, whatever the cause, the effect was produced, and it was permanent. Jean Jacques remained for Madame Récamier a most devoted friend, and this friendship prevented his marriage, so far keeping him unsettled; but from the end of the year 1827 his attachment to her was no longer painful or dangerous, and his fine mind, by this time very richly stored with material, was free to concentrate its energies on great intellectual labors.

In the autumn of 1828, Jean Jacques went to Normandy to study the traces of Scandinavian influence in France. He fixed his residence for this purpose in the old castle of Bretteville, near Cherbourg, on the seashore, making excursions in various directions. He came to the conclusion that "a little Scandinavia" existed at the most northern extremity of lower Normandy. Here he found Danish and Swedish words in the *patois*, popular superstitions resembling those of the north, stone altars like those often found near Copenhagen and in Norway; and so he got valuable materials for a chapter on Scandinavia in France, all which delighted him exceedingly.

Soon after his return to Paris, he was called away again by other considerations. His father suffered from chronic bronchitis, and was ordered to pass a winter in the south. They were neither of them in very easy

circumstances, but Jean Jacques managed to buy a carriage for twelve pounds, a "calèche," and they set off in
this vehicle with a friend. André Ampère was very
talkative during the journey, notwithstanding the state
of his throat, and his talk is said to have been mar
vellous; the subject being that immense one, the classification of human knowledge. They went to Hyères,
where Jean Jacques frequently visited the great historian
of the Norman conquest, Augustin Thierry, whose labors
had cost him his eyesight, and besides that brought on
a nervous malady which compelled him to allow his
brain some rest. "It is a most painful spectacle," wrote
Jean Jacques, "to see him dragging himself along, supported by a companion, without eyes, almost without
legs, yet with a healthy mind and clear thoughts." Young
Ampère made it his business at Hyères to devote himself absolutely to his father, keeping the accounts of
their little expenses,* playing eight or ten games at

---

* Much to J. J. Ampère's credit, he seriously endeavored on several
different occasions to make himself master of the difficult art of housekeeping, but always with little success. The most astonishing stories,
well authenticated, remain to testify to his singular natural incapacity
for managing the affairs of common life. His father's household was
very badly managed at all times; and it needed all the respect felt by
his guests for such distinguished scientific talents, to enable them to
pardon the roughness and want of form in his hospitality. On his
return from Italy in 1824, Jean Jacques was determined to show how
useful he could make himself as butler, so he went to the cellar to fetch
wine, but found that the key would not turn in the lock. He had
another key made, and things went on very well for some time, when, lo!
one day he observed that the stock of wine was diminishing with a
rapidity which suddenly surprised him. The day following, to his still
greater surprise, the empty bins were full again: yesterday, only twenty-
five bottles could be counted; to-day, several hundreds! He rushes

chess every day with him, and even allowing himself to be upset in their drives ; for André was singularly rash in a carriage, and his son thought that filial piety required him to be upset too, for company.

Our hero's money matters at this time were not in a very satisfactory condition. He had possessed a little capital, but this gradually melted away with the expenses of his studies and travels. That journey to Hyères with

up-stairs to tell the wondrous tale, — two witnesses go down with him, and confirm it, — they count hundreds of bottles !

The explanation was that Jean Jacques had with the most perfect innocence got a key made to open the door of a neighbor's well-stocked cellar, whilst he kept the old key of their own, thus going one day (just as it might happen) to the meagre Ampère stock, and another helping himself freely to the more abundant supplies of a neighbor and tenant called Fresnel. " I ought to have been tried for it at the Assizes," said poor Jean Jacques ; " but the affair was hushed up, and restitution made."

He did worse than this, if possible, in Rome, in 1862, where he became a house-breaker *avec effraction*. It was in the month of March, at two o'clock in the morning ; so he took a fancy to smoke a cigar on his balcony. The night was dark, and the wind high : he believed that he had turned the key in his glass door to prevent it from slamming behind him. After walking and smoking on the balcony a quarter of an hour, he thought he would go in again ; but the door was completely shut against him, and no key to be found ! In order not to pass the night on the balcony, he boldly takes the resolution of breaking a pane of glass, so as to get at the inside handle : this done, he enters and strikes a light, when, lo ! he is not in his own apartment at all, but in a bedroom belonging to some neighbor,—the bed, most fortunately, unoccupied. His own door was wide open all the time !

This absence of mind may have been hereditary, for André Ampère had it in a still worse degree, as a hundred legends tell. One of the best of these is that he once at a cab-stand began to calculate with a piece of chalk on the back of a stationary vehicle ; and when the cabman got a fare, and drove away at the usual slow pace of the French *fiacre*, the philosopher, not to be interrupted by so little, ran after it unconsciously, and (in a double sense) *pursued* his calculation.

his father was paid for with some of his last bank-notes, and ruin seemed very near. Jean Jacques looked it calmly in the face, and said, "When I am utterly ruined, I hope to make a fortune." One of his latest steps on the downward road was to pay his father's most pressing debts ; for André, entirely absorbed in his scientific occupations, was quite unable to attend to ordinary household economy. There is nothing at all surprising in these pecuniary difficulties. Jean Jacques lived in the best society in Europe ; he earned nothing ; he was always ready to make a sacrifice of money in favor of his mental culture; and, as his capital from the beginning had been small, of course it rapidly melted. In October, 1830, he got an honorable situation as Maître de Conférence at the École Normale. He kept this appointment for three years, and was also appointed to replace M. Fauriel and M. Villemain at the Faculté des Lettres. In 1833, the chair of French literature at the Collége de France became vacant, and J. J. Ampère was chosen as Professor. By these and other employments suitable for a man devoted to literary pursuits, he contrived to get through life without positive inconvenience from poverty ; and by good luck he found in J. Mohl, the well-known Orientalist, a friend who both could and would take charge of his money matters for him, and keep them clear and straight.

This appointment at the Collége de France prevented Jean Jacques from accompanying his father to the south in 1836, on his tour of inspection of the southern lyceums. André was not in good health when he started.

He had almost lost his voice, and was troubled with a constant cough. He arrived at Lyons in a state of extreme weakness, and when he got to Marseilles was quite unfit for his duties as inspector, and took refuge in the college infirmary, where he was tended with the most anxious care. Then came a violent inflammation of the throat, strong fever, and finally pneumonia. The pneumonia was overcome, and on the 6th of June the patient was able to write a letter on matters of important business; but the effort was immediately followed by a burning fever, which began with the chest, and finally attacked the brain with a fatal result. Jean Jacques received the sad news at Paris, and had the misery of thinking that, after travelling so much about Europe at different times, he had been prevented from taking that one journey which would have enabled him to watch by his father's death-bed.

Bredin, an intimate friend of the elder Ampère, was with him as he passed through St. Étienne, and told an anecdote afterwards, which is finely characteristic of a great thinker. Bredin tried to avoid conversations on the important subjects which most interested his friend, from a dread of the effects on his precarious physical condition. " My health! my health !" said Ampère. " What does my health signify? There ought to be no consideration here, between us two, about any thing but the eternal truths, about the men and things which have been useful or hurtful to humanity !"

When the elder Ampère died, he left hardly any money, having always been generous to poorer friends,

and an unskilful economist also. Jean Jacques was himself ruined, or very nearly so, as we have already seen, in
consequence of his travels and unremunerative intellectual pursuits. But the situation was even worse than
this simple statement implies. The reader may remember that André had a daughter by his second wife. This
daughter, Albine, had been married at the time of her
brother's return from Norway; and she and her husband
were a constant burden to Jean Jacques. It was a
most unfortunate union in every way. The husband,
whose name was Ride, turned out idle, drunken, and a
gambler, and finally lost his reason in consequence of
his evil habits. His wife, being ruined and wretched,
fell into bad health and low spirits, finally becoming half
insane herself. Jean Jacques had to keep both of them ;
and, since his little capital was gone, this had to be done
out of his earnings. Besides these relations, Jean
Jacques was afflicted with another, a cousin named De
Soutières, an eccentric being, of no use to any one ; who,
without being precisely mad, had a wild imagination,
which education, instead of sobering, had excited. In
his youth, he had tried to make use of chemistry to trans-
mute substances into gold ; and, at a more advanced age,
he studied algebra with a view to winning money by
its help in gambling. Besides this unlucky tendency to
make the most foolish possible use of whatever knowledge he possessed, this De Soutières was intensely disagreeable, perfectly uncompanionable, utterly incorrigible,
and simply an affliction to his friends. André Ampère
had helped him from 1812 to 1836, and from that date

till 1848, he was kept by Jean Jacques, who finally paid for his interment. With these burdens, and the narrow income of a French professor, it is not surprising that our hero should have desired some piece of good fortune outside of his ordinary resources. There was a chance that he might win the Gobert prize of 9000 francs for his historical labors, and luckily he did win it in the year 1840. Not only did he receive the prize once, but it was accorded to him for two successive years on account of the same work, his " Literary History of France before the Twelfth Century." This work was itself a result of his labors for his professorship. His labors in teaching were indeed useful to him in various ways, both by solidifying his own acquirements, by making him better known in Paris, and also by revealing a great special talent for lucid oral exposition, which had been unsuspected even by himself. Few learned men have ever been so much liked by their audiences.

The remainder of J. J. Ampère's life is a tangle of various threads, which it may be more convenient to follow separately. The most important of these threads are: 1. His intellectual pursuits ; 2. His friendships; 3. His travels.

He was naturally gifted for all three ; naturally a hard student, a devoted friend, an eager, observant, and courageous traveller. By simply following these natural instincts, he lived in a state of constant activity, so that the current of his existence was always swift and clear, without repose enough for stagnation at any time. Every year, every month even, was filled with the

labors which instruct and elevate the mind, and brightened by those pleasures which keep it cheerful and
healthy. J. J. Ampère, so far as we can judge from the
abundant materials in our possession, escaped the dulness of the ignorant, because of his extensive knowledge,
and never suffered from the listlessness of the learned,
because, so soon as one pursuit became somewhat less
attractive, it was immediately succeeded by a fresh object of enthusiasm. Whilst his studies led him to a
minute and careful exploration of the past, his daily
habits brought him into contact with all that is best and
most interesting in the present. He read the best literature in many languages, visited the most remarkable
scenes and cities of many countries, and had for his
intimate friends the most cultivated and companionable
people wherever he went. He retained to the last a
quite youthful power of enjoying all the advantages
which were opened to him by his scholarship, his travels,
and his friendships, so that there has seldom been so
complete a realization of an intelligent bachelor's existence.

I will endeavor to give, in a short space, some faint
idea of Ampère's intellectual activity. If all his studies,
on the one hand, were pleasures to him, so on the other
his pleasures easily became studies. He increased the
interest of his travels by having some special intellectual
object in each excursion: for example, in September,
1838, he went with two learned friends to Italy, where
they carried into execution what they called a "*voyage
Dantesque*," a scheme of travel guided entirely by the

wish to elucidate some points in the life and works of
Dante. His travels in Germany and in Sweden and
Norway had for their leading motives the German
language and the history of Scandinavian literature;
his residence in lower Normandy was suggested to
him by the desire to follow up the traces of Scandinavia
in France. Every journey which he undertook in after
life had in like manner some intellectual object; and
that not a mere pretext to add the pleasures of dilettanteism to the charms of travel, but a serious purpose
connected with the traveller's labors as a writer·and
professor. Whilst actually on the road, he was always
thinking and observing; and, when the body had its
necessary intervals of rest, the mind was active in
literary studies. At Malta, for example, in 1841, when
condemned to an involuntary repose by the quarantine,
he settled down to sedentary work at once. "I feel a
sort of pleasure" — he wrote to a dear friend — "in
being imprisoned, in no longer having to go and see,
but in resting body and mind. This rest is far from
being complete; for I had hardly time to re-establish
myself in sedentary life before the rage for work took
hold of me again. I am arranging part of my studies
on Greek poetry in Greece. I am preparing my lectures
in studying Rabelais. The Chinese language, which I
had abandoned for some months, and which it would
have been an impiety to remember in Greece, has put
in its claims again. With all these, time passes quickly
in my magnificent prison." Whilst travelling in Southern Italy, in the burning month of August of the same

year, and soon afterwards in Turkey and Greece, he read and wrote in every available interval. " If ever I have been without liberty," he said, " it has been in this journey, so constantly filled by the impressions of the mind and the fatigues of the body." In the same letter, he says, "I hope that God will preserve to me strength and sufficient length of years for me to concentrate all my labors in a work, — labors various in their purpose, but which have a tendency to unity." Even the facility with which he resigned appointments that were of value to him was generally dictated by the desire to allow himself more leisure for his studies. When he gave up the post of Maître de Conférence at the École Normale, it was in order that he might the better investigate the early history of French literature. "At all times of his life," wrote Madame Lenormant, who knew him well, "Ampère, whose disinterestedness was unequalled, was ready to resign any employment which did not seem strictly necessary, for the dissemination of the ideas or doctrines which were dear to him." He had in an equal degree the two distinct enthusiasms of literature and archæology. Even so recently as the days of Ampère's activity, archæology was an infant science. It has since then wonderfully grown and developed itself, but in those days the few archæologists there were had comparatively little aid from the investigations of others; and they were not helped, as in the present day, by innumerable photographs. Ampère was a most industrious archæologist, and seized on all opportunities. For example, when detained by a contrary wind at Leghorn, he immediately hunted up antiquities; and, having discovered some hieroglyphics, lay down amongst spiders and dust for six days to copy them. "It is not merely notes that I take," he says, "but texts. I am in the position of copyists, before the invention of printing; and, as the manuscripts I have to deal with are in stone, it is still more necessary to copy them completely, as there is no means of carrying them off." He wrote from Paris to Alexis de Tocqueville: "I have great need of breathing a little, — of breathing the air of the fields with you. I have just written two articles, one of which required much study. At the same time, the subjects I lecture upon compel me to undertake great labors. I sleep very little, and am ready to drop with fatigue." This weariness was only temporary; for, even so late as the year 1862, he was still capable of feeling all the glow and enthusiasm which animate the energies of the best workmen. "I felt within me an extraordinary *entrain.* Rome had become the sole object of my toils. I buckled myself to the *Roman History at Rome*, and intended to enlarge the plan." The prodigious activity of Ampère's mind alarmed his friend, De Tocqueville, who sent him this good advice: "Whatever may be the great facility which God has given you, be careful not to abuse it; and mind you do not tire, if not the angel, at least the animal, which is necessary to the angel. You have appeared to me for the last twelve months in the condition of an intellectual volcano. This sort of over-excitement, with

the admirable sureness of taste which you have acquired, makes you in my opinion very superior to what
you have ever been. But life should be so ordered that
it may last : one should keep his strength, and be careful of his *verve*, so that neither the one nor the other
may become weary." Advice such as this may be
listened to by those to whom work is difficult; but
Ampère had such facility that he never could properly
distinguish between work and play. De Tocqueville
once asked him the question, "Que faites-vous, vous
qui avez l'art de faire beaucoup, vite et bien ?" Some
people can escape from work by a simple change of
place ; but this resource was denied to Ampère, for the
peculiar reason that he had the gift of working in all
places with equal facility : so that the first chance room
in an inn became like his own study for him in five
minutes ; that is, as soon as he had spread some books
and papers on the table. He did not get enough sleep,
being a night-worker, and in the constant habit of reading and writing till four or five o'clock in the morning.
Far from betraying the slightest sign of cerebral exhaustion, he was never so productive as during the
last decade of his life. He used society as a tonic
and stimulant, and had a complete belief in its efficacy;
but we must remember that the society he frequented
was the brightest and most animating in Europe. On
his return to Paris from a country house near Compiègne,
he lectured better than usual, and said about this
success: "M. Hochet, who had not approved of my
first manner, told me that it was my best lesson.

That's what it is to have passed several days in the country with dear friends, to have good conversations, and hear beautiful readings. All that electrifies one, and enables one to do well in public." From his infancy, Jean Jacques had been surrounded by eminent men; and half his ability was due to the constant influence of this society. Much of that talent for exposition, which made him the best professor of his time, may also have been due to his constant practice in conversation. He hardly ever passed a day, except on those rare occasions when he was travelling alone, without talking to some listener who was capable of appreciating him at his best; and he thus became one of the most perfect talkers in the world. When once a certain natural modesty and diffidence had been overcome by his interest in the subject, his talk became inexhausti-ble, — full of imagination, yet accurate in matters of fact, with an ardent enthusiasm, a power of lively indignation against what seemed wrong to him, always tempered by good taste and an exquisite sense of what was delicate and becoming. He represented in all the capitals of Europe the perfection of French grace and culture, yet remained to the last without vanity, though petted by the best society everywhere. You may seek through all that he wrote, and through all that was written about him, without finding any trace-of that self-importance which success in the pursuits of literature and erudition so often develops in those who have attained it. He had, no doubt, a natural satisfaction in success; but the delight of his life was first in his affections, and after that in his labors for themselves, with little reference to the external rewards they brought. The unfailing charm of his society, which was acknowledged by all who knew him, would have been entirely incompatible with any thing approaching to conceit. Jean Jacques was remarkable for many things, but chiefly for having reconciled, with the happiest facility, certain qualities which it is hard to reconcile at all. He was at the same time one of the most learned men in the world, and one of the least pedantic ; one of the most brilliant ornaments of society, and one of its most simple and unassuming members.

Ampère's warmest friendship, and probably that in which his affections were placed most wisely, was his friendship with Alexis de Tocqueville. His name is known beyond the limits of his native country, but only those who have attentively studied his character can know how near he came to realizing the ideal of a high-minded, liberal, and accomplished gentleman. The best and finest qualities which belong to an aristocracy were joined in De Tocqueville to the open intelligence of a fearless thinker and the wide sympathies of one who really desired the greatest good for the greatest number. His manners, though distinguished, were somewhat cold ; yet Ampère loved him from the day of their first meeting at the Abbaye au Bois, in 1836. Soon afterwards, De Tocqueville took possession of his ancestral estate and château of Tocqueville near Cherbourg ; and in 1839 he invited Ampère to go and visit him there. The invitation was gladly accepted, and the visit cemented their friendship. Alterations were going forward in the château; and the host in subsequent letters affects to believe that it must have been difficult for the guest to enjoy any quietness with the noise of hammers going on about him. He is to be protected from disturbance in future visits by having a room expressly prepared for him, to be called " *la chambre d'Ampère.*" The room is prepared accordingly in the first floor of a tower, because the guest is likely to find it warmer and pleasanter there than higher up; but he is to be allowed to climb up into his " roost," whenever he likes. " What a pleasant life it is at Tocqueville," wrote De Loménie, dating his letter "from Ampère's tower," " where the hosts impose upon you no other duty than those of 'l'Abbaye de Thélème,' *Fais ce que voudras!* The kindness and serenity of the master harmonize perfectly with the peaceful beauty of the place. Here nature seems to invite you to throw off every care : the nerves take rest, the blood is refreshed, one passes happily from reverie to work, and from work to reverie, only to recreate and renew the faculties by gay and varied conversations." De Tocqueville himself wrote to Ampère long afterwards : " Whenever you come, you are sure to find open arms ready to receive you. Summer or winter will be alike to us ; and ' *la chambre Ampère*' will never lose its name, even if you do not inhabit it for years." This kindness produced in Jean Jacques so strong a feeling of affection that he declared he was bound up in the lives of De Tocqueville and his wife. The happiest time they ever spent together appears to have been a space of between two and three months at Sorrento, at the end of 1850 and beginning of 1851. De Tocqueville rented a house with a "*chambre d'Ampère*" in it; the chosen dwelling being above the road, a little before Sorrento, on the first slope of the hill. The roof was terraced; and from it they could see Naples and Vesuvius to the right, with valleys of orange-trees to the left. This roof was a favorite place for their conversations, but they also walked a great deal upon the hills. Ampère speaks of the charm of De Tocqueville's society, of his inexhaustible mind, which allowed itself free play in the company of his friend, and of his admirable style of expression, which, though easy and unstudied, was just as pure and refined with a single hearer as if he had been in a *salon* or at the Academy. Elegance and perfection in language were a necessity to the refined taste of De Tocqueville. Whilst he talked as they were seated together on some rock on the hillside at Sorrento, his sentences were so pure and perfect that they might have been reported word for word. "He hated phrase-making, yet I have never heard him begin a phrase without finishing it."

One of the best and most characteristic passages in De Tocqueville's letters to Ampère is that in which he speaks of the aristocracy that he liked, and another kind of aristocracy with which he had little or nothing in common : —

"You have seen that M. Molé was gone. His death will shut up one of the last salons where people could talk. *With him we had the aristocracy which loved ideas and letters,* with others we have *the aristocracy which likes equipage, fine liveries, great names, titles, holy works, all mixed up and kneaded together."*

De Tocqueville's health began to break down in 1858 from bronchitis, and in 1859 he was seriously ill at Cannes. This disquieted Ampère, then in Rome ; and, in the month of April, he went to Cannes on purpose to see him. When he arrived, his friend was already dead. And so ended a life of perfect dignity, which had been brightened by well-deserved fame, but never lowered by any unworthy condescension,—the life of a philosopher, who, though his name was celebrated, knew the value of tranquillity, and loved the penumbra of personal obscurity, estimating public opinion at its just value, and taking fame for no more than what it is really worth.

I may now tell what remains to be told about the friendship between Jean Jacques and Madame Récamier. We left that subject soon after her indiscretion in publishing part of a letter from Weimar. When Ampère returned from Sweden, the friendship was re-established, but from that date it was never any thing more than a friendship on either side. The evenings at the Abbaye were a necessity to Ampère when in Paris, and he remained pathetically faithful. He had now, however, sufficient liberty of heart and mind to permit occasional absences for travelling ; and Madame Récamier "knew that, to retain one's friends, it is necessary above all things to respect their liberty, and not to clip their wings." She still exercised her old arts, and with

the old success; the whole of them being reducible to
the one principle of taking an interest in what interested
her friends, and giving them the sympathy of the most
agreeable listener in the world. Nevertheless, life was
a disappointment to her as she drew towards the close
of her extraordinary career. After having received
adulation from royal and noble personages, and (what
she probably valued more) after having been the centre
for many years of the most brilliant little circle in
Europe, infirmity came to her at length in the shape of
increasing blindness; and her life was saddened by the
death of some friends and the failing health of others.
An operation partially restored her sight, when, having
heard that her friend Ballanche was seized with inflammation of the lungs, she committed the imprudence of
going to see him, and lost her sight altogether. Ballanche died. Chateaubriand (the friend she really cared
for most) was old, dull, melancholy, and almost helpless.
Her own health confined her to a sedentary existence,
and nothing remained for her but the thickening dregs
of life. In the dark hours of these latter days, Jean
Jacques devoted himself to her like a son. Instead of
being jealous of Chateaubriand, he respected him as his
friend's friend; and, when Chateaubriand died in 1848,
Ampère, who had been recently elected Academician,
represented the French Academy ostensibly and Madame Récamier privately, and accompanied the remains
to their final resting-place on the rock in the sea near
St. Malo. In his speech over the grave, he spoke of the
long friendship between the author of " Atala " and the

lady whose sightless eyes shed tears for him at the Abbaye au Bois.*

After this loss, Madame Récamier was more than ever cared for by her surviving friends, especially by Ampère, who, to remain near her, accepted the post of librarian at the Bibliothèque Mazarine, thus binding himself to renounce his travelling propensities. So her life went on in sadness, yet cheered by the fidelity of her friends, till 1849, the cholera year. It was the only malady that she dreaded, but she dreaded it with ungovernable fear. There were many cholera cases round about the Abbaye, and soon the contagion penetrated even within its walls. In her alarm, she went to stay with a niece at the National Library in the Rue Richelieu; and, after living there a month, she herself was seized by the terrible disease, and died, after frightful tortures, on the 11th of May. The shock of the final separation produced in Ampère, as did all violent shocks of sorrow, an immediate desire for travel as the only possible way of partially escaping from the pain. He at once threw up his appointment of librarian (which in many ways was exactly suitable for him), and set off to Spain and Portugal. From Cadiz, he sailed for England, thinking that the bustling civilization of London might be of use in turning his thoughts away from the misfortune which had befallen him; but in London the same need of

---

* Notwithstanding its intimacy, there had always been a curious formality and ceremony in this friendship. For example, every evening Madame Récamier formally inquired, in two separate questions, if Monsieur de Chateaubriand took cream and sugar in his tea, and always received the same formal and polite replies to both interrogatories.

change pursued him, and he went to Scotland, seeking forgetfulness even amongst the Highland glens and mountains. We may vainly ransack the records of the human heart for another instance of a man who throws up his employment and crosses seas and kingdoms because of the violence of his grief for the death of a blind old woman of seventy-two, who had only liked him, and to whom he was bound by no tie of relationship. Yet Thiers was right when he said that Madame Récamier was all Ampère's family. Jean Jacques had a most affectionate nature. In his own family, he had nothing but wretched burdens : his father was dead, his sister Albine was dead, his poor young mother had died long, long ago ; he had no wife or children of his own, and he lavished on Madame Récamier the affection which might, in happier circumstances, have been divided amongst his own kindred.

The best proof that the affection which Jean Jacques bestowed on Madame Récamier was rather an outcome of his own nature than the result of any unique attractiveness in hers is that she had a successor. He could not live without being part of a circle ; and, in the year 1853, he gave himself in this way to a whole family, who accepted and returned his affection with the most perfect good-will. This family, whose home was in the south of France, near Pau, but who passed much of their time in Italy, were intelligent and cultivated people, with that social ease and frankness which suited Ampère's taste. There were three generations in the little circle, and he soon gave his affection to all three. When in Rome, he kept up an appearance of independence by dining occasionally at a restaurant, which his friends laughingly called "the rival;" but at length a member of the household, Madame L., whose health was the reason for their stay in Italy, became so much worse that the shadow of coming sorrow made him a less inconstant guest. As it became more and more evident that the lady would soon be removed from those who loved her, Ampère's friendship for her quickly ripened into a sentiment of melancholy tenderness. The most austere of judges, provided that his austerity did not develop itself into calumny, could find nothing to reprove in this sad friendship in the Valley of the Shadow of Death. Even so pure a mind as that of Perreyve only spoke of it as "most sacred," his allusion to it being in these words: "tous les amours les plus sacrés."

Madame L. was the daughter of M. and Mme. Cheuvreux. Her own name is not printed in full in the Ampère correspondence, a discretion which shall be imitated here. Her influence on Ampère was like that of some calm and beautiful summer evening, when the night comes on in peace, and we feel saddened and sobered, yet strangely near to an ideal happiness; when visible things are mysterious, and things unseen are no longer hopelessly remote, — no longer beyond the reach of imagination. Ampère, who, with all his good breeding, was often vehement and violent when very much in earnest, learned from this lady, though late, a delicate temperance. "Thanks to her," he said, "I feel that I can change my ways and habits, that my violence may be subdued, because I so much loved her mildness, — her mildness, which was not weakness, which extinguished neither the fire of her soul nor the charm of her intelligence."

The winter of 1857 was passed at Rome, and Madame L. was sufficiently strong to bear society. In April, it was decided to go to Como, where a charming villa was taken near the lake. The journey from Rome began pleasantly in a great travelling carriage; the party taking lunch every day in the carriage on a silver picnic service, and enjoying themselves as people sometimes contrive to do, by shutting their eyes to an approaching evil. At Venice, Madame L. seemed wonderfully well; and the week they passed there was strangely happy, with that too perfect happiness which northern superstition (or perhaps simple experience of life) considers of evil omen. Her worst month every year was August. They were at Como in August, and it seemed as if this year the malady would deal with her more gently. It struck her, on the contrary, with redoubled severity; and they had to leave Como suddenly, travelling hundreds of miles to Rome, full of anxiety for their suffering charge. They reached at length the end of their weary journey, and after that no illusion was any longer possible. Ampère, in alluding to these sad recollections afterwards, speaks of the sleepless nights which he vainly tried to turn into nights of labor, disturbed by the most opposite sounds, the thrilling song of the nightingales in the shrubberies, the discordant voices of the contadini, the barking of the dogs, and then the sun rising radiant and gay whilst they were all so sad. The dying lady retained her clear intelligence to the end, and occupied much of his thoughts by her undiminished interest in others, both in public matters, such as the future of Italy, and in the private affairs of those nearest to her. At length, the end came; and the event left Ampère in a sort of religious melancholy, not unsuitable for the later years of life. Henri Perreyve delivered to him a message from Madame L., which was her desire that Ampère should be a Christian. He was one already in sentiment and conduct, but was unable to give his assent to the dogmas of the Church. Perreyve neither exaggerated the interval which separated Ampère's religion from his own, nor affected to consider it nearer to Catholic orthodoxy than it really was. "I well know that you are a Christian," he says, "but you are so by the intellect; and it is not by the intellect that one can come near to God." *

---

* The question of J. J. Ampère's religious belief is settled by a written paper found since his death. He says, speaking of the Roman Catholic faith, —

"This faith would alter nothing in my way of life: it would not require me to renounce any one kind of happiness, and it would introduce into my life the only happiness which I could now enjoy. I have no pride in not possessing this faith. Such a pride would be an absurdity. The greatest geniuses, the greatest philosophers, the greatest *savants*, the greatest poets, the greatest artists, have had this faith. One must be stupid to despise it, to find in it a limit to the intelligence, myself especially, since I have seen my father believe, and believe as a Catholic, —and Ballanche, and Ozanam, and Madame L., and the Abbé Perreyve."

"I believe in God, in his providence, in a future life, in the recompense of the good, in the punishment of the wicked, in the sublimity and

After the death of Madame L., Ampère looked upon the house of her father and mother as his own home. Besides these friends, he had an unfailing resource in the two allied ducal families of De Mouchy and De Noailles, who in that generation belonged to the same order of cultivated and intelligent nobility as the De Tocquevilles. In the year 1856, the Duchess de Mouchy offered Ampère a set of rooms in her town house at Paris, to be his own town residence; but he declined, on the ground that it was too distant from the libraries, where he worked. Jean Jacques was always rather a pet of great ladies, who treated him as they generally treat nice priests. The above-mentioned Duchess got the tailor at Mouchy to make him a comfortable dressing-gown out of the cloth of the country: it was a fancy of hers to give these garments to men she esteemed, just as Oriental potentates bestow robes of honor. Her

truth of the Christian doctrine (he means moral doctrine, not dogma), in a revelation of this doctrine by a special inspiration of Divine Providence for the salvation of the human race; that is to say, in an action of God upon the soul, producing in it what it is not in our own power to produce therein. But I do not indulge the illusion that I am a believer in the exact sense which the Church teaches."

"You know that I do not exaggerate the power of reason. My own humbles itself before the mystery where it stops short; that is to say, very near to its point of departure. What it does not see is infinite; but, where it does not see, it does not believe."

From this and the passages immediately following, the conclusion is that J. J. Ampère was what we in England should call a good Unitarian; yet as his father and most of his friends were Roman Catholics, and as he was baptized and confirmed in the Church of Rome, he continued to conform to her rites in some measure externally, but with a minimum of hypocrisy, as his real opinions were not at any time a secret, though he did not obtrude them on others.

mother, the Viscountess de Noailles, was another great
friend of Jean Jacques. After a dangerous illness in
1846, he first went to stay a month in the pretty valley
of the Rille ; but after that he went to be nursed in the
magnificent château at Mouchy, during his slow and
tedious convalescence. He had to lie down constantly,
and was hard to manage; but the noble ladies who took
care of him maintained the severity of the prescribed
regimen, and gradually brought him round. After this,
they assumed something like parental rights over him,
and remained his faithful friends till death separated
them. Madame de Noailles was a woman of uncommon
intelligence, and quite superior to the political prejudices
of her class, whilst she had sufficient strength of mind
to resist the prejudices of other classes. Her intellectual position enabled her to see the faults of both sides.
She saw the evil done by the fanaticism of the first
republicans ; and she clearly perceived, at the same time,
both the degradation of the monarchy and the immi-
nence of what she called "an American era" for France,
that era in which the French people are now actually
living.

I have already mentioned Ampère's friendship with
J. Mohl, the Orientalist, who, being a better economist
than Jean Jacques, very kindly took charge of his money
matters for him. They first met in Cuvier's drawing-
room in 1824, when Ampère had just returned from
Italy. Mohl, who belonged to Stuttgart, had come to
France to study Arabic and Persian ; and he found in
Ampère a nature which, though entirely different from

his own, pleased him so much that a lasting friendship
followed. The two even lived together under the same
roof in the Rue du Bac, from 1831 until Mohl married
Miss Clarke, in 1847. There are some good stories of
their housekeeping, which was not always without inconveniences. Amongst other incidents is the following:
Jean Jacques, coming home on a very cold night in January, lighted his fire with waste paper, and so successfully that he set fire to the chimney, thereby much
disturbing Mohl, who was lying in bed with the tooth
ache, and exclaimed, as he came to the rescue, flushed
with pain, anxiety, and annoyance, "Decidedly, the situation is *intolerable !*" *

I have purposely, for the reader's convenience, post-
poned till now the consideration of Ampère's rank as a
traveller, and have even intentionally omitted one or two
of his most important journeys, when we were occupied

* Mohl was not only a distinguished Orientalist, he was also master
of several European languages ; and I remember receiving a word of
encouragement from him, which the reader may thank me for commu-
nicating. I was at his rooms in the Rue du Bac (I am afraid to think
how many years ago); and, as at that time I spoke French imperfectly, I
preferred English, which Mohl spoke very correctly. He asked me if I
found that I made progress in French, and, on receiving an uncertain
reply, asked if I understood French conversations thoroughly when I
overheard them. "Yes, every word." "Very well," he went on to say,
"then rely upon it that you will soon speak fluently yourself ; for, when
the ear misses nothing, the tongue is sure to follow, but it always lags
a little behind. For the present you should listen attentively." The
encouragement and advice here given are excellent, and founded on
accurate observation. People are generally very ready to say that they
understand a foreign language when they can catch about one word in
three ; but I never knew any one who really understood every word
spoken by natives, without being able to speak well himself very soon
after having reached that point.

with other matters. We might easily underrate him, in an age which has been astonished by the discoveries of the great African explorers. Ampère made no geographical discoveries: his travels were never any thing more than excursions, or periods of residence in foreign countries, but they have an important peculiarity which ought not to be overlooked. He was one of the first Frenchmen, he was even one of the first Europeans, who made travelling an integral part of an intellectual life; one of the first men who would go hundreds or even thousands of miles at any time, merely to get more perfect light on an object of intellectual pursuit. His interest in Roman history was fed and strengthened by long study on the spot, and study so painstaking and accurate that he came to know the remains of ancient Rome better than any of his contemporaries. His studies of Grecian literature led him to Greece itself, that he might read the Greek authors with the light of Hellas on the page and its own scenery around him. He studied German literature in Germany, in personal intimacy with its living leaders. His interest in Scandinavian .lore took him, as we have seen, to Sweden and Norway, as far north as Drontheim. After that, instead of contenting himself simply with the historical fact that there had been a little Scandinavia in Northern France, he went to live in it, and explore it as a linguist and archæologist. In 1843, he studied Egyptian hieroglyphics in the Italian museums; but, not being satisfied with that, he went in 1844 to study Egypt in Egypt itself. It is easy, of course, for people who never felt any noble intellectual enthusiasm to depreciate these studies as different varieties of dilettanteism ; but what do they say to this ? Ampère, when in Egypt in 1845, was reduced to great physical weakness by a dangerous attack of dysentery ; but there were certain tombs which he greatly desired to see, and, to reach them, he had to cross a burning plain of sand. Being determined not to leave the country without accomplishing this purpose, he had his body covered with laudanum, and made his attendant tie him on the back of his camel, that he might not fall from weakness, having for his only consolation the company of an unhopeful doctor, who told him that in the Egyptian climate dysentery was generally fatal, but that human life was not worth much at the best, and that dying was less difficult than people generally believed. The visit to the tombs cost Ampère fifteen months of acute suffering, but it clearly proves the vigor of his resolution as a travelling student. It was rash ; but the rashness was the heroism of intellectual energy, which will be turned aside by no fear of personal risk or inconvenience.

Travelling usually produced a good effect on Ampère, both physically and mentally. " Les voyages," he said, " me donnent toujours de la force." Besides this, he had an intensely sensitive nature, which caused him to feel the need for travel at certain times of trial, as an escape from the pressure of grief. We have seen that the death of Madame Récamier sent him into Spain and Portugal, and thence to London, and thence again to the Highlands of Scotland, in the mere restlessness of sorrow. "I dread Paris," he said at such times, "and yet I have true friends there." Even after his return, he finds it impossible to settle in Paris permanently, and takes flight across the Atlantic in 1851, lands at Boston, and makes an excursion of more than a thousand leagues, including Quebec, Illinois, and Cincinnati ; then he sets off on another great excursion southwards.

The cause of many travels which Jean Jacques undertook as he advanced in life was one very familiar to all wanderers. A peculiar form of nostalgia seized him from time to time, — not the nostalgia which desires home and the native land, but the longing to see once again the scenes which are associated with recollections of other years, the longing to roll back the mist which gathers between us and the past.* This desire came upon the affectionate, regretful nature of Jean Jacques from time to time with an irresistible force. When tired of the straight and monotonous streets of Paris, with their wearisome succession of ever similar splendors, his thoughts would turn to the tortuous but picturesque *vicoli* of Rome and her horizon of distant hills. Rome called him in this way repeatedly : it was the place he loved best in the world ; and he went there many times, always to work. "Unluckily," he said, "I cannot imitate the hurried tourist, who said to Madame C. in Rome, ' In order to see more, I have made up my mind not to look at any bas-reliefs.' Now it so happens that there are many bas-reliefs in Rome ; and, when one has to

* Tennyson has exquisitely described this melancholy satisfaction in one of the most perfect of his minor poems, " In the Valley of Cauteretz."

study them in detail, it is a long business." The desire
to do again what one has done before was curiously
manifested in 1854, when Ampère wanted to go and
study again at some German university.

At length, all these wanderings drew towards the
inevitable rest. Ampère was working again at Rome,
early in 1861. " I am lodged," he wrote, " on the Tar-
peian Rock, in the German house. I have certainly the
most beautiful view of Rome, — the mountains in the distance, the Forum at my feet, the Palatine, the Aventine,
the Tiber. Through my window I see the palm-tree of
Saint Peter *in Vincoli.* I am next door to Henzen. I
have all the books that I can wish for. Alas! how
much more beautiful all this would be, and lighted by
another light, if my friends were in this Rome where
they are no more!" The next year, 1862, he revisited
his favorite city, and lodged in the same rooms, working
still with the energy of youth, — " Je travaille de toutes
mes forces." This was his last residence in Rome ; and
afterwards he remained more faithful to his friends at
Pau, telling them that formerly he had never dreaded
the possibility of dying on the road, to which every
traveller is exposed, but that now their affection had so
spoiled him that he wanted to die " *en famille.*" This
event was nearer than he may have anticipated. One
night in March, 1864, he had been working as usual, and
was seized with sudden pain about the heart. It passed
away ; and he resumed his ordinary life, saying that he
had still ten volumes in his head on Rome. Nevertheless, being warned by the attack of pain, he now made

his will, and was seized again in the night preceding
Easter day. He rang the bell violently; and, when his
friends ran to his assistance, they found him unconscious and dying, his lamp still burning, the counterpane
of his bed all covered with books and papers, and the
pencil he wrote with just fallen from his hand. He died
in harness, laboring to the last.

In the month of August in the same year, a good man,
well known to the readers of this volume, Henri Perreyve, preached a sermon in the chapel at Stors, in
which he gave his best eloquence to celebrate the virtues of Jean Jacques Ampère, dwelling chiefly on his
courageous probity, his generosity, his gracious and
simple goodness, and, above all, on "the infinite delicacy
of his sure friendship, which, once given, was never
retracted. He was faithful in sorrow as others are in
prosperity." "I do not fear," said the preacher, "to recall his beloved face even in Thy presence, O Jesus! for
Thou wert, in Thy mortal days, an incomparable friend."

It is evident from this and other passages in the same
sermon that Perreyve saw no evil in Ampère's friendships with women. We all seek happiness in some form;
and Jean Jacques Ampère sought it chiefly in friendship,
choosing his friends in both sexes. Amongst men,
he was warmly attached to De Tocqueville, Mohl, the
learned Italian Marquis Capponi, and others; amongst
women, to Madame Récamier, Madame L., the Viscountess de Noailles, and the Duchess de Mouchy.
Honi soit qui mal y pense. It seems to me that, when
a man of Ampère's brilliant intellect and all but bound-

less learning delights in endless conversations with cultivated women, such intercourse may be honorable to both parties.

The life we have been following was one of the best adapted for culture that could be led by a human being. From his childhood, J. J. Ampère lived in the kind of society which is at the same time the best informed and the most perfectly communicative. His time was so beautifully divided between acquisition and communication that the blue mould of ignorance could never grow upon him, and his intellectual armor could never be rusted by reserve. He was neither, on the one hand, the silent scholar, incapable of imparting what he knows, nor, on the other, the copious chatterer, whose words are empty and vain. His acquirements were so great that the strongest epithets are not too much to express the vast extent of his knowledge : it was enormous, prodigious, what you will ; and his facility of utterance, in public speaking, in private conversation, or by means of books and articles, was like the flowing of perennial springs. He had access to every thing : he was not tied down, like many an earnest student, to the wretched resources of some third-rate provincial city ; he was not even limited to the noble museums and libraries of Paris or to the help of the learned men who lived there. Every country in Europe was open to him, and he was at home in many capitals. Though never wealthy, he contrived always to have money enough for his wants, including a reserve for sudden journeys of great length, which he undertook as readily as a queen's messenger, whenever Minerva commanded. His health was not what is called robust, and yet his physical powers were always equal to his large and incessant demands upon them. He could travel night and day, with little regard to comfort, before railways were common on the Continent; whilst all places and all hours were alike to him for his intellectual work. His life, therefore, as a perpetual student, was one of rare advantages, — a life of extraordinary powers in conjunction with extraordinary opportunities.

Nevertheless, if a wise man were asked whether he would accept or decline such a life, with all its advantages, I think he would surely decline it, and for this one sufficient reason: that it had no centre of its own. Jean Jacques Ampère was a homeless being; so homeless, that merely to write or read his biography gives one a feeling of restlessness, which only ends when he is quiet at last in his grave. The need of affection, which in others so often leads to the happiness of marriage and the inestimable benefit of a settled existence in quiet independence of society, was always compelling Ampère to revolve like a satellite round somebody. Had he been the only satellite, as the moon is to the earth, the situation would have been more acceptable. Had he been even the nearest, as Mercury is to the sun, the position might have been tolerable still. But he was an outer satellite, like Jupiter, without the planet's happy unconsciousness of cold. Not only this, but his imperious need of family life compelled him to be a parasite. I use the word, in reference to him, without either contempt or blame ; for he certainly never attached himself to any house or family where he was not heartily welcome when he came, and sincerely regretted when he went away. His friends, too, being chiefly French people of the best kind, had too much real delicacy to let him feel any thing approaching to patronage ; and his high Academic rank, added to the scientific fame of his illustrious father, gave him a social position which, in France, is really and substantially equivalent to that of a great nobleman. Nevertheless, he was a parasite still, — not for the sake of money, which he earned honorably by labor, but for the sake of that human love and affection without which he found life a desert. Most men would rather die under their own roof than as a guest in the house of another ; but Jean Jacques wished more than ever to be near his friends in the last hour, although they were comparatively recent friends ; and he passed away, surrounded by those who were not of his kindred, and who had only known him in his age. So lonely was he, except for their kindness, that he left them all he had, to be employed. after some posthumous publications, in any work of charity they might prefer. Small as are the earnings of the highest intellectual labor, and small as were Ampère's talents for money-making, with his large generosity, he owed no man any thing when he died, and even left a little *peculium*, now yielding an annual interest of eighty pounds, which is employed as a prize held for two years by a young writer, artist, or *savant*, chosen by the Academy of Lyons.

HENRI REGNAULT.

JACOTOT'S theory that all intelligences are equal, and Rude's simple belief that the only difference between men is that occasioned by labor, were alike disproved by the childhood and early manhood of Henri Regnault, who gave evidence from the first of natural gifts so visibly different from those of ordinary humanity, that only the strongest prejudice could refuse to see a special favor of nature in his singularly artistic organization. Labor, indeed! Why, there are old artists in every capital of Europe who have gone through three times the amount of labor that Regnault ever gave to his art, and who at sixty have not attained either the skill or the knowledge which he possessed at twenty-five. Industry is a good practical virtue, and a habit which, no doubt, is useful in enabling us to make the most of our time; but genius, or inborn faculty, whatever moralists may say, is more effectual as to results than the most laborious application. Landseer, who led the life of a London bachelor in easy circumstances, was, I believe, very generally in bed during those morning hours which it is the pride of Industry to utilize; and, instead of working late at night, he generally went into society. His work was done in a few hours between his late breakfast and his ride before dinner. A very highly gifted etcher of my acquaintance — there can be no harm in naming Paul Rajon — works a couple of hours or so in the best daylight, and then rides out in the Bois de Boulogne, doing more work in a year, and better, than some laborious and respectable followers of the craft who wear out their eyesight under the lamp. But it is needless to multiply examples. Both for acquisition and for production also, natural faculty and aptitude are worth any quantity of toil. The gifted man will work, of course, because he cannot help it, and sometimes he will work with tremendous energy and magnificent perseverance ; but the difference between him and the dull struggler is that he simply exercises a power, whilst the other tries painfully to acquire one.

Dulness and difficulty are so common in the world, — there are so many aspirants whose natural gifts are manifestly insufficient for the tasks they undertake, — that we all feel a profound satisfaction when we see a man whose powers have authorized his desires. We feel, with regard to Regnault, that he had a clear right to lead the kind of life he chose, and to indulge the hopes which encouraged him. Seldom has any artist been more abundantly endowed with all the aptitudes which belong especially to the painter. His passionate delight in the pleasures of the eye was the first and most necessary gift of the true painter which he possessed ; but, besides this, he had that close sympathy with the physical half of life, which is so much rarer in our civilization than it was in ancient Greece, to our great loss and detriment as artists. In these days, it is rare to find a painter who can keep sufficiently clear of literary influences, who can really live the life of a painter, in the frank enjoyment of his eyesight, without half-blinding himself by thinking. Again, that closeness of sympathy with the physical, which I have just alluded to, is impossible for any one whose own bodily frame is not capable of a very high degree of activity; the habits of sedentary life are injurious to it, confinement in a great modern city may easily extinguish it altogether.

Henri Regnault was born in 1843, at the end of October, and was the second son of Victor Regnault, whose name is as famous in the scientific world as his son's name has since become in the world of art.

The reader may have observed that, as some evidence of the facility with which talent becomes hereditary, every subject of the biographies in this volume had a more or less distinguished father. Victor Jacquemont's father was a man of great acquirements and stoical courage, an able and voluminous writer, a patriot, with manhood enough in him to bear prison and exile rather than sacrifice his political convictions. The son, in turn, was also a man of great acquirements and stoical courage, was also an able and voluminous writer, and, though he lived in milder political times, proved his manhood by his unflinching resolution as a traveller The father of Henri Perreyve was not celebrated, but he was able and learned. Rude's father was not learned, being in humble life; but there is evidence that his intelligence was above mediocrity, as he introduced an invention into France which at the present day is most extensively useful. Jean Jacques Ampère had for his father one of the most illustrious scientific discoverers who ever lived. And now we come to Henri Regnault, whose father rendered such services to science that a mere enumeration of them occupied, when he died, three or four columns in each of the leading newspapers.

I have not space to enumerate them here; but a very brief outline of Victor Regnault's career will not be out of place.

He was born in 1810 at Aix-la-Chapelle, where his father, who was an officer in the French army, happened to be stationed with his regiment. By the time the child was eight years old, his father and mother were both dead; and he was left with all the difficulties of youth and poverty before him. He became a shop-boy, and carried parcels; but, notwithstanding what appear all but insuperable obstacles, he worked so resolutely at his own education that in 1830 he accomplished the feat of getting admitted into the École Polytechnique, as one of the first on the list of candidates. As this book is intended for readers outside of France, I may pause to explain that the École Polytechnique is a mathematical college, which has a limited number of vacancies every year, and that admission is won by a severe competitive examination, which only the most brilliant students have a chance of passing at all, — mediocrities never attempt it. The story of a poor parcel-carrying shop-boy in a provincial town getting into "Polytechnique"* by dint of hard labor, and in amongst the first, would be scouted as utterly improbable in a novel. However, Regnault got in, as we see; and, when he came out again, he was a student of mining (*élève des mines*). He advanced so rapidly in this profession that he became, in 1847, *Ingénieur en chef des Mines.* After that, his labors were purely scientific. His splendid experiments on the carburets of hydrogen, which, according to Berthelot, have become classical in the history of chemistry, led to his nomination to the chair of chemistry at the Polytechnic, and elevated him to the rank of Member of the Academy of Sciences in 1840. Thus he won, at the age of thirty, and at the very beginning of his scientific career, a position which others are happy to attain as the reward of a long life.

Then came a series of important researches on heat, and in 1841 he was appointed Professor of Physics at the Collége de France, where he set up his elaborately furnished laboratory; and in this laboratory he continued his investigations on heat, with practical studies relating to steam-engines and the dilatation and compressibility of elastic fluids, investigations which have since led to marvellous results in the liquefaction of gases. His study of steam advanced the theory of the steam-engine; and the practical tendencies of his scientific intellect led to his appointment, in 1854, as Director of the National Porcelain Factory, at Sèvres. The great scientific dis-

---

* Into "Polytechnique" is a customary form in France.

tinction of Victor Regnault is (according to those who are capable of judging these things) that he was one of the best makers of experiments who ever lived, that he made thousands of experiments with the greatest acumen, patience, and care.

In his own departments of intellectual labor, he was so eminent that he is constantly called "illustrious," an epithet always reserved for the greatest. He was a foreign member of the English Royal Society, and received the Copley and Rumford medals. He was also Corresponding Member of the Academies of Berlin and St. Petersburg.

Even this hasty sketch is enough to show that Henri Regnault was born in the aristocracy of intellect ; that the sentiment expressed in the glorious old motto, *noblesse oblige*, was likely to make itself felt in the young man's consciousness, so that he would desire "nothing common to do, nor mean." There is no place in the world where the son of a man of great intellectual eminence feels that stimulus so strongly as in Paris, because there a reputation stands firmly on its own basis, and is real substantial greatness in itself without the adjuncts of rank and wealth. Young Regnault, then, came into the world very like a young prince who has a great name to maintain by personal courage and effort.

His passion for drawing displayed itself very early, for when quite a child he would draw from memory what he had seen in his walks, especially horses and dogs. This love of animals lasted through life, and even influenced his choice of human subjects, directing his attention more especially to those Oriental races which, by their indolence in repose and their violent ferocity in action, most nearly resemble the wild beasts.   In his childhood, Henri was constantly asking to be taken to the Jardin des Plantes, where he delighted in watching the animals in their dens.   He observed their movements with persistent attention, so that it was difficult to get him away. So early as 1857, he wanted to be an artist, but at that time thought of sculpture rather than painting.   His father did not put any obstacle in his way, did not try to prevent him from becoming an artist, but, knowing the value of a good general education, required that Henri should complete his classical studies before en tering upon the special education of art.   M. Victor Regnault fixed upon the degree of *bachelier ès lettres* as the point to be attained before abandoning literary studies.   It is the lowest of the university degrees in France, and requires a very thorough knowledge of French, much Latin, and a little Greek, besides many other matters.   The paternal intention was simply to prevent his boy from growing up illiterate, as so many do who are carried away by a passion for the fine arts. Henri submitted to this as readily as Henri Perreyve submitted to pass his examination for the bar ; and, more than this, he gave his best efforts to his work, and succeeded in winning a good many prizes at the Lycée Napoléon, where he was one of the cleverest pupils.   He left school in 1859.

His father did not like him to enter one of the great studios of Paris, so he applied to Ingres and Flandrin for advice. As Flandrin could not take him, he being at that time occupied with the frescoes in St. Germain des Prés, he recommended M. Lamothe as a master. Lamothe was an old pupil of Ingres, and had the classical and religious traditions.

Henri Regnault set to work very ardently, and was admitted in 1862 to try for the *Prix de Rome*. He missed it twice, but had the courage to present himself a third time, in 1866, and succeeded. The subject was "Thetis brings to Achilles the arms forged by Vulcan." There is a pretty story connected with this success. He worked at first with great energy, but soon became dissatisfied with his composition, and expected a third failure. He lost hope, indeed, to such a degree that he thought it useless to go on. After he had renounced the attempt, but before the expiration of the time allowed for the contest (a few days yet remained), he went with his friend, Arthur Duparc, to pass the evening at a friend's house, and met a young lady whose face struck him forcibly by its uncommon aspect and its remarkable expression. He immediately made two sketches, and his friend observed that he became pensive. The next day he went back to his cell,* and resumed the abandoned picture, changing its form from an upright to an oblong, and "giving Thetis the delicate and distinguished profile of the young lady he had met the evening before." He worked like one in a fever: in twelve days, the new picture was finished, and it won the prize.

* The competitors are shut up in cells, and have to paint from memory, in complete isolation.

He had been working very hard in the year 1865, rising early and making the best of the daylight hours. This application had compelled him to renounce the pleasures of society. "I tried at first," he said, "to bear both the day's work and the fatigues of *soirées*, but found it impossible, and have decided to give up *le monde.*" After winning his prize, he went to Brittany, where he passed the month of September, and early in October he was called to Sèvres by a telegram which informed him that his mother was dying from inflammation of the lungs. He set off immediately, of course, but was stopped at Nantes by an inundation of the Loire, and obliged to go back to take the line from Quimper to Paris, so that he only arrived at Sèvres on the night of the 13th. By that time, his mother was lying in her place in the cemetery. On the 21st of the same month, an old aunt, for whom he had the most lively affection, was suddenly carried off. At five o'clock she was walking about, at six she was lying dead. So that the year which was brightened by the *Prix de Rome* was grievously darkened afterwards by these losses, which were dreadful blows to Henri, with his affectionate disposition.

He set off for Rome in March, 1867, suffering dreadfully from the cold on the line between Paris and Marseilles, a night journey which he afterwards compared to Napoleon's retreat from Russia. "I never was so frozen," he said, "in my life."

I may here remark that it was a peculiarity of his physical constitution to be exceedingly sensitive to cold, a fact of some importance, as it inclined him always to prefer southern regions, such as Italy, Spain, and Africa ; and this preference had a great influence on his destiny as an artist. Besides his physical dislike to cold, he had an intense natural repugnance to bad weather of all kinds, and would have been utterly incapable of any sympathy with those English and Scottish landscape-painters who delight in effects of rain. " Bad weather has followed us everywhere," he wrote. " We have been drowned at Nice, drowned at Genoa, drowned at La Spezzia, drowned at Rome: Florence alone had a kind smile for us."

The life of a *Prix de Rome*, when once settled there, is as charming as any existence that can be imagined. He lives with his comrades in a beautiful palace, with a fine park and garden ; a life adorned by painting and music, without a single material care, for the repasts in the refectory are better than those of the Roman restaurants.

The love of practical jokes, which is a defect of boys in general, and of young artists in particular, led to a very curious and cleverly imagined custom in former times, now fallen, I believe, into desuetude. New comers from Paris arrived generally in a carriage, and the old pupils went to meet them at Storta, fifteen miles from Rome. Then they escorted them to the Academy, where every thing was purposely made as wretched as possible for their reception. The rooms which were shown to them had been previously cleared of all but a little miserable furniture ; they dined in the worst room that could be found in the whole building, on a poor table, surrounded by broken chairs and lighted by dirty tallow candles, stuck in common glass bottles. The plates were all cracked, the forks were pewter, twisted and broken. The students quarrelled during dinner-time to make matters as uncomfortable as possible ; and one of them, dressed as a monk, read out aloud from the most tiresome Italian book that could be found.

Whilst Henri Regnault was at Rome in 1867, a story got about in Paris to the effect that he had been assassinated. Hébert received almost daily telegrams from Paris, asking if it were true. Regnault at last answered himself that "his monument would not be erected, *this year at least*, near to the one which was to be inaugurated to the memory of his comrade Deschamps," a ceremony for which he was requested to sing a requiem. What is really remarkable in this answer is that it looks prophetic to us, who know that a monument to Regnault's memory has been erected subsequently *in that very church, and close to that of the above-mentioned Deschamps !*

There is a time in the life of all intelligent young men when they are sure to idle, if they have the opportunity ; and, although such times are often bitterly regretted in after-life as lost months or years, the probability is that they have a special utility, and contribute an element not otherwise obtainable to the ultimate development of the man. I have touched upon this subject in the "Intellectual Life," and will not quote myself ; but I will quote once again the excellent assertion of Töpffer, that

" a year of downright loitering is a desirable element in
a liberal education." If it is so in the training of men
devoted to what may be called positive pursuits, it is so
still more decidedly in the education of authors and
artists, who require impressions and materials which are
often only hit upon by accident, and are not always to
be come by at the easel or the desk., In 1867, Henri
Regnault spent a great deal of time in intelligent *flânerie*
at Rome. He rose early, and immediately set off on
horseback for a long ride, coming back to *déjeuner* at
eleven, and visiting galleries and churches in the afternoon. These explorations of the neighborhood of
Rome, and of the artistic treasures in the city itself,
occupied the whole of his time till dinner; and then,
after a little music, he went early to bed. This is not
exactly the life of a hard-working painter : it is rather
that of a tourist of independent fortune, who is making
the most of a residence in the historic city by diligently
seeing what is to be seen ; but it was of use to Regnault,
who, of course, was incessantly observing. The mere
physical exercise was good for him also, even as an
artist, because it kept up his sympathy with animal life,
and also with human activity. I may mention as evidence of his interest in what was to be seen that he
and some comrades went to a country fair purposely to
observe the popular types and costume. They found
very little costume and very little beauty, the only feminine beauty discernible being that of some English
ladies, who had gone there, like themselves, from curiosity.
En revanche, if the people were not beautiful, they were

dirty, being obstinately conservative, if not of costume, at least of the ancient antipathy to cleanliness. " Our Bretons of Plogoff," said Regnault, "are refined marquises in comparison with them. What a distance between the peasant women of Rome and the fine, tall Breton women of the Pointe du Raz and the Isle of Sein!"

Soon after the opening of the Universal Exhibition of 1867 in Paris, the French art students of the Villa Medicis (the French Academy at Rome) obtained leave of absence. This was granted for two reasons, both in order that the young painters might see the collection of all the schools of Europe at Paris, and also because the cholera had attacked the Roman population, and the inhabitants of the Villa Medicis were in some danger of contagion. This upset Regnault's plans, and he returned to Paris, where he remained from June to December. He was in Rome again before the end of the year; and in January, 1868, he, with eleven of his fellow-students, went to see the eruption of Vesuvius. Seven of them ascended, including, of course, our hero, whilst the mountain was in full eruption; and he compared it to climbing coke in a coal-scuttle with a very steep slope. Regnault used his pen very cleverly, and described his impressions well. Perhaps the reader may like to have his description of this wonderful scene in the original:—

" Pour nous récompenser de nos fatigues, nous étions devant un spectacle vraiment infernal. La lave sortait en bouillonnant d'une sorte de tunnel, et coulait comme un torrent, avec l'éclat d'un métal fondu, rougi à blanc.

Par moments elle ralentissait sa course, se soulevait à plusieurs reprises comme la poitrine d'un géant essoufflé, et chaque fois laissait échapper comme un gros soupir de vapeurs sulfureuses que le vent chassait loin de nous.

"Au-dessus de nos têtes s'étendait un grand panache de vapeur éclairé par les reflets rouges de la lave. Toutes les dix ou quinze secondes le cratère vomissait un immense plumet noir foncé qui s'élevait comme un arbre colossal et retombait en cendres. Du milieu de ce jet noir sautaient des pierres enflammées qui montaient à une assez grande hauteur et retombaient en roulant sur les flancs du petit cône; c'était en grand un bouquet de feu d'artifice partant avec un vacarme proportionné à sa taille.

"Nous sommes restés là à peu près une demi-heure, jusqu'à ce que la nuit fut venue. Nos bâtons, trempés dans la lave, flambaient immédiatement comme des allumettes, et le courant était si rapide qu'il entraînait la pointe des bâtons sans qu'il fut possible de résister à sa force."

Regnault had been painting the portrait of a lady (Madame Duparc); and Hébert, the Director of the French Academy at Rome, was so pleased with this performance that he invited many great ladies to come and see it at the Villa Medicis.

"My humble student's rooms," Regnault wrote to a friend, "are always full of people, and my bare straw chairs have the honor of carrying Polish princesses in *ska*, the Princess de Sc——, the Countess de G——, the

Marchioness de No——, &c.　The prettiest ladies of Rome and the world in general (especially of America) pass before the portrait.　This enchanting public makes me compliments which I am not going to repeat.　They are too much exaggerated.　I content myself with virgin blushes ; and, truly, I am sometimes much embarrassed."

The interest which Regnault took in every thing at Rome led him to produce a great number of drawings on wood, representing the life and aspects of the wonderful old city.　Luckily for his purpose, the Pope had not yet in those days quite shut himself up in the Vatican, and Rome was still the unique ecclesiastical city, with that wonderful mixture of majesty and oddity which is not to be found elsewhere.　Regnault, who had explored every corner, and noted down in his retentive memory every bit of originality in the people, from the Pope and Cardinals down to the dirtiest beggar, found it a mere amusement to make many drawings on wood ; but he did them with so much vivacity and truth that he had a right to expect some recognition.　The woodcuts were exhibited at the Salon of 1868 ; and, by a strange caprice of the jury, the wood-engraver got a medal, whilst no notice whatever was taken of the brilliant designer, without whom it is probable that the wood-cutter would have been able to do very little.　As matters were, the original drawings were not improved by his treatment ; for one who had seen the drawings before they were operated upon by the burin and scalpel says that they were full of delicacy and intelligence when fresh from Regnault's pencil, but became heavy and vulgar when translated.

An odd accident happened to a picture which he had nearly completed in June, 1868, "Automedon breaking the Horses of Achilles." This picture was on a large scale, and was painted in a studio at a considerable height from the ground. The paint was not sufficiently dry to allow of its being rolled, the window of the studio was too big for it to pass on the stretching-frame, so it had to be detached, and then nailed by top and bottom to two cross-pieces, so that it might be neatly folded without creasing it, and then put out on the roof. Once there, the canvas was stretched out again, and let down by cords into the yard below. The operation was the more delicate that the figure of Automedon was not dry at all. Unluckily, there was a wind ; and everybody who has managed a sail knows what wind on canvas is. A single gust was enough to tear off the heads of the nails, to twist the canvas like a dish-cloth, and send it rattling down on the pavement far below in a state not at all adapted for public exhibition, the figure spoiled, and the rest cracked with great fissures. Regnault immediately decided to paint the whole over again in dead color, and send it to the exhibition as a sketch ; but afterwards he resumed work upon it ; and, as soon as it was finished, there was another fall, — not of the picture, this time, but the painter.

Henri Regnault had from childhood been passionately fond of horses, and now in the freedom of his student life at Rome he indulged this passion as much as his time and means would allow. There was an exceedingly handsome horse in Rome, belonging to a French officer, a commandant of Zouaves. This lovely but lively creature nearly killed its master on the day of the *Fête Dieu*, and when Regnault saw this outburst of equine energy he admired the animal more than ever, and the temptation to get upon his back became absolutely irresistible. He tried him, and found him "charming, — charming again the next day, pretty as the heart's desire, elegant, docile, graceful; just a little lively, but well deserving a prize for irreproachable conduct."

After that there were some little difficulties. This union of all perfections had a temper, and began to show it by stopping in an unreasonable manner, which led to some use of the spur. One day, Regnault had made an appointment for a ride with a gentleman and his wife, and they were waiting for him on the road at Ponte Molle. To his vexation, the horse kept him in a contest which lasted three-quarters of an hour, after which he rushed into the Via Flaminia as if he were racing. Regnault avoided the first carriage he met, but came into full collision with the second, which was a cart full of sand. The horse stopped as a cannon-ball stops when it hits a bastion, but Regnault was projected forwards with terrible force, alighting on his head near the feet of the cart-horse before him. He was brought back to the Villa Medicis covered with blood, but not insensible. His servant, Lagraine, nearly fainted on seeing him. The doctor found no bones broken, and put his head for forty-eight hours under ice, "like *champagne frappé.*" Four days afterwards, he left his bed.

The accident was of importance, because, in combination with frequent attacks of Roman fever, it led to a decisive medical order that the young painter should quit Rome. Persistent rumors had gained currency in Paris to the effect that he had been assassinated, a revival of the same rumor which had been so generally believed in 1867. Fortunately, a telegraph was there to admit of an early contradiction, and Regnault amused himself by writing a letter in the character of his own ghost. There is something sinister in these rumors, idle as they were; for they too soon associated the name of Henri Regnault with the idea of violent death.

Having quitted Rome on the 6th of August, 1868, Regnault first went to Marseilles by sea, and, after staying a week in a château in the south of France, went to Bayonne to join his friend Clairin, with whom he was to go to Spain. Clairin, who had been waiting a whole fortnight, lost patience, and pushed on; but they met afterwards. Regnault reached Bilbao some time in September, just in time to see a bull-fight, in which he took a passionate interest. The reader would, I believe, mistake the character of Regnault, if he concluded that horrible things had an attraction for him because they were horrible. Feats of strength and activity delighted him immensely, so much so that, although he disliked horrors, he could not tear himself away from them when they were associated with human or even animal agility and courage. This, I believe, is the true explanation of what has frequently been taken for a morbid pleasure in horror in Regnault's choice of studies and subjects. The following expression of his feelings about bull-fights, in a letter to his father, will, I think, set this in its true light : —

" I confess that the struggle with the picadors is very disagreeable to me ; the disembowelled horses, the men knocked down at every instant, and who run great risks in falling, all that produced a painful impression upon me. But the game of the matadors, banderilleros, espadados, &c., is really very effective. There were costumes marvellous for the richness and originality with which the tones of color were arranged. Unhappily, all the bulls were not completely killed. It is frightful to see the poor beasts tormented and made quite giddy by their enemies with cloaks and by the cries of the crowd. All this seems to me very sad, and yet I was glad to have seen it, and shall return to-morrow. The bull has sometimes fine movements, and amongst the men there are some who present themselves with such ease and such elegance that, although one regrets from the moral and humanitarian point of view that such things can be, one finds in them a most interesting spectacle from the artistic point of view."

Nothing can be clearer than this expression of opinion, which is evidently an exact account of the state of Regnault's mind. He could and did feel pity for suffering and a repugnance to the sight of even animal pain ; but his artistic admiration for courage, fine movements, and brilliant costumes, overcame his repugnance (without by any means extinguishing it) just sufficiently to attract him to the dreadful and beautiful scene again.

I feel it necessary to insist rather strongly on the artistic side of Regnault's strong and ardent temperament, because, if we lost sight of it, we should so easily misunderstand him. No men are so much exposed to this kind of misunderstanding as artists. Their interest in certain kinds of material for their art often becomes an overmastering passion, and impels them to frequent places for purposes of study which no one but an artist would select. In this way, landscape painters often bury themselves in the most outlandish villages, where there is no society, where there are no books or intelligent amusements of any kind, and they easily acquire a reputation for unsociableness and a desire to shun their kind, when the real explanation is probably nothing but the irresistible attractiveness of a very picturesque spot where a painter may work in peace. Figure painters are liable to misinterpretations of a still more damaging kind; for, when they have a taste for the picturesque in figures, they may be led, not to "talk with rocks and trees," "on lonely mountain ground," but to talk with very low people in dirty dwellings and popular drinking-places. Henri Regnault, who was one of the most thorough gentlemen of his time, — Henri Regnault, who was perfectly happy and at ease in the highest society in Paris and Rome, — had a passion, at Madrid, for the very lowest society that could be found, simply because it was so interesting to him as an artist. There was one place especially, no better than a hovel, in the Plaza de

la Cevada, much frequented by horsebreakers, coach-
men, porters, and fruit-sellers. "Frightful types are to
be seen there," said Regnault, "but there is a certain
Dolores, who sings Seguedillas, Gitanas, Malaguenas,
Rondenas, Palas, with a splendid contralto voice, such
as one can hear nowhere else, for it is almost a tenor,
and what a tenor! a voice that makes the whole place
vibrate! She is beautiful as the most beautiful antique
statue, more beautiful even, for she has eyes that see, a
mouth and lips that breathe, hair whose locks undulate
like serpents, and of a brilliant black. I want to make
a study of her for my 'Judith.'

"The Spaniards are truly a strange people. You cannot imagine the native distinction and politeness of all
these rascals, whom one would not be happy to meet
on the outskirts of a wood. They live *en famille* in that
wine-shop. The other evening, an Aragonese offered us
preserved fruits at the end of a *navaja* as big as a cavalry sabre. Every time we go there, we exchange little
courtesies. They are very hospitable, and in the low
class I find few who are not cordial and frank. They
are elegant and handsome, with their silk kerchiefs and
their vests of *majo*. They offer you their glasses to
drink from. Listen to the beautiful Lola, listen to her
singing, with her superb contralto-tenor voice, long
melancholy ballads, Gitanas, or Juguetas, interrupted by
great sighs on the lower notes, whilst the guitar embroid-
ers its variations on the same monotonous theme, which
transports you you know not whither. Then *hole, hole,
hole*, the audience become excited, the hands applaud,

and keep time as they applaud. One hears the footsteps of a handsome picador who stands up to dance, showing his white teeth and his broad silken girdle, on which fall two great chains of gold. Then Lola jumps on a bench or a table, and begins the same rhythmic movements."

Soon these picturesque people gained confidence enough in Regnault and his friend to come to the studio and *pose* in their curious costumes. Regnault went so far in the way of sociability that he actually became godfather to a little *gitano*, and here is a description of the manner in which the family lived : —

" I have been to see the mother, under the guidance of her husband, a good fellow, who took me to the little town inhabited by the *gitanos*, close to Madrid, near Retuan. It was night. We entered a large house all in a ground floor, divided into many small chambers. Each family occupies one. A fire of embers was in the middle of the room, on the brick floor. On one side were the straw mattresses they sleep upon. They were seated round the fire, the children with nothing on but ragged little shirts. The donkeys walk about freely in the rooms, and pass from one to another, eating the bits of straw which they find. We had brought three bottles of wine, which we distributed to these good folks. A handsome young man played the guitar, another sang, the women marked the rhythm by clapping their hands, the children danced. We sat on the ground in the biggest room round the fire, except the mother, who was ill and lay down. The scene was lighted by a little antique lamp, and the wine went round. Nothing can be more curious than these interiors, where the most wretched poverty reigns. The men are almost all dealers in asses and mules. They have the reputation of being able to bring dead donkeys to life, and of riding at full gallop on the corpses of mules. I belong to the family now, and they treat me in the most friendly way, wishing me health every time they meet me. They talk like high-priests, with a certain emphasis, and noble, majestic gestures. They often repeat to me ' *Señor Don Enrique, vaia usted con Dios y con salud.*' They never jest ; and one has to be very careful not to treat them too lightly, for they are prodigiously proud, and fear nothing."

Regnault lived so much *by the eyes* when in Spain that his letters are almost incessant descriptions of external things, touched lightly and rapidly with a master hand ; for he had a great literary gift, though there is no reason to suppose that he ever suspected it, absorbed as he was by the more attractive and amusing art of the painter. Every thing strikes him. He puts himself in the way of the popular festivals, and is glad to be out in the streets, seeing all that goes on. There is at the Academy of San Fernando, in Madrid, a little picture by Goya repre-senting an episode of the popular *fête*, the *Burial of the Sardine*. Regnault witnessed the same festival, and saw on Shrove Tuesday another episode, thoroughly Spanish, very strange and very paintable.

"In Spain (at Madrid at any rate), when the last sac-raments are taken to a sick person, the priest gets into a cab, and is escorted to the house of the dying person by men who carry torches and ring little bells. It was almost night: the crowd was leaving the Prado, and going down the Carrera San Geronimo, when the tinkling of the little bells became audible. The *cortége* passed; and, according to Spanish usage, both men and women fell on their knees. It is impossible to imagine any thing more grotesque than these maskers, with heads of camels, heads of monkeys, heads of devils, and big heads of Englishmen * in cardboard, throwing themselves on their knees."

The same Shrove Tuesday five frightful masks came bursting into the studio, and shook hands violently with Regnault and his friend. One of them represented a horrible-looking marquis, and turned out to be the beau tiful Dolores, the enchanting singer, accompanied by her guitar-player, her father, her cousin, and her cousin's cousin. After this, the whole party went the round of the cafés, in the low quarters of Madrid.

Regnault had a strong admiration for the politeness of the lower classes in Spain. "What astonishes me most," he said, "is the inborn distinction of all these good people. They are truly elegant, generous, polished. Oh, if I were king of Spain!" And again, in another letter: "The lowest has something of Don Quixote about him. He is never *canaille*, never mean, and a grandee does not consider himself dishonored because he allows a beggar to light a cigarette at his. I like the

---

* I hope the English reader feels flattered by the association with devils, monkeys, and camels. This may be taken as an illustration of international caricature.

people much : their politeness is exquisite, and they are obliging to a degree which is absolutely unknown to the French. For a whole fortnight, the town was in the hands of the lowest class, armed to the teeth, and yet there was neither a single robbery, nor any excess whatever. As I said to my father : Put Paris in the same state, and you would soon see what would happen." *

The costume of the women pleased Regnault as much as the popular manners. "The dress worn by ladies is very simple ; and, as the work-women wear it just as gracefully, with the same ease, the same natural distinction, different classes can mix together in public without incongruity, and even an inhabitant of Madrid may mistake one class for another."

I have mentioned already the ominous rumors which were current at Paris in two different years, to the effect that Regnault had been assassinated in Rome. In Madrid, he was nearly poisoned. One day, being very hungry, and at the same time too much interested in his work to take a regular meal, he took a piece of bread and cut it with his palette-knife whilst painting. The same evening he was in convulsions, and suffering from horrible pains, poisoned by some color which had been transferred from the palette-knife to the bread. The next day, fortunately, he was well again ; "but " — he wrote with a foreboding which (with our knowledge of his ultimate fate) seems prophetic—"*it is written that I shall die a violent death !*"

---

* This has been since confirmed by the outrages under the Commune, though even that was, on the whole, better than might have been expected.

Our hero was at Madrid during the revolution, which, in comparison with French ones, turned out to be a remarkably quiet affair. He called it "a model revolution, —the first wise and reasonable revolution that ever was." Not a drop of blood was shed, and the principal occupation of the people was the protection of property, the working-men and shopkeepers doing duty everywhere as armed policemen. We have just said that no blood was shed, but there was one exception. A thief had stolen an Englishman's gold watch, and was immediately shot. The watch was laid on his body in the public street, and left there till the owner claimed it. The incidents of the revolution delighted Regnault, because of their incessant picturesque interest.

"We do not lose our time," he wrote: "we visit all the *corps de garde* and the bivouacs ; we take notes, and on our return to the studio we sketch all that has most struck us in our walks. Madrid, just at present, is full of superb pictures ; the variety of costumes, the mixture of arms and rags, the courtyards, the streets, often very picturesque, are so many interesting motives."

The reader will observe in all the passages which I have quoted a remarkable combination of delicacy of taste with a spirit which does not shrink in the least from contact with the common people, but greatly enjoys its own interest in the living world around it, as we can imagine Shakespeare doing, or Cervantes. Himself a thoroughly well-bred person, and yet at the same time overflowing with a vigorous vitality, the young artist is delighted with a populace which gratifies his love of the

picturesque and his sympathy with life and movement
without offending his good taste. It would, however, be
a complete mistake to conclude from what has just been
said of Regnault's interest in the common people that
he abandoned his own rank in society. At the very
time when he would pass an evening with the *gitanos*, to
whose child he had become godfather, he would spend
two or three evenings in the same week in the saloons
of great ladies amongst the most aristocratic society of
the Spanish capital. These contrasts amused him, as
they generally do amuse men who have sympathy and
versatility enough to adapt themselves easily to such
widely different surroundings. It was in one of these
aristocratic drawing-rooms that Regnault first made the
acquaintance of General Prim. "He is very simple and
distinguished," Regnault wrote in a letter: "he has told
us all his adventures in detail; his life is a perfect
romance."

Regnault's friends, Count and Countess B——, saved
Prim in 1866, and induced him to come back to Spain in
1867. In 1868, they brought him from London to Spain
in the character of their domestic. He played his part
admirably and with imperturbable coolness.

"In their first retreat," Regnault wrote to his father,
"they ran great risks. Catalonia was full of spies
seeking for Prim, and orders were given to shoot him
wherever found. He had shaved his beard, and he
served the Count and Countess as if he had done nothing
else all his life.

"At *table d'hôte* in the hotels, he heard (with a napkin

on his arm and a plate in his hand) all that was said about him; and at that time people talked of nobody else. He knew how he was tracked, and it was only by discretion and precaution that he crossed the frontier. Even in France, he was not safe; and he was not at ease till he got to London."

In 1868, Prim came to Spain as a domestic, with a livery and a yellow waistcoat, and lived with his own servant, who was wretched at being compelled to treat his master as a comrade. At Cadiz, he changed his menial uniform for that of a general.

As soon as Regnault had made Prim's acquaintance, he wanted to paint his portrait, and obtained the Marshal's consent. I defer for the present what will have to be said about this work, when we have to consider Regnault's labors as an artist. The portrait is equestrian, which interested the young artist all the more, as he was so passionately fond of horses. All the horses in the royal stables were placed at his disposal as models to choose from, and this delighted him. His canvas was set up in a great coach-house; and near it there was a riding-school, in which grooms exercised the animals on purpose for the artist to observe their action. These facilities, in combination with Regnault's passion for the animal and his intense sympathy with and full understanding of noble horsemanship, made the Andalusian horse in the picture, as well as the movements of its rider, a striking and unquestionable success; but Prim disliked the picture, and refused it somewhat roughly. All the reasons for this refusal are not precisely known;

but it is thought probable that the principal one was because there were a number of armed Catalans in the distance, peasants with flags, recalling the revolutionary origin of the Marshal's power, which his aristocratic feeling did not quite like to be reminded of. Another reason was probably because his military love of smartness was rather hurt by an absence of neatness in the painted hero. Regnault had represented the general, not as he might appear at a review, but as he most probably was in real warfare, his hair not neatly brushed, but rather blown into disorder by the mountain wind, his hat off, and that general appearance of untidiness which every officer has in a real campaign, and which every officer is so careful to avoid in times of peace. It is highly probable that Prim's artistic sense may have been much inferior to his faculties for ruling men (the two gifts, as Leslie remarked, are scarcely compatible),* and that the picturesque element in the portrait may have offended a taste which was more military than artistic. Regnault resolutely refused to make the slightest alteration, and the picture remained on his hands. He and the Marshal exchanged letters, in which the forms of politeness were duly maintained on both sides ; but there the acquaintance ended. Before leaving the subject, I may mention a remark about Prim, which Regnault quoted as sagacious. He was really

---

* "The abilities required to govern a country are so far from including the accomplishments necessary to the formation of a fine collection of works of art, that it may be safely asserted they are scarcely compatible." — *Preface to the " Handbook for Young Painters."*

sovereign of Spain,—too much the sovereign, and some
people were remarking that he committed mistakes
which he might perhaps pay dearly for some day.

Regnault had left a good deal behind him in Rome,
—his servant and model, Lagraine, his dog, a black
greyhound, and a little collection of artistic properties,
such as carpets, tissues, &c., all which he desired to
bring away. Besides these things, there was his unfin-
ished picture of Judith and Holofernes, which he was
now anxious to complete. He therefore returned to
Rome in the spring of 1869, with the intention of doing
what remained to be done, settling his affairs finally,
and removing his effects to Spain. During this his
last residence in Italy,—a country which had strongly
interested him at first, but which now held a secondary
place in his artistic affections,—he received from Paris
the news of the effect produced by his portrait of Prim
in the Salon of 1869. There are a good many clever
portrait painters in France; but, notwithstanding the
great merit of much that they do, the Parisian public is
not accustomed to performances of such unquestionable,
irresistible power as the masterpiece which the Marshal
had refused. No sooner had it appeared than it made
a sensation from which no visitor escaped. Some were
delighted, others perplexed and astonished, as people so
often are by decided, self-asserting originality, — " indifference alone was impossible." Victor Regnault, with
paternal exultation, made a collection of the newspaper
articles in which his son's work was mentioned, and sent
them all to him in a packet. The effect was different,

perhaps, from what the reader may imagine. Notwithstanding the audacity of his manner of painting, which,
though it is only due to the strength and vivacity of the
young artist's sensations, may easily be mistaken for
effrontery, he was really and truly modest, — far more
modest, it is probable, than many whose ability and natural genius were considerably inferior to his own. In a
letter which occupies more than four pages of print, he
gives five lines to a commentary on his critics. "Those
Parisians must be mad to concern themselves so much
about me : *they must have very little to do.*"

He left Rome in the beginning of August, his sentiments about the place having undergone a complete
revolution since Spain had so much enchanted him ; and
his passion for Spain, though strong enough already,
was weak at that time in comparison to what it was
soon afterwards destined to become. He landed on
Spanish soil on the 9th of August, and at Alicante
divided his time between painting and photography.
Nothing could be more remote from the rigidity of the
photograph than Regnault's style in painting; but he
despised nothing that could help him, and applied himself to the photographic business, which was new to him,
with his usual *entrain* and energy. His father, as a man
of science, knew all about the scientific details of photography, and gave his son instructions by letter. A local
photographer kindly helped him over a great preliminary
difficulty, occasioned by the use of unsuitable water.

"We lead," he wrote, "the existence that I love. At
six in the morning, we set off with a guide and a donkey,

laden with an apparatus for painting and photography. We remain out all day ; and it is hot, I assure you. The evening, at nine o'clock, we return to Alicante : we plunge into the sea, and come back to supper at the hotel. After supper, we go up to develop our proofs in our own room."

" The country is superb : it is Africa, Egypt. Arid grounds of a marvellous form and color, a dazzling light, mountain outlines, wild and grand, palm-trees, nopals, fig-trees ! There is work enough for ten years, without going two leagues from Alicante."

This is from a letter to his father. At Elche, he writes to a friend, M. Cazalis, about delightful baths by moon-light, or when there was no moon ; but the sea was so starred with phosphorescence that there were times when he thought he was swimming in the Milky Way. " The beautiful country ! It is Africa already ! The nopals are familiar to us, and for the last three weeks we feed on delicious fruits, which must descend in a direct line from those of the Promised Land ! "

The two friends then travel over the mountains to Granada. They were by no means rich, having for the moment, between two of them, a sum of less than three pounds to take them about two hundred miles ; but they expected to find money at Granada. This tempo-rary poverty was caused by a voyage to Majorca, which I have passed in silence, as it gave little satisfaction to Regnault. Though naturally rather expensive in his tastes (having those of an artist and those of a gentle-man in combination), he could live gayly enough on

short commons, when the occasion required it; and the
two friends, with their servants (four persons to keep),
managed not only to do the journey on the sum just
mentioned, but actually arrived at Granada with a
balance of eighteen francs in hand, a feat of economy
which has few parallels even in the biographies of
artists.

Not only was the journey surprisingly cheap, but it
was a constant intoxication of delight. They slept on
the ground, wrapped in their cloaks, by the side of their
carriole (hired for a small sum for the journey); they ate
bread and figs, and it is probable that they drank nothing more expensive than water: yet notwithstanding
these little privations, which the exuberant good spirits
of youth and health only considered amusing, they were
in a state of such passionate enthusiasm about the glorious scenery, that they enjoyed their days of travel immensely, and might have sung after them with Byron :—

> "Whether we lay in the cave or the shed,
>   Our sleep fell soft on the hardest bed.
>
>   .   .   .   .   .   .
>
>   Fresh we awoke on the morrow.
>   All our thoughts and words had scope ;
>   We had health, and we had hope,
>   Toil and travel, but no sorrow."

"We have seen marvellous things!" he wrote to his
father from Granada, "of an incredible grandeur and
novelty. We must come back to them! Cular de Baza
and Guadix! they are written in my memory. I shall
never find in any land, not even in Africa and Syria,
any thing more imposing or more beautiful. What a

country! The inhabitants are not remarkable, but the country! the country!"

At Granada, Regnault found the supreme delight of his life as traveller and artist. The enthusiasm of poets, in their most powerful verses, has never surpassed in strength and intensity Regnault's fiery but careless prose, written rapidly in letters to his most intimate friends, and as little intended for the public eye as the Indian letters of Jacquemont. As Tennyson declared himself a Mussulman when his imagination was filled by the Arabian Nights, so Regnault fancifully affirmed his adhesion to Mahomet, because he had "inspired such a work as that!" The eloquence of his enthusiasm filled his letters with all the hyperbole of Oriental fancy. He wrote like one possessed by the Muse, and with splendid though unconscious ability. The temptation to make quotations is here stronger than ever; but I resist it for the present to advance with the story of the life. The same shadow of early death, which we have noticed once or twice already, broods even over these, the most brilliant of all his letters. "And then," he says, speaking of his companion, "Clairin and I are destined to a short existence. We lead too vagabond a life, we spare ourselves too little, we have too much ambition, too many desires, to attain old age. It is probable that we shall not die together."

He had always this mournful sense of the shortness of life in general, and the special, exceptional brevity of his own. Here is a note, written by him in Spain: —

"*Life being short*, one must paint as much as his eyesight will permit. Consequently, one ought not to fatigue them by reading stupid newspapers."

Here is another extract, evidence of the same state of feeling : —

"An idea which pursues me and pains me is the fear of breaking down on the journey of life before having seen all I want to see, and especially before having made use of my materials. I am wretched not to be able to see into the future, and not to be sure that time will not be wanting for the accomplishment of what I desire to do. If I could but say to myself : 'In two or three years, you will come back laden with materials ; you will know a good deal, and you will have twenty-five years to express what you know.' Oh, then all would go well ; but the notion of dying on the road, — it is *that* which crumples me up."

A little later, being still pursued by the apprehension of not having time enough in his life to do what he wanted to do, he wrote the following remarkable sentences : —

"I have but a single thought now, and that is to make up for lost time. Oh, if I could but make the years of six hundred days, and the days of forty-eight hours ! Life is short." And then he adds, "*Perhaps it will be shorter for me than for others.*" Then he takes a firm resolution to live more seriously in future: there is to be no more idle gayety, no more riding of horses, no more gymnastics, no more music, — he is to be dedicated exclusively to his art !

He was at Granada in September ; and in December we find him at Gibraltar, greatly enjoying the society of British officers there, especially of some Scottish officers, who were very hospitable to him, as they probably soon found out that he was a manly fellow, and a gentleman. Perhaps his horsemanship won their hearts, for he hunted with them.

English hospitality seemed to him "charming, but too feeding ; one has to be always eating and drinking." He bathed every day in the sea, and wondered how he would endure a Parisian winter after that.

He chose Granada rather than Seville for his head-quarters, because in the first place there was the Alhambra, — an inexhaustible mine of treasure, and also because his friend Clairin and he could live in the most undisturbed solitude, "in an excellent hotel, where we shall see nobody during the winter, and where we are separated from the town by magnificent trees, which cover the hill on which the Alhambra is built. Here we feel far from mankind ; for one has few opportunities for seeing humanity up there, above the noise of the streets, and one is sure to enjoy that peace which is necessary to the regular pursuit of work."

I like these two opposite qualities in Regnault's character, — his appreciation of the value of solitude, and his hearty interest in human life. At Madrid, instead of shunning the crowd, he had sought it on every possible occasion, and observed life in all classes of society, from the drawing-rooms of duchesses to the miserable hovel of the *gitano*. At the Alhambra, he is happy to be alone with his friend Clairin, that he may work on undisturbed. His appreciation of the value of solitude was simply that of the worker who knows that results are always greater when the hours of labor are unbroken.

Much as Regnault loved Spain, he had looked beyond it from Gibraltar to the African shores of the Mediterranean; and the passion for light — intense, regular, splendid light — which was in his nature, and which made him prefer Italy to France, and Spain to Italy, disposed him also to prefer some city of Morocco even to his enchanting Granada. The gradation is clearly marked in a letter to M. Montfort: —

" I confess that Italy, after Spain, seems to me very dull, too well known, and used up. The Italians, both men and women, weary me: their costumes seem to me black, dull, or glaring, without harmony. What a difference from Spain, *which nevertheless is but a stepping-stone!* It is the East which I call for, which I desire, and will have! It is there only, I believe, that I shall really feel my own powers." Even in April, 1869, he writes to M. Duparc, " I wish I were already in Morocco!"

He visited Tangier for the first time in December, 1869, to make arrangements for a long stay. His servant, Lagraine, was to have arrived at Gibraltar from Rome in the beginning of December, but there was no news of him, nor could any news be obtained, with all the facilities of the telegraph. He ascertained that the boat which left Marseilles at the time when Lagraine would be ready to leave, according to the programme

of his voyage, was the " Sonerah ; " and, as the sea had
been rough, it was thought probable that this vessel had
taken shelter somewhere on the coast of Spain. Regnault accordingly left for Tangier by himself, after
waiting two days at Gibraltar for the missing steamer.
At Tangier, he got a telegram announcing that the
"Sonerah" had gone to the bottom without leaving a
single survivor to tell the tale or send a message. The
effect of this news may be best described in his own
words : —

"I passed a terrible, agitated night. I felt remorse
for having caused the poor young fellow to leave Rome
to make him perish so miserably. I thought of the last
moments of this creature, who loved me so much, and
who must have so much suffered from the thought that
he would never see me again, and that all the things
which I had intrusted to him and recommended to his
care would go down with him and be lost. Perhaps
it was in the endeavor to save the case which contained
my picture that he had missed the opportunity of saving
his own life. I made to myself a horrible drama in my
brain."

These words convey something ; but I have no doubt
they fall far short of the truth. We must remember
that Regnault's memory and imagination were far more
powerful than those of ordinary humanity, and that his
power of realizing scenes and absent persons as if he
saw them, already remarkable by nature, had been enor-
mously increased and intensified by his studies as a
painter. He would, therefore, during that terrible night

at Tangier, as he lay sleepless on his bed, not imagine vaguely, as less gifted and cultivated persons might imagine, but actually *see* the shipwreck and his good servant's struggles and death with the vividness which belongs to the eye of the painter only.

Regnault went back to Gibraltar by the next steamer, and there beheld on the beach a tall man, who gesticulated violently as soon as he recognized him. This man was the interpreter at the Club House Hotel, who knew Regnault ; and, as soon as the steamer was near enough for a human voice to reach it, the good, kind-hearted fellow shouted with all his might, " He is not lost : he is gone to Tangier this morning ! " — for everybody at Gibraltar had heard of Regnault's supposed misfortune. He could not believe the good news ; but, when he landed, other witnesses confirmed it. The explanation was, that although the " Sonerah " had, unhappily, really foundered, Lagraine was not on board. He had had the good luck to take another boat, which had missed the correspondence at Oran for Tangier ; and this had caused a week's delay, besides four days at Malaga.

When Regnault got back to Tangier, behold, Lagraine and his dog were waiting for him on the shore ! The dog nearly devoured him in its joy (the poor creature had not seen its master since he left Italy, and dogs have not the consolation of letters), whilst Lagraine seized Regnault's hand, and shook it so that he said, " Il me brisa la main d'amitié."

The joy at the recovery of his servant, his dog, his picture, and all the belongings of his studio, added to

the delight of finding himself in the clear African sunshine, and surrounded by the sort of material for his art
which most interested him, made the time he spent at
Tangier the happiest of his brief existence. He wrote
to Clairin, who still remained at Granada, urging him to
come to Africa, as Granada was a cold place at that
season, whereas the temperature of Tangier was of a
delicious mildness. "In the spring," says Regnault,
"I shall leave my establishment here to go and finish
at Granada what I have begun there. So my dream
will be realized! I shall sketch some scenes here, and
then go to the Alhambra to paint pieces of architecture
which belong to the subjects, after which I shall return
here to put the last touch to the figures. All will be
arranged for the best."

The two friends set up house at Tangier in rather
handsome style. They rented a delightful old Moorish house, which was already admirably adapted for a
painter's needs. It was very conveniently situated, and
had a *patio* or court, which they covered with a glass
roof, so that it made a splendid studio, and the glass
was so arranged that it could be removed at will. The
two artists permitted themselves some Oriental comforts
and splendors in their sufficiently spacious rooms; but
their good taste, and artistic dislike to the incongruous,
made them reject European furniture. "There are no
chairs in the establishment," says Regnault: "all European ugliness is prohibited." Their establishment of
servants was rather numerous for two devotees of a

proverbially unremunerative art ; * but Regnault had a
right to be hopeful now.   There was Lagraine, to begin
with, too ingenious to be employed in merely menial
occupations, and "exclusively occupied with photography, joinering, care of stretching frames, canvases,
colors, and accounts."   A man able to attend efficiently
to all these superior matters must have been a treasure
indeed.   Then there was Nana, a Christian cook, the
wife of an ex-consul, who had fallen into poverty, a
youth called Khadder, who went on errands and kept
the house clean, a maid called Aïscha Tchama, who was
laundress.   Regnault had also a Master of the Horse in
the person of his groom, Ali Pata, "a little fellow fifty
years old, monstrously ugly, four feet high, a real Tri-
boulet, gifted with a charming originality, with a great intelligence, and an elephantiasis into the bargain, which
makes one of his legs as big as his body, whilst the other
is shrivelled, and no bigger than a *thin* lucifer match."
This grotesque personage comes in capitally in the description of an Oriental establishment, and I hope the
reader notices the exquisite exaggeration in the last
adjective.   A common lucifer match is too thick to give
a just-idea of the meagreness of poor Ali Pata's limb,
which is like a *thin* lucifer, no more.   Ugly as Ali Pata
may have been, he was recommended to Regnault by
an ambassador as *a pearl.*   Let us remember there are

---

* In France, *pauvre comme un peintre* is a well-known proverb, and,
notwithstanding the large incomes made by a few, I fear that the proverb
is still too near the truth.

ugly pearls as well as pretty ones. He spoke Spanish well, and was interpreter, besides which he had the reputation of being the best horseman in Tangier, notwithstanding his deformity. It is scarcely necessary to say that Regnault had a horse, and that the horse had the most charming qualities in his eyes. " I have a love of a little horse, quiet, intelligent, and strong." And, besides his own dog, he has a leash of greyhounds. With this establishment in the ancient Moorish dwelling, the two young friends lived like princes, and had ideal delights in the exercise of their talents and the passion for their art which many a prince might envy. The glory of the African sunshine made the place a paradise to Regnault.

" Every time we go upon our terrace we are dazzled by the brilliance of this City of Snow, which goes down from our feet to the sea like a great staircase of white marble, or a covey of white sea-gulls.* I do believe that the sun which lights you is not the same as ours."

The reader is probably aware that the art students of the French Academy at Rome have to send a picture every year to the École des Beaux Arts at Paris, as evidence of industry and progress, in return for their pension and the facilities for living and study afforded at the Villa Medicis. This annual picture is always called the *Envoi*, and it is supposed to be painted in Rome ; but, by the connivance of the Director, it may, of course, be

---

* Regnault's earnest desire to convey the idea of whiteness overpowers, in this instance, his literary judgment. Snow is too chilly to be introduced here, and the sea-gulls too restless for houses to be compared to them. The staircase of white marble would have been sufficient.

executed elsewhere, in which case, however, the student, to keep up appearances, would add the finishing touches in Rome itself, where the *envois* are exhibited before they go to Paris. Regnault, by his residence in Spain and Tangier, was in fact a sort of truant from the Academy, to which he still belonged, and from which he drew an annual allowance ; but, to conciliate his taste for Africa with the duties of his position, he wrote to M. Hébert, the Director, begging him to permit the continuation of his residence at Tangier, where he had every thing necessary for his work, and promising that, when his picture was nearly finished, he would go with it to Rome. His own private intention was to finish the picture as nearly as possible at Tangier, and only to go to Rome in the beginning of 1871. "The first necessity for working well," he said, "is to like the place where one is at work, and to feel sustained by the material that the eyes can dwell upon. Now I feel myself well off here, and so I remain."

He had some little commissions to execute at Tangier, and when these were finished he started for the Alhambra at the end of March, but passed some time at Seville, where he found a new pleasure in studying the Murillos, which gave him a new and much higher idea of the master. The two friends arrived at Granada on the 21st of April. After staying there till the 5th of May, they rode to Guadix, on the other side of the Sierra Nevada, being nine hours on horseback in hail, rain, snow, and wind. All the landscapes in that part of Spain excited Regnault's enthusiasm to a high degree,

for he was almost as much alive to the beauty and sublimity of landscape as he was to the strength and grace
of human beings and animals. Cular de Baza was one
of his favorite places in Spain for landscape, and it was
Regnault's intention to paint a great picture of its
scenery, a pure landscape. He drew many landscape
studies in a powerful and simple manner.

Leaving Spain at the end of May, 1870, Regnault
returned to Tangier, where he bought some land and
erected upon it an immense studio, to paint a very big
picture in. He had quitted the Alhambra before quite
finishing his studies there, being full of ardor about the
magnum opus, and anxious to begin. His anxiety to do
something of great size and fine quality was much increased in the present instance by the knowledge that
it was to be the last of his *envois* as *Prix de Rome*, and
was to be purchased by the Minister of Fine Arts for
the Luxembourg collection. "Je suis pris," he said, "de
la rage de mon tableau, il faut que je parte, il faut que
je commence."

His building scheme at Tangier included not only a
painting-room, but also a residence, which Regnault
playfully called a little palace. Its situation was outside
the city on the road to Fez, sufficiently near town for
convenience, and near the road, which Regnault found to
be an advantage artistically, as he could see the passers-
by, the groups of peasants, the caravans of camels, and
all the other elements of the picturesque Oriental life.
There was a fine view, too, of the citadel and across the
channel ; and the situation was so much in the country

that there were no houses in the neighborhood. He had unfailing water on his little property, with a few fig-trees and pomegranate-trees. The painting-room was of quite magnificent dimensions, being fifty-two feet long by thirty-four wide, with a height of thirty-three feet. This was the important building; for Regnault, like all true painters, very wisely and properly thought of his studio first and his home after. The "little palace" was to be merely a cottage; but here again the decided personal tastes of the young gentleman display themselves, for he carefully plans his stabling and dog-kennels.

All this may seem somewhat extravagant; but every profession has its own kind of economy, and Regnault understood a painter's economy very clearly. His intention was to keep this studio at Tangier all his life, and return to it to paint all his *large* pictures. He would thus have no need of a large studio at Paris, where the rent of such a place amounts to at least £150. The expense and loss of time occasioned by long journeys from Paris to Tangier were to be, in Regnault's project, more than compensated for by cheapness of living, in a delightful climate, and by the regularity of the light, which never fails in Morocco. Besides these considerations, there was the certainty of tranquillity favorable to work, and all possible elements for the kind of pictures which Regnault desired to paint. "Always fine forms, fine tones, interesting groups before one's eyes! One cannot open the door without seeing pictures ready-made."

I have gone into the details of this scheme because

it throws a strong light on Regnault's character. The reader may remember (for he is sure to have heard it) the common assertion that Frenchmen love Paris more than any other place, and are unhappy at a distance from it. I know a good many quiet country folks in France who find ample happiness in their own fields, and in the nearest little country town, without ever thinking of Paris, except to wish it would keep quiet and not trouble them with explosive revolutions. Here you have a brilliant young painter, the son of a man with a splendid scientific reputation, with access to the society of the capital and its pleasures, who tranquilly turns his back on both, and builds a studio on the opposite shore of the Mediterranean (not even in the French colony), that he may be able to work in peace, and a good light. "J'aime autant cela que vos revolutionnaires parisiens. Ici nous ne faisons pas de politique."

There was one practical difficulty in living at such an out-of-the-way place as Tangier, which Regnault had not foreseen, — the distance from an artists' color-maker. He ran short of white (painters always run short of white), and wrote pressing notes to his father about that and other materials. Meanwhile, he had to go on working as he could, and said that his picture would have been " bien plus éxecuté," if he had not been deprived of white so long.

The flight of time now brought Regnault to an epoch in the history of his country when he and every Frenchman worthy of the name had other things to think about than private inconveniences, be they even so irritating as the want of white to a painter. War was declared whilst he was still at Tangier, and his distance from France left him exposed to anxieties which sprang from the imagination as well as to those which were only too fully justified by facts. False news came to him from all quarters, to be contradicted the next day by other news which agitated him, although it might be equally untrue.

"We have hardly the heart to paint," he wrote home to his father : "we await the arrival of every steamer from Gibraltar, and seize the newspapers and letters ; we hurry to the Embassy in the hope of a little news. We consult maps, we discuss the probabilities of strategic marches, we compare the different despatches."

At the outbreak of the war, Regnault's *envoi* picture, a copy of the famous *Lances* of Velasquez, was exhibited at Paris along with an original work of his which has since become celebrated, the *Exécution sans Jugement.*

I shall not pause to speak of these at present, for art was completely forgotten in those days of intense national excitement. Who would care about pictures by young Academy students in London, if a Russian army, two or three hundred thousand strong, were advancing on London through the green lanes of Kent?

When it became evident that Paris would be invested, Regnault could bear his voluntary exile no longer, and quitted the charming new studio, the bright atmosphere of Tangier, the devoted servants, the picturesque people, the animals that he loved, never to see them more. Never more was he to work in the great studio, never again to sit in the shadow of his own fig-tree, near his well, when the day's work was over, and watch as he smoked his pipe of peace the last rays of splendid sun-shine redden the rock of Gibraltar across the purple waters.

His constitution delighted, as I have said, in heat, and was so ill-adapted to the cold that he could not endure it without much inconvenience, amounting, when it was prolonged, to positive suffering. This tendency had been greatly augmented by his residence in warm climates. The mild winters of Tangier delighted him ; but, whilst they did not enervate, they certainly left him less than ever adapted to the severity of a Parisian winter, and that of 1870–71 was of quite exceptional severity. He accepted, nevertheless, all his military duties without a murmur, only observing to one of his correspondents that he was ill-prepared for the cold nights.

" We have slept under canvas at the foot of Mount Valerien, at the Folie-Nanterre, exposed to the most icy and violent wind during the three coldest nights of the year. In those nights, many soldiers were frozen. It was rather a hard trial for us, and especially for me, who had passed four winters running in hot countries."

Scarcely expecting to get through the terrible cam-paign alive, he concerned himself about all his affairs, writing to a friend at Tangier to see his servant La-graine, and mind that he had money enough for the current expenses. He added, " In case I should die during the war, Clairin's father will have a paper on which I have expressed my last wishes."

A marriage of affection had been arranged since Regnault's return from Africa between him and a young
lady whom he greatly esteemed and had long thought
of seriously in his own mind. This engagement gave
him an additional reason, and a powerful one, for desiring
to live; yet he exposed himself as freely as if he had
been completely indifferent to existence. He saw the
young lady every day when his duties permitted a short
absence from the front, and returned to his post encouraged by the expression of an affection which in those
terrible times may have been more freely and unre-
servedly demonstrated than in the formality of ordinary
existence.

Regnault served as a private soldier. He had first
enrolled himself as a *franc-tireur*, but afterwards yielded
to the solicitations of his friends, and entered the *Garde
Nationale sédentaire.* This, however, was too quiet for
him, and he soon entered a marching battalion. It was
obvious that such a man as Regnault ought to have been
an officer; and this rank was offered to him, but he
simply declined it, both on the ground of his want of
military experience, and also because he thought his
example in the ranks might be of more use than his
command. "Being decided to undergo without flinching
the fatigues and disagreeables of the business, without
shirking any one of them, to be the first at fatigue duties
and the foremost under fire, I hope to induce others to
come with me who might be disposed to grumble and
hold back. There are a good many of us who are
animated by these sentiments, but they can never be

sufficiently numerous. You have a good common soldier in me : do not lose him to make a mediocre officer."

This is exactly the temper which I have been praising in Rude, the sculptor, — the temper which is satisfied with its rank, and has no desire to rise above it, yet has the strongest possible desire to do what is most honorable, most worthy of a man, in the rank, however humble, which he happens to occupy.

Meanwhile, in the meetings with his betrothed, Regnault indulged in dreams of future happiness and plans of travel. They were to visit Spain together, of that we may be quite sure, to stay at Granada and see the wonderful Alhambra. They were to cross the Narrow Sea between the Pillars of Hercules and see the little property on the road from Tangier to Fez, where Lagraine was thinking anxiously of his young master, and the dogs were wearily awaiting his return.

He had need of all these hopes to comfort him a little in the fearful reality of those nights of cold.* "Oh! I can speak with full knowledge of the cold, and I know this morning what it is to pass a night on the hard

---

* In connection with this subject, I give myself the pleasure of relating a little anecdote. A young friend of mine who was in the Mobiles was seized during one of those terrible nights in the outskirts of Paris with an attack of illness brought on by the cold, so severe that he thought himself dying, and would most probably have died before morning, had not a man come to him with a large can of hot tea, which he no more expected than he expected a supper from Véfour's. This was due to the exquisitely thoughtful benevolence of Sir Richard Wallace, who saved many a life in this and other ways during the siege. All France honors his name, and all England ought to be proud of it.

ground, exposed to an icy wind. Four of our men are frozen."

On Tuesday, the 17th of January, 1871, the battalion was ordered to the outposts. About noon, Regnault went to say good-bye to the family of his betrothed. The parting was sad and ominous. He knew that he was going to the combat, and took the precaution of having the following words sewed on the lining of his tunic : " Henri Regnault, painter, son of M. Victor Reg-nault, of the Institute," adding the address of the house he had just left, and requesting that his body might be brought back to it. He took with him a little packet of letters and portraits, on which he had written, " For my betrothed." The combat took place on the Thursday, and his betrothed had news of him at noon that day by a servant who had come for a horse, and who was in good spirits, announcing that the redoubt of Montretout had been carried. Clairin was with Regnault, by his side. I now quote the account given by M. Cazalis :—

" About four — night was falling — the fight raged furiously in a wood near the park of Buzenval. In the tumult of the engagement, the two friends, who had hitherto kept near to each other, were separated. The retreat was sounded. Clairin sought Regnault, and could not find him : he ran to the front, called, rejoined his company, still could not find him, returned between the trees which the dying were supporting their backs against, went from one body to another, calling his friend's name all through the gloomy wood, and hearing no answering voice."

Clairin sought anxiously the whole night through. At last, he found a man who had seen Regnault, just when the retreat was sounded, go near the wall behind which the Prussians were hiding themselves. Regnault had been called for at this moment, but he had answered, " I shall fire my last shot, and come immediately." The man believed that an instant after this he had seen Regnault fall.

Clairin returned to Paris after a fruitless search, and at six all his worst apprehensions were fully confirmed. News was brought in by an *ambulancier* that Regnault had been found, and in evidence he brought a little chain with a silver tear. This tear had been given to him by his betrothed ; and when she gave it she had said, " Take it, now that I am happy, but you must give it back to me the first time you make me weep." And now the tear was brought back to her, and she wept.

The *ambulancier* who brought this souvenir of the dead had left the body, which was still not easy to find, as it had been subsequently removed with about two hundred others. This was on the Saturday, and on Sunday morning the bodies were laid on the ground at the cemetery of Père-la-Chaise; and here Clairin found what remained of his friend, and kissed the beloved face, all soiled with the earth of the battle-field. There was but one wound, in the left temple. Death had been instantaneous, and without pain.

When Regnault's betrothed heard where his body lay, she went in person to pay it the last duty of her love.

She bore the trial with heroic fortitude. Father Gratry, who was to have married them, wrote a noble letter to her, touching the right chord. "Lift up your soul!" he said. "This world is not a cruel game nor a vain appearance. To die for a sacred cause cannot be nothingness and vanity. It is a great thing which has results. Such an act, such a gift of self, has a reality which subsists. No small thing is lost, still less any thing great. Every martyr has his eternal life in full and substantial truth."

What shall I say of this premature death, — this sacrifice of life just when it was promising all its richest and fairest gifts: the joy of triumphant labor; the satisfaction of reputation won fairly and honorably, without the slightest intrigue, without a moment's abandonment of dignity; the enjoyment of all the innocent pleasures which belong to a robust and vigorous manhood, joined to an exquisite organization, — horsemanship, swimming, music, travel in the noblest scenery, or tranquil residence in the places that he loved best, — a life, too, already brightened by a hope of that which in its quiet reality is better than all else which this world has to give, — the supreme felicity of a marriage neither arranged as a matter of interest nor entered into from thoughtless passion, but founded on clear knowledge and firm affection, — what shall I say of a death by which all these fair possessions and still fairer anticipations were sacrificed, and sacrificed to a hopeless cause in the last combat of a weary war, which from first to last had been nothing but discouragement and disaster?

Simply this, that such a death is better than the happiest, the most prosperous life that the whole world can offer. It is better to die like Regnault, slain in the flower of manhood, than to live, like Titian, to one's hundredth year.

I can imagine some cool person answering that this is exaggerated, because, after all, there was nothing exceptional in Regnault's conduct, — that when his body was laid in Père-la-Chaise two hundred others were laid there with him, who died for their country as he did.

God forbid that I should undervalue the humblest of these lives that were laid down for their country then ! I would not rate them the less because they had not skill and genius, for the dullest and least gifted may have been Regnault's equals in moral worth and virtue and patriotism. But there are two or three things to be specially considered in his case, and which account in some degree for the exceptional fame which has followed the death of Regnault, whilst others have passed into oblivion.

In the first place, he was under no legal obligation to serve in the army at all. As a *Prix de Rome*, he was entirely exempt, that being one of the great privileges of the *Prix de Rome*. People were sometimes sufficiently ill-advised to remind him of this, and say : " But why risk yourself ? You need not serve : don't you know that your prize exempts you ? " He used to answer such people with perfect silence and a *look*. What the look expressed I leave the reader to imagine.

In the second place, whilst serving, he might easily

have avoided extraordinary risks, but incurred them voluntarily, as a hundred instances testify, for the express purpose of keeping up the courage of less spirited comrades, his aim being to set an example as a model private soldier.

In the third place, he was a Frenchman absent from France when the war began, living in great ease and comfort an ideally charming existence in a delightful climate where he had established a home exactly suited to his tastes. At a time when many other comfortable people went away from Paris, as far as they could for safety, he came to the city on purpose to be shut up during the siege and suffer cold and hunger, and expose his life day and night upon her ramparts.

Again, life offered far more alluring prospects to him than it does to most men, far more of those attractions which turn heroism into prudence. The reader knows this already, and I need not dwell upon it.

Since Henri Regnault's death, the merit of his heroism has been greatly augmented in the eyes of thoughtful people by the discovery from certain passages in his papers that it was not mere animal courage, not merely the instinct of combativeness, but that it sprang from a firm though quiet conviction in his own breast, and as deep a sense of duty as ever animated the most resolute of patriots. Several such passages might be quoted. I select one written upon a paper which was found on his dead body : —

"We have lost many men, and must now endeavor to replace them by others, stronger and better. The lesson ought to be of use to us. Let us no longer soften ourselves by the pleasures of ease. Life for one's self alone is no longer allowable. Some time ago, it was the fashion to believe in nothing but enjoyment, and in all vicious passions. Egotism should be put to flight, and with it that fatal habit of glorying in the contempt for all that is honorable and good. To-day, the Republic commands to all of us a serious, pure, and honorable life. We ought to pay to our country, and above our country to free humanity, the tribute of our body and our mind. We ought to give what these can effect together. All our forces should work together for the good of the great family, whilst we ourselves practise and develop in others the sentiment of honor and the love of work."

The reader will please to remember that this is not a public speech, but a strictly private, sincere expression of the writer's most intimate thought. He expected the same patriotism in others, in those nearest to him, and said, at the beginning of the war, "I shall be very glad to know that Eugène (his brother) is in the camp, — *under fire*, if necessary."

How true the metal rings! There is no base mixture of self-interest or family interest here! The sound is clear as the trumpet, pure as the melody "that's sweetly sung in tune."

The Friday after Regnault's death, the very morning when the capitulation of Paris became generally known, a funeral service for the repose of his soul took place in that large new church of St. Augustine, which every

26

visitor to Paris will remember. It is one of the strangest
things in the history of that strange and terrible time
that, although Paris had lost its inhabitants by hundreds
and by thousands during the siege, and had become
deadened to the sense of calamity, a thrill of pain — pain
of a kind not felt before in all that miserable experience
— ran through the city when public rumor first told of
Regnault's death. Even the humiliating news of the
capitulation could not make Paris indifferent to the
mournful ceremony at the church of St. Augustine.
His own family, being absent, were still uninformed of
their loss ; but every famous man then in the capital
came to mourn for him as for a younger brother. The
nave of the church was so thronged that it could not
hold the people. His comrades in arms were there *en
tenue de campagne.* Drums, muffled with crape, filled
the church with their lugubrious noise, and — sadder
than all the black hangings and the crape and the
chanting and the drumming — close by the bier lay one
little fragrant bouquet of white lilac, sent by his betrothed.

From that day, Regnault's name, partly from his own
indisputable merits as an artist, and partly from the
striking circumstances of his death, passed into the
rank of the immortals. His country had a real though
mournful satisfaction in the sacrifice of one of her
noblest and best. Popular feeling took Regnault's name,
and inscribed it in the national memory. Englishmen
may smile at this national idolatry of the brilliant young
artist, soldier, gentleman, and it may be conclusively

proved that he was not the only patriot in France; but England has Sir Philip Sidney, and there is this analogy between the two, — that in both cases a man of genius, adorned with all knightly and graceful accomplishments, admirably fitted for the enjoyment of life, threw life away for his country. I cannot blame the popular tendency to select from the multitude of the slain a few of the best and bravest to be remembered ever after as examples. Many an English officer may have been more thoughtful for his troops, because he remembered the beautiful humanity of the dying Sidney, and many a Frenchman, in times to come, may more willingly accept hard months or years of military service when he remembers the self-sacrifice of Regnault.

It would be somewhat out of place, in a volume of this kind (which is not intended exclusively for readers who take a lively interest in the fine arts), to develop at any great length whatever estimate I may be able to form of Regnault's capacity as an artist ; but, on the other hand, it is difficult for me to leave him with such scant notice of his artistic powers as I have given in the course of this biography. I will therefore say something about his artistic abilities, though in a short space.

He was really a born painter: the evidence of this is abundant. He had the natural instincts and enthusiasms of a painter, especially the intense enjoyment of the sense of sight. Many of his letters, in which this enjoyment is frankly expressed, will seem wildly exaggerated to those who have not, at least in some inferior degree, a share of the same faculties; but many have had something of this intense delight in seeing who were unable to paint pictures. The delight of the eyes, before passing into good artistic production, requires other faculties and some accomplishments: it requires memory, invention, and technical skill.

Regnault's artistic memory was extraordinary, and the strength of it was proved in his earliest youth. When a child, he would not copy drawings or engravings, but went to look at Nature (chiefly animals, at that time), and then drew them, with striking fidelity, at home. When he was twelve years old, his father had an accident; and the boy was troublesome in the house, so to keep him quiet it was suggested that he should occupy himself in art. He accordingly modelled in clay the portrait of a horse belonging to the Emperor. This was done entirely from memory, the horse being at St. Cloud and the young artist at Sèvres. He went to see the animal from time to time, but that was all. The result astonished the artists, and some casts of Regnault's horse were taken for their gratification. The portrait of Prim was executed in the same way from memory; for, although the artist had facilities for painting the horse in the royal stables at Madrid, the General never once sat to him.

In Italy and Spain, Regnault would sketch in the evening, in his studio, the figures and groups which he had particularly noticed during the day. Another decided mark of artistic genius in Regnault was what people call precocity. This word is often used by mediocrity to insinuate that the fruit is ripe before its time ; the truth being that, as genius is destined to a far grander development than mediocrity, it begins to develop soon, just as a young giant who has a greal deal of growing to do will generally shoot up pretty quickly from the first.

I may refer the reader to two drawings published by *L'Art* in 1876. One is a tiger drawn by Regnault at eight. The beast is something like the groom at Tangier, Ali Pata, he has one leg thinner than the other ; but he is a real tiger nevertheless, stealthily moving towards his prey, and right in local color with an approach to rightness in modelling. The other sketch was done at the age of thirteen, and represents a French colonel on horseback with his soldiers on foot, standing at ease, and wearily waiting for the arrival of the Queen of England, that trying exercise of patience which every middle-aged Parisian remembers to this day. For delicate humor, close observation, and fairly good drawing, this sketch might well be admitted as an illustration to some popular book or periodical, and the boy could probably have earned his living already, as a draughtsman, if he had not been occupied with other studies.

From his earliest youth, he had the most ambitious intentions as an artist ; and, whilst his teachers were giving him lessons in history, he would compose and sketch historical pictures, intending to paint them some day. When he had a little leisure, he amused himself by composing on a more important scale, and there are still in existence large battle-pieces in charcoal or chalk, such as the battles of Issus, Arbelles, and Rocroy, done with great dash and energy, and not a little knowledge, considering the young artist's opportunities, between the ages of eleven and thirteen.

All study requires some courage and determination, but the studies of painters unquestionably require far more than literary pursuits. If you want to read a poet, however difficult, you may read him in your own library, in an easy-chair ; but, if you want to draw a landscape, you must go out, and the study of men and animals will take you into the street, the stable, and the menagerie. It is always one sign of the true painter's temperament to stick at no trouble or inconvenience where his studies are concerned. Regnault had this kind of resolution in the supreme degree : he shrank from nothing which could give him the sort of knowledge that he wanted. When a boy, he used to go to the Jardin des Plantes to study the animals, and was well known to the keepers, who let him do as he liked. On one occasion, he found it inconvenient to draw a young lioness through the bars, so to avoid the difficulty he went inside the cage, and tranquilly completed his drawing there. The lioness had a good reputation for mildness, and did not betray his confidence.

He left a great number of sketches and studies, which prove the incessant artistic activity of his mind. For one picture, the " Entombment," there are sixty drawings. Wherever he happened to be, he observed and watched, sometimes painting elaborate studies in oil or water-colors, at others sketching swiftly with pen or pencil. There are a hundred sketches by him done in Normandy only. During the bombardment of Sèvres, no less than six hundred photographic. negatives taken from Regnault's paintings and drawings were entirely broken to pieces.

With the pencil or chalk, he drew rapidly and decisively ; but he had to fight a good deal with his pictures, notwithstanding their appearance of ease. The portrait of Madame Duparc occupied him from August to December, except three weeks of holiday in the country. Regnault said, " Ah, if I could paint as I draw, I should be really happy. Perhaps that may come to me by hard work." He had endless difficulties with his picture of " Holofernes." " I am trying," he said, " to fill the immense void in the upper part of the picture without arriving at any good result. I change its position, I raise and lower, I cut away canvas and add fresh canvas, but have not yet made it answer."

There were times in his life when the desire for a more complete and satisfactory expression of his genius made him grave and taciturn. In 1865, he said that he had become silent, and would willingly be invisible like Æneas surrounded by his cloud ; " nay, often it is painful for me to speak. I like to listen and say nothing. I know not if it is from studying art, that rich and infinite language, but I have taken a dislike to the every-day language that all people speak and hear. Artists and poets ought to have dwellings above the clouds, noiseless, smokeless, where they might retreat in their fits of madness, and lose themselves in the purity above them. I would only allow the noise of bells to rise in all but inaudible harmonies."

Every physician who reads this will at once see in this desire for silence a result of too much effort. Regnault's critics were always talking of his facility. He really possessed facility, and executed quickly; but his friend M. Duparc, who knew his ways of work, gives the following explanation on this point : —

"Every piece of painting that he worked upon was executed at speed; but he was only the more severe upon himself, and sacrificed without hesitation the result of considerable labors, if he perceived that a change could produce a better effect. Each work of his was the subject of long meditation and patient study before it was given to the public, and he counted neither his time nor his trouble." He gave concentrated expression to this in a single sentence : " Il faut chercher lentement, longuement, puis produire vite." But, notwithstanding his love of rapidity in execution, he hated hurry, and particularly disliked being obliged to send in a work at a fixed time, when he would rather have improved himself by study. When pressed in this way, he said, " There is no good in working like an express train." His most earnest longing was for such a degree of technical accomplishment, such mastery of matter in his own materials and the objects he painted, that he might *begin* to express his thoughts. This beginning had been fairly made at the time of his death ; but it was only a beginning, and yet how unmistakably powerful! It is easy to see that he worked with passionate inspiration, even if we had not the testimony of eye-witnesses to prove it. " Indefatigable, seizing all things passionately, he almost always worked with furious energy, forgetting all else, unable to quit his canvas, leaving his meals, or eating pieces of bread hastily, without interrupting his work."

He himself said that he considered painting to be a decoration ; and he sought decorative materials, such as beautiful tissues, and decorative backgrounds, such as the halls of the Alhambra. He had a passionate fondness for all things which delight the eye by a play of color, such as fish, for instance, which might often be seen on the table of his painting-room.* Here is a description of his studio at Paris, which exhibits this taste in its intensity : —

" How can we give an idea of the disorder which reigned in this *atelier ?* Precious stuffs, sumptuous carpets, all sorts of curious objects, tables covered with game and fish, waiting to be painted, all was confused together in one indescribable chaos. Day by day the strange collection was renewed. If the carp of the Seine seemed too commonplace, and not brilliant enough, splendid sea-fish replaced them, and the most different kinds of game exhibited in turn their plumage or their fur."

At Tangier, he and Clairin set to work to decorate the *patio* which served them at first for a studio, in the style of the Alhambra. The reader will remember that this was before decoration became a fashion.

* This taste, however, is by no means confined to painters of decorative subjects. Theodore Rousseau, the landscape painter, used to keep a stock of stuffed humming-birds in a drawer.

The decorative tendency may be noticed in most of his pictures. In the "Salomé," we have a scheme of black and yellow, the black being repeated in the frame, and all the details of costume and furniture are decorative. In the "Execution without Trial," the decorative element is in the background, which is a study in the Alhambra; in the water-color of "Hassan and Namouna," it is principally in the tapestry. I believe there are a few paintings by Regnault in which this decorative element is not to be found; but they are exceptions, and certainly do not express his prevailing taste. His fundamental tastes as a painter were expressed by him once very clearly in words when writing to his friend, M. Cazalis, about a large picture which he intended to compose. Here is an abridgment of it. I have italicized the points which appear to me specially characteristic : —

"The two immense blue and gold folding-doors of the Hall of Ambassadors have just been opened. The Moorish king appears between them, armed, and *covered with his most delicate tissues, on a richly caparisoned horse.* At his horse's feet a hero, the general-in-chief of the army, is ḥumbly prostrated, and offers his sword. He has conquered a province for his master, and offers it to him whom none may look at but in trembling, and on their knees.

"On the steps of white marble, on which *sumptuous carpets are thrown,* warriors stand in order with *flags taken from the enemy.* The steps go down to the water, and two boats are moored to them. The general and his suite have descended from one, in the other five negroes guard a group of captive women. On the prow of one of the boats, a *severed head* will be nailed, the head of a Christian chief. *All is gold, precious stuffs, all is elegant and precious — architecture, arms, jewels — and in the midst Mahometan despotism and indifference."*

The two notes struck upon here are evidently decorative elegance and a certain repulsive moral side of Oriental civilization, which at once repelled and fascinated Regnault, as it did Byron. In two subsequent sentences, the two notes were struck still more decidedly. Regnault says : —

" Their *civilization* is expressed by the artistic elegance of all that surrounds them. They have even more beautiful and more elegant armor than that of the Christians of those days, and all covered with precious tissues."

" Their *cruelty :* a severed head is nailed as a trophy on the boat, but the heads of obscure warriors have been cut off and nailed on the walls and doors of the captured city."

The reader will find these two elements in much of Regnault's work. They were both present in the " Salomé," both in the " Judith," both in the " Execution without Trial." When the last-named picture was exhibited in London, English taste was shocked by the dreadful severed head on the step, and the too successfully imitated trickling of the blood. I think much of this feeling must have been due to the unaccustomed nature of the subject; for there are crucifixions and martyrdoms in every public gallery in Europe, which would be far more painful, if we were not so used to them. The death inflicted in Regnault's picture is instantaneous, and probably painless : his real motive was not so much the death itself as the irresponsible despotism of the tyrant who commanded it, and the impassible coolness of the fearfully strong and skilful swordsman who carried out the order. Why Regnault liked dwelling upon despotism of this kind I do not know, for it was repugnant to all his feelings, which were tender and kind, and to all his principles, which were those, not of a Saracen or Turk, but of a liberal European. I suppose that his early taste for tigers and lionesses led him to a similar interest in man, consid· ered as a strong and sanguinary animal.*

Though Regnault never succeeded in quite satisfying himself with the technical quality of his work, he reached an uncommon vigor of style, both in oil and in water-color ; whilst his power as a sketcher in black and white has seldom been surpassed. He had a keen sense of color, and might ultimately have become a really great colorist : even the works he left behind him, immature as they all must be considered, are as strong and original in color conception as they are in grasp of subject and power of manual execution.

There is a certain manner of translating nature into art, which, although it varies infinitely with different masters, is still always recognizable as the sign-manual

* In " Hassan and Namouna," Hassan is really nothing but the human animal in repose.

of the true painter, that manner which looks confused and unmeaning when the spectator is too near, but justifies itself by startling force and truth at the right distance. Regnault fully possessed this power, as the reader may judge for himself the next time he goes to the Luxembourg. Let him examine *too* near and at the right distance the painting of the magnificent Andalusian charger under General Prim, he will at once perceive that Regnault possessed already in full strength the wonderful power of painting wrong to look right, which is the evidence of accomplishment with the brush.

He disliked reasoning about art, and said with perfect truth : "If we were to reason about painting, we should not dare to do any thing. If you reason before the works of the masters, you will find plenty of things which have no *raison d'être*, and which are where they are because they do well there. *Voilà tout !*" This is excellent. We begin to learn art criticism by reasoning about art ; but after infinite labor we come exactly to Regnault's conclusion, that the artist is always justified, if what he puts in his picture *does well* in it.

Regnault was frank enough in the expression of his opinion about the great masters. For Raphael and Michael Angelo his admiration was limited, attaching itself to some of their works, and not to others. For example, he considered the "David" of Michael Angelo "atrocious," but was overwhelmed by the magnificence of the Sistine Chapel. "That ceiling," he said, " is unimaginably grand, it is the marvel of marvels, it strikes you like a thunderbolt. I came out from under it half dead."

The pictures by Raphael at Madrid pleased Regnault little, but he warmly admired the Raphael frescoes at the Vatican. He did not at first like Murillo and Goya, but came to them afterwards. The one great painter for whom he had an unlimited and passionate admiration was the majestic, sober-minded Velasquez. "He is the first painter in the world. His style is easy without negligence ; strong without bombast ; his language is pure without pretension. Ah! Velasquez, Velasquez!"

Again he writes, when at work copying his favorite master : " It is very interesting to copy Velasquez. What a master! what frankness in his execution! what truth, what heart, what *go!* It is not precisely easy to copy him, but it impassions one."

Notwithstanding this admiration for Velasquez, Regnault never allowed himself to become a mere follower of a dead master. " All those geniuses," he said, " who have exhausted a vein in art are like blind alleys (*culs-de-sac*). After them come their imitators, who go and break their noses at the end of the said blind alley. To do any thing in art, a man must imagine that he is going to take a step in a new direction."

This may partly account for Regnault's wildly generous admiration of Fortuny, who had really taken a step in a new direction. " I have seen studies by Fortuny which are prodigious in color and vigor of execution. What a painter that fellow is! I have seen,

too, some charming etchings by him. What skill! what
amusing color! What wit and accuracy in touch!"

Elsewhere he exclaims, "Ah, Fortuny, you disturb
my sleep." "J'ai passé avant-hier la journée chez
Fortuny, et cela m'a cassé bras et jambes. Il est éton-
nant ce gaillard-là! Il a des merveilles chez lui! C'est
notre maître à tous."

Regnault was equally prepared to receive impressions
from all the arts. Architecture affected him quite as
powerfully as painting, and music as powerfully as
architecture. In both, he liked the picturesque and the
original rather than the severe. At Genoa, he is struck
by the staircase in the courtyard of the University,
which has for its rails two lions of colossal proportions,
which descend the steps head downwards, meeting the
spectator "avec une hardiesse étonnante." In the cathedral there he admired the use of color in the marbles.
" Ses marbres blancs et noirs alternés lui donnent une
sévérité imposante dans une harmonie sombre où la
plus petite note rouge ou violette prend une puissance
incroyable."

Regnault was so constituted that prettiness, or even
elegance and good taste, were insufficient for him. His
mind needed grandeur and sublimity in the objects of
its admiration. As he loved Beethoven in music, so
in architecture he sought an irregular vastness full
of fantastic and prodigal invention. A Greek temple,
however pure, would have left him cold: the prodigious
temples of India, with their shadowy vistas and infinite
mystery of sculptured ornamentation, would have driven

him wild with delight. The *littleness* of the Roman remains was a disappointment to him : the Arch of Titus
seemed a plaything; the Coliseum alone answered to
the needs of his imagination.

Before the smaller works of the Romans, he called to
mind the colossal magnificence of the Egyptian temples,
with their huge statues of granite, the vast courts and
broad flights of stairs : he remembered that twenty-five
chariots could be driven abreast on the tremendous
walls of Nineveh; he thought of the great terraces of
the many-storied Indian temples, with troops of priests
and multitudes of people ; and then, with all these
recollections of the colossal in his mind magnified to
still greater immensity by the heat of his own imagination, he turned to the little Roman arches of triumph,
and wondered how the gigantic heroes who had conquered the world could walk under them without
knocking their heads !

Even St. Peter's was scarcely vast enough for him in
itself, but needed the fog of incense smoke to increase
its apparent size. "I have seen marvellous effects
there," he says; "and at certain times the marvellous
basilica, which at first scarcely gives a religious impression, assumes a mysterious and imposing aspect still
further increased by the smoke of incense and the great
shadows of the vaults."

"It was wonderful on Easter day. I was in the vestibule when the great doors were opened, and the end of
the church became visible in a luminous mist, in which
rose the great baldachino with its tinted columns. Thanks

to the incense smoke, and to the rays of sunshine which crossed it, the length of the cathedral was more than tripled."

The strange mixtures in Spanish cathedral architecture were not offensive to Regnault, who found in it much that delighted him in varied and picturesque detail. But all this is as nothing in comparison with his enthusiasm for the Alhambra. "How shall we render," he says, "the rosy light which fills this enchanted palace and the golden reflections in the shadows? There can be nothing more exquisitely strange."

Elsewhere he says, "Let the earth turn no more, let the stars fall, let cities crumble, let the hills become valleys: what matters it to us, if only the Alhambra be spared for us and for our friends!"

"Every day we go to the Alcazar in the divine Alhambra, where the walls are a lace of amethysts and roses in the morning, of diamonds at noon, and of green gold and ruddy copper at sunset. We stay there till the moon comes to see us; and when she has kissed us, and sent to rest the fairies and the genii who chiselled this marvellous palace, we depart, regretfully looking back at every step, unable to turn our eyes from those columns of rosy marble which take at times the hues of mother of pearl."

Sometimes his language reaches the passionate utterance of truly Oriental hyperbole. "When the sun shines in the morning," he says, "my divine mistress, the Alhambra, calls me: she has sent me one of her lovers, the sun, to tell me that she is dressed and beautiful. I love thee, O Mahomet, because thou art the father of my fair and beloved Alhambra!"

He has the deepest sympathy with the last of the Moorish kings, who wept when the fortune of war drove him away from this palace of delight. "I understand the tears of Abu Abdillah when he left his dear Alhambra to fly before the armies of the Catholic sovereigns."

For a while, Regnault and Clairin had this wondrous place to themselves, and possessed it with the most absolute of all possessions, that of perfect appreciation.

"In *our beautiful palace* of the Alhambra, where we live so happy and at ease, we are not even troubled by the noise of revolutions. Men may dispute about government, and strive together in civil conflict ; but, as for us, we admire the genius of the Moors: we daily discover new splendors, more incredible combinations, profounder design in the invention of doors and ceilings. It is a labyrinth where we lose ourselves."

"And then the glimpses through every door and window, and the panorama of splendid mountains all around! And that immense plain of the Vega, which stretches away to infinity; and those trees, as green as if it were spring, and water everywhere, everywhere plenteous springs! To the left, under the walls of the Alhambra, the Darro with gold in its sands ; to the right, the silver-bearing Genil. What a land!" Regnault said elsewhere that "a palace not surrounded with water was not a palace for him."

It would have been impossible for a nature so richly and variously endowed to keep strictly to a single art, or to a single branch of study. Regnault loved music scarcely less than painting, and had a fine voice. One of his friends says that he would pass whole nights in music. There was a piano in his studio at Paris, and he knew some excellent musicians. When they came to visit him, the palette was often laid aside, and all his enthusiasm and energy were given to Beethoven, or some other mighty "inventor of harmonies."

I have no doubt that Regnault might have won a position in literature, if painting had not been the stronger attraction. He wrote both gracefully and powerfully, as the reader may have judged in some degree from what has been quoted here; but there are pages too long to quote, which prove a sustained energy, an abundance of diction, far above ordinary letter-writing. There are, of course, the usual faults of untrained literary energy, such as a multiplication of similes or an occasional mixture of metaphors; but that is nothing. He had an extensive literary education, having seriously studied four languages besides his own; namely, Latin, Italian, Spanish, and Arabic. His bodily activity is proved by a single detail: he could leap over two chairs, *à pieds joints*,* and he could leap over five with a run.

---

* Leaping *à pieds joints* means not only leaping without a run, but without the slight impetus gained by putting one foot before another. A very intimate friend of mine, a French gentleman, now dead, would stand quietly before a drawing room chimney-piece, his feet close together, and then suddenly spring up in the air and land with his feet on the mantel-shelf without disturbing any of the ornaments. The reader will probably find it difficult to do as much.

Besides this, he was a first-rate horseman, ready to mount any thing that came in his way.

Travelling, which exercises both body and mind, seemed to Regnault an essential part of education. He called it "the true school of the artist and the man," adding that, "if education were better understood, young men would be more rapidly formed, and become serious earlier in life."

In the École des Beaux Arts at Paris, there are cloisters or *loggie*, of a simple but graceful character, decorated with a good sense suitable to the place; and at the end of one of these arcades may now be seen a monument erected to the memory of the pupils slain in the Franco-German war. The principal object in this monument is a bronze bust of Henri Regnault, by Degeorge; and an exquisitely beautiful female figure in white marble, by Chapu, the idealization of *La Jeunesse*, is holding a branch of golden bays up towards the honored head. The bronze features have something of the energy and resolution, the artistic heat and fire, which animated the young genius who fell at Buzenval. Thus, ever young, with the thick hair and short crisp beard of early manhood, the enduring bronze will recall to future generations on the threshold of manly life the virile virtue which sacrificed both art and love to patriotism.

And now the reader in some distant land, to whom the incidents of the Parisian world are not of necessity familiar, may remember Victor Regnault, and ask if he lived long enough for these pains and pleasures to affect his declining years. Yes: he died in January, 1878, saddened but not broken by a burden of many sorrows. Not only had his son been killed in the war, but the manufactory of Sèvres, of which he was director, had been sacked by the German soldiery, and all his instruments, the result of a life of labor, barbarously destroyed. "When he returned to Sèvres," says M. Berthelot, "he found his apparatus broken with strokes of a hammer, his thermometers methodically divided into fragments of equal length, the registers of his experiments burnt or torn with the precaution of a hatred which appeared intentional. The results of six hundred experiments on gases, executed with the precision of a master whose skill increased with his years, are thus irrevocably lost."

What remains to be said reminds one of the terrible conception of some imaginative poet, who closes his tragedy by successive strokes of pitiless, implacable fate. Victor Regnault's other son, Léon, had been attacked by a mental malady, which appears to have in some measure affected two others of his four children.* His wife was dead, his daughter was dead, and he himself was stricken by paralysis, so that he could not move. Still, he had himself carried to the meetings at the Institute, and placed in his chair by a lay brother of the order of St. Jean de Dieu, who constantly accompanied him. At length, feeling that life had little more usefulness in reserve for him, he quitted Paris to spend his last years in a calm retreat near Bourg, the place where André

---

* Son fils Henri, *le seul qui eût échappé à la fatalité morale acharnée sur ses autres enfants.* — M. Berthelot.

Ampère lived when he was separated from Julie. Here
he may have thought that beyond his own death, which
he awaited with serene patience, no further trial was in
store for him ; but one day his sister came to see him,
and, during her visit, she died before his eyes.

It is a custom of Henri Regnault's friends to meet at
Buzenval on the 19th of January, the day he fell, to
celebrate his memory. When they met in 1878, seven
years after the event their piety thus commemorates, I
say when they met, at the very hour, Victor Regnault
died suddenly from apoplexy, in his retreat near Bourg-
en-Bresse. It may be that the sadness of the anniver-
sary, in addition to the accumulated weight of many
sorrows, had weakened the last poor thread of worn and
weary life, and prepared him for the final deliverance.

THE END.

MR. HAMERTON'S WORKS.

———◆———

———◆———

" The style of this writer is a truly admirable one, light and pictur-esque, without being shallow, and dealing with all subjects in a charming way. Whenever our readers see or hear of one of Mr. Hamerton's books, we advise them to read it." — SPRINGFIELD REPUBLICAN.

THE INTELLECTUAL LIFE. Square 12mo. Price $2.00.

" Not every day do we take hold of a book that we would fain have always near us, a book that we read only to want to read again and again, that is so vitalized with truth, so helpful in its relation to humanity, that we would almost sooner buy it for our friend than spare him our copy to read. Such a book is 'The Intellectual Life,' by Philip Gilbert Hamerton, itself one of the rarest and noblest fruits of that life of which it treats.

" Just how much this book would be worth to each individual reader it would be quite im-possible to say; but we can hardly conceive of any human mind, born with the irresistible instincts toward the intellectual life, that would not find in it not only ample food for deep reflection, but also living waters of the sweetest consolation and encouragement.

" We wonder how many readers of this noble volume, under a sense of personal gratitude, have stopped to exclaim with its author, in a similar position, 'Now the only Crœsus that I envy is he who is reading a better book than this.' " — *From the Children's Friend.*

THE SYLVAN YEAR. Leaves from the Note-Book of

RAOUL DUBOIS. With Twenty Etchings by the Author and other Artists. 8vo. Cloth, gilt edges. Price $5.50. A cheaper edition, square 12mo. Price $2.00.

" 'The Sylvan Year' is one of Mr. Hamerton's best books ; and Mr. Hamerton, at his best, is one of the most charming modern writers. . . . A record rich in intelligent observation of animals, trees, and all the forest world ; rich, too, in the literary beauty, the artistic touches, and the sentiment that mark Mr. Hamerton's style." — *From the Boston Daily Advertiser.*

" Its author lived a year in the Val Sainte Veronique, watching the forest through all its changes, and adding to his already large stock of woods lore. He has enough scientific knowl-edge, but, in talking of nature, he adds to that the observation of the artist, and the sentiment of the poet and the man of true feeling. Then he knows the literature of the woods, the flowers, and the seasons. The style is very quiet ; one reads it with a slow sort of delight that nothing else gives, and the enjoyment of it grows with every new book that the author writes. These out-door books of Mr. Hamerton are more attractive than his graver works which treat of the Intellectual Life and of Art, although those are admirable in their way. But 'The Unknown River,' 'Chapters on Animals,' and 'The Sylvan Year,' have a sim-plicity, a delicacy, a depth of feeling, and a wealth of literary beauty that are very rarely found united " — *Boston Correspondent of the Worcester Spy.*

THOUGHTS ABOUT ART. New Edition, Revised, with

Notes and an Introduction. "Fortunate is he who at an early age knows what *art* is." — GOETHE. Square 12mo. Price $2.00.

"The whole volume is adapted to give a wholesome stimulus to the taste for art, and to place it in an intelligent and wise direction. With a knowledge of the principles, which it sets forth in a style of peculiar fascination, the reader is prepared to enjoy the wonders of ancient and modern art, with a fresh sense of their beauty, and a critical recognition of the sources of their power." — *New York Tribune.*

A PAINTER'S CAMP. A New Edition, in 1 vol. 16mo

Price $1.50. Square 12mo. Price $2.00.

"If any reader whose eye chances to meet this article has read 'The Painter's Camp,' by Mr. Philip Gilbert Hamerton, he will need but little stimulus to feel assured that the same author's work, entitled 'Thoughts about Art,' is worth his attention. The former, I confess, was so unique that no author should be expected to repeat the sensation produced by it. Like the 'Adventures of Robinson Crusoe,' or the 'Swiss Family Robinson,' it brought to maturer minds, as those do to all, the flavor of breezy out-of-door experiences, — an aroma of poetry and adventure combined. It was full of art, and art-discussions too; and yet it needed no rare technical knowledge to understand and enjoy it." — *Joel Benton.*

"They ('A Painter's Camp' and 'Thoughts about Art') are the most useful books that could be placed in the hands of the American art public. If we were asked where the most intelligent, the most trustworthy, the most practical, and the most interesting exposition of modern art and cognate subjects is to be found, we should point to Hamerton's writings." — *The Atlantic Monthly.*

THE UNKNOWN RIVER: An Etcher's Voyage of Discov-

ery. With an original Preface for the American Edition, and Thirty-seven Plates etched by the Author. One elegant 8vo volume, bound in cloth, extra, gilt, and gilt edges. Price $6.00. A cheaper edition, square 12mo. Price $2.00.

"Wordsworth might like to come back to earth for a summer, and voyage with Philip Gilbert Hamerton down some 'Unknown River'! If this supposition seem extravagant to any man, let him buy and read 'The Unknown River, an Etcher's Voyage of Discovery,' by P. G. Hamerton. It is not easy to write soberly about this book while fresh from its presence The subtle charm of the very title is indescribable; it lays hold in the outset on the deepest romance in every heart; it is the very voyage we are all yearning for. When, later on, we are told that this 'Unknown River' is the Arroux, in the eastern highlands of France, that it empties into the Loire, and has on its shores ancient towns of historic interest, we do not quite believe it. Mr. Hamerton has flung a stronger spell by his first word than he knew." — *Scribner's Monthly.*

CHAPTERS ON ANIMALS. With Eight Illustrations by

J. VEYRASSAT and KARL BODMER. Square 12mo. Price $2.00.

"This is a choice book. Only such a man as Hamerton could have written it, who, by virtue of his great love of art, has been a quick and keen observer of nature, who has lived with and loved animal nature, and made friends and companions of the dog and horse and bird. And of such, how few there are! Mr. Hamerton has observed to much purpose, for he has a curious sympathy with the 'painful mystery of brute creation,' as Dr. Arnold called it. He recognizes the beauty and the burden of that life which is bounded by so fine and sensitive a mortality. He finds in the uses of the domestic animal something supplementary to his own manhood, and which develops both the head and heart of the good master. We have been often reminded of Montaigne in reading this book, as we always associate him with his cat." — *Boston Courier.*

THE LIFE OF J. M. W. TURNER, R. A. Square 12mo.

Price $2.00.

"We have found his volume thoroughly fascinating, and think that no open-minded reader of the 'Modern Painters' should neglect to read this 'Life.' In it he will find Turner dethroned from the pinnacle of a demi-god on which Ruskin has set him (greatly to the artist's disadvantage), but he will also find him placed on another reasonably high pedestal where one may admire him intelligently and lovingly, in spite of the defects in drawing, the occasional lapses of coloring and the other peculiarities, which are made clear to his observation by Mr. Hamerton's discussion." — *Boston Courier*.

ETCHING AND ETCHERS. Illustrated with Etchings

printed in Paris under the supervision of Mr. HAMERTON. A new, revised, and enlarged Edition. 8vo. Cloth, gilt and black. Price $5.00.

"We are not in the habit of overpraising publishers or authors, but we have no hesitation in saying that Mr. Hamerton's 'Etching and Etchers' will henceforth deserve to have, and certainly obtain, a place in every gentleman's library in the country who can afford to buy the book. The subject is treated so conscientiously; there is such a maturity and repose of thought and exposition, and in every page, whether you agree or disagree, so much to think over with luxurious reflection, besides which the illustrations are so valuable and delicately chosen for the object in view, that the book rather resembles the mediæval labors of life-long devotion, than a nineteenth-century forty-steam-power of ephemeral production." — *The Spectator*.

THE GRAPHIC ARTS: A Treatise on the Varieties of

Drawing, Painting, and Engraving in Comparison with each other and with Nature. Square 12mo. Price $2.00.

"Few books have issued from the American press of more deserved and general interest and value. The volume displays a vast amount of artistic knowledge and research, and a thorough familiarity with all the literature of the subject, and with general literature as well, besides showing his own conspicuous and graceful literary accomplishment. It is a volume most to be welcomed, however, for its probable effect in widening the respect for graphic art in its various forms through making men and women of some literary culture better acquainted with its reason and method as well as its beauty." — *Chicago Times*.

ROUND MY HOUSE. Notes of Rural Life in France in

Peace and War. Square 12mo. Price $2.00.

"Whatever the subject he chooses, and he is at home with a good many, Mr. Hamerton is pretty sure to write an entertaining book, and this one, which gives an account of his life in France, is no exception. He takes the reader into his confidence, and tells him just how hard it was to find exactly the sort of house he wanted. . . . After describing this tempting place, the author goes on to give his readers just that full record of what he saw in his daily life, which is most interesting and useful to an outsider. The merit of this part is, that it so exactly resembles the talk of a sensible man whose tact enables him to know just what his hearers would like to hear." — *Atlantic Monthly*.

WENDERHOLME: a Tale of Yorkshire and Lancashire.

Square 12mo. Price $2.00.

"To those who are familiar with other works by Mr. Hamerton, it may be sufficient, in a general way, to say that 'Wenderholme' is characterized by the same thoroughness, the same simplicity, the same artistic flavor that make 'Round my House' so delightful; by the same love of nature, the same appreciation of the beautiful, the same refinement that mark 'The Unknown River' and 'A Painter's Camp;' and there are not wanting evidences of the wide reading, the proofs of culture and earnestness that are conspicuous in ' Intellectual Life.' " — *Cincinnati, O., Times*.

FRENCH AND ENGLISH : A COMPARISON. Square 12mo.
Price $2.00.

"Mr. Hamerton's comparison of the two nations follows a very methodical order. He compares them, step by step, in reference to education, patriotism, politics, religion, virtues, customs, and society. The chapters on the virtues — which are philosophically classified under the heads of truth, justice, purity, temperance, thrift, cleanliness, and courage — abound in suggestive observations." — *Academy.*

"A most interesting and instructive work. Mr. Hamerton has lived long in France; and he is not only a close observer, but a thinker. . . . Like everything that comes from his pen, this work is distinguished by a literary style of remarkable clearness and grace, while in substance it is equally distinguished by the sound basis of its criticisms in experience and their general impartiality." — *The Scotsman.*

"As its title indicates, it is in the nature of a comparison; but while its plan accommodates itself to this indication, it makes no attempt to do so stiffly. On the contrary, its treatment is delightfully free and easy. The scope of the work may be gathered from the fact that the comparison of the two peoples refers to their education, patriotism, politics, religion, virtues, custom, society, success, and variety, — this last implying their diversity as peoples, that is, the degrees in which portions of them vary from the common type. But this enumeration utterly fails to give any adequate idea of the intimate knowledge, the multiplicity of details, the shrewd observation of a multitude of matters, and the kindly criticism of a thousand points, which have contributed to make this a most readable book. The subject of the volume is intrinsically interesting, but it is rendered additionally so by the graceful and easy method of its presentation. There is everywhere evidence of the author's extensive knowledge of literature, and his close observation of men, institutions, and manners. At the same time, the topics which come within his range are of the highest importance, and such as are now attracting the widest attention. There is not a dull statement nor an uninstructive observation in the book, and in it Mr. Hamerton has made a valuable addition to the volumes on kindred subjects with which he has already delighted readers." — *Exchange.*

PARIS. In Old and Present Times. Profusely illustrated with
woodcut engravings and 12 superb full-page etchings. 4to. $6.50. Library Edition with all the woodcuts. 8vo. $3.00.

"It is neither a history of, nor a guide-book to, the gay and giddy French capital, although it partakes in some degree of the nature of both; but it is a very pleasant, instructive volume, brimful of information about the famous buildings, parks, squares, and places of Paris, which those who have seen them, as well as those who have not, will be glad to have described by pen and pencil in so attractive and convenient a manner. . . . He invites his readers to accompany him in a lazy boat-ride around the city; and during the progress of this journey, he points out the different historic buildings to be seen from the water, tells the story connected with them, explains their architectural details, and secures the excellent engravings which beautify his book. . . . He traces with historic accuracy the erection, decoration, decay, and restoration of those magnificent temples. The parks and gardens and the streets are treated in separate chapters, particular attention being paid to landscape effects, drainage, paving, etc. The book is written in a graceful and spirited style; it is handsomely bound and printed, copiously and artistically illustrated, and cannot fail to be a useful and instructive, as well as ornamental, addition to the library." — *Saturday Evening Gazette.*

"Paris is so rich in historical association, so full of important buildings, so carefully planned and arranged, so brilliantly decorated, and so perfectly cared for and kept up — in short, is so clearly the nearest approach yet made to the idea. city, — that one is never weary of reading about it. Mr. Hamerton knows his Paris well, her history and her aspect, without being so narrow in his exclusive devotion as the pure Paris-lover gets to be; and he is a very observant and sagacious judge of architectural effects, even if a little too catholic. The book is in nearly all respects just what that fortunate person needs who means to reside in Paris a while, with leisure to study it; it can hardly fail to give him generally sound notions of what the famous city has that is most admirable in its external aspects." — *N. Y. Evening Post.*

A SUMMER VOYAGE ON THE RIVER SAÔNE. With

152 illustrations by Joseph Pennell and the Author. 4to. Cloth, gilt. Price $2.50.

" Mr. Hamerton has written his book in the easy style of familiar letters addressed to Mr. Richmond Seeley, his 'friend and publisher.' These stand in the place of chapters, and allow the writer greater latitude and more intimacy in the treatment of his subject. The voyage divided itself naturally into two sections. The upper part of the river, from Corre to Châlons, was navigated in a long, narrow barge, called a *berrichon*, as from the character of the river and the lack of inns a small sailing-boat would have been objectionable. From Châlons to Lyons, Mr. Hamerton descended the Saône, with his son and nephew, in his own steel catamaran, the *Arar*. The first part of the book is full of anecdotes of the travellers, — their ' Pilot,' their ' Patron,' their domestic arrangements on the barge, their methods of killing time, and their passages of diplomacy and courtesy with bargemen, gendarmes, and other officials. The whole history of their difficulties with the authorities on the question of sketching is given at full length. . . . Four maps and a hundred and forty-eight pen-and-ink drawings illustrate the expedition. Of these, a hundred and two are original drawings by Mr. Joseph Pennell, twenty-four compositions by Mr. Pennell after Mr. Hamerton, nineteen original works by Mr. Hamerton, while three are drawings by Mr. Hamerton after Messrs. Jules Chevrier and J. P. Pettitt. Mr. Pennell's work, as might be expected, shines in the qualities of elegance, taste, and judicious finish. He seems to have surpassed all his previous achievements in daintiness of style and fineness of workmanship. He has found some quaint compositions, chosen from unusual points of view, wherewith to illustrate the appearance of the river seen from the end of a gang of barges." — *Athenæum.*

PORTFOLIO PAPERS. Square 12mo. Price $2.00.

" Mr. Hamerton has done more to familiarize reading people with the principles and methods of art than any other writer. Mr. Ruskin's genius gave the impulse to a wide-spread interest in art years ago; and, by a very happy sequence, Mr. Hamerton has appeared to do the secondary work of education. He lacks almost entirely Mr. Ruskin's genius; but he possesses in large measure that sound judgment which Mr. Ruskin often conspicuously lacks, a thorough knowledge of his subjects, and the rare ability to write from the standpoint of his readers. Mr. Hamerton's great quality as a teacher has been this ability to put himself in the place of the man who is ignorant of art, and expound to him in the simplest fashion things which to Mr. Hamerton himself must be obvious and elementary. In this volume, Mr. Hamerton writes interestingly about five artists, — Constable, Etty, Chintreuil, Guignet, and Goya. The volume also contains ' Notes on Æsthetics,' ' Essays,' and ' Conversations.' Among the subjects which appear in the division of ' Essays ' are ' Style,' ' Soul and Matter in the Fine Arts,' ' The Nature of the Fine Arts,' and ' Can Science Help Art?' On all these subjects Mr. Hamerton is thoroughly at home; and the book is, on the whole, the utterance of a large-minded and catholic critic and student." — *Christian Union.*

IMAGINATION IN LANDSCAPE PAINTING. An elegant

folio volume, fully illustrated, and bound in cloth. Gilt. $6.50. (Limited edition.)

" The very interesting folio in which this eminent artist and art-writer discusses Imagination in Landscape Painting, like everything that comes from his hand, has a popular, quite as much as a technical, interest. The keynote of Mr. Hamerton's work is found in the sentence, 'The power of recalling images with clearness is imagination of the more ordinary kind, though it is usually called memory; whilst the power of combining these images in such a manner as to make them into works of art is the gift of artistic invention, which is very much rarer than the other.' This thought Mr. Hamerton elaborates at length, and with all the charming simplicity and ample resources of his admirable style. The value of the book is very much increased by fourteen illustrations reproduced by various processes, besides a number of pen-and-ink drawings."

MODERN FRENCHMEN.

MODERN FRENCHMEN. Five Biographies: Victor Jacquemont, Traveller and Naturalist; Henri Perrevve, Ecclesiastic and Orator; François Rude, Sculptor; Jean Jacques Ampère, Historian, Archæologist, and Traveller; Henri Regnault, Painter and Patriot. By PHILIP GILBERT HAMERTON. Uniform with "The Intellectual Life," &c. Square 12mo. Price $2.00.

"Philip Gilbert Hamerton has the faculty (not common to all authors) of making everything he touches interesting. Best known as a writer on art, his works upon that subject have come to be recognized as standards. His novels and essays are always full of meat, and his works generally are characterized by a fairness and impartiality which give them peculiar value. His latest work, 'Modern Frenchmen,' is made up of five biographies." — *Boston Transcript.*

HUMAN INTERCOURSE.

HUMAN INTERCOURSE. Square 12mo. Price $2.00.

"He has the art of presenting to our minds a hundred paths into which every subject opens. . . . In writing about 'Human Intercourse,' Mr. Hamerton has the always significant facts of human nature to deal with, — those eternally interesting creatures, men and women. . . . Occasionally, too, there are sentences that suggest by their felicity the rhythm of poetry. Better than all, in this, as in every one of Mr. Hamerton's works, we feel that we are dealing with a man who, besides his grace, his wit, or his keen observation, is always on the side of simple truth and purity of living, and possesses a high-minded faith in the power of the Best, and a determination to aid in its final victory." — *Philadelphia Press.*

LANDSCAPE.

LANDSCAPE. Square 12mo. Price $2.00.

"Mr. Hamerton in sending to his publishers, Messrs. Roberts Brothers, a complete set of proofs for the library edition, says: 'I have done all in my power to make "Landscape" a readable book. It is not mere letter-press to illustrations, or anything of the kind, but a book which, I hope, anybody who takes any interest in landscape would be glad to possess.' . . . The subject is treated from all sides which have any contact with art or sentiment, — from the side of our illusions; our love for nature; the power of nature over us; nature as subjective; verbal description, 'word-painting;' nature as reflected by Homer, as the type of Greek nature-impression; by Virgil or Latin, Ariosto or Mediæval; then as studied by Wordsworth and Lamartine, as types of English and French; from its relation to the various graphic arts, its characteristics in Great Britain and in France, and from the geography of beauty and art. Mountains are weighed in the art balances; lakes, brooks, rivulets, and rivers in their degrees of magnitude. Then man's work on rivers and their use in art are considered; then trees, under their various aspects; then the effect of agriculture on landscape, of figures and animals, and of architecture. 'The two immensities,' sea and sky, conclude." — *The Nation.*

Mr. Hamerton's Works (not including "Etchers and Etching," "Imagination in Landscape Painting," "Paris," and "A Summer Voyage on the Saône") may be had in uniform binding. 14 vols. Square 12mo. Cloth, price $28.00; half calf, price $56.00. A cheaper edition 14 vols., 16mo, cloth, Oxford style, $17.50; cloth, imitation half calf, $21.00.

For sale by all booksellers. Mailed, post-paid, on receipt of advertised price, by

ROBERTS BROTHERS, PUBLISHERS,
Boston.

[*From the* NEW YORK TRIBUNE *of October* 13, 1885.]

BALZAC IN ENGLISH.

PÈRE GORIOT. HONORÉ DE BALZAC. Translated.
Boston : Roberts Brothers.

IN publishing a translation of Balzac's " Père Goriot," the Boston firm
undertaking the enterprise seems to feel that there is some doubt as to
the success of the experiment, which includes, if the public approve the
initial essay, the presentation in English of several of the great Frenchman's other works. Perhaps the slow recognition of Balzac's genius by
the American and English public may be capable of intelligible explanation. The magnitude of his work is alone sufficient to repel such as only
look to French fiction for ephemeral sensation, while the seriousness of
his purpose might intimidate those who imagined that he was didactic and
therefore dull. *But the time should now be ripe for the introduction of
English-speaking people to an author who by right of genius stands alone
among his contemporaries, and whose marvellous knowledge of human nature, subtle analytic power, encyclopædic learning, and brilliant descriptive
talent justify the daring comparison of his productive force with that of
Shakespeare.*
To understand Balzac thoroughly, indeed, he must be read in the
original and as a whole. Selected pieces from the " Comédie Humaine "
may convey a sufficiently clear apprehension, for the public, of his powers,
but a careful study of that wonderful scheme throughout is indispensable
to a real knowledge of his aim and scope. The " Comédie Humaine " is
the most remarkable work of its kind extant. It is not mere fiction. It
is, as Balzac intended it to be, a faithful history of the France of his
time ; a history so faithful and so detailed that were all other contemporary literature destroyed, posterity could from this work reconstruct an
exact and finished picture of the age. In his general preface (which the
American publishers have judiciously prefixed to their translation of
" Père Goriot ") the author gives some account of his plan. His aim was
to do for society what Buffon had done for the animal kingdom. Since,
however, men and women are complex creatures, and since their acts and

sufferings are caused mainly by the influence of passions whose treatment demands a profound study of psychology, it is evident that the task of the novelist, or, as he might be better named, the social historian, must be much more difficult than that of the naturalist.

Balzac, however, supported by that confidence in its own powers which so often characterizes genius, grappled boldly with this arduous undertaking. He was to write the history of his time, nothing extenuating, and setting down nought in malice, painting in their due proportions the vices and the virtùes of the period, showing the springs that moved society, the passions that furnished motives to action, the meannesses, the magnanimities, the rapacity, the self-sacrifice, the sensuality, the purity, the piety, the heathenism of his fellow men and women. His equipment for the work was splendid. His erudition was both extensive and curious. He knew not only common but recondite things. In science he had outstripped his generation. In the " Comédie Humaine " may be recognized the practical embodiment of evolutionary philosophy. The influence of the environment upon character and conduct is always insisted upon by him. And because he never loses sight of the natural processes through which character is moulded and changed, his characters possess a peculiar reality and vitality. To him they were indeed living, and the rare faculty by which, in the alembic of his mind, all the complex influences and agencies concerned went to form, complete, and vivify these creations, has endowed them with so strong an individuality that they live and move still for the reader. Nothing that belonged to Balzac's time escaped him, and he explored the obscurer lines of research as conscientiously as those more open and clear. Thus it is that there is to be found in his work: references to what are now thought the supernatural theories of the day, and he has sounded the depths of mysticism with the same devotion shown in his pursuit of physical science.

Critics have regretted that he had no high moral aim; but this regret seems to imply misapprehension of his purpose not less than error as to his achievements. His aim was to describe life as it was being lived under his eyes. That his tendencies were not debasing is shown by the striking contrast between his work and that of Zola. In the latter's writings the ugly, vile, and horrible is so elaborated, exaggerated, and kept in the foreground that it colors and characterizes everything. In Balzac there is not less realism, and nothing more graphic than his descriptions of the seamy side of life has ever been written. But there is no taint of lubricity and no suggestion of liking for the scenes so depicted. A sombre fire runs through all the pictures of low and vicious life, which, while enhancing the skill of the artist, moves to pity or indignation because of the destinies so sadly fixed. Perhaps no better example of his style than " Père Goriot " could be selected. Père Goriot is the Lear of modern society; and though the passions which move the characters are for the most part sordid and base, the pathos and power of the story are so great, that even in translation the genius of the master is unmistakable. There is nothing in fiction more pitiful than the figure of old Goriot and the skill of the creator, which sets down all the defects and limitations of the hero, thereby accentuates his devotion and the ignoble tragedy of his fate.

Balzac, however, never adopted the modern vice known as the "star system" in dramatic management. There were no "sticks" in his company. Every character is complete, intelligible, consistent, progressive Neither does he pad. From beginning to end, save as regards his descriptions of things and places, every sentence has direct relation to the working out of the plot. And as to those long and minute descriptions, which have vexed some critics, they were written with the distinct and avowed purpose of preserving faithful likenesses which should be of use to the historian of the future. Nor are they tiresome, but often seem to sharpen the realization of the story, and in all cases increase the general impression of fidelity to facts. *The style of Balzac is very remarkable for its power. It is nervous, full of suppressed fire, suggesting a brain so prolific of thoughts that the utmost care had to be exercised to prevent them from overcrowding one another. The concentrated force of expression frequently reminds one of Shakespeare, and bursts of marvellous impassioned eloquence — not of the frothy kind, but presenting truths deep as the centre — at intervals flash out, adding to the sense of repressed volcanic power which pervades these works.*

The defects of Balzac are those of his time and country. It is curious that while he himself finds no really lofty female characters in English fiction, even belittling the heroines of Scott, and advancing the strange theory that the neglect by Protestant peoples of the worship of the Virgin has lowered their standard of womanhood, — his own most ambitious types of piety and purity in woman exhibit less of his characteristic knowledge of human nature than any of his other characters. This type, in fact, he appears to have described from pure imagination, with the result that his creations of this class are cold, unapproachable, abnormal, bloodless' beings, whose goodness does not impress us as meritorious, because they are essentially incapable of wrong-doing. In a word, he has filled up the vacant niche with conventional angels, only removing their wings. As to the low plane of the ambitions which move so many of his characters, no doubt he would have said that he merely took the world as he found it; that these were the prevailing ambitions, and that he could not make society better than it was. And doubtless there is much force in this, though it must be acknowledged that the France of Balzac's time afforded almost as abundant material for satire as the Rome of Juvenal.

Taking him at his own estimate, however, and accepting his view of the duties of the novelist under the given conditions,— a view, be it said, which is always open to doubt and dispute, — it is impossible not to admire the depth of his insight and the marvellous scope and comprehensiveness of his genius. The enterprise he undertook was gigantic, yet what he accomplished was so monumental a work as to prove the justness of his self-appreciation. Some day, perhaps, a complete translation of the "Comédie Humaine" will be undertaken. Possibly the success of Messrs. Roberts' venture may induce them to extend their enterprise. "César Birotteau," and one or two more of Balzac's stories, have been put into English already, though inadequately. There ought to be, in the United States and England, at the present time enough lovers of good literature to make such an undertaking as a complete translation of this author remunerative. When we consider what masses of trash pour from modern presses, and what capital is employed in reproductions of so-called classics which have become rare and obscure because they deserved oblivion, it seems reasonable to expect that Balzac would find purchasers if issued in the form suggested.

The translation of "Père Goriot" is very good, and Balzac is not the easiest author to translate. The publishers cannot do better than to intrust the succeeding volumes to the same capable hands, and it would be only justice to the translator to put his or her name on the titlepage. For it is a meritorious deed to have turned into excellent, nervous English the prose of this great Frenchman, whose fire and fervor, clear sight and powerful description, when contrasted with the average novel of the day, shine forth with redoubled splendor, and whose brilliant genius in the analysis of human character casts altogether into the shade the amateurish essays at psychologic fiction which are gravely spoken of in these degenerate times as the promising productions of a new and higher school of literary art.

———◆———

PÈRE GORIOT. A Novel. By HONORÉ DE BALZAC. 12mo. 349 pages. Prefaced with Balzac's own account of his plan in writing the "Comédie Humaine," xix pages. Half-bound in morocco, French style. Price $1.50.

ROBERTS BROTHERS, PUBLISHERS, *Boston*

www.ingramcontent.com/pod-product-compliance
Lightning Source LLC
Chambersburg PA
CBHW031059110726
47900CB00003B/993